COMPLETE ABANDON

NORMAN ISAACSON

iUniverse LLC
Bloomington

COMPLETE ABANDON

iUniverse books may be ordered through booksellers or by contacting:

iUniverse
1663 Liberty Drive
Bloomington, IN 47403
www.iuniverse.com
1-800-Authors (1-800-288-4677)

ISBN: 978-1-4917-1423-2 (sc)
ISBN: 978-1-4917-1425-6 (hc)
ISBN: 978-1-4917-1424-9 (e)

Library of Congress Control Number: 2013920807

Printed in the United States of America.

iUniverse rev. date: 11/19/2013

Dedication

To my wife Susan, and other smart, tough cookies…

Chapter 1

Watching the clock, he thought about that hour's lecture. Aphasia is a terrible problem. Knowing what you want to say but unable to say it is a horror. He was glad he took the course. The subject was important and he admired the professor.

The clock had no second hand so it was impossible to know exactly when the course would close. As he stared at the clock, the bell rang.

Almost in unison the class stood and headed for the door. He wondered why the classes weren't staggered. If they were, there wouldn't be the mad dash for the stairs as those inside hurried to get out as an equal number of students rushed in. It was chaos in the hallway. Everyone is going up and down the stairs at the same time.

Out in the corridor he saw the girl coming toward him. He thought her stunning, absolutely beautiful. He knew he had never seen her before because he knew he could never forget her if he had. He thought he would stop her and boldly ask her for a date. There was nothing to lose.

As she came alongside he started to speak, but was paralyzed by a beautiful smell. He sniffed the air. Where is it from? As he wondered, the smell turned pink. How can a smell have a color? It was from her, he realized. The smell and the color were coming from her. I have to get my arms around her. I have to hold her. I have to kiss her.

I have to kiss her breasts. I want to kiss her breasts. Everything has changed color. I want to kiss her breasts and her chest. I must. Why is everything pink?

She's in my arms and I smell that pink smell. She looks scared. Her eyes are wide open. I think I should not be trying to kiss her breasts. I can't help myself. Why am I trying to tear away her blouse? I must get to her beasts. I must get her nipple in my mouth. I can't stop. I don't want to stop. I want to suck her breast. She is so pretty and smells so good.

Someone is grabbing me. Why are they grabbing me? They are pulling me away from her. Don't stop me, please don't. They're holding me and there's the security guard from downstairs. I want that pink smell back.

Those guys are talking to the guard. Where did she go?

The guard wants to know why I attacked her. Did I attack her? All I wanted to do was kiss her beautiful tits. Oh god, what have I done. I bet I'm in trouble. Could I get kicked out of school?

He wants my student ID card. Oh shit, I bet I am in trouble. What happened? Those guys are looking at me like I'm a nutcase. Hey, all I wanted to do was kiss her breasts. All I wanted was to keep that beautiful pink smell. How can a smell be a color?

Where did she go? Who is she?

I want my degree. They can't throw me out of school.

How can a smell have a color? How can a color have a smell? What the hell happened?

University Campus Security

Building Report

Location	Date	Time
Postman Hall	3/19	2:00 pm

I was on door guard during the 2:00 class change when an event was reported to me by a student who came down stairs with the outgoing group. I was told by that student (ID # 374 56 9822) that some sort of altercation between a male and female student had taken place outside room 204.

I immediately left my door post and reported to the second floor. At the entrance to room 204 I saw three male students holding another male student while a female student was trying to arrange her torn blouse.

(Three male students: A/B/C/ = ID #'s--- A) 374 17 9851, B) 516 61 3251, C) 523 95 1792.

One Female Student: D = ID # 095 27 9551- Susan Merrill, Male student being held: E = ID # 571 34 6191 - Paul Coleman.

After identifying all students involved I gathered the following information.

Male student E grabbed ("hugged") female student D in the hallway at class change. He tried to take off her blouse. She resisted and backed up from hallway into room 204.

Students A, B, & C seeing event subdued student E and sent messenger (ID #374 56 9822) to get me at my door guard post.

I took charge when I got to the second floor and the subdued male was turned over to my control. He seemed confused and almost unaware of what he had done. The female student seemed only a trifle embarrassed and stated the event "was no big deal."

Since no harm had befallen the female student, I asked if she wanted to press charges, she replied "no." At that point, I gathered the ID numbers of all involved and released them. The three males left the second floor. The female student went to her class.

Male student E kept shaking his head from side to side as if to clear his confusion. He stated, "I lost control and couldn't help myself." I detected no alcohol odor and did not suspect he was high from drugs. I walked him to the building exit door and told him my report to Campus Security would be filed that afternoon. He grew nervous and asked if he would be kicked out of school. I told him that was not my decision to make. He left Postman Hall no longer exhibiting the confusion I had seen when first I encountered him.

I called for relief, and when Officer Melendez arrived, I went to the Postman Hall Security Office to type this report. When finished, I reported back to my post as Door Guard at Postman Hall. Officer Melendez left at approximately 2:37pm. This report was filed at the main Campus Security office at 5:17 pm the same day.

Signed   Lawrence Scott Badge # 484

CHAPTER 2

Dean of Students Harvey Grossman sat at his desk thankful this morning did not provide a situation comparable to yesterday's adventure, which found him calling the parents of a freshman girl who had sexually accommodated the entire men's varsity debate team during the first two weeks of the semester. He was pleased the parents agreed to immediately retrieve their daughter.

As he pondered being a parent, his secretary handed him a security guard's report about a male-female incident. After reading it, he thought it might be serious enough to qualify as an assault case and that would mean the police would get involved.

Prior to his position at New York University, he had been dean of students at a New York State teacher's college near Buffalo. While that school had its share of male-female events, the local police were mindful of the college's position in the town and never wanted to act against the school or the student body. But New York City was not a small town near Buffalo and the NYPD pulled no punches when it came to arrests that all too often led to a prosecution. So, he thought, it would be best if he could arrange to have campus personnel deal with this new muddle and eliminate the need to involve the local precinct.

Being extremely practical, he figured those who had resolved similar cases before could do it again. He picked up the phone and called the English Department seeking Professor Solomon Woodrow.

Almost every member of the administration and faculty held Professor Woodrow in high esteem. Dean Grossman remembered hearing about Professor Woodrow when he first arrived at the University. He was one of the few professors greatly appreciated and respected by faculty and administration members who had never yet met him. And that was quite the opposite from so many other faculty members who were intensely disliked by people who

4

had never met them. The dean knew that faculty reputations spread at about the same rate as fire in a dry forest, but they were invariably accurate. If you had a "bad" reputation, you deserved it!

Having just finished class Professor Woodrow entered his office as the phone was ringing. "Hello, Professor Woodrow here."

"Professor Woodrow, this is Dean Grossman. I need your help."

"What is it now, Harvey? Did someone steal your Mont Blanc pen?"

"Please, professor, this could be serious. I have received a security guard's report detailing a male student attacking a female student in Postman Hall… and the affair could be a police matter."

"Then why don't you call them?"

"I don't want the police involved because what happened could give us a PR black eye which as you realize must be avoided. Therefore, I was hoping you could gather your adjudication squad or whatever you call yourselves, and rectify the problem on campus as you have done in the past."

"I see no problem with that, but I want to know what happened. It would be silly to arrange anything without knowing what took place."

"I understand and will send a copy of the guard's report to you. Now, could you tell me who you will select to work with you?"

"As I have before, I will seek the help of Professor Lehman of Chemistry and Professor David of the Speech Department.

"Why do you need three?"

"Well, as you know Professor Lehman is self-admittedly difficult so we agreed to have a more youthful and less-explosive faculty member on board. In that way Professor Lehman and I will not endlessly argue. We have both agreed to bow to Professor David's views so we can bring matters to a close."

"Yes, I understand Professor Lehman can be a chore."

"Harvey, you don't know the half of it. She is gloriously bright and genius smart, but when she gets an idea in her head nothing less than dynamite can dislodge it."

"So this Professor David is the dynamite?"

"I wouldn't go that far, but he is sweet, very sharp, charming, and she likes him. We three worked very well together the last time when we located the source of and reason for the rat poisoning in the Psychology Department."

"Oh God, yes, please don't remind me."

Okay, I won't. Please send the guard's report to me and let us get started."

"You will have the report in less than an hour."

"Fine."

He waited a few minutes before using the phone. She answered on the third ring. "Professor Lehman speaking."

"Gertrude this is Sol. I want to—"

She broke in. "Sol don't you get going with that Gertrude crap. The name is Gert and you know it. Okay?"

Broadly smiling he said, "My, my, aren't we touchy this morning?"

"I can hear the smile in your voice, wise guy. Are you ever going to stop trying to get my goat?"

"Gert, my dear, I cannot…not while your goat is so easy to get."

"Okay, you've had your fun. Now, what is it? Why'd you call?"

"I just spoke to Harvey Grossman. He needs us to settle another case of student impropriety."

"What happened?"

"I don't yet know. He's sending over a security guard's report. I will fill you in when I get it. Also, I intend to involve Winthrop David. Is he still okay as our third?"

"Oh, yes. He's a smart guy. And don't forget to call him Win. He bridles at Winthrop."

Smiling again, Professor Woodrow said, "What is it with academics? Gertrude is Gert, Winthrop is Win? What *is* your problem?"

Laughing, she replied, "My friend, that's a hard question to answer, since I am speaking to a Solomon who, for some unknown reason prefers Sol. What is *your* problem?"

"Ah, Gert, you are a treasure. I'll call when I get the guard's report."

CHAPTER 3

As Sol again dialed Gert's extension, he stared at the security guard's report and didn't know quite what to make of it. What kind of attack takes place in a crowded hallway? An attacker with serious intent would certainly pick a better place than that. So, he thought, either we have an idiot for an attacker or what the guard said was true, that an alcohol and drug free student lost control and couldn't help himself. But what would make a student lose control? And, why did that confusion so quickly pass and enable the student to leave Postman Hall no longer displaying any indication of confusion?

When she picked up, he said, "Gert, I have the guard's report and it does not make sense to me."

"Why not?"

"Well, it's just too stupid. It concerns a male student attacking a female student in a corridor of Postman Hall. That's the gist of it."

"So why is that stupid?"

Well, first, the attack is in a crowded corridor, second, the young woman who was attacked seemed not to mind what happened, and third, the attacker was overwhelmed by something that rather quickly dissipated, and there seems to be no involved drugs or alcohol."

"Do you have the ID numbers of the students?"

"Yes, the guard put them in his report."

"Did you check the IDs and find out the names?"

"Yes, the girl's name is Susan Merrill and the boy's name is Paul Coleman."

"Good. Once I have their numbers I will contact the girl and have Win contact the boy. We will then set a meeting at my place which they both will attend so we can get to the truth of this situation. Is that satisfactory?"

"Absolutely. I will immediately fax the guard's report to you. All the information you'll need is in it. Right now I'm off to class, so I'll talk to you later." He hung up and gathered the materials he needed, left his office and walked to the classroom.

Today's class and the previous one dealt with ambiguity in language and he knew to make clear the idea that a word could have more than one meaning was not as simple as it sounded. To discover ambiguity one must step away from their usual pattern of analysis to seek other meanings or referents that are or can be contained in the language under investigation. All too often students were not quick to see the variations and tended to dismiss interpretations other than their own, so Sol slogged his way through the hour and was pleased to realize the class was almost finished.

One of his most precious moments was ending a class. Though he rarely prepared a lesson plan, he was most acutely aware of the exact ending for every session. In his judgment, show business sayings were not very useful, but two applied to his class endings—'Always leave 'em wanting more' and 'Always leave 'em laughing.' In that light, he had developed what he thought was a smashing riddle and hitting the class with the puzzle was going to be today's finale.

Standing in one of his Oxford don poses, he said, "In a moment, I am going to offer a riddle, the answer to which I want no one seeking right now. Let me repeat, I do not want anyone crying out with the answer or what they think is the answer as soon as I finish." He strolled to the other side of the room and with his hands grasping his jacket's lapels, he continued. "What I do want is the correct answer and the reasoning as to why it is the correct answer—but I want it for our next class meeting. Clear?"

The student's grunt-like murmurs did not dissuade him even though Sol's estimation of the intellectual prowess of his students was far in excess of the potency they actually possessed. If anything, that assumption was, if not the prime dilemma, certainly one of the major problems confronting almost all professors who had been on the front lines for more than a while. Years before, they had started with students who had been educationally prepared to handle collegiate academic demands. That was no longer the case. Far too many present-day students couldn't write very well, didn't read much, couldn't spell, knew little history, and were not overly concerned with what they could not do or did not know. They were not curious about why they were not curious.

"Are you ready?" he asked. Their lack of response created a dark cloud in his mind, but nevertheless, he continued. "You should copy the riddle if you think you will need to look at it before our next meeting."

"Is this homework?" asked the redhead in the first row.

"No. This is not really homework. It is merely a riddle which, if solved, will help you better understand what we have been saying about ambiguity."

"So we don't have to do it, right?" asked the same girl.

"Yes, you do have to do it—solve it. I want you to work out the answer."

"Here or at the dorm?"

Sol looked at his watch and then at the wall clock. "Since we have about three minutes remaining for class, I don't think there will be time to work it out here."

"So it's homework." stated a voice from the rear of the room.

Sol closed his eyes, uttered an under-the-breath oath and rather than say anything else, hit them with it. "Here is the riddle. Three monks were passing a tree where three pears were hanging. Each took one and that left two."

There was a bleak silence before the room filled with distress. "But Professor Woodrow, you said it was a riddle that would help us understand ambiguity, right?" said the red-haired girl.

"That's right."

"Well, I don't understand ambiguity and I don't understand the riddle. What do I do?"

Sol's response was never offered because the ten-to-the-hour buzzer rang at that moment and the students stampeded from the room.

CHAPTER 4

Following the students, he left the class room and was confronted in the corridor by a person he took to be a clown. Standing before him was a young man with rings in his ears and nose, wearing large thick-soled work shoes, baggy jeans, and a purple sweatshirt. His sartorial outfit was completed by his quite long hair and scraggly beard.

"I bring you regards, Professor." The young man said.

"From whom, may I ask?"

"From my father. He said I would undoubtedly see you and that I must remember to mention him when I do. So...I have."

"And what is your father's name?"

"Merriweather Sloan."

Sol was silent as the name registered and then he burst out, "You are Merewether's son?"

"That's correct, sir."

"I remember meeting you many years ago when you were younger, quite a bit younger."

"I also remember those days when my dad would bring me here. I remember meeting you."

Sol stared intently, trying hard to reconcile the boy he had met with the man standing in front of him. It was impossible. "It's good to see you again." Sol said. "Now, tell me about your father. Where and how is he?"

"He is fine and he's living in a beautiful place outside of London. He said he misses the Village and especially, you."

"Yes, your father and I were very close, very close." Sol's mind flashed through a typical drunken weekend with Merri—one of so, so many. How wonderful he was, how romantic and beautiful, how willing a lover.

"I miss your father. I miss him more than I can possibly say."

"Maybe you should go over for a visit."

"No…" said Sol, shaking his head, "no matter how wonderful a moment in time may be, or may have been…once it is over, it is over. The moment is gone and only a fool thinks there is a chance to recapture it."

"Well, I can give you their address, if you like."

"Their address?"

"Of course, he's there with my mother."

"Your mother, how stupid of me. Well, yes, maybe I could write a short note. We were good friends."

The young man took a slip of paper from a book and leaning on the wall, wrote quickly. Then he handed it to Sol who looked at the neat script seeking a similarity that wasn't there.

"Now, let me ask, are you a student here?"

Almost laughing, the young man said, "No sir, I teach here. I just started as an assistant professor in the History Department."

"Well, that is wonderful. I'm sure your father is very proud."

"I'm not so sure about that. I think he would have preferred I become a plumber or an electrician. He always said it was very special to be able to work with your hands."

Sol briefly closed his eyes as he recollected Merriweather's hands—those wonderful hands. "Your father may be right, you know. Teaching at a university is not what it used to be. When he and I started, everything was different…everything. The job was rewarding, prestigious and meaningful. No longer true, I'm afraid."

"Be that as it may, I've found my life's work. I love history and I love to teach it."

"Well, you couldn't find a better bunch in need of instruction. Most of them think the world began three days or so before they were born."

"Oh, I don't know about that. They seem to be on the ball. So far, it's been thrilling."

"Really? Well… that's very nice…"

The young man looked at his watch. "Oh, I have a class now. It was great to see you and I'll tell my father I ran into you."

"Yes, please do."

As the young man made his way down the corridor, Sol thought about him. Assistant Professor…what was his name? He pumped through his memory and then it came to him. Stanley, Stanley Sloan, Assistant Professor Stanley Sloan. How about that?

At sixty-four, Sol wasn't old, but that young man made him feel very old. Why don't I retire and like Merriweather go to England, he asked himself. I could write another book… another perfectly useless book about clear thinking and the spoken word. He laughed to himself. When he started teaching he had speeches of every type to analyze…political speeches, inspirational speeches, instance after instance of learned people speaking intelligently to those who understood the subtlety and beauty of language and also, how it was used to make a point. Now the world was confronted with sound bites.

Because of television, most of his students had never seen a human being stand before others to deliver a speech aside from inaugurals and maybe a State of the Union. They knew what a speech was, but had no real understanding or appreciation of the complexity involved in a good one. C-Span provided coverage of congress and nothing more boring had yet been developed. The average politician made people happy that public speaking was a lost art. Those Washington jokers needed to make sense for a minute or two, at best, since the average person didn't or maybe couldn't pay attention longer than that, and the journalists who covered the political goings on, didn't care much for style. They were ready to dispute facts. Everything else seemed irrelevant to them.

He opened his office door and marched in, threw his books on the desk and plunked into the chair. He hadn't felt this lousy in a long time. Meeting that Sloan boy made it worse. It was all behind…over…done. All that remained was dying. He wondered if a lot of people his age looked at their life and realized how stupid and meaningless it had been. But was it meaningless? he asked himself. Was teaching these people worth anything? Was his research a waste of time? If he had never been here, someone else would have taught what he had; someone else would have written what he did; someone else would have had this office. A replaceable part… a well-engineered, but absolutely replaceable part… How sweet.

The telephone rang. He stared at it wondering if he should answer. Shrugging, he picked it up. "Hello."

"This is you know who and you know what you know who is holding in his hand."

Sol laughed. "How wonderful. You could not have called at a better time. I was ready to go out the window."

"Don't do something so stupid, you silly ass. Just get over here and take my you know what out of my hand. It's burning hot."

"Absolutely the right moment…and absolutely the right offer. I'll be over in fifteen minutes."

Smiling now, Sol hung up the phone, took a deep breath and said aloud, "Damn. That is just what the doctor ordered."

He looked at the pile of papers on his desk and the books he had just added to the pile. Not now, he thought. Why waste more of my life? He checked his pocket to make certain he had sufficient cigars for the evening. He had two. He opened a mahogany humidor on his desk and took three more which he carefully put into the fitted cigar holder built into his attaché case. He rubbed his hand across the smooth, lustrous leather and saw an analogy to his life… a case inside a case… a life inside a life.

Leaving his office and the school was always a pleasure. Rather than walk down, he grabbed the elevator. Outside, students were gathered by the bookstore discussing something with great vigor. At one time, it would have been whether the government's foreign policy would accomplish its stated goals. Now, he'd bet, it was more likely an assessment of the latest pot shipment to hit the Village.

In the same instant he realized he was being unfair. They might very well be arguing about movies, television, or which of the freshman girls gave a better blow job. He admitted he may not know their subject, but he knew with the wisdom of a shaman, their discussion most certainly had nothing to do with anything outside their immediate existence.

He walked across Mercer to Washington Square Village, two blocks away. He was sorry he had not gotten an apartment there when he had the chance, since it was so close and convenient, but… always a "but"… it would have put him in the thick of the academic circle. He was better off over on thirteenth. It was just far enough away to be handy, yet not an open declaration of affiliation with NYU. His distaste for the academic life had grown throughout the years as the students changed, but the faculty had changed even more. They were no longer humble or appreciative of creativity. Pomposity, bombast, arrogance, piled onto an unwarranted certainty that any position they took was correct. There was no longer the opportunity for debate. Debate could not exist when neither side would acknowledge the opposition could have a point. These people were by no means intellectual. In fact, they abhorred intellectuality. They sought a dictatorial construct with themselves as ringmasters. "Fuck 'em all." He muttered.

The elevator stopped at seventeen and he sauntered toward Cyril's apartment which had a terrace Sol liked. Cyril lived way up high because he needed the height. He needed the occasional sun. Who wouldn't after a full day and often a full night at dimly lit funeral parlors? Maybe it was the undertaking business that made Cyril so much fun. Sol wondered if dealing with death on a daily basis made one a better living person. That was a hard question to figure out, but in Cyril's case, it didn't matter. He was a joy.

He rang the bell and heard a distant voice yell, "Come in." He turned the knob and was amazed that the door opened. How wonderful and how foolish of him to leave the door unlocked. Cyril's refusal to come to the door could only mean he was unable to do so. And that would mean one of two things, he was in bed and wouldn't come out or, and what Sol hoped was true, he was in the Jacuzzi.

Sol closed and locked the door behind him. Then walked across the thick carpet to the bedroom where he saw the undisturbed bed. Turning and walking to what was once the dining room, he entered a stupendous bathroom. There in the center of it was a pink and blue tub; in it was Cyril.

"Come in, my love. Undress and join me."

Sol needed no additional urging. He perched on a velvet-covered stool and stripped. As he lowered himself into the hot water, the rich smells of the oils Cyril had added, reached his nostrils.

"You put in vanilla, and... and what is that? I know it, but I can't..."

"Cinnamon. Isn't it lovely?"

"It's lovely and you're lovely," he said, as he leaned to Cyril and kissed him. "You have no idea how welcome this is and how wonderful was your call. I was very, very low."

As Cyril leaned against Sol and slowly rubbed some oil onto his chest, he said, "I could ask what the trouble is, but that would mean you'd have to go through it as you tell me, so I'm not going to ask and I don't want you to think about it. Just lean back and let me massage you into a good mood."

Cyril's hands caressed the flesh of Sol's chest, his stomach and then lovingly fondled his testicles. "Oh...that's lovely, just lovely" Sol murmured. "Just let me float here forever with your hands where they now are. What more could I ask?"

Cyril kissed him and said softly, "There's no need to be upset, dear. All you have to do is float here with me and let me hold you."

They stayed in the tub for the remainder of the afternoon.

CHAPTER 5

"Please come in and sit down." Win said to Paul Coleman.

Coleman did and looked around Win's office, taking in the bare walls save for a large poster listing more than fifty ways to state Murphy's Law. Gesturing at the poster with his thumb, Coleman said, "I feel like that damn thing was written for me."

Win glanced at it. "Yeah, I've had days like that. I know what you mean."

"Professor, no disrespect, but I don't think you have any idea of the way my world has gone upside down."

"Out of joint, huh?"

"Oh yeah, since the damn thing happened, I'm like a jinx. The people in the program think I'm some kind of rapist or nutcase. It's the NYU–Greenwich Village version of the treatment they dish out at West Point."

Win felt sorry for him but kept his poker face because Coleman could actually be guilty. The last thing Win wanted was to feel sorry for a guy who did deserve to have the book thrown at him.

"Look, Mr. Coleman, why don't you tell me what happened the other day."

"Before I do, can I ask you some questions?"

"Certainly."

"Well, did you ever do anything and then wonder…why the hell did I do that? Or did you eat something you knew would disagree with you, but you ate it anyway? Or know you shouldn't do something because it was stupid or dangerous, but went right ahead and did it… or… oh, damn… this is so crazy."

"Wait a minute, Coleman, wait a minute. I'm beginning to catch your drift. Are you saying that what took place was something your conscious mind told you not to do, but you did anyway?"

"Well…yes and no. Once I started tearing at her clothes, I knew I shouldn't be doing that, but I couldn't stop."

"So… you were in some sort of fit. You were semi-aware of what you were doing but didn't have the…the…whatever to stop?"

"Yes…yes, something like that. I can't explain it. I don't even know what happened. All I remember is that this girl passed me in the hall…lingered a moment and then walked on. I was completely overcome by something and the next thing I knew I was grabbing her and trying to kiss her chest… her breasts."

Win leaned back in his chair. "You wanted to kiss her breasts?"

"Yeah, that's what they told me. Evidently I had torn her blouse at the neck and was trying to kiss her breasts."

"What the hell for?"

"You tell me. Someone tell me." He put his hands to his face and rocked in the chair. "I don't know what the hell is going on."

Win realized that whatever was going on was not something he understood either. Acting against better judgment was something everyone did at times, but this other business, the breast kissing. That was odd.

"Tell me, what did you mean when you said you were completely overcome by something?"

"I've been thinking about that and all I remember is a wonderful smell. The girl passed me and this wonderful, amazing smell came next. It was like she was being followed by a cloud."

"What kind of smell?"

"I don't know… a smell."

"Was it sweet, like flowers or perfume or like fresh bread or cake?"

"No… nothing like that. It wasn't a smell I could name. It was just a great and warm and wonderful pink smell. Oh, shit, I don't know what to say. How do you describe a colored smell you can't name?"

"To be sure, that's not easy."

Win had seen good acting and felt he was a decent judge. Coleman's tale wasn't a phony concoction to explain away what happened. His face had helplessness all over it and it suddenly hit Win that he believed the young man.

"Professor David, you gotta help me. I don't know what to do. If they throw me out, my whole future is smoke. How could I get into another grad school?"

"The police have not been brought into this, right?"

"No…I mean, yes… the police aren't involved. The guys in the hall who pulled me off never thought about calling the cops. Most of them said what I did was cool. You know… a college guy with uncontrollable gonads…that sort of thing. I don't think the girl talked about it to anyone besides the security guard, but I don't know." He paused. "Damn, I don't even know who she is."

"Well, this much I can tell you. The incident was reported to campus security and that's how word of what happened was spread. But right now, with the serial murderers and rapists around, what you did wouldn't rate much attention at the local precinct."

"Well, that's good, but I wish I could meet and talk to her. You know, to apologize." He sighed, stood and paced the few feet to the window. Win never fully realized how small his office was, but seeing Coleman trying to walk off his frustration made it clear. All he managed were three full steps before he had to turn around. This is not an office, Win thought, it's a cell.

When Coleman returned to the chair, he said, "Damn, I feel like shit over this. I don't know what to do."

"Tell me again. Try to remember what happened when she passed. Close your eyes if that'll help and try to recall what you felt and what you saw in your mind."

Coleman stared at him for a moment. Then leaned back in the chair, closed his eyes, took a deep breath, and started to talk.

"Okay. I just finished the aphasia class with Professor Conroy, and after saying a few things to one of the guys, I headed out. I was going to meet a girl for a cup of coffee at Bernie's. Anyway, I leave the room…204, the one with the piano in it, and I head down the hall for the staircase. There were people coming up and going down…the hallway was busy. Best as I can remember, I was walking close to the wall and passed another room…I guess 203 or 202, I don't remember which. There was a class letting out. So I moved to the center of the hallway to give the people coming out more room. And I think I even stopped to let a few girls get in front of me. Suddenly, this girl comes the other way. Maybe she came out of 201 or came up from downstairs, anyway, she's going the other way and she passes me on my left. Just as she passed I took a deep breath and whoa…lights flashed and everything seemed to turn one color…"

"What…everything turned a color?"

"Yeah."

"What color?"

"I don't know…sort of pink…a light pink I'd say."

17

"Not a dark color?"

"Oh no, that's clear. The color and the smell seemed to come together, but the color came first. Then this smell hits me."

"It was a pleasant smell… right?"

"Oh yeah, I never had a feeling like that smell created. First everything gets kind of pink-white and then wham, this wonderful smell joins in. My mind was racing and I remember now that I was sort of talkin' to myself. I remember asking myself if this smell was better than the smell of the perfumes and stuff the girls used when I was a kid."

"What do you mean by stuff?"

"You know the smell of their lipstick, hair spray, powder, rouge, make-up—all that. I remember that clearly. When I was first goin' out with girls and used to neck, they used to smell great. How they smelled was hard to beat."

"But this smell was better?"

"The smell had me swaying. I think I could have passed out. One second there's nothing and then bam, all of a sudden it hits and I feel warm, relaxed, secure, safe…can you get that? I feel all that in an instant. Like one breath it's not there and then another breath… it's all over the place." He stopped and shook his head. Then he leaned forward and spoke very slowly.

"This is crazy, right? I bet you never heard anything like this, right?"

"Take it easy, Paul, take it easy." Win stood and walked the few steps to the window. Turning back, he asked, "Would you like to go for a walk? Would that make it easier for you?"

"No. I'm okay. This place is fine…small, but fine."

Win took his seat. "Okay now, what happened next?"

"Best as I can remember, I stop in my tracks and turn to my left. I must have moved very quickly because this girl, the one, she jumps a bit and then she stops. She's looking at me. In an instant I know the smell is from her. There is absolutely no doubt in my mind and even though there are lots of people in the hallway, I know she's the one. So I throw my arms around her." He closed his eyes, but craned his neck forward like he was trying to see.

"She starts to scream and back up. Now, I have her in my arms and she is backing up so we are sort of tied together, dancing across the hallway. We would bounce into the wall, but there is an open door behind her so we go right into that room. She stops…I guess she pushed back and I stopped moving forward…so she stops and I try to nuzzle my head onto her boobs… her breasts. And before I know what the hell I am doing, I reach up and tear away her blouse. All the time I am trying to kiss her boobs, but before I am able to get my hands on her bra, a couple of guys who must have seen the whole thing, came into the room and pulled me away."

"What did she do at that moment?"

"Well, you got to realize this whole thing took...probably less than thirty seconds. It was like a flash. All the time, she was screaming and her eyes were as big as saucers. She was terrified... that's what I really feel bad about. She was really scared and... I guess she had a right to be." He paused. "Professor, you got anything to drink in here?"

"No. I'm sorry, but come on, let's walk down the hall to the lounge. I'll buy you one."

As they walked, Win stared at Coleman and realized he was just a normal guy. Just a decent guy caught in something he couldn't understand. Win laughed to himself. Coleman wasn't the only one who didn't understand what was going on.

They got to the lounge and Win bought two cans of soda from the machine. Then he sat facing Coleman and for a moment neither said anything. They opened the cans and drank.

Then Win asked, "Tell me, do you remember having feelings like that before, even close to what you felt in the hallway?"

"I thought about that and the only thing that's close is when I was a kid... a little kid."

"How little?"

"I don't know, but young. Really young."

"Was what you recalled a good feeling? Was it a pleasant memory?"

"Oh yeah, though it's really confusing, but smelling that girl and those kid memories all seem to be related in some way. It was like every question you ever asked was answered and every answer was the one you wanted. It was all about peace and security."

Win could not remember if he ever had a feeling that matched Coleman's description. He thought back to his early days of pot smoking—not even then would he have described his highs with those words.

"Do you have anything to add? Is there anything you haven't told me?"

"No, Professor, that's what happened—every weird bit of it."

"Okay. Now I'm going to call a colleague who will have a meeting with the young lady. When that is done, I'll let you know what's going to happen next."

Win could see Coleman wanted to say something else, but was hesitating. "What is it, Paul? Have you left something out?"

"No Sir, it's that I want a favor. Could you get me the name of the girl so I can apologize to her?"

"Well, I'll ask. She may not want to meet with you, you know, but I'll ask. Also, if things work out as I think they will, I'll want you and the girl to come to a meeting with some colleagues of mine so we can learn more about all of this. If we have that meeting, then you can apologize to her."

"Okay." Said Coleman, "that'll be fine."

"Before you leave give me your phone number so I can call you directly."

"Hey, Professor David, I feel a lot better. I don't know what to say except, thanks."

"You're very welcome, Paul, and if it will help, I do believe what you told me was the truth and I hope we can make this incident a thing of the past in a short time."

"That would be great." He wrote his phone number on a slip of paper and after handing it over, got up, smiled, shook Win's hand and left the lounge.

Win finished his soda and walked back to his office to call Gert. "Well, what did that little shit have to say for himself?" she asked.

He told her that Coleman did not seem to be a nut or a pervert and that the entire affair could be easily dealt with once they had a meeting with the girl. Gert told him she had already arranged that meeting and it would take place shortly.

Win related what Coleman had said and added that he didn't think Coleman was a liar, a nut or a criminal. As they spoke, Win could tell Gert was uneasy and wondered if she wanted Coleman to be guilty so she could arrange a lynching or its Greenwich Village equivalent. Eventually, though, he sensed she accepted the idea of Coleman's innocence and promised to call after she talked to the girl.

CHAPTER 6

Gert trudged into her office and released an armload of books onto the table alongside her desk. Then, turning toward her computer, she wondered how long it would take for her books to be scanned so she could trade the weighty cargo for a few discs. One of these days, she hoped.

She cleared the top of her desk by pushing everything on it to one side to make room for the papers she intended to grade. As she was about to start, the phone rang. It was Win telling her he had completed the conference with Coleman and that he believed the boy to be innocent of any criminal action. Since Gert had immediately taken sides, she was now stuck with her guilty verdict, but out of respect for Win, she promised him and herself to listen to the girl's story.

Meeting with the young lady would be important because they had been assured the administration would abide by their collective decision. Win was dubious about that because he said he would never fully trust any administration. As he, she knew the administration played the game for their personal benefit and were not zealous about policies or programs helpful to the only group that mattered—the students. Too many administrators thought they were the reason for the university's existence and that their work would be better recognized and certainly more appreciated if they could eliminate students and the faculty from the campus.

However, if it ever came to taking sides, Gert knew she'd be more comfortable with the administration because she shared Sol's view of the faculty as a loose-knit bunch of pompous, arrogant snobs. Though, to be honest, she thought the administration only slightly less awful. Being part of a group you didn't want to be part of echoed Groucho's famous observation, but it was the truth. Her way to deal with it was to hang out with the rebels like Sol and Winthrop and to keep a distance from both the faculty and the administration.

A knock on the door pulled her away from her thoughts.

"Come," she shouted.

The door opened slowly and framed a sweet-looking young lady who Gert assumed to be Susan Merrill, the attacked.

"Miss Merrill?" Gert asked.

"Yes, Professor Lehman. May I come in?"

Gert was astonished by the question. The typical student barged in and took a seat—any seat. Once she had to hoist an overgrown lardass from her chair, because he had marched in and sat at her desk while she was across the room. Eventually, she realized this typical bozo didn't have bad manners, rather, he didn't know right from wrong. There had been no social instruction from his parents and since this particular behavior wasn't featured on TV or in some stupid movie, how could he learn of it.

"Yes, Miss Merrill, please come in and sit there." Gert pointed to a chair. The girl entered and rather stiffly sat. She crossed her legs at the ankle, folded her hands in her lap, and then looked at Gert with a slight, but friendly smile. Gert enjoyed the show. Miss Merrill acted like she was auditioning for the lead in a British boarding school movie.

Her manner was as appropriate as her outfit. She was wearing brown leather boots, neatly pressed jeans, a red and white checked blouse, and a navy blazer—fashion smart and quite collegiate. Dark, well-coiffed hair framed pink skin and dark green eyes. The bright smile was an added plus. Gert liked her immediately and wondered if Coleman's little escapade was nothing but a sham so he could get his paws on her. It wouldn't be the first time some smart-ass came up with a novel self-introduction.

"Miss Merrill, do you understand why you have been told to see me?"

"Yes, Professor Lehman, Dean Grossman explained that this affair should be handled at the faculty level, with formal authorities kept out of it. He said that if there would be criminal charges or anything like that, then his office and the police would have to get involved. He also told me the boy's name is Paul Coleman."

"That's right, Miss Merrill, for once the administration has used its collective head and kept things off the hot burner. It is possible, however, for things to get messy."

"I guess a lot of it depends on what I say, right?"

"Absolutely, since you haven't formally pressed charges, the event is unsettled, a non-affair, but something did happen and a resolution is necessary."

"Yes, but you have to understand, what happened the other day was more of a surprise than anything. I wasn't hurt or anything and the only damage were three buttons torn off my blouse."

"Aside from a sexual assault, of course. But tell me, had you met Mr. Coleman before?"

"No, but I'd seen him a few times coming from his class as I was going to mine."

"I see." Gert sensed no outrage or anger in the girl, so the incident would probably blow over. Nonetheless, it was important they do the job they set out to do.

"Miss Merrill, why don't you tell me what happened. Take your time, try to leave nothing out and starting from when you entered the building tell me what took place." Gert was pleased with her little speech. It had a professional polish, like the good TV cop.

"Okay, that won't be hard" The girl uncrossed her ankles and planted both feet on the floor.

"I was going to class in that building. It's on the second floor and I was going down the corridor past a lot of people going the other way from classes that had let out. It was the usual mob scene. Everyone was trying to get out at one time. I remember I passed a few guys and a few girls and then this guy…he stops short. I noticed that because everyone else was walking. He just froze." She paused, took a deep breath and crossed her legs at the knee.

"It was like he had just heard a noise, you know, like maybe you're out someplace quiet and then suddenly there's a loud noise and you'd turn your head in the direction where the noise came from. You know what I mean? You'd try to pinpoint the source of the sound?" Gert nodded.

"Well, that's what he did. He stopped short, stuck his neck out and then turned and looked straight at me. His eyes were wide open, really bright. He's got nice eyes."

"I haven't seen them yet." said Gert.

"Oh, well, I guess you will. Anyway, he's kind of cute."

Gert laughed. "Miss Merrill, let's try to stick to the facts, okay?" Gert realized at that moment there would be no police involved in this affair… maybe a motel clerk, but no cops. "What happened next?" she asked.

"Well, like I said, he stopped short. Then he turned toward me, hesitated for a second or two and then lunged and grabbed me. I screamed, I guess, and tried to back up. You know, to get away from him."

"Did he say anything?"

"Oh, no. His eyes were closed and he was sniffing."

"Sniffing?"

"Yes. His eyes were closed and his nose was kind of up in the air, like this." She raised her chin, pointed her nose frontward and took in three short bursts of air. Gert was watching closely and understood exactly what Miss Merrill meant…sniffing.

"So while he was…sniffing…where was his head? Was it at your neck? Where?"

"No. All the time he was sniffing he was trying to kiss my breasts."

"Both? Was he trying to kiss both of them at the same time? Was his face in the middle of your bosom?"

"No. I would have to say he was trying harder to kiss the left one more than the right."

"Okay," said Gert. She thought this was getting a little weird, but she had volunteered to do her part. "Okay. So he was trying to kiss your left breast more than the right. Then what?"

"Well, as I said, I started to back up and he was pushing forward so we kind of bounced out of the hallway into a classroom behind me. When I realized we were in a room and not in the hall any longer, I got real nervous, so I started to fight back and scream louder. Nothing seemed to get through to him and it wasn't until some of the other students pulled him away that he seemed to understand what he had done."

"What do you mean?"

"Like I said, he pulled a few buttons from my blouse and… that's it." Sheepishly, she added, "I hope this doesn't give you the wrong impression of me, Professor Lehman, but to be truthful, I think I kind of enjoyed it all. Never before did a guy go into a trance on me. It was weird."

"But aren't you even a little angry at him?"

"Oh, no…well, I guess I am a little upset, but…ugh…I think I'd like to go out with him or something."

"Or something?"

"Well, I've been to fraternity parties and had more than a few buttons off my clothes at the end of the night. I never complained to anyone about that and those parties are fun. I think this whole thing just took me by surprise. Maybe that's what the issue really is."

Gert got the very clear impression that Mr. Coleman had scored a home run. Certainly this young girl thought him far more attractive now than she would have if she just bumped into him on the stairs. There was no case here and there was no way there would be any charges pressed.

"Well, Miss Merrill, I think what you're trying to tell me…is number one, you're not overly upset about any of this. Number two, you'd like a date with Mr. Coleman, and, number three, you enjoyed the whole thing…right?"

Miss Merrill smiled and the room lit up. Quite clearly this young lady was bathing in the juices Mr. Coleman had stirred. The guy really had scored.

After what Gert thought a pregnant pause, she smiled, and asked, "Is there anything else you feel worth mentioning?"

Miss Merrill looked at the floor and then at the wall. Her face seemed to flush with embarrassment. Then she looked at Gert and said, "I thought about this and I know you'll think I'm crazy, but since you asked. In the park, you know, Washington Square, well, I've seen mothers nursing and that's what I think he had on his mind. It wasn't a sexual thing with him. I think he wanted to nurse."

Gert stared at her thinking we've crossed the line…we have definitely moved into another dimension. Then, after a moment, Gert asked the only thing she could think to ask "Miss Merrill have you ever had a child?"

"No, and I know what you're thinking. That's what I thought also. How could I know that? How could I know what that felt like? Well, it's like all the things I've read about breast feeding. The baby is peaceful, blissful. Its eyes are shut and there's lots of sniffing and sucking. That's what happened. I'm sure that's what was on his mind." She paused and then burst out. "You're going to think me terrible, but I really got aroused. He didn't seem aroused, but I was. It was kind of wonderful."

Okay, Gert said to herself, okay. Here is this young lady who thinks the guy who attacked her was really after milk for his Wheaties. Therefore, there was no way this, this…whatever it was…could possibly be seen as criminal. Gert thought a moment and then asked, "Tell me, if you can, Miss Merrill, why did he want to nurse at your breasts and not someone else's?"

"Oh, yes, I did think about that and I have no idea. We must have passed each other in the hall three times a week for the last six weeks. Now that's a lot and he never noticed me before."

"Had you noticed him?"

25

"Well…yes…I guess I did."

"Well, that really doesn't matter since you didn't attack him…he attacked you."

"Yes, I see your point."

"Tell me, was there anything you did that day or that morning that was different from what you usually did… anything that was not like the day before?"

She looked at the ceiling, the floor, the walls, focusing on the array of diplomas, awards, certificates, and framed letters celebrating Gert's contributions to science and to the chemical industry.

"Anything?" Gert asked once more.

"Well, the thing I can think of is a new perfume. My mother sent it to me and I used it that day. Everything else was usual, my clothes, my makeup, and so on. The only different thing would have to be that perfume."

"Well," Gert said, smirking, "That's very, very interesting." She paused for a moment, then said, "Well, maybe your perfume clouded Mr. Coleman's mind and caused him to lose control, and not only that, but the smell of it took him back to when he was a baby nursing at his mother's breast."

The young lady looked perplexed. "Is something like that possible? Could my perfume cause him to do that?"

"Miss Merrill, as you can understand, anything is possible, but I don't think that's what happened."

They sat looking at each other wondering if Gert's estimation could in any way be true. Then after a moment Gert shook her head. "No. That would really be crazy, so I'm going to forget I said it. I think you should forget about it as well."

Miss Merrill closed her eyes, shook her head and smiled that beautiful smile. "That would be goofy, wouldn't it?"

Nodding, Gert said, "Okay, let's wrap this up, shall we? Is it fair for me to say you don't want to press charges or demand any disciplinary action be taken against Mr. Coleman?"

"Right, I really wasn't hurt and I still think he's kind of cute."

"Okay, Miss Merrill, you've made yourself abundantly clear. Let me get back to my colleague who interviewed Mr. Coleman. After I have spoken to him, I'll get back to you. Will that be satisfactory?"

"Oh sure, that'll be fine."

She stood and extended her hand which Gert shook. Then she turned, opened the door, and gracefully left the room.

Gert stared at the wall for a moment and then called the dean.

CHAPTER 7

Gert checked the room to see if everything was where she wanted it. Cheese, crackers, and wine were on the small table by the sofa, the music was on, the lights were adjusted, and Sol's ashtray was placed so he wouldn't miss it. She smiled at that thought because the rug alongside the chair where Sol usually sat showed a blotchy gray square from the pounds of ash deposited there. A spot Sol referred to as the Greenwich Village answer to Mount Saint Helens.

A while back Gert insisted Sol provide his own ashtray, and he had done himself proud. He paid a local potter to make an ashtray that looked like human lungs, and because Sol was no cheapskate, the result was an anatomical dead ringer for the real thing. The potter added black to the pink glaze so the lungs looked not only real, but sick. It was grotesque and Sol loved it. Gert also liked it, particularly when other guests spied it under the chair (where it was kept) and jumped about a foot.

The plan for the evening was to conclude the Coleman—Merrill calamity, because a rapid resolution would make everyone happy. Dean Grossman was nervous and wanted everything settled before any negative publicity surfaced.

At ten minutes to seven, there was a double ring from downstairs and Gert knew it was Sol. The intercom system in the entrance held a hidden TV that sent a signal to a monitor in her bedroom closet. After checking that screen, she hit the button opening the downstairs door.

Sol was always early, because he lived half a block away in one of those white-brick rabbit warrens that had been built all over the city in the early sixties. Fortunately for him, his particular building was substantial. So many look-alikes on the Upper East side were poorly made. A toilet flush on an upper floor sounded like Niagara Falls as liquids plummeted down to the sewers. It was crazy, but whenever the penthouse tenants had diarrhea, the entire building lost sleep listening, throughout the night, to cascading fluids.

Gert knew she could never deal with anything like that so she got her own place…her very own brownstone. She bought it when one of her patents was licensed by a major cosmetic conglomerate and the flow of endless dollars started. Since that time, Gert had developed other items for the same organization bringing in even more money. Her financial position went far to explain her independence. She had enough money to say anything to anyone.

Maybe twice a year Gert would travel uptown to Bloomingdale's and Bergdorf's to watch the action at the cosmetic counters and make notes of the prices. She did not understand women's need to spend what they did for such products, but her glee watching the extravaganza was hard to match. As a chemist, she approached almost every product as nothing more than a mixture of raw materials. Creams, lotions, balms, and applications of all types were as easy to knock off in her lab as it was to make pancake batter in the kitchen. Once, for fun, she made two pounds of cold cream for the same money an ounce cost in an East-side boutique.

Thankfully, the cosmetic company money permitted her to redesign, rebuild, and refurbish her brownstone following a plan she created. There were living quarters on the street level and the third floor and a state of the art laboratory in between. The lab was completely sealed off except for a door behind false windows facing the street. The only other way in was by an elevator built into the wall of Gert's bedroom. She never forgot the look of disbelief on the faces of the elevator company people when she explained what she wanted and how it was to be built. They thought her crazy, but when she waved the checkbook, she got exactly what she wanted.

Sol thumped the door and when she opened it, he swirled into the room.

"Good to see you, my dear," he said and offered a cheek to cheek on either side.

"Come in, come in. Sit down and eat, drink, and smoke that dirty cigar."

"Oh, you're a darling. It's at a point out there where lighting up has become a capital crime."

Gert nodded. "Don't forget, Sol, tonight is business so please limit your drinks."

"Okay, Sarge, I'll take it easy."

"Please do, I want to get this out of the way so we can attend to our own business. Volunteering for this was okay, but I don't want to start doing the administration's work. They do shit little now, and if they find out we actually can do something, they'll jump at every opportunity for us to do more of their work."

Sol smiled as he walked across the room to "his" chair and plopped into it. The cigar was in his mouth a few seconds later.

"Red or white?" Gert asked.

"Some red, if you would. I feel rather continental tonight" She brought him a glass and he placed it on the table alongside the lung-like ashtray. Lighting up, he blew a cloud of smoke into the room and said, "I had a nice shock earlier today."

"What?" she asked, sitting across from him.

"I ran into Merriweather Sloan's son, Stanley. Believe it or not, he's an assistant prof. in the History Department and he told me Merri is living outside of London with his wife. What do you think of that?"

Gert looked surprised. "No shit? Merriweather Sloan's kid? I remember him when he was about nine or ten."

"Same here…I couldn't believe he's grown up and teaching here."

"You had a good thing with Merri, didn't you?"

"Oh, Gert what can I say? I was depressed all day, as usual, because the Sloan boy brought back so many things I had stashed away."

"You seem okay now. What did you do? A handful of ups?"

"No. I skipped my dance lesson and spent the afternoon with Cyril. He called at exactly the right moment and we spent delicious hours in his tub. Talk about good timing."

As he said that the downstairs bell rang. Gert went to the extension intercom by the door and asked who was there. Win's metallic voice resounded from the small speaker. Gert buzzed him, and a moment later he walked in. He nodded to Sol, and, following Gert's pointed finger, sat on the sofa. "Help yourself—red or white. And the cheese is fresh, so fill up. I'm sure you haven't eaten."

"Don't mind if I do," Win answered, pouring wine and then heaping a one- inch layer of cheese on a cracker, which he stuffed into his mouth. Two chews and he washed it down with a gulp of wine. "That's good cheese, Gert…where?"

"Balducci's. You shouldn't have to ask."

"I know, I know, but I always ask and I always tell myself I'll go there and buy some stuff, but then I get busy and, well, you know."

"Right, but sooner or later, you'll move your butt and buy a quarter pound of something."

"I won't hold my breath," said Sol.

They were silent for just the right amount of time for Gert to call their meeting to order. "Win, tell us about your talk with Coleman."

"There's nothing much to say. The guy is as sorry as can be and afraid he'll get thrown out of school. I don't think he had any evil or even any sexual intentions. What happened is a real aberration, a total anomaly. He can't explain it and after listening to him relate what happened, neither can I. He seems to have gone blank as the girl passed and then he grabbed her so he–I'm quoting now–'so he could kiss her chest, her breasts.'"

Sol looked owlish in surprise. "He wanted to kiss her breasts?" he asked in a tone mingling disbelief and delight. "He wanted to kiss her titties? My oh my, what a crafty ploy."

Shaking his head, Win said, "No, Sol, I think you're wrong. He was not working a pickup or a weird hello. I think he was just trying to get out of the building when she walked by and caused him to have some sort of fit. He went blank, until he realized what was going on, but by then he was already nuzzling away." Win sipped more wine, smeared cheese on another cracker and went on. "This is the part that has me buffaloed. He said the whole event was prompted by the girl's smell."

As they stared at him, he said, "I know what you're going to ask and he has no idea what the smell was. He said it was not perfume like, not food like…just an overpowering, sweet smell that he found unbelievably pleasant." He sipped more wine, and then said, "The smell is the key. That's what set him off." Win shrugged and stuffed another cheese-covered cracker into his mouth.

"That's it?" Gert asked. "That's all he had to say?"

"That's right. He doesn't deny a thing, but he says he doesn't know why he did it."

"Well then…how the hell can we make a decision?" Sol asked.

"Our job as I see it," Win said, "is not to look for motivation or explanation, but rather, to focus on the outcome. Mr. Coleman is ready to take the leap. He's really broken up and sorry as hell." He started to lather another cracker as he looked at Gert.

"What did you find out from the girl?"

"She's a real cutie, has enough manners and style for the entire freshman class, and, hold onto your hats… is ready to run off with Mr. Coleman the instant he asks."

"No kidding?" asked Sol.

"Deadly serious. The whole thing is funny because Miss Merrill was quite as surprised at what happened as the boy said he was. She had seen him coming from class a few times, but she said he never gave her a tumble. I can't say she has a crush on him, but right now, he's very high on her list."

Sol picked up his wine glass and dipped the end of his cigar into it. After a soaking, he put the glass down and the cigar back into his mouth. Working the end of it with his teeth and tongue, he inhaled deeply and blew out a plume of smoke. "Quite obviously," he said, "there is no reason to call the police or alert the administration. This is a non-issue."

"That's how I feel," said Win, as he and Sol looked at Gert.

"Okay. That's what I thought would be the case. All that happened here was a loss of three buttons, and that's no big deal, since Miss Merrill stated she had lost far more than that at fraternity parties."

Sol giggled. "Neither of you would believe what I lost at a fraternity party."

"Stop!" called out Gert. "I don't want to hear that story. You know damn well you never lost a thing. All your life you've been giving things away."

CHAPTER 8

Sol laughed out loud and with his glass offered a midair toast to Gert. Win also laughed and asked, "Okay, what's our next move?"

Gert stood and faced them. "Now, don't get pissed, but I invited them both to join us. They should be here about eight or so."

Looking more surprised than Win, Sol asked, "Why did you do that?"

"There's more to this than you think. At first, I wrote it off as a wiseass student who figured out a great pickup move. But after talking to the girl and hearing what Win learned from the boy, well... something else is going on."

"What?" asked Win, but before Gert could answer, he blurted out, "I bet you mean something with the smell business, right?"

"Exactly."

"Okay, it is the basis for Coleman's actions. He says the smell was what set him off."

"Right, and Miss Merrill said the only thing she did differently that day compared to other days, was to use a perfume her mother had recently sent."

Sol huffed. "You two are just barely making sense. Win, are you saying the boy said the girl's smell was what triggered his actions? And you," he said, turning to Gert, "are you saying the girl used a special perfume that day?"

"Right you are," said Gert. "But I don't know if the girl's perfume is special or just plain old perfume. Or maybe the boy has a weird affinity for a particular odor or odor component."

"Well," said Sol, "if you don't know what's going on, what makes you think those kids will know?"

"That's not really the only reason I asked them over. There's something else...something I want Miss Merrill to tell you about. I've told her not to mention it to anyone and she promised she wouldn't."

"By the way," asked Win, "are they coming together?"

"No. I thought it would be best if they met here. I particularly want Mr. Coleman to hear Miss Merrill's ideas about what she thinks he was doing."

"What is that?" asked Sol.

"I'm not going to tell you. I'd like both of you to hear it as he does."

Sol nodded and stuck the tip of his cigar back into his wine, Win said, "Well, that's okay with me."

As they waited, Gert brought out what she called a sandwich buffet—plates of cold cuts, bread, pickles, coleslaw, potato salad, paper plates, plastic knives and forks, napkins, soda and cups.

"My God," said Sol. "This is a he-man picnic. Shall I run off to the park and get some ants?"

As they admired Gert's handiwork, the downstairs bell rang. "Win, would you go down and let Mr. Coleman in?"

"Sure, but how do you know it's him?"

"He was told to come at eight. She at eight-fifteen. I stressed the time difference."

Win went downstairs, and after a few moments, ushered Mr. Coleman into the room.

"Professor Gert Lehman and Professor Solomon Woodrow...this is Mr. Paul Coleman." Coleman nodded at them both and stood frozen by the door looking like a private meeting generals for the very first time.

"Come in, Mr. Coleman," said Gert. "Take a seat there by the counter and make yourself a sandwich. We were just about to do the same."

"Gert," said Sol, "Don't you think we should wait for Miss Merrill before we chow down?"

Gert looked at Sol the same way she used to look at her mother when her mother would put her down. "Okay, okay, I guess you're right. We probably should wait."

"You mean she's coming here?" asked Coleman. "Oh, god, is she bringing the cops? Am I history?"

"Hey, take it easy," said Win. "Professor Lehman invited you both because there's a mystery in all this... and secondly, there are no cops and no problems. The entire incident will be very quickly forgotten."

Coleman's face lit up and a yard-wide smile spread over it. "Wow, that's great. I've been so upset...so worried I couldn't sleep." He blinked, looked at the ceiling, then at Gert. "You know, it would be one thing to tell my folks I screwed up and flunked out, but to tell them I got booted because I molested a girl would not be very cool."

"No question about that young man," said Sol. "Just forget about going home. Your "problem" is over. Tomorrow we will tell Dean Grossman that the incident has been adjudicated."

"So," said Gert, "that's that." As if planned, the downstairs bell rang. "I'll go," said Win. A moment later, he escorted Miss Merrill into the room.

Everyone, especially Mr. Coleman, sat up. Miss Merrill looked wonderful. She was wearing heels; dark hose; a slim, dark skirt; and a, light-blue sweater. She wore just the right amount of makeup and had fashioned her hair to frame her face. Quite a pretty picture, thought Gert.

Win, a step behind Miss Merrill facing the "audience," noticed their varied facial expressions. Gert's face registered approval, as did Sol's, while Mr. Coleman looked like Columbus sighting land.

"How good of you to come," Gert said, walking to Miss Merrill. Then she introduced the others. Everyone smiled except Paul, who looked at the floor when Susan looked at him. While she continued to stare at him, he looked up and then quickly looked down at the floor. Then, quite softly, he said, "Miss Merrill, I'm really sorry about what happened. I feel terrible and I hope you will forgive me."

She walked across the short space separating them to a spot directly in front of him. "I think I know how embarrassed you must be, but I want you to know I accept your apology and hope we can be friends."

He looked up and smiled. "I sure hope so. I really do."

"Now… that that's settled," said Gert, "we can get on with the evening. Right now, please come and grab something to eat. After, we'll talk."

They filled their plates and said little while they ate because they were joyously watching Mr. Coleman create and eat two monstrous sandwiches. He relished the food, but his eyes broadcast his real desire. If there were a law against staring, he would have been stood against a wall and shot. But that is not to say Susan was trying to hide. She managed to place her anatomy in just the right spot for his close and unswerving observations.

"In a bit," announced Gert, "we'll have some coffee and dessert and then we'll talk about this business." Everyone nodded and kept chewing. Fifteen minutes later they were in a circle around the sofa, scraping cake remains off the paper plates.

"Okay, now that the food is out of the way, let's try to make some sense of this."

Looking at Sol, she said, "You're the only one who did not have a chance to speak directly to either of these young people, so you have no accurate idea of what transpired. Let me bring you up to speed." Gert told Sol what she recalled and Win added what he had learned. When they finished, they invited both Susan and Paul to fill in gaps or clarify whatever needed it.

"So," said Sol, "what we have here is a case of Mr. Coleman violently reacting to an olfactory stimulus provided by Miss Merrill's perfume, which she is obviously not wearing tonight." Everyone smiled. "The perfume," he continued, "is no doubt the causative agent and managed to overcome Mr. Coleman's sense of propriety. If I recall properly, that sort of thing is not unheard of. Many native cultures use hallucinogenic potions that have wildly prominent odors and produce exceedingly exotic results."

"I think we all understand that, Sol, but what is special here is not that Mr. Coleman reacted as he did, rather, what Miss Merrill told me she believes he was trying to do."

Paul looked at Susan and asked, "Do you think I was trying to do something other than just...umm...undress you and...umm...well, you know?"

Before she could answer, Gert said, "Mr. Coleman, I think we all assumed you were trying to get into her pants, no more no less."

"Now wait a minute, Gert. What other reason could there be?" Win asked.

"Yes," added Sol. "I'll second that."

Gert turned to Susan, "Why don't you tell them what you told me? Tell them your theory."

The young girl was obviously embarrassed, but she said, "I told Professor Lehman that the bliss or ecstasy Mr. Coleman experienced, that he told you about, and what we've talked about was not pleasure derived from sexual satisfaction, either actual or expected."

"Then what was it from, my dear?" asked Sol.

"Well, I told Professor Lehman that after I had a chance to think about what happened and his expression, I felt he looked and acted like babies nursing at their mother's breasts." There was silence.

"You can go down to the park any afternoon and watch, I have. The babies snuggle up. They sort of burrow in to their mother's breasts and suckle. When they do that, they're totally at peace, completely relaxed and detached from the world. It's wonderful to see and...and that's the way Mr. Coleman looked. He didn't seem to be after a cheap sex thing. I think he wanted to nurse at my breasts."

"You think I wanted what?" Mr. Coleman blurted out.

She turned to him and with a look of absolute certainty on her face said, "Well, you may not realize the truth, but I know. You were too busy to understand what you were doing."

Paul shook his head and then shrugged his shoulders. "I'd like to say you're wrong, but why not? That explanation makes as much sense as what I did."

"But why?" asked Win. "What would have caused him to seek..." He paused and, turning to Coleman, said, "You told me you were overcome by a wonderful smell and that things turned pinkish, right?"

"Pinkish?" asked Sol. "Shouldn't it have been blue?"

"You mean I should have been thinking of a boy's blanket, something typically blue?" asked Paul.

"Yes," said Gert, "that's what I also thought, the typical color."

"But," Susan said, "if I were the typical mother, nursing him about ..." she looked at Mr. Coleman..."about twenty-five years ago?" He nodded. She smiled triumphantly and then said, "I would be wearing a white bra, but my skin was pink. That would explain his recollection of the pinkish-white color."

"Mr. Coleman," asked Win, "were you nursed as a child?"

"I don't remember. I'd have to call home."

"Please do that. I'm really interested in knowing."

"Okay."

They sat staring at each other. All of them confused except Miss Merrill, who looked the picture of satisfaction.

"Mr. Coleman, tell me, do you have any desire right now..." asked Gert, "to nuzzle, suckle, kiss, whatever? Do you have any immediate desire to jump on Miss Merrill's chest?"

He looked at Miss Merrill and smiled. "No, I can safely say that what I feel right now about Miss Merrill has nothing to do with breast-feeding." The smile turned into a leer. "Nothing that wholesome." He softly added.

Miss Merrill flashed a smile and then blushed.

"Hold on, hold on," said Gert. "Let's put a damper on that for the moment. I still have a couple of questions—well, more requests than questions."

They all looked at her. "Mr. Coleman, I want you to find out two things for me. One, call home and find out if you were, in fact, breast fed, and two, what, if any, was the brand of perfume your mother wore during that time of her life. Would you do that for me... for us?"

"Sure...that'd be no problem, I guess."

"Fine. Now, Miss Merrill, I would love to get my hands on that perfume your mother sent. Would it be possible for you to bring it to me so I can analyze it? Would you do that?"

"Of course, that would be the least I could do to repay your kindness."

CHAPTER 9

Because the carrot cake was a hit, Gert started another pot of coffee. While it dripped, Win asked Gert if he could invite Lydia to hear about Paul's trance and Susan's theory. Gert agreed and a few minutes later Lydia joined them. Win introduced her telling Susan and Paul that she was Gert's tenant in the downstairs apartment and that she was also an executive in an advertising agency.

Win could never get enough of Lydia. Her beauty constantly amazed him for he thought no woman was as perfectly formed. Try as he might to establish a relationship with her, she never offered herself beyond an occasional admittance to her private world. She was as ambitious as she was stunning and everyone but Win could see he did not figure in her long-term plans.

Quickly and precisely, he told her what had happened and about the "why" of tonight's meeting. Lydia's inquisitiveness was immediate.

"You mean, Mr. Coleman, when you passed Miss Merrill in the corridor— just passed her," she repeated, her voice colored with awe, "and you got a whiff of the perfume she was wearing, you freaked?"

"That's about the size of it, Miss Cornell. It was like a blanket over my head. Everything else was blotted out. The only important thing was getting close to more of that wonderful smell."

From under the umbrella of hovering blue smoke, Sol said, "You know Lydia, when I recall years long past, I remember moments when I allowed myself to completely abandon my morality, my judgment… call it what you will… and fling myself at the object of my desire. What Mr. Coleman did is not so remarkable when viewed through an historical lens. Nowadays, unfortunately, actions such as his seem odd because so many are terrified of' "offending" a living creature by committing a politically incorrect act."

"Living creature?" asked Win.

"Of course. It's not just people nervous about dealing with other people. My god, that's the least of it. Every day, I see people talking to their pets, pleading for absolution or seeking forgiveness for a transgression." He stood and struck a pose as if talking to an imaginary dog. "You've all seen the blue-haired ladies and their little beasts, 'Oh poochy woochy, forgive mommykins for stepping on your toesey-woesey'. Or, 'Next time I will remember to be nice to your pal Fido and not be angry when he poops on my four-hundred dollar shoes. Forgive me, pooch-woochy. Please forgive mommykins. My god, it's obvious that slighting poochy woochy is just awful, but," He turned to face them. "The reverse is true. Dogs are trying so hard to please they are having heart attacks and now require counselors and psychiatrists."

"God, Sol, is it that bad?" asked Lydia, trying hard to stop laughing.

"That, my dear, is just the half of it."

"Well," said Gert, "I haven't heard one of your monologues for quite a while. You must be pretty well relaxed."

"Yes…yes… the fruit of the vine."

"Professor Woodrow, you're funny. I never thought professors could be funny. None of mine ever smile or crack a joke."

"My dear, Miss Merrill," announced Sol, in his best oratorical style, "in this room you have three of the wisest, most human, fun-loving members of the faculty of this most refined and esteemed institution." He paused to take another gulp of wine. "Maybe a bit later, I will do my snake dance for you."

"Hey Sol, take it easy, you'll scare them." Gert said, pouring coffee for him as she removed his wine glass from the side table.

While she finished her cake, Lydia, desiring more information, arranged a meeting with Miss Merrill. "I want to hear more of your reactions to everything," she said to the younger girl. Then turning to the group, she said, "You wouldn't know, but I've been handed a new work assignment that ties in with all this."

"Tell us, dear girl, Tell us how the hucksters will be appropriating my funds as I sleep."

"Oh, come on Sol, advertising is not the enemy."

"Not the enemy you say? Not the enemy?" He sat up straight, leaned forward, and energetically used his cigar to punctuate his words. "Let us not forget what Lord Halsbury said to the House of Lords."

Before he could continue, Gert interrupted him. "Don't blame her. Just because she works in advertising doesn't mean she created the industry, and my friend… as you well know, there are good and bad guys everywhere." Then, she turned to Lydia "Tell us, what about this new assignment?"

"Well, my agency handles the Allison-Taylor account, and their new division is trying to come up with a new fragrance. When they do, I have to develop a promotional rationale for it. But if I can find a product as well as produce the copy, well, that would be fantastic."

Win laughed. "Can you imagine a manufactured product that would replicate what happened to Mr. Coleman?"

"Oh that would be wonderful," said Susan, "It could be called Complete Abandon."

Lydia froze and stared at her for a long moment. "Please say that again!"

"All I said was that I thought Complete Abandon would be a good name for a perfume that would or could produce such a reaction."

Lydia looked at Gert and then at Win. "Out of the mouths of babes."

"Do you think that's a good name?"

"Miss Merrill, if things turn out as they might and as I hope they will, that could be a great name and you'll be in for a piece of change for coming up with it."

"Are you serious? I could get paid for just saying what I did?" she asked incredulously.

"Oh, sure. Many people get paid a lot for saying far less than that."

As Susan smiled, Paul said, "You know, I've been wondering about all this and something keeps nagging at me."

"What is it?" asked Win.

"Well, let's say that Miss Merrill's…that Susan's perfume…" When he said "Susan," she smiled and leaned closer to him. Then he smiled and leaned closer to her, so their shoulders were touching. "Let's say that Susan used a perfume that somehow lit up my memories of breast-feeding and since those were pleasant memories, I responded positively. But, let's say I hated my mother or that breast-feeding was a disaster and the odor set off the exact opposite reaction. Could I have done something bad? Could I have done a criminal thing with the impetus…the cause being…my bad memories?"

"Your memories that were previously repressed," Win broke in, "But now, because of the fragrance they were released and you reacted in a way that would not have occurred because of the repression."

"Exactly. And, if I did do something really screwy, am I to blame or is it the fragrance?"

"Young man," injected Sol, "an odor cannot be convicted of a crime."

"True," said Gert, "but could you prosecute the people or the agency that released the odor? In other words, is Lydia responsible for an act caused by her perfume's effect on Mr. Coleman or me...or anyone?"

Lydia, looking confused said, "You guys are getting too deep for me, and I have no answers except to say that we are all personally responsible for our actions. I can't see it any other way."

"Wow!" said Mr. Coleman. "I hope I'm never in a position to find out what would happen in a situation like that."

"Mr. Coleman," said Sol, unmistakably poised to offer another pearl of wisdom, "Mr. Coleman, you must never forget that men who do not make advances to women are apt to become victims of women who make advances to them."

"And who, may I ask, is the author of that gem?"

"My dear Gert," he said, blowing smoke everywhere, "that was mine. I said that just now, right here, while sitting in this chair."

Looking at Sol with a half smile, Gert said slowly, "I think it's time to bring this wild party to an end. I'm sure we all have mountains of work to get to."

"You're right about that, Professor Lehman," said Susan, as she stood. "I want to thank you all for you hospitality and I must say that I was nervous about coming over because I've never spent any time with professors. But I'm glad I came, because you people are great."

"That goes double for me." said Mr. Coleman. "I'm glad things worked out as they did and I thank you all."

"Mr. Coleman," said Sol, "Mr. Coleman and Miss Merrill," he repeated. "I'm glad you both came. You represent the best of this institution in that you are intelligent and sincere. I leave you both with these words since soon you sleep: The waking have one and the same world, the sleeping turn aside each into a world of their own."

After a profound silence, Gert said, "Right... time to go."

She rose from the sofa and extended her hand to both Paul and Susan. The two thanked everyone, shook hands with all, and then, holding hands and warmly smiling at one another, left.

"Those are nice kids." Win said. "I'm glad things worked out."

"Boy," said Lydia, "that young lady has quite a crush on that Mr. Coleman and I've got a feeling they'll be far better pals in the morning."

"Like us?" Win asked.

Gert jumped in and said, "Why don't you two escort Sol downstairs. I've got some work to do after I clean up."

A few moments later, Sol, Lydia, and Win were thumping down the stairs to the front door where Sol set out to walk the half block to his place. Win put his arms around Lydia. "You know, I was hoping we could be together. Watching those kids brought back a lot of memories and I would love to do some necking."

"Well, lover boy, I take that as a compliment. But I have a lot of office work to do and, I think, the beginnings of a mean headache. You don't want to be with me when I get a nasty headache. They're not as bad as migraines, but they make me a wreck, and you don't want to see me like that"

Win would be the first to admit he didn't know much about women, but he had seen enough movies to know that when a female invoked the headache ploy, it was a signal to hit the road.

"As much as I'd like to, I will never argue with a headache." He leaned down and kissed her. "Are you sure you want me to go?"

"Oh, Win, please…if I ask you in, you won't leave and I have all that work."

"And that potential headache⊠"

"Oh, Win, please, I'm not feeling well."

"Okay…okay." He kissed her cheek and saying he'd call the next day, left."

CHAPTER 10

In her apartment, Lydia thought about what had been said. Was it possible the girl was right? Was it possible her mother's perfume triggered a memory in that guy that turned him into a breast-feeding baby, or was it all nuts?

She was determined to get answers, not only because she needed clarification, but also because she was going to tell a company vice president what she had learned and didn't want to look stupid. If she was smart about this, it could mean a major promotion. Eventually, she would get what she wanted, but she had to be smart.

He picked up on the third ring. "Randall."

"Tom, this is Lydia. Are you busy?"

"The world won't end. What is it?"

"I'd like to come over and talk about the new perfume project."

"Now? Won't it keep till tomorrow?"

"I'd like to keep this idea out of the office for a while, okay?"

"Is that the only reason you want to come over?"

"My, my, whatever do you mean? Could there be another reason for my coming to your apartment?"

He laughed. "Okay, Lydia, why don't you put on perfume, fresh lipstick, that slinky beaded dress and grab a cab? I'll change the music and chill the wine."

"Twenty minutes."

"Fine."

The dress he called "slinky" was the one she wore the third time she went to his place. The third date was the culmination of her holy trinity—a formula she used since high school. It was how she decided who was a bed partner and who was not. Early in her social life she learned that first dates could often seem better than they really were. The second date emotions were less likely to be caused by any extraneous elements because now she was in better control. Third dates were the key. If she still was aroused, still in control and recognized the benefits as real, she would let him gain what had now become a craved prize. Her precise judgment made clear that giving anything away was stupid when a considered exchange could achieve real advantage.

A quick shower, perfume and the dress. As she slipped it over her head she smiled recalling Monroe's answer of "radio" when asked what she had on when she posed. Lydia stood before the full-length mirror and examined the pluses of her figure. Good legs, proper hips, small waist and breasts just a bit large for the package. When men said her shape was magnificent she was pleased, but the compliment and her body weren't by themselves, meaningful. For what those men craved—her body, her sexuality—were what she considered tools she had to wisely use.

When wearing the dress, underwear was out because it hindered the fabric's movement. Three panels of beads front and back let the dress flow like liquid when she moved. Once she put it on for Win and enjoyed his eyes glazing before his glands ignited. Tom reacted similarly when he saw her wearing it for the first time. Being wanted by men was pleasant, but being in control was far more glorious…that was the kick for her. She knew the magic would not last, but while she owned it, she would use it to her best advantage.

Wearing a long raincoat over the dress, she walked to Sixth Avenue, grabbed a cab, and in less than ten minutes the cab turned from Twenty-third into Irving Place. Tom's penthouse was in one of those fabulous prewar buildings with sunken living rooms, marble baths, plenty of closets, and more than enough rooms.

When the taxi pulled up to the building, one of the evening doormen greeted her as he opened the cab's door.

"Good evening, Miss Cornell Mr. Randall sent word that you would be arriving." With a radiant confidence, she strode through the lobby, passing the inside man who smiled, nodded and gestured for her to enter the express elevator. Inside, the operator made it a point to keep his eyes on the controls and said nothing but, "Please watch your step," as she exited.

She figured Tom must have been lurking by the door, for he opened it after one knock. "Come in, come in," he said. "Let me take that coat." With his help, she shrugged it off and waited in the entry hall as he hung it in the closet. Turning back to her, he lecherously stared. "Goddamn, I love you in that dress. It really turns me on."

With her eyes averted, she demurely said, "Oh you're being silly. How can a dress get you excited? It's just some cloth and beads."

"Right, like the fucking Hope Diamond is just a lump of coal." As he said that, he took her in his arms and kissed her slowly yet eagerly. And as she responded, he reached down and slid his hand under the hem of her dress, to her center. For an instant, he hesitated expecting underwear, but finding none, he leaned closer and whispered in her ear, "I think a woman's nakedness is marvelous—so smooth and sleek. God damn, you really turn me on."

He took a small step backward and let the dress glide downward through his fingers until he held it at the hem with both of his hands. Then he slowly raised his arms. Deliciously, inch by inch, her nakedness was revealed as is the stage for the opening night audience eager for a glimpse of their expected prize.

"Beautiful, just beautiful," he said, as he knelt in front of her. She moved her hand to his chin, gently raised his head, and looking into his eyes, said, "Tom, I want to talk first I think this is important."

"You're goddamn right this is important. There's nothing more important in the whole fucking world." As he said that, he kissed the skin of her thighs and then slowly let his tongue inch upward. Then he slid his hands up the back of her legs until he was firmly holding her. With gentle pressure, he pressed her against his mouth. She shivered and felt her knees tremble.

"God, Tom."

Not answering, he pushed forward until he pinned her to the wall. Gently and relentlessly, he loved her flesh until her body responded with wrenching spasms. Only then did he take her into his arms and carry her to the bedroom.

CHAPTER 11

Lydia didn't understand why decorating her place should be so hard. She had the money and the time and she thought, the taste, but she could not please herself. Win thought her place was fun and imaginative, but coming from Win, that wasn't much of a compliment. He was like a parched man who drinks from a muddy puddle and thinks it champagne.

She thought her couch and chairs, her lamps and tables, everything she bought was okay, except for the bed. Her bed was practical, functional. It had come with a headboard, a footboard, and a thick mattress. It was decent, but Tom's bed... it was memorable.

"You like the bed, don't you?" he asked.

"How did you know?"

"I wish you could see you. You squirm around on it like it was a playground. Like you were a honey bee dropped onto the biggest and sweetest flower in the garden." He paused, sat up and looked at her. "God damn, its wild watching you twist and coil."

"Twist and coil, you make me sound like a snake."

"Oh, but you are. You're Eve and the serpent." She grinned as he went on. "Everyone's got that Adam and Eve and the snake story all fucked up. When Eve realized what was up, she invented the bullshit about the snake and ate the apple because she damn well wanted to. The snake was nothing more than a made-up excuse for self-indulgence."

"But Adam believed her."

"Adam was a schmuck. Like the dopey husband whose wife comes back from the mall with a couple of grand worth of doodads and he believes her when she tells him she spent twenty bucks. The fact that she spent the afternoon in bed with a couple of cross-country truckers whose payoff got her to that mall never occurs to Mr. Adam. He's so busy believing her he doesn't even think she could be putting him on."

"Boy, I thought I was cynical."

"That's not cynicism, that's just marketing. Adam bought the line about dutiful, faithful little women. Never forget... advertising works. Once our little tales turn them on, they believe any bullshit that comes along next. The public is putty—moldable, thick and brainless."

His attitude, his blatant fearlessness and disregard excited her. It resonated so thoroughly that she thought there was a male part of her that could never accept the role females had been handed.

She stretched. How lovely she felt. He was right, she thought. I am a snake and I love it. She reached for him and kissed him hard on the mouth. Then she pushed him down onto the shiny sheets.

"Now lay still while I tell you what I came here to tell you."

"That's right," he said smiling broadly. "You did come over to tell me something. I forgot about that. When I get wrapped up in satin sheets, my mind leaves the present." Now it was her turn to smile and as she did, she moved her hand and cradled his scrotum. Tenderly squeezing, she said, "This should keep your mind completely in the here and now."

"Baby, you keep your hand right where it is now and you'll always have my full and undivided attention. There's no question about that, I—" She squeezed again. "Shut up and listen," she said, as he grinned.

"Tonight, I discovered a name for the new perfume. I want to call it Complete Abandon and I know the fundamental idea for the entire product line. That name was dropped by a girl who was kind of attacked by a guy. Now get this, he didn't want to rape her or anything like that. He wanted to, no lie, nurse at her breasts. He was so turned on he grabbed her in a college corridor and nothing mattered but getting his hands on her and his mouth on her nipples. He totally lost control. He freaked out!"

"Totally lost control?" he asked, incredulously, and sat up. She moved her hand to his chest. "Yes, that's it exactly. He literally went after her like a baby fighting to get the nipple back after losing it."

"What happened?"

"Nothing much because some guys grabbed him and then he... he, I guess you can say, he came to his senses."

"What caused his reaction?"

"Best as I can determine right now, it was a perfume the girl was wearing. It was a gift from her mom and was a brand new for her. The commotion started when he walked into her odor field."

He slid backward and leaned against the headboard. She snuggled alongside, drawing the sheet up to cover them. "I don't want to burst your balloon, babe," he said, "but every perfume under the sun has tried to hit the magic pheromone, the one that rings a guy's gong."

"I know," she said, "but I don't care about that. I believe no one will ever be able to find that magic bullet. What I'm thinking about is what this guy was after. He decidedly did not want to grab her and slide it in. He wanted to snuggle, to be close. He said he sensed security and warmth from the odor."

"So you're saying forget trying to get a scent that will turn men into raging bulls. Instead, go after the product that will turn them into little boys who come to mommy for a cuddle and a kiss. What comes after the cuddle and the kiss is not our business... that's their business."

"Exactly. You're so right there. That's it exactly. Every woman wants a strong man... a real man... but one who will listen to what she has to say... who'll do what she wants. Every woman wants to tame the beast. If we can work the formula that can get guys to come to mama with their thing still in their pants... well, we'll win the gold."

"You know, that's really interesting...what you said about what women want. I think that's the same with fags. So many try to pick up a 'real man' and take him to bed, but that game puts them in a bind. If they actually pick up a real man, he'll turn them down, but when they do get a guy in bed, he isn't what they're after... a real man. It's endless frustration for them."

She stared at him, wondering where that example came from, but deciding to pay it no mind, she said, "If we can pull this off, we'll be able to write a big ticket. God, it would be fantastic."

"Sure, but how?"

"Well, I scheduled a meeting with the girl and I'm going to try to get the perfume her mother sent. It shouldn't be that difficult to get my hands on it and once I have, we can analyze it and isolate whatever is in it that's out of the ordinary."

"Will she give it to you?"

"I don't see why not. I whet her appetite when she tagged it Complete Abandon. I told her there might be some money in it for her, if we use it as a name for the new fragrance. She was excited at that prospect. It shouldn't be so hard to buy her off."

"You know you really are a snake. And when you talk like that I get nervous. How do I know you won't use me and then when you don't need me, I'm out with the garbage?"

She pulled away from him and sat up. The little girl sexiness that turned him on was gone. Now she looked like one of the corporate guys he faced throughout the year.

"Tom, understand me and listen carefully. I enjoy our little romps, but love is not involved. I respect you, you're smart and you know advertising. You've taught me a lot and I appreciate that, but my under-the-sheets feelings are separate from business." She paused then slowly continued. "In business, well… I'm serious about business. I know what I want and I'm sure you can help me get it. All I'll demand from you or anyone is loyalty. Don't screw with me and I'll be there for you."

She stretched out beside him. "Some people are stupid about their ambitions. They act like they have two lifetimes. You know them—I'll get it done eventually; what's the rush? Well, I'm not like that. I know what I want and I intend to have it." She raised her body and leaned on her elbow. Staring directly at him, she said, "We can pull this off. We can make it happen. Do you believe that?"

He felt like he was back in the Army listening to the C.O. tell the unit how they were going to kick ass and achieve their objective. How nothing was going to stand in their way and that they would blast to shit anything or anyone who was between them and what they were after. The Army made him tough and it made him realistic. Killing people made him pragmatic. He learned early you set your sights and you took the shot. She was just like the hard-ass commanders he stuck with in combat—the ones who got him through. He looked at her alongside him, the sleek and beautiful body and her sincere and perfectly featured face. She was special. He knew that. He had always known that.

He sat up and gently placed his hands on the sides of her face. "You know, babe, I learned in the Army, when you're fighting for your life, nothing else matters. Think about something else and you're finished. I learned to stay alive in combat and I learned who and what would keep me alive. You're charmed. I knew that the first day I saw you. I'll follow you. I'll follow anyone who's going to keep me alive." He stared into her eyes. "Do you believe that? Do you understand I'm as serious as you are?" As he spoke he felt a surge of power making him erect.

She relished his strength. "I do believe you and I know we can do it. No bullshit. No nonsense. No stupid jealous fighting." She pushed him down onto the glistening sheets, raised herself up and then slowly lowered her body until she felt him slide into her. With their eyes closed and their lips apart, they lunged at each other. And, tied together in passion, they sealed their contract with sweaty moans and bursting orgasms

Later, wrapped in heavy robes, they sat on his terrace and looked into the night around them. Pointing to his left, he said, "That's Brooklyn over there." Then he swiveled the chair and pointed in the opposite direction. "And that's New Jersey."

She stared into the blackness where he had pointed. "Brooklyn and New Jersey, why would anyone want to live there?"

"People don't want to live there. They…wait, wait…that's not fair. Probably some people do, you know, like die-hard old Dodger fans, but most don't. Most of them want to live right here, in this apartment and be able to look into the blackness and see the lights from places they'd rather not be."

"I have never been to Brooklyn and I don't ever want to go there. Whenever I hear about it on the news, they're always counting bodies."

"Life is very tough for a lot of people, Lydia. You know that."

"Certainly, I know that, but I don't give a damn about them. They're customers… nothing more than that. Our job is to get them to buy what we sell."

"Right…whether they need it or not." He said.

"Look, you know as well as I do, they have no idea what they want. If we didn't tell them what they're supposed to want or do, they'd walk around banging into walls." She picked up the wine glass, drank some and then turned to him. "Everyday I go into stores and see the shop-girls wearing those stupid long nails with pictures on them. Can you believe that? With those nails they can't eat, they can't wipe their asses, they can't type, they can't do almost anything, but they have to have them. Why? Because the campaigns make it look glamorous. It's the same with their hair and ugly clothes. God, they're all such cowards. You go into a department store and watch what they buy. They have no taste, no idea at all about what's fashionable. If some Hollywood bimbo wore a grass skirt to a premier, the next day they'd all look like refugees from Pago Pago."

"Hey, you don't have to sell me. I'm on your side."

"I know, I know. It's just I get so angry." She drank more wine and pushed back into the deep cushions. "I guess I am conflicted about this, but once in a while I hope people will be brave and make their own decisions and not let us tell them what they want, what they should buy."

He looked at her and smiled. "But that moment passes, doesn't it? And then you realize that's the way it's supposed to be. We suggest and they do."

She looked up at the black sky. "You're goddamn right the moment passes and I'm glad it does. And you're right again when you say, 'that's the way it's supposed to be.' Without us to tell them what their lives are all about, they'd be lost."

"Don't think I'm trying to be cute, but I really do love it when you talk that way. It's like hearing my thoughts come to life."

"That's why we're good together. We think alike and we want the same thing."

He nodded. "I hope this idea pans out. No one has ever proposed a fragrance line that doesn't promise sex, sex, and more sex."

"It will succeed because everyone has always known those promises about sex were bullshit."

They sat in silence until he asked, "Okay, what's next?"

"I have to give it more thought. But first off, I have to get that perfume from the girl. Once we analyze it, we can better understand what the hell is in it that produced that stupendous effect."

"What if you can't get it?"

"Don't you worry, I'll get it. One way or another, I always get what I want."

CHAPTER 12

After returning from Gert's, Sol wistfully stared at the barren wall, mourning the painting that once hung there. He knew he had bad habits with one of his worst trying to buy people. The missing painting was one of a list of items he lost in similar futile attempts to gain favor. Nevertheless, with his hopes flying high, he disregarded basic truths and continually tried to secure companions from the open market.

Most people know it's a loser's game to be sad and that happiness is at the core of everyone's make-believe world. The hucksters and the sloganeers endlessly sing, "One must continually strive for the good life." Sol had tried his best, performed as instructed, and always lost. Yet, he was cornered by the huckster's continual efforts to convince us that sadness is to be avoided and that happiness is the grand prize. It was no surprise seeing people striving to avoid the dark and dismal dumps.

But for every person who tries not to be sad, there are others who strangely relish the grief. They come to life and glisten in the glow of misfortune's halo. These are people so busy with distress, so deep in the pit that they would never—probably could never—recognize moments free of anguish. Life, to them, is tough and relentlessly hard. A miserable bloody battle all too often already lost.

Sol was such a person. He was a man who had never really experienced the joy of his homosexuality. He was cheated out of it by the "well-meaning" people, who, when he was young, managed to convince him that homosexuality was indeed an aberration and a violation in God's world. He was caught in an awful paradox. The more he enjoyed his true self, the more he denied his true self.

His life had not been easy. He never had a meaningful long-term private relationship. He could never find a suitable mate. He was always wrong. Always just a little too smart, too energetic, too dull, too lazy, too intimidating, too judgmental, too needy, too alone, too much a part of things, too schooled, too dumb, too rich, too poor—never quite right.

Fortunately though, he had a good brain and found his niche in academia, one of the few places where misfits are not cast out. Colleges and universities are still prime sanctuaries for those hiding from the usual and the typical. He had spent his working life at significant academic institutions developing an admirable reputation and becoming well known in his field. He was an acknowledged expert in rhetoric and public address.

Year by year it saddened him to see his cherished chosen field, his life's work, become part of the wasteland created by popular culture. As a young man, he was influenced by Aristotle's view that rhetoric was the art of observing in any given case, all the available means of persuasion. Being able to influence others with well-tailored and cogent argument was a greatly admired skill.

He was steeped in the nineteenth century and longed for a time of public lectures, political debate, and orations like the July 4th speech delivered by the local celebrity on the village square. Reading those preserved speeches moved him in a way known only to those who love an art form of old. Sol was also an expert in the field of radio speech-making. He knew all about the 1920s and the new perspective radio brought to speech, especially to the political speech. At one time only those within earshot of the speaker could be influenced, but with radio, millions from every area of the country were available as an audience. Then, along came television with commercials that signaled the end of eloquence.

Where once the spoken word was invested with reasoned argument, imaginative design, and spectacular delivery, it was now reduced to thirty seconds of glaring stupidity and the never-ending drone of buy, buy, buy.

The few students who saw the value of his knowledge were those planning to be corporate executives or legal stars glittering at the Supreme Court. Typical students avoided his courses because they demanded a reasoned and thoughtful use of language. Clearly, students who thought "duh" and "you know" were utterances of significance and usable in any sentence were not ready or able to appreciate the spoken words of Washington, Lincoln, Douglas, or Twain.

Viewing his social life and his work life side by side, one might wonder why he had not jumped from a high window. Those who understood him felt with little doubt he would have done so had he not had the opportunity to be a ham and stride about the classroom doing his credible imitations of Darrow and company.

Living alone was not a problem for many people and for those like Sol, it was a blessing. Living with another person eventually forces a self-acknowledgment of the effect of one's moods. Living with another eliminates the narcissistic ability to strike whatever emotional pose becomes appealing. Having another living thing around was just too much of a responsibility. Sol was even unable to own a cat or a dog, because even those dumb animals would demand in their particularly ignorant way, a joyous approach to the next hour or day. Sol once did own tropical fish, but he lost them because when feeling sorry for himself he forgot to feed them. But in his favor, he did made amends by donating a hefty sum to the city's aquarium.

Now, staring at the wall, he wished he had not traded the painting for what he thought was a bargain. People are not bargains. People can never be bargains. Whatever benefits they may momentarily provide are amply balanced by the craziness they impose. As he stared, he recalled the painting's scene—a smooth, but not friendly looking sea. Not one that would put up with a casual swim. Its oily black surface clearly warned of awaiting death. The salvation was the ship, a schooner under full sail tilted to starboard by the wind's weight. The white water pushed up by its bow was a shower of foam.

Three figures were there on its deck. Who were they? Where were they going? Where had they been? Often, he refused to look at the crew, focusing instead on the ship. Where was it going? Where had it been? He lost count of the days and nights he stared at that painting dreaming about its last port of call.

I'm like that ship, he thought. I'm always coming from someplace, but where I'm going is not known. Like a ship without a chart, I'm tossed from port to port, hoping the next will be better. Always filled with hope of a new land, but tortured with the unmerciful knowing there are never new lands, at best, merely some new geography.

He picked up the phone and dialed Gert. One ring, two, three, four, five rings.

"What?" she said. Before he could answer, she asked, "Sol? It's you isn't it?"

"How did you know?"

"I saw you leave tonight. I've seen you leave like that many times before and I know you well enough to recognize the blues. What brought it on this time?"

"Oh, Gert," he said slowly. "I saw those two kids and I fell apart. My whole life has been spent trying to find someone the way those two kids found each other."

"Oh, Sol, please. We've been over and over and over this. Whenever you see a couple, any kind of couple, sparks fly. You want what they have. You never had what they have. God, Sol how many times are we going to go through this?"

"Gert, I'm an old man…no…I'm an old queen. Oh my god, that's worse, much worse. What the hell is going to happen to me?"

With more than a hint of anger in her voice, she said, "You know, sometimes you are a gigantic pain in the ass. You are so incredibly selfish. It's me, me, me, me, me. Do you ever stop and think what it's like to be me? What it's like to live my life? Has that ever gotten into your selfish skull?"

He was stopped cold and instantly realized, not once, not even for a moment, had he ever considered her situation. How could that be? Instantly, in every cell in his body, he knew she was right.

Was it worse for a woman? He chided himself. Damn it, we are two women. With almost no trace of the sorrow of the moments before, he said, "Gert, I truly apologize. Not once did I ever think about you, not once. My god, I am so stupid and inconsiderate and as you say, selfish."

There was a long silence. Then, softly she said, "It's great to hear you say that. Those few words might just be turning points. You might now begin to realize I'm as screwed up as you." She paused. "You might also begin to see that three-quarters of the people we know are all fucked up. If you would stop being so caught up with yourself, you might see who is standing next to you, neck deep in the same pile of shit."

He closed his eyes and took a breath. "Gert, how do you live with it? How do you live with no mate… alone?"

"It isn't easy pal, and it won't get better. The younger you are, the easier it is, but when you get old, like we are, living alone or with someone else is no longer important. Certain things are easier when another person is around, but that's it. Everything else is bullshit. What you have to do is accept yourself as you are."

"What does that mean?"

"Look in the mirror, goddammit. You aren't a dashing thirty-year-old anymore. You're an old man. On other continents, you'd have been dead for years."

He stared at the phone. What could he say? "Are you telling me my life is over?"

"Well, tonight when you came over, you said you were really depressed. When I hear that kind of talk, I see feet on the window sill. Luckily, Cyril bailed you out this time." Her voice softened and he recognized her concern. "Look, Sol, your life isn't over. Far from it, but if you think it is, you're a goner. At this point, nobody but you can help you."

"God, I feel like the country mouse dodging traffic on Broadway. What do I do?"

"First thing is to spend a buck and see a good shrink. Second thing is to listen to what she tells you."

"She?"

"Absolutely, don't go near a man. Knowing you, you'll be sitting there trying to look fetching and cute, figuring ways to get into his pants. Go to a woman and tell her your troubles. They're probably the same as hers."

"Do you know someone?"

"Of course I do. See me tomorrow and I'll give you some references."

He closed his eyes and realized she's thrown me a life preserver, that's what she did. She plucked me right off the edge.

"Gert, I don't know what to say. You must think of me as Old Granny with a runny nose. And that's exactly what I am... an old lady pain in the ass."

"Sol, don't be so hard on your self. Try to be your own friend. If *you* can't be nice to you, why should anyone else even try?"

"Oh, god, there's so much going on in my head, but you saved me. How can I thank you? What can I say?"

"Sol, say 'goodnight.' That'll be fine for starters."

"Gert, you're a magic woman and..." He stopped when he heard her inhale and knew she was going to break in and tell him to shut up. "Okay, okay," he said... "Goodnight, I'll see you tomorrow and I... I ..."

"Goodnight, Sol...sweet dreams"

She hung up as he stared at the handset. This piece of plastic, he thought, this piece of cheap plastic was my lifeboat, my rescue. Apart from that realization, his thoughts were jumbled, but another came through clearly when he realized that without the phone call, it might have been impossible for him to discover what her friendship meant to him. "I'm not alone," he said aloud. "I'm not alone anymore."

CHAPTER 13

"Hey, how ya doin?"

"Paul. Is that you?"

"Yeah, Mom. You win the cigar."

"It's late, Paul. What's wrong?" Her concern was clear in her voice.

Reassuringly, he said, "Nothing's wrong and believe it or not, everything is really great. I met this absolutely fantastic girl. We really hit it off."

Releasing her breath, she asked, "Is that why you're calling...to tell me you met a girl?"

"Not entirely. There is something else."

"What is it?"

"Did you nurse me when I was a baby?"

After a hesitation, she asked, "Did I... what? Paul, is this some sort of prank? You know... an initiation or something?"

"No, Mom, believe me. I really need to know. Was I nursed? Did I... ugh... breast feed?"

"What a question to ask at a quarter to twelve?" He was pleased to hear the usual humor back in her voice.

"C'mon, Ma, did I? Did you?"

"Well, I really don't understand this, but...yes, you did. You nursed a long time... until you were... about a year and a half."

"Why did I stop? Was it normal to stop then? What happened?"

"What happened was simple. You grew too many teeth and decided that feeding was more fun with a little meat added to the menu."

"What do you mean? I bit you?"

"Darn right you did. You would bite me and then look up to see my reaction...such a cutie. You were a monster," she said, laughing.

"Ma… hey, you know I love you. I guess I was biting because… I… because I didn't know I wasn't supposed to."

"Oh, no, you knew what you were doing. That little devil face. That little smile. You knew."

"I was really a monster, huh?"

"Well… not a very terrible one. Anyway…" She stopped, the memories fading. "Paul, what is this all about?" she asked more firmly.

"I'll write it all down. I promise. Tonight, before I go to sleep, I'll write it down and mail it first thing tomorrow. It's just too complicated and crazy to go into over the phone."

"Is this girl involved? And who is she. Where does she come from? What's her name?"

"Easy…take it easy. I'll write and explain everything… and her name is Susan, Susan Merrill. She's great. You're gonna love her."

"Paul, this sounds serious."

"Well, Ma, I just met her, but there's a real chemistry between us… really. She's really special."

"I'm happy for you, Paul, and I hope she is special."

"Mom, I'm gonna sit down right now and write everything and tell you what happened. It's kind of funny, how we met, I mean. I think you'll get a kick out of it."

"Well, as long as everything is all right, Paul…" Again, he could hear the concern in her voice. "But what is it? Are you eating okay? Please make sure you eat properly…please."

"Mom, c'mon, I'm twenty-four. Mom, I know how to feed myself."

"I know that, Mr. Big Shot, but listen to me. Don't stuff yourself with that fast food."

"Don't sweat it. I'm doing well and I love you."

"We love you too. I'll tell Dad you called, but I won't tell him what you asked."

"It'll be clear when you read my letter."

"Okay. Goodnight Paul. Sleep well."

He hung up and stared at the bare wall. He felt good. Warm would be a good word to describe how I feel, he thought. I feel warm and smiley. Goddamn, smiley…I feel smiley and warm. Am I in love? He was smiling broadly as he picked his pen and began to write.

"Hello, Mom?"

"Susan is that you? What is it? What's the matter?" she asked in one breath.

"I'm okay. Nothing's wrong. I just want to ask you a couple of questions."

"Is that why you're calling? It's late."

"I know, but I won't be long."

"What do you want to ask?"

"It's about that perfume you sent. Where did you get it?"

"Oh, that. I've had that around for a long time. It's old, but it's wonderful. I've always loved that smell. To be honest, I'm not sure when I got it, but I do know it was a long time ago. Why? Is something wrong with it?"

"On the contrary, I think it's wonderful. I wore some the other day and … well… I met this wonderful boy."

"He's a student I hope and not one of those Village people."

With slight protest, she said, "Mom he's a graduate student and very nice."

"Well, that's good. How did you meet and what's the connection?"

"What connection? What do you mean?"

"Well, Susan, in one breath you ask me about the perfume and then you tell me you met this boy. What's the connection?"

"Oh, well, I wore some of the perfume and he attacked me. He attacked me in a hallway at school."

The silence lasted more than a moment. "He did what?"

"Oh, Mom it isn't like it sounds. He didn't really attack me. He, well, it wasn't a nasty attack."

"What did he do?"

"He tried to nurse at my breasts."

This silence lasted for far more than a moment. "Susan, are you joking? You aren't tipsy or something?"

"Oh, Mom."

"Susan, are you telling me this 'nice' boy tried to nurse at your breasts? Is that what goes on now? God, when I was your age, we would shake hands."

"Mom, it isn't like that. It's just too complicated and I can't explain it over the phone. I'll write you a letter."

"I hope you do. It sounds like it should be interesting reading."

"Anyway, tell me about the perfume. Is there anything special about it?"

"Oh, the perfume, yes, well, I think your father gave me that bottle after you were born and I hid it away… never used it. I bought others, but never used that particular bottle."

"Why didn't you use it? I once read that you're supposed to use perfume or it spoils...or something like that."

"I don't know if it does or doesn't. That bottle was special. I think I did something kind of weird and a little foolish with that bottle, if I correctly recall... I have to think a bit."

"What did you do?" There was silence.

"Mom... what's the matter... Mom."

"Oh, my, Susan, I just remembered about the perfume....why I hid it away. If I had remembered I never would have sent it to you."

"What did you do?"

"I didn't do anything, really. It was a joke... your father's sense of humor... you know." She paused and took a deep breath. "When I was nursing you, I would often use a breast pump at work to save the milk so you could have it when I got home. Anyway, one night, your father... Mr. Cute... took some breast milk and added it to a perfume he was concocting from rose petals. His usual efforts were clear liquids, but the milk made this one cloudy. Even though it had a nice smell, I guess I figured the perfume was ruined and probably hid it away for sentimental reasons. That's why it was still around after all this time."

"That's amazing. I bet that explains everything."

"Explains everything? Explains what?" Before Susan could answer, her mother said, "Oh, you mean about the boy? Were you wearing the perfume when it happened, when he attacked you in a not very nasty way?"

"Oh, Mom... please. Well, yes... I was... and oh, Mom, this is so strange."

"Strange is a mild word, Susan. This is weird. When your father played cute with the perfume, I was sure it was spoiled. Now you're telling me it has magic powers? Well, I don't know anything about any of this, but I think whatever's in milk that makes it milk must have been killed off after sitting in a bottle filled with alcohol for almost twenty years."

"Look, Mom, I'm going to give the perfume to a chemistry professor I met today. She's going to analyze it and I'm sure we'll find the answer. I'll keep you posted."

"You do that, dear. And, make sure that boy doesn't 'attack you again. What am I saying?"

"I know what you mean, Mom, but don't worry. I can handle myself."

"Oh, Susan ...life used to be so simple."

"I know... I know. Goodnight. I love you. Say hi to Dad."

"Yes dear. Take care. Sleep well and don't eat too much junky food, please."

"Night, Mom. Love ya."

"Goodnight, Susan."

She hung up the phone and picked up her pen. After three attempts at writing the day's events, she gave up and went to sleep. I'll write tomorrow, she told herself.

CHAPTER 14

"Professor David speaking."

"Win, this is Sol. Are you free or do you have an office filled with young starlets fluttering their eyelashes while trying to properly pronounce?"

"I'm free, and Sol, supposedly pronunciation no longer matters—content is king."

"Well ith that tho? Woo don't care about pro-noun-zee-ay-shun?"

"Very funny, very funny, now, what can I do for you?"

"I'm calling to tell you I was really in the pits last night and I called Gert for help… late as usual, but good old Gert… she absolutely straightened me out."

"What do you mean? How did she do that?"

"Win, there is something you may not understand about me. In my world and in my life, grand quantities of self-concern are involved. Endless mirror gazing, endless how do I look? What shall I wear? All that infernal business and then, with that, there's the other side. What's going to happen to me? Will I ever find someone? Can I be happy?" He paused. "Oh, Win, it's been never-ending torture. I envy the others who don't have the grief I do. But me… well, I've been feeling so sorry for myself for so long. I never gave a moment's thought to other people and how life treated them. People I know and love, Gert and you, for two immediate examples."

"Sol, where is this leading?"

"What I am trying to say is simply I have been a selfish pig who has failed to understand what friendship is. You and Gert… wonderful Gert…you are both very important to me and I am apologizing for not realizing how lucky I am to have you both as friends."

Win smiled. "Sol, it's great to hear that and I'm glad you realize the worth of the friendships you do have."

"Oh, wonderful…wonderful. Now, later today, can I treat you to lunch?"

"Why not…at two?"

"Fine, I'll meet you at… no … you name the place."

"Okay, let's meet at La Sala Di Mangia."

There was a pause. "My boy, are you mad? I'd have to cash in my government bonds to pay the check."

"Just joking, just joking. Let's make it Burger and Bun."

"Right you are. Far more suitable for my salary."

"Is Gert coming?"

"I am going to call her this minute. If the Burger and Bun disgusts her, I'll let her choose and call you right back. If I don't call, we'll meet there at two."

"Okay. I'll be in my office for another hour before class."

When Sol hung up, Win thought it was a very interesting call. How often does someone admit they've been an ass? He wondered whether he had guts to take a good look at his own life. Look at me, thirty-five, unmarried, living like a hermit crab, why? Why can't I do what I want? What the hell is my problem? "Wait," he said aloud. He knew what would come next and this was not the time for a self-pity session. His mind shifted back to Sol and he wondered what could have prompted such a sudden change. Last night Sol seemed his usual self. What happened after he left Gert's to bring about so profound a reversal?

He put his feet up on the desk and stared at the Murphy's Law poster. Why the change? He knew any behavioral change involved a shift in beliefs that then led to a change of attitude. What did Sol confront that altered his thinking about himself? It had to be Gert, Win realized. She must have said something or did something that turned him around. Maybe I'll find out at lunch. A knock on the door interrupted his thinking.

"Come."

The door opened and Coleman walked in looking relaxed.

"Mr. Coleman, good morning."

"Good morning to you, Professor. I hope you slept well."

Win smiled to himself. This was a changed person—no question.

"I get by, but you…obviously you had a very good sleep. You seem less tense."

Sitting down, he said, "Professor, you have no idea. These last few days were a living hell. But now… well, things are great. I think Susan Merrill is super. If this whole crazy business didn't happen, I never would have met her."

"Yes, she seems nice. But aside from that, what can I do for you?"

"Well, I called my mother last night and she did nurse me for a year and a half. I don't know what that has to do with what happened, but well… that's it. Maybe it's important."

"I'd guess it matters. The act of nursing is one none of us can recall, but you doing it and how that ties in with Miss Merrill's perfume are questions we have to answer."

"So it all depends on my mammary memory…right?" he said, laughing.

Win groaned. "Mr. Coleman, be strong and resist the temptation to repeat that."

Still smiling, Coleman nodded and got up. "Professor, if there's nothing else, I've got to go to the library."

"You go. I'll pass the word about your nursing to Professor Lehman— she's the one who's going to make sense of all this. I'll be in touch if she wants more info."

"Okay. I'll see you."

When Coleman opened the door to leave, Win spotted painters in the hallway and immediately moved to his office window. He struggled to open it, knowing if he did, his choice would be lumpy Greenwich Village air or paint that smelled like bananas. He couldn't guess the ingredient that made paint smell like bananas, but it did and it was awful. He wondered if others thought it smelled like bananas.

Suddenly, his mind flashed back a few years to a small town where he once stopped to get gas. As he held the pump nozzle, he smelled cherries instead of gasoline. His immediate reaction was fear, because he knew that stroke patients often reported a strong odor just before they stroked out. But fortunately, the attendant saw the fear on his face and told him to relax. That part of town housed a company that manufactured smells. They produced the chemical substances that gave products specific odors—like aerosols that made an old car smell new or a bathroom smell like roses. Wondering if the banana smell was manufactured by that company, he thought it weird that cleaning products had a lemon smell and his talcum smelled like pears. The supermarket had become the bastion of phony smells—everything seemed to smell like fruit except the fruit.

He moved back to his desk to grade papers, knowing the banana odor would no longer register in a short time, since human adaptation to odor is rapid. Thankfully, the worst smells are accommodated in minutes. Walk into a slaughter house and your stomach turns, but stay there for ten minutes and you adjust. The first whiff registers and then little by little, the brain's reception of it vanishes. He figured that somewhere in our evolutionary ladder such a specific ability was important. He wondered why. Most likely, it had to do with recognizable pack odors and the new odors of strangers.

After class he headed out to meet Gert and Sol at the Burger and Bun which was a typical diner that had stopped competing with other diners by specializing in burgers. You could get burgers made from chicken, turkey, duck, tuna, lamb, beef, pork, veggies, shrimp, and if the owner trusted you, rattlesnake. There were always rumors about goat meat, horse meat and other exotics, but Win always ordered beef hoping nothing "extra" was ever added.

When he got there, Gert and Sol were already seated in the first booth across from the counter. This particular booth had a permanent reserved sign on it and it was available only to regulars who were important, but not important enough for the booth in the window. That one was reserved for those who were TV recognizable or were sufficiently photogenic to create envy in the passersby. The last time they were in, a local rock legend was allowed to sit in the window booth. His tattooed and disheveled persona created enough agitation in the street to bring in at least fifty acolytes who would eat sawdust burgers if he would bless the dish.

"Hey, you two, slide over so I can squeeze in." Win flopped onto the seat so that Gert was in the middle of the booth which was a semicircle made for seeing and being seen. Gert loved it because it made her feel important though she knew if she won the Nobel Prize, no one in the joint would know anything more about her than they did now.

"Ah, the three mad professors. What can I get you?" The question was asked by Frankie, the waiter, who unlike the other service people was really a waiter. At least that was the occupation on the form supplied to his parole officer. Not being an idiot, he figured "waiter" was a wiser choice than "thief," which was the truth, but a dumb thing to write down. The rest of the service staff were typical Village and New York—writers, actors, musicians, oil painters, sculptors, water colorists, designers—all waiting for the right moment when the world recognized them.

"Hey Frankie, what's happening?" Gert called out.

One of Frankie's eyebrows went up with Gert's exuberance. "Hey, yourself, Prof. What'd you do, get high in the lab this mornin'?"

"No. I definitely did not, but that's not a bad idea for this afternoon."

"Make sure you mix up a big batch; this joint could use a lift." As he said that, he brought his order book up to meet his pencil which was poised in midair like a mantis waiting for the exact moment. "What's it gonna be?"

Gert said, "I'll have a tuna burger, well, fries, house dressing on the side for the salad, and tea."

He looked at Sol, who said, "I'll have the same."

Win didn't wait. He said, "I'll have a well-done beef burger on a toasted bun, crisp fries, Russian dressing on the salad, black coffee now and a cherry coke with the food."

"Well done, well done. You guys are well trained, not like the damn tourists who carry on like they're at the Waldorf."

As he turned to leave, Gert called out, "Hey, Frankie, what's that on your neck?"

Win and Sol both stared up at the waiter and recoiled when they saw what looked like a giant roach crawling up his neck from under his collar. He turned back to them with a broad smile on his face.

"Ain't it a pisser? It's new. The greatest tattoo I have. He pulled at his collar exposing a multicolored tattoo of one of those New York City water bugs—about two inches long and completely grotesque.

"Now why the hell did you do that?" Gert asked.

"Well, I figured I needed some way to make sure I only work in the kind of places I enjoy, like this joint." He waved his arm and continued. "With this thing creepin' up my neck, I would never get hired at any upscale joint. And I don't want to work in no such joint like that, but I have my weak moments— so I figured a gross tattoo would be a great way to guarantee never gettin' hired at some kind of fancy place."

Screwing up his face, Win asked, "But doesn't it bother you, having a thing like that on your neck?"

"Shit, no. I can't see it." He hesitated and then asked in a voice oozing with concern, "It doesn't bother you guys, does it?"

Sol raised his eyebrows. "Oh no, young man, personal adornment can be a very interesting way to express individuality."

The waiter smiled and stepping back said, "Exactly. That was my feeling from the get-go. And if you think this baby is weird, you should see what some of the guys in the joint have. Man, this is nothin'."

As Frankie turned and headed for the kitchen, Gert asked Win, "Do you have a tattoo?"

"No, and I never gave the subject a serious moment."

"I have one." said Sol. Gert and Win started at him. "It's the name of my first great love." Sol looked down, and then slowly moved his hand to the edge of his napkin. "It was a love that was never going to end. We both got the same tattoo."

"What happened?" Gert asked.

"Who knows?" Sol picked up the napkin and dabbed at the corner of his right eye. "One day, a sunny day, as I remember, it was over. He was gone and that was that."

"Have you tried to locate him?"

"Win, my boy, we're talking thirty years ago. It's too late. It was too late the next week." He stared at the napkin. "Some things aren't meant to be… that's all."

Speaking softly, Gert said, "Now let's not get morose. You invited us here because you were feeling good—let's keep it that way, okay?"

Straightening and sitting back, Sol smiled. "Gert… wonderful Gert, you always know what's right." He took a deep breath then announced, "Yes, I did invite you both because I want to tell you I am delighted to have you as my friends. Last night I realized I have very little in this world except Cyril, a few distant relations and you two. I fear I overlooked how important you are to me." Then, in a firmer voice, he added, "That will not happen again. You will always be able to count on me."

Gert reached across the table and took his hand in both of hers. "Oh, Sol, Sol, I'm so glad to hear that. We all of us have very little except…" She hesitated, and then very slowly added, "…except for Win, we probably have all we're ever going to get."

"Yes, Gert, that's the conclusion I reached last night. There isn't a hell of a lot that's going to happen in my life from here on out… even my dance lessons don't perk me up as they once did. As much as I don't want to think of it as all downhill, I can't think of a better or more accurate metaphor."

Win listened, passing over Sol's remark about dance lessons, but he thought they were talking more to each other than to him, but what Gert had said really struck home. His mind raced through the usual list—his age, his inability to get a girl who wanted to get married, his inability to understand why he couldn't do what thousands of guys did all over the country every single day. Was he just a younger version of Gert and Sol? Was he going to be sitting here twenty years from now, still alone… still unable to find someone?

Softly, Win said, "Gert, I wouldn't be so sure of me. I don't seem to have much luck with long-standing relationships."

They both turned to look at him.

"Oh, Win, don't be an ass. Your life is unfolding more and more each day. The best is still on its way."

"I wish I had your confidence, Gert, but more and more I'm preparing myself to be alone. I hate the thought of it because I don't want to be alone, but that seems to be the way the cards are falling."

"Win, wait a minute. What about Lydia? You look at her with love in your eyes."

"I don't think so, Sol. We get along, but I feel what Lydia wants I will never be able to give her."

"And what is that?"

"Position and money, but most of all power. Advertising is a power-hungry business. Her eyes light up with more voltage when she talks about campaigns than when she talks to me or with me. I think I'm just a convenient stop on her ride."

They were silent, each feeling for the other and each unable to do anything more than that. A few moments later, when the food arrived, they were still searching for the right things to say.

"I think we better eat." Sol said. "And I think we better talk about other things while we do or we'll all start crying."

"You're right, Sol…absolutely right." And then taking a bite of his burger, Win added, "Coleman came to see me this morning and told me he called his mother and she said he was nursed, and for quite a while too."

"So," said Gert, putting her burger back on the plate. "Coleman was nursed and when Miss Merrill brought me the perfume this morning she told me a very interesting story. It seems the perfume her mother sent was a bottle long unused. A bottle put away because Miss Merrill's father, who made his own perfumes, put breast milk into a perfume he made as a joke and his wife stashed it away thinking it was ruined. She never used it again and when she recently came across it, she sent it to her daughter thinking she might use it. She had completely forgotten about the breast milk addition."

"Do you think the breast milk affected the perfume?"

"Well, Sol, you know what happened."

"But is that possible? Why didn't it spoil? When I leave milk in the back of my fridge for too long, it turns into a science fiction movie. How come it didn't turn rancid?"

"That's part of the mystery," said Gert. "Eventually, we might find out."

"Look," said Win. "If Coleman reacted to the perfume because it had breast milk in it and that brought back memories of his nursing, why didn't it affect any of the other guys? Why was Mr. Coleman the only one who had that whacked-out reaction?"

Gert looked blank. "I can't answer those questions. The perfume should have gone bad, but it didn't. I think we probably don't have all the facts... anyway...my immediate theory is that it was a combination of events. It was that perfume *and* Mr. Coleman. He seems to be the ingredient that completes the reaction. No one else reacted, so Coleman is the key and what really took place is still unknown."

"Okay, so what do we do?"

"First thing tomorrow. I'm going to start analyzing that perfume. In a day or two I'll know what's in it and when I have it properly evaluated, we'll be able to answer some of the nagging questions."

They nodded to each other. Now caught in the mystery, they were able to let go of the thoughts that had made them so blue moments before. They returned their burgers to the kitchen for reheating and when they got them back, attacked them with real hunger.

CHAPTER 15

As the cab bounced, Lydia wondered if opening up to Tom had been the smart move. She wondered if he was bastard enough to cut me out. The big neon sign question of the day was simply put, could that oversexed office boy be trusted? When the taxi sped through a red light, she concluded it was too late to worry about whether she should have told him. She had, and that was that. Now she must cover her ass. She had to see Dunn. If she could get an audience with that son of a bitch, she could fix things so Tom would be reporting to her. All she needed was twenty minutes.

Twenty minutes with the big boss. Would that be enough time? She would tell him the exact truth and convince him this was her big moment. If he let her have this account, she would bring it home for him and the ATD Agency. It would be the golden egg and it would solidify her position with the agency and with Metropolitan Brands. She shifted so she could see herself in the cab's rearview mirror. Staring at her image, she vowed this plan would work and then she could tell the gropers to "fuck off" and go screw a steno.

There was and would be no limit. If it played out, she might step from the agency into Metro Brands itself. V. P. in charge of cosmetic marketing would be a nice title and a nice place to start in that monster company.

The first thing to do is see Dunn—he's the key. The cab screeched when it pulled up.

"There you go, babe. I told you I could get you here in twelve minutes." He was the total cabby, with his cigar stub, three days of beard, and his last meals all over his shirt. He was as much a local icon as the Statue of Liberty.

"You earned the tip." She tossed the twenty onto the front seat. He glanced at it as it floated down, but she could tell he was more interested in her than the cash. She smiled. It made her feel wonderful to know all she had to do was "be" and they would jump. "I told you there'd be a good tip if you got me here in less than fifteen, but don't get your hopes interplanetary. What you want isn't available for any amount of money."

"Hey, lady, you're breakin' my heart. How could you think I wanted anythin' more than the cash money layin' there?" His beaver teeth glinted in the morning light. "You are outa my league. I know that, but I still love to think of what it could be like."

"Well, well," she said, smiling. "a little honesty. It's nice to meet a man who speaks the truth, but it'll do you no good. As they say, virtue is its own reward."

"Lady, I think the wise guys who say that are playin' jerky-jerky too much."

Lydia laughed and slid across the seat, opened the door and stepped from the cab into the morning. As she turned to close the door, the cabby picked up the bill and stuffed it into his shirt pocket. Then, in one fluid motion, he killed the meter, shifted into drive and pulled into the early traffic.

The ride to the seventeenth floor was quiet. It was early—only 7:45. Like water is wet, it was a known fact that Alexander T. Dunn always got in before 7:30. When she first heard that, she wondered if it was bullshit. Spread the myth that the boss is working his balls off and the Lilliputians will slave even harder. She did believe he was working at 7:30, but she couldn't shake the idea he had one of those Murphy beds up there that vanished in the wall. Well, this might be just the morning to find out, since the secretaries weren't in till nine.

She made her way to her office. It wasn't big, but it had good points like its East-side location which meant it got morning sun. When things worked out, she promised herself a twentieth floor corner office so she could watch the sun move around the building. After dropping her briefcase on the desk, she went to the ladies room, touched up her makeup and adjusted her outfit. The dress was one of her favorites, a shirtwaist in navy silk. Nice and quiet, respectful, formal, no overt sexiness, but able to show every line of her figure. It was cut like a man's shirt, but on a woman, it was so filled with understatement, it poured out sex.

The only person on the executive level was a retired cop-security guard by the elevator. He sat at a small desk, empty except for a telephone. As she exited the elevator, he rose to greet her, "May I help you Miss? These offices aren't formally open till nine."

"I know that." She held her ID tag for him to see. "I'm Lydia Cornell from the seventeenth. I have to see Mr. Dunn. It's urgent."

The guard's police background showed itself when she said "urgent." He moved toward her. "Is anything wrong?" He asked.

"Oh, no, I just have to see Mr. Dunn."

He sat, picked up the phone and dialed. After a moment, he said, "Mr. Dunn, there's a Lydia Cornell here who says she must see you on an urgent matter." The silence was a mere moment while the guard waited for an answer, but it was a breathtaking eternity for Lydia. The answer came when the guard smiled at her. He pointed down the corridor. "Do you know which it is?"

"Yes I do." As she slowly walked away, her heels clicked on the marble tiles, a slow steady tick, tick, tick. Approaching his door, her confidence never waned.

His office was one removed from the corridor, so Lydia opened the outer door and walked in, strode to his door, and knocked. When she heard him say, "Come," she opened the inner door, but she hesitated in the doorway as she appraised what she saw.

His office was about thirty feet long. Between her and Dunn were a polished wooden floor and a grand-looking Oriental rug. At one time, Orientals were authentic and expensive, but she knew you could get a good-looking copy on Fourteenth Street, so she dismissed the carpet. The wooden floor was another matter. The dark, wide, reddish-brown boards were obviously costly. Probably ripped out of some old farmhouse, sanded, refinished. and then custom installed for dollars an inch.

The rug and the floor's grain forced the eye straight ahead, like in a bowling alley. There were no pins, only the boss sitting at an antique desk so big it looked like a car. His jacket was off, his sleeves rolled to the cuff. Clearly, he was working, but nonetheless he looked fresh. She wondered if maybe the guy did get it all done before the rest of the world woke up. There had to be a reason for his success. There are a lot of smart people, but ingenious, hard-working compulsives are another story.

"What's so urgent it couldn't wait for regular hours?" he asked.

Lydia took a deep breath and blurted out, "I need twenty minutes of your time to explain a plan I have for the Metro Brand fragrance account. I know it will work and I believe it will revolutionize the industry. It's a new approach and we can be the first to get control. I'm not chemist enough to know if patents are a possibility, but they could happen in the future."

"Now that's the way every salesman should talk—right to the fucking point. No bullshit. No nonsense." He leaned back into his chair and then rocked back and forth. "Why are you telling me? Why aren't you telling Tom Randall? He's your immediate supervisor on the Metro account."

He motioned her to the desk with a wave of his hand and she walked forward slowly, deliberately casual so as not to display her unease. The wooden slab desk top was covered with loose sheets of yellow paper. It was clear he was working, and judging by the amount of paper on the desk, he had been at it for quite a while. The rumors were true.

She stopped about a foot away and slowly said, "I have told Tom. He knows about it, but I want to run it myself. I want to control what goes on. It was my find and I want to be in charge. Playing second-in-command is not for me." She paused and then added, "Does that sound unreasonable?"

"Shit no. I would do exactly what you're doing if the tables were turned." He stood and motioned for her to follow. To the right, there were leather chairs, sofas, tables, lamps, and ash trays. It looked to her like a movie set interior of a ritzy British club.

He sat in a chair and pointed with his chin to the one across from his. She sat, crossed her legs, and waited. After ten seconds of silence, she realized he was not going to ask any questions until he heard what she had to say, so she started with Coleman's attack on Miss Merrill.

"Why do you think what happened can be repeated? What if this event was a one time and will never happen again with anyone, including those two?"

"That's what I want to find out. I will need chemists to determine what's in that perfume. And, if what I suspect is true, and there is something odd in it, I want to know if the addition creates an odor that triggers latent memories."

"You aren't concerned with the potential sexual excitation?"

"Absolutely not. That's what every fragrance manufacturer is breaking balls to do. They all want the magic pheromone that makes men screaming crazies. That's not going to be found, because I don't think it exists." She shifted her body and recrossed her legs. He was watching her. He was looking at her legs. Let him look, she thought, it couldn't hurt. "But," she continued, "the odors of childhood, the odors that represented peace, comfort, and most of all warmth and security, they were the important odors. That's what everyone should be after."

"You don't think sexual excitation can be achieved through a great-smelling perfume?"

"No I don't. All a perfume has to do is maintain what already exists. When a man looks at a woman and starts to get an urge, only a truly negative odor will eliminate it." He smiled at her. She figured this was the moment to gamble. "Like the way you're looking at me, now. Did you need a perfume to generate what you're thinking?"

"You're right. I'll admit that. You're a great-looking woman, and when I look at you I get the hots, there's no denying that. And you're right about the negative odor. I can't even think of a smell that would turn me off right now."

"Exactly, exactly." She was eager now; the fervor of her desire was potent. She leaned forward in the chair and stared into his eyes. "Let's say we meet and are very much attracted to each other. We have the opportunity for a sexual encounter and we consummate the moment. Okay. Perfume helps in a minor way by adding a touch of the exotic. But let's say we meet at a place so public or inconvenient, that there is no possibility of sexual consummation. A pheromone, if it exists at all, would be wasted, but an odor that creates an absolutely pleasant sensation wouldn't be wasted. The closer you get to me the more peaceful and serene is the moment. Why would a man pass up a chance to repeat that feeling?"

He was looking at her with great interest. A half smile on his lips. "They told me you were smart, a real hot shot, but I had no idea. Jesus Christ, you remind me of me."

"I'll take that as a compliment."

"As you should." He got up and slowly walked back toward his desk. Half way there, he stopped, turned and came back. "What are you going to call it?"

"Complete Abandon."

"I don't think that's an appropriate name for an item that, if it works, will create feelings of serenity."

"You're right, it isn't. We should deliberately market the item against itself. Sell it as a hot, sex item. Play it up with all the ceremony and celebrity we can muster. The school girls, the shop-girls, the long- suffering wives will buy it expecting men and boys to fall at their feet." She paused and then said emphatically, "Don't make a mistake and think they're stupid. They may be ignorant, but they're shrewd. They don't really believe any perfume can be so effective it would immediately intoxicate a guy and drop him in his tracks. They know we're playing with them. They know we're appealing to their fantasies. But if this product works, we'll be giving them something that isn't bullshit."

"Let me get this straight. A perfume does exist that got a guy to want to suckle at the breast of the girl who was wearing it, right?" She nodded. "And you want to duplicate the product…get chemists to create a formula that will do the same thing. You then want to market a full line…?" She nodded again. "… and call it Complete Abandon. It will be a total line, perfume, toilet water, splash, powder, all the facial stuff, the works. And you want to market it as an item in line with its name, knowing it will not do that… not create complete abandon, but if anything, the exact opposite… moments of peaceful warmth, right?"

"Exactly. And if you're wondering why I want to market it that way, I don't think women will buy an item called Peace or Serenity. Deep down, they're torn. They might truly want that, but they crave the wild side. When it comes to the battle, the fantasy always wins. No one always wants to play it safe. So we'll sell the fantasy, give them Complete Abandon and make them think they're getting sexual magic. What we'll give them is a safer and more subtle satisfaction, which, they certainly also want."

"Do you think men will buy the stuff for them?"

"Wouldn't you if you thought it would get the girl you're after into bed, the backseat or… on the top of a desk?"

He smiled. "You really are hot shit. Are you offering yourself to me?"

"Mr. Dunn, I'm trying to get you to understand the strength of my desire. I'm not fooling around. I want this opportunity."

"Don't call me Mr. Dunn. From now on call me Tee."

"From now on… Tee?"

"Yes," he said, "Tee. From now on, we're going to be working closely and Mr. Dunn is too formal."

"Does that mean you'll okay it all?"

"I'd be an asshole to say no, Lydia. No one has come into this office in years with the moxie, the balls, and the sheer guts you've showed me. I want people around me who are as hungry as you are. Self-satisfied people aren't looking to own the world." He stood and walked back to the desk motioning her to follow. He sat and looked up at her.

"Let me ask you a question, Lydia. What is it you want?"

She looked at him, at his smooth, shiny hair, the firm, tanned flesh of his face, the stark white collar of his shirt and the lavender tie. She looked out the window behind him at the sky and the regal buildings of New York money. Then she looked back at him, looked as deeply into his eyes as she could. "What I want, Tee, is simple. I want everything."

He whooped out a laugh. "That's my kind of worker. That's my kind of girl." He smiled and stood up. "If I have anything to do with it, you're going to get just that…everything you ever dreamed of and more." He thrust out his right hand across the desktop. Lydia stared at it for a moment not understanding and then, smiling, grasped it and shook it, sealing the deal.

He sat down once again and said, "Okay. Now go back to your office and write it up…everything. I want to look at it on paper. Specify personnel, office space, equipment, and whatever the hell you think you will need. Don't skimp—first class. Let's get cracking on this."

"Do you want it this morning or this afternoon?"

"I learned one important lesson when I was teaching at Columbia, all over the world people are simultaneously working on similar projects. The ones who bring it in first are the winners. The longer you take the less you gain. Catch my drift?"

"You bet I do. It'll be on your desk before lunch." She turned to leave.

"One more thing," he said. She stopped and turned. "Were you serious about the offer?"

Slowly and softly, she replied, "I'm serious about everything connected with this project."

He grinned. "Fantastic, but down the path. That would get in the way right now. This is not the time for distractions."

She smiled and sucked in breath between her teeth. This is a real man, she thought. This is the kind of person who builds an international agency.

"What about Tom Randall?"

"I'll talk to him this morning. You go and get everything on paper."

CHAPTER 16

Lydia closed her eyes and gave thanks. She had been given the magic formula for her heart's desire. I have the chance, she said to herself. I finally have the chance. Retracing her steps to the office door, she looked back at him before she opened it. He was penciling something on a yellow sheet, but sensing she was looking at him, he looked up, smiled and waved her away with his free hand.

She walked back down the corridor and when she got to the security guard, he asked "Was the urgent matter settled, Miss Cornell?"

"Yes, it was...quite satisfactorily."

"Great. That's the way to start the day." Lydia smiled at him.

Back in her office she listed everything she thought she might need, from chemists to desks. So much of it was still a mystery there were blank spaces at the bottom of her list, but the marketing plan and the advertising concept were sketched out. Line by line the strategy took shape.

She knew it would depend upon the odor actually producing the desired action. It still seemed fantastic to her, but it happened. It did happen. Mr. Coleman did attack Miss Merrill. And he did because of the scent she was wearing. That was the secret of the entire affair—that scent. The structure of that perfume has to be analyzed and the exact proportions of everything in it have to be determined. Getting her hands on that perfume was vital and she figured no difficulty getting it from Miss Merrill. The girl seemed straightforward and guileless. Lydia could not imagine a reason why she would not hand it over. If necessary, I could arrange a swap, she thought. I'll buy her any perfume she wants.

Turning back to her list of necessaries, Lydia carefully spelled out her reasoning for the marketing procedures. She knew she was right about it by the way everything fell into place. She reasoned out approaches for women buying it for themselves or as a gift, for men buying it for girlfriends or wives and not least, plans for teens and seniors. She gingerly ventured into schemes to offer it to racial and ethnic groups she knew little about except that they existed. Also mentioned was the need for a first-class social psychologist who thoroughly understood the ethnic groups that were out there. Looking up at the clock she was amazed it was almost eleven. She called Win hoping he'd be in his office.

He answered, "Professor David, here."

She purred, "Good morning to you, lover."

"Lydia, what a nice surprise. For a moment I thought it was Miss Conroy."

"Is she your present student of the moment?"

"Just joking, just joking, there's no one but you." He paused, waiting for her to say something, but she remained silent. "So, I must ask to what do I owe the pleasure of your interrupting your morning at your fantasy factory?"

"Mr. Sweet, I need a favor. I want to talk to that Miss Merrill, Mr. Coleman's love interest."

"Well, I know she lives in one of the dorms, but not which one. Anyway, she's probably not there now. She's probably in class or hanging out someplace."

"It's important."

"Okay. I'll see what I can do. If I locate her I'll tell her to call you direct, okay?"

"That'll be great and I thank you in advance, lover man."

"Don't say things like that; you'll get me excited."

"Not much you can do over the phone."

"You're right, but I could run out and find Miss Conroy. I'll bet she's ready for some private tutoring."

"Is that what they call it now?"

"That's what they've always called it."

"That's cute, very cute."

"Get together later tonight?"

"I don't know. Work has taken on a new twist with little time left for anything but office."

"You know about all work and no fooling around?"

"Yes I do. You will try to locate her, won't you?"

"Don't worry, I'll locate her."

"Okay...bye now."

She hung up hoping he'll be able to find her quickly, because so much depended on that perfume. Then she wondered if there was such a thing as a formula that could not be duplicated—maybe "created" was a better word—if it turned out Miss Merrill wouldn't part with the stuff. Her thoughts were interrupted by a knock on her door. "Come," she said. The door opened and Tom Randall came in.

"Tom. What's up?"

"I got to hand it to you, baby. You are the real thing. Just came from A.T. Dunn himself and he told me I was to help you as much as I could and eventually I'll get another account to work on. And that the Metro Brands deal was all yours... alone."

"Are you angry?" She thought about getting up, but chose to remain seated.

"No, I'm not angry. I'm a company man and I do what I'm told. If he wants you to handle the deal on your own...he gets what he wants. He is the boss."

"I know that, but that's not the issue. I thought you might be sore because I jumped you and went directly to him."

"Look, Lydia, I know that's the way to do things. If I felt as you do, I would've done exactly the same thing. I just stopped by to tell you I am not angry and I'm willing to do what I can to help." She was far more pleased than surprised, because he could have easily managed to screw things up for her.

"I'm glad you feel that way and if there is a way we can work together, I'll let you know. Okay?"

She stood and came from behind the desk to face him. He smiled and extended his hand, probably expecting her to shake. Instead, she took his hand in both of hers and pulled it to her breast. "I'm sure we'll have a chance to work closely together," she said softly.

"Damn, you are one hot babe...damn!" She let go of his hand and smiled.

"I better get out of here, right now or I'll stretch you out on that desk and show you just how close I can work." Moving quickly, he turned and walked out.

Back at her desk, she had started to look over the proposal when the phone rang.

"Miss Cornell?" a female voice asked.

"Yes, who's calling?"

"Miss Cornell, this is Susan Merrill Professor David said you wanted to talk to me."

"Yes, Miss Merrill, I do, but first, I want to thank you for taking the time to call. I know you're busy."

"I'm not that busy."

"Great, because I need a favor and I thought we could talk about it over dinner."

"Over dinner?"

"Absolutely. My treat. You name the place and I'll pay the bill. I can clearly remember my college days and a free meal was always cool. Has that changed?"

"Absolutely not. When?"

"How about tonight?"

"Super."

"Okay if we meet in front of the Cedar Street Tavern at… what's a good time for you?"

"Six thirty?"

"Fine. I'll see you in front at six thirty and don't forget…you pick the restaurant and… one more thing… I'd like to wear jeans so don't pick the Waldorf."

"Me too…and don't worry… I'm not the Waldorf type."

"Great. See you at six thirty."

Dunn lit the short, fat cigar and realized as he held it, how ridiculous he probably looked. But that's the price. Leaning back in his chair, he smiled. Got to be part of what's happening. If you're behind the times, you're out of the times. It was really that simple. Everything else is bullshit…in or out. End of story. There was a buzz and a moment later, a knock.

"Come," he said. The door opened and Tom Randall strolled in. As he approached the desk, Dunn asked, "Did you speak to her?"

"Just now. I left her office about five minutes ago."

"How did she act?"

"She's no fool. Right off she apologized for leap-frogging, I graciously accepted and agreed to everything, because I am a considerate and obliging fellow."

Dunn laughed. "Oh for sure, you're all that, but you are also a fucking snake of the first order.

"But Mr. Dunn," Randall comically protested, "don't forget…I'm your snake."

"Yes, you sure are and let's keep it that way. Knowing Lydia Cornell as I think I do, I'm sure she's going to spread her legs and offer you deep involvement in her project. How you handle that is your business, but remember I want to know what is going on. When you find out anything, tell me. I don't want to run after you, so keep me posted."

"Absolutely, but what do you want me to work on?"

"Start work on the copy for her campaign and keep in mind that selling discontent is our primary and basic mission," Dunn got up, and using the cigar like a sword, he pointed it at Randall. "Our goal is dissatisfaction. If you ever find a contented consumer, it is your sworn duty to create enough immediate doubt and worry to dispel that momentary feeling of contentment. Remember, a disgruntled consumer is our prime customer."

Randall smiled. "Mr. Dunn, you have a grasp of the advertising business second to none."

Dunn flopped back into his chair and said, "Okay, get out of here, go back to your office and start thinking of copy for Cornell's project. I like the name Complete Abandon, so start your gray cells to work on a campaign with that idea as its central focus."

"Done!" Randal said, walking to the door.

But Randall stopped and turned back when Dunn said, "Don't forget, Tom… keep me posted on her progress. I'm serious about this, so no fucking up…okay?"

Randall saluted with military precision and left the office.

CHAPTER 17

University Place had an endless flow of people lurching ahead on both sides of the street, marking a transition from a New York City blatant for the native, but a blank to the tourist. For the unaware visitor, it was a picture of similarity where everything looked and sounded exactly the same. A green grocer's neatly arranged fruits and vegetables looked like another display, unless the viewer noticed the subtle variations at a similar store three blocks away. The differences in each food store, dress shop, pharmacy, or travel agency emphasized their particular connections to the old country—to the home country. For those who knew how to see, those differences were signs as obvious as diplomatic plates for UN big shots.

The careful eye took in the signs, the symbols, the clothing, even the trash piles on the street. Walking slowly provided even the tin ear with the accents and dialects of languages usually relegated to cable TV at weird hours. Like smoke from camp fires, smells enveloped the sidewalks and seeped into everything. After some time in a neighborhood, each person took on the smell of those streets. If anything, the smells were badges of belonging, like an animal's pack smell, a routine device for separating out who was welcome and who was not.

The foreignization of the city was as vibrant now as it was in the early 1900s. There were people from everywhere, everywhere. New York City had become an all-season version of California, where a true native was as hard to find as a nugget of gold.

As Lydia sauntered, the street hustlers aimed their appraising gazes at her. Their hungry eyes considered her status as a student and then quickly dismissed that idea. She was too well dressed, too assured and far too insolent in her visible dismissal of their stares. Her cold eyes and attitude transmitted a flagrant defiance that so intimidated the street guys that they cursed her when she passed. She wondered how many "smart" girls from colleges fell into the traps these parasites presented. Not only that, but why did these girls fall for the bullshit these wise guys delivered? One day she would find out. There could be good advertising copy in the pitch these predators had developed.

But what was the quid pro quo for the girls? It was easy to understand what these guys wanted—a quick push in the sack and one more college girl added to the scorecard. In the sixties, the girl's were conned into sex by a clever mix of civil rights, freedom and the pill. But now, in the early teens, the reasons for girls getting conned were different. Now it might be sheer stupidity, a nose-thumbing at parents, or any of the readily available drugs.

Lydia sighed when she thought about addictive drugs. How wonderful an addicted customer was for the bottom line. Once bitten… a lifelong advocate. Maybe it could be that way with this perfume. No! She reminded herself, not just a perfume, but a complete line, like Avon pushing clothes and jewelry.

Looking down the street, Lydia saw Susan Merrill waiting outside the bar and wondered about her. She seemed like a sweet kid. No pretensions, at least none easily seen. What might she want, Lydia wondered, and then tried to figure what might be a wedge she could use? I'll have to wait for the moment, she realized.

When she was about two feet away, Lydia extended her hand and Susan Merrill reached out for it.

"Hi, Miss Cornell. It's so good to see you again."

"Oh, please don't call me Miss Cornell. It's Lydia."

"Okay, as long as you call me Susan."

"Fair enough, first names it is." Although they looked relatively similar, an astute observer could see the overt innocence of one and the wise, calculating aspect of the other.

"How about the restaurant, did you make a decision?" Lydia asked.

"There are so many places, I get confused. Back home we have one of this and one of that. Limited choices made my life easy."

"That may be so, but here you have everything. I bet you could find food from every UN country right here in Manhattan." She paused, raised her eyebrows and asked, "Does anything special appeal to you?"

"Well…"

"Come on, don't be bashful."

"Well, I've never had New York Chinese food and I wondered if there was a place nearby?"

"You have had Chinese food, though?"

"Oh, yes, but the town I come from just got its first Asian place a year ago. They serve everything... you know... Chinese dishes, Korean dishes, Japanese, Thai, everything that isn't American or European. And...well...I'm not so sure about their cooking, everything I had there tasted the same."

"Well, Chinese is a good choice. I know a great place. Follow me." Playfully, Lydia took Susan's hand and led the way uptown.

They walked up University to Thirteenth and then cut over to Fifth. To an onlooker, they could have been sisters. They made a nice pair, both knowingly pretty and able to project a positive image. They looked like a couple everyone would want at their next party.

At the corner of Thirteenth and Fifth was a brand new Chinese Restaurant, the Li Brothers. It was a chopstick away from the *Forbes Magazine* galleries and had quickly established itself as a "smart" New York dining room. Lydia loved such places, because the staff's bowing and scraping was equivalent to the money you dropped into their palms. The first time Lydia was at this place, she slipped the maitre d' a fifty on nothing more than a whim. She had been back only three times since and each time the staff behaved like she was Mao's best girlfriend. She was treated like royalty and couldn't figure out how the different shifts knew who she was until a restaurant owner told her they took photographs of those deserving special treatment and pinned those photos to a kitchen bulletin board for all to see. Lydia didn't know if that was true, but it sounded smart and to survive in the New York restaurant business, being smart was a prime requisite.

Since it was dinnertime when they arrived, Lydia didn't expect to receive the level of attention she had before, but she was wrong. The particular maitre d' who had taken her money was on duty and snapped to attention when he saw her. He stepped down into the roped-off waiting area where several couples were biding their time and bowed to her.

"Ah, Miss Cornell," he said, "how wonderful to see you once again, Please follow me." He led them to the velvet rope which he ceremoniously swung aside and, with much deference, escorted them to a table near the center of the dining area. A reserved sign was swept away as they took seats. He bowed to Lydia and snapped some authoritative words to a waiter, who had materialized out of the dark rear of the room. As water was poured by the busboy, the waiter cleared extra settings and handed out oversized menus. As the other diners watched them scan the menus, Lydia could see Susan was impressed by the treatment they received.

"It's nice to be treated like that, isn't it?" she asked.

"Oh, I'm awed. He marched us right by all the other people who were waiting." She paused, a quizzical look on her face. "But how did they know you were coming? You said I should pick the restaurant."

"They didn't know and neither did I till you said you wanted Chinese food."

Susan stared at her. "They treat you like that whenever you come in?"

"That's right. I treat them properly and they treat me with respect."

"I don't understand that."

"It's simple. I gave them enough money for them to roll out the red carpet whenever."

"You mean you gave them a large tip the last time?"

"Not really, I gave money in addition to the tip. In other words, I paid for the treatment we received. And they'll keep treating me that way because they always expect to get more money."

A combination of astonishment melted into envy on Susan's face. "Wow, I would love to get treated like that."

"You would?"

"Of course, wouldn't anyone?"

"Well yes, I guess you're right, but right now let's order. What would you like?"

"I know so little about this food. Why don't you order for us both?"

Lydia smiled. "Okay." She signaled the waiter who leaned over with pen and pad at the ready. After asking Susan some questions, Lydia managed to order won ton soup, steamed dumplings, Seafood Fantasia in garlic sauce, and Mandarin Delight in ginger sauce. The waiter vanished and in a few minutes the soup started the food parade. There was little time for detailed conversation, but finally after the seafood, but before the Mandarin Delight, Lydia asked about the perfume.

"Oh, yes, well... I gave the bottle to Professor Lehman this morning. She said she would need it if she was going to make a detailed analysis."

"Did you discuss when you would get it back?"

"No. I just gave it to her. I guess she'll give it back when she's finished with it."

"She's not going to use it all, is she?"

Shrugging, Susan said, "I don't know how much she needs to do whatever she's going to do." She paused and stared at Lydia. "You want some of it, don't you?"

"I guess it couldn't hurt. I mean… it may come in handy as an example for some work I'm doing at the agency."

"You like working in advertising?"

"Oh, yes, and I have just been given a great deal of responsibility with a new line. I was hoping to use some of your perfume as a reference point for the fragrance."

"Would you use the fragrance for the entire line?"

"Sure, as long as it isn't a copy of something that's popular. Every perfume that makes it now has to have a singular scent. If the perfume is good, a whole line develops around it, even baby powder."

"You really think you could use it for baby powder?"

"Why not, and from what I picked up the other night, your perfume has a lot to do with babies."

Susan smiled. "I guess it does. Look what it caused Paul to do. That is so crazy. I can hardly believe it happened." She sipped some tea and then asked, "Is it possible to copy a scent? You know, take the smell from one thing and transfer it to another?"

"Oh, sure, most smells are just specific molecules from different substances—like oils from flowers or spices. Your perfume must be special in a strange way. I'd love to get some to sample and then copy its properties."

"Gee, I don't know what to do. I guess I could get it back from Professor Lehman."

"I would be glad to give you something for it."

"You mean money? Do you mean you want to buy it?"

"Well, I could get you some money, the agency always pays for anything it uses, but I thought that maybe you'd like something else instead of money."

"What else, for instance?"

"Well," Lydia paused, and looked at Susan from one angle, then shifted in her seat to look at her from another. In almost a whisper, but loud enough for Susan to hear, Lydia said, "So pretty." Then in a full voice, she said, "I could get an agency photographer to take professional pictures of you after—don't take this wrong—after one of the professional makeup artists does a full-fledged and magical transformation. Would you like that?"

"You mean like one of those television makeovers?"

"Sure, if you'd like that." Lydia paused, and then said, "You know, I bet I could get you a closet of new clothes and maybe even a chance to model those clothes in one of the magazines we have ties with."

"Model in a magazine ….me?" Susan gasped.

"Why not, you're certainly pretty enough. You'd be a natural."

Lydia sat back in her seat and looked at Susan as if she was a museum piece. "You know, you are a natural. I bet I could get you an audition. We use so many of the same models in our ads and the art directors and account executives are always screaming for new faces, new talent."

"You really think I could be a model? I always thought I'm too short for that sort of thing."

"You might not be tall enough for runway work, but for magazines, you're perfect. I wish I had your looks."

"How can you say that? You're so beautiful."

Lydia laughed. "I may have good points, but… not like you. You're so fresh and young. You're just what they're looking for. Next to you, I'm an old lady."

"Oh, don't be silly." Susan said.

At that moment, Lydia thought Susan looked and sounded like it was the moment when all her dreams came true. Her wide open eyes and flushed skin were pure and wholesome expectation. Her face was showing pure joy.

"Hey," Lydia said, "We'd better eat or all this food will get cold. We can discuss this more, if you like, over dessert."

"Oh, God, yes, imagine me… a model."

As Lydia ate more of Mandarin Delight, she looked at Susan and said, "Not a model, Susan… a top model. There's quite a difference."

To Lydia it was plain Susan wanted to say something but didn't know what to say. She just stared at Lydia with an expression of surprise and gratitude on her face.

When they finished the main dishes, they considered dessert. Susan said she never thought Chinese restaurant desserts mattered because she'd never heard of anything besides almond cookies and ice cream. But to her amazement and joy, Li Brothers had four that sounded wonderful. While deciding, they giggled over Eight Treasure Rice Pudding, Peking Dust, Almond Float and Spun Apples.

They decided on the rice pudding and were thrilled when the waiter delivered a bowl for two. The rice pudding looked like rice pudding, but it was covered with different candied fruits and nuts. It tasted as good as it looked.

When they were finished, Susan said, "Oh. Lydia, how can I thank you? That was wonderful, absolutely wonderful. I've never had such great food." Susan reached across the table and covered Lydia's hand with her own.

"It was my pleasure, Susan. I remember how boring college food can get."

"You know it. The dorm food is okay, but it's always the same. This is a welcome change."

"Good. I'm glad you enjoyed it." The waiter brought the check and Lydia paid with a credit card.

"This may sound silly, but I get a kick out of seeing you pay for a meal like this. My mother never worked and she never had a nickel my Dad didn't give her. I really like seeing single women able to afford what they want."

Lydia smiled and got up. Susan followed as they walked through the dining room to the main entrance. The maitre d' did his act and Lydia handed him some money as they got to the front door. Her rushed to open it for them and oozed a goodnight as they walked into the evening.

Outside, Lydia said, "Susan, never forget the feeling you have about being independent. Never put yourself in the hands of a man so completely, you can't decide what you want."

"I know what you mean. The girls in the dorm talk about that all the time. I'm going to have a life for myself, man or no man."

"Good for you. If this model business works out, money will not be a problem. Maybe it will never be a problem."

"God, could that be possible?"

"It's possible, believe me."

They walked a block before Susan asked, "When could I get those pictures taken?"

"I'll need a few days to arrange it, but this week probably. You can bring the perfume to the agency when you come for the pictures, okay?"

"Oh, sure, I'll talk to Professor Lehman tonight and get it back from her as soon as she's finished with it."

"Great. I can't wait to find out if the chemists think it might help with the baby powder and the rest of the line."

Susan stopped and took hold of Lydia's hand. "I want to thank you for the dinner and I want to thank you for the chance at modeling. Whatever happens, I want you to know I'm grateful."

Lydia, tried hard to match her sincerity. "I'm glad you feel that way. You might become a model and then again you might not. I'll be happy to do what I can, so at least you'll have a good shot at it."

"You bet I will." Susan said. Then hand in hand, they resumed their walk down Fifth Avenue toward the Arch.

An hour later in her apartment, Lydia wondered if Gert would make a hassle about the perfume. Probably not, since her involvement is nothing more than curiosity and the analysis is her game of let's find out what's in the perfume. Lydia realized Gert was not alone in that, for she was also deeply interested in the answer.

CHAPTER 18

Gert stared at the perfume, a nondescript glass bottle with a white plastic spin-on cap which she twisted off and took a quick sniff. Her immediate impression was floral. It was a sweet and wholesome combination of odors from which Gert quickly identified the primary one—roses.

Comparing it to today's perfume brought a smile to her face, for now, a typical scent came in a package that was far more expensive than the cost of the old bottle and the old perfume combined. Packaging and promotion were the ways to sell now. Television had changed everything by focusing attention on the package, not the contents. There was little difference from the way TV programs were packaged to the way goods were packaged. If the hype was sufficiently intense, the public bought into the trumped-up importance.

Gert laughed. Things were not always like that. When she was young it had been easy to grow up. She thought about Susan Merrill. She seemed like a nice, sweet kid… almost too nice and sweet…a throwback to her mother's time. Gert wondered how long it would take for the Greenwich Village milieu to crush that pleasant small-town quality. But maybe she'd be lucky. Maybe she was stronger than she looked and could hold her own against the hipsters and the freaks.

The laboratory Gert had created in her building was better equipped than her lab at school, so she had taken the perfume there. Analyzing it would not be a difficult chore. Standard procedures would yield the usual and expected quantities of essential oils in an alcohol solution. The problem would be isolating the breast milk and determining its properties, particularly the properties that had such a significant effect upon Mr. Coleman.

Every aspect of Susan Merrill's mother's life would have some effect upon the composition of her breast milk like her diet, or whether her life was easy or tension filled, and what drugs she took or was taking at that time. As now, with expectant mothers being told not to smoke, drink alcohol, or use addictive drugs, mothers to be in the seventies were warned about the same potential dangers. Did Susan Merrill's mother abide the warnings or was she a rebel who did what she pleased?

Gert started separating out the components of the perfume and was not surprised at finding the three-level arrangement typically used: the top note which is perceived immediately; a middle note, or heart, used as a modifier and available when the top note impact flashed away after ten minutes or so. And finally, there was the base note or end note which is most persistent and can still be whiffed after an hour or so when the top and middle notes fade.

In this case, the most blatant odor component—the top note, roses, drew immediate attention. The middle note or the heart note was a floral – also roses. The base note was sweet, maybe vanilla.

Essentially, the perfume was common: a rose and vanilla combination. All in all, it was the typical fragrance of a seventies housewife As Gert looked at the liquid, she pondered the real mystery, which was why and how it remained a perfume. By rights, it should have spoiled—deteriorated and turned into a gloppy brown lump.

Gert was proud of her analytical work and regarded every analysis she completed as intellectual property no different from the way an author viewed a just completed novel. Her analysis was a product of her intelligence and sharing what she had accomplished was rare. In the past only one analytical adventure, as she thought of her work, was ever shared with anyone. Sharing was not a habit she relished.

Years of training took over and Gert wrote detailed notes of the procedures she had used and the results she obtained. After she finished, she got a split of red wine from a small refrigerator and sipped some as she pondered the results.

Timing was the key. If Miss Merrill had put on that perfume first thing in the morning, then the base note would be the available fragrance component that had hit Coleman. If she put it on a few minutes before they came together, that would be different. Then the top note would be just as significant as the other two. But, if she had put it on an hour or two before, well, then it would be a combination of roses and the "magic" ingredient that hit him.

After several more hours of work, Gert managed to separate out some natural fats that looked like milk fat. She knew it would be very difficult and maybe unnecessary to analyze which of the 142 fatty acids involved in this complex mixture had played a part in Coleman's reaction. What made more sense to her was to see if any of the known constituents of human milk were present in a quantity beyond normal expectations.

Human and cow's milk are similar but differ in specific ways. The major differences are that cow's milk has significantly more calcium, thiamin, and riboflavin while human milk has about double the amount of niacin. What she found surprised her. The level of carbohydrates was unexplainably high. She wondered if there had been augmented fermentation. Whatever the reason for the differences, the perfume had broken chemical rules and turned into something strange.

Was it possible Merrill's mother was one of those high-carbo freaks on one of those hyped diets that "guaranteed" strength, agility, brains, freedom from all diseases, and nice tits? Was it a joke? Those diets didn't do much except make the writer and the book publisher smile.

While thinking about the results, she wondered if Merrill's mother had some metabolic imbalance that screwed up her digestion or maybe she had inadequate carbohydrate utilization. There could be many reasons. But then it dawned on her that Merrill's mother was not the loose cannon in this case… it was Coleman's mother. She was the one who developed his nutritional base line. It hinged on Coleman. If he hadn't reacted as he did, then the entire situation would not have happened. Coleman's the key. He nursed at his mother's breast and he wanted to nurse at Merrill's. The perfume was merely a catalyst, some sort of bridge between his childhood nursing and his attempt to get at Merrill.

The specific ingredients of Merrill's perfume are vital, but it's Coleman's reaction to what's in it that brought this all about. It's him and the perfume! Separate them and neither factor holds any weight as explanation. He's the ingredient that must be analyzed. He's the loose cannon as is any guy nursed by a mother with a high carb preference. Gert realized that specific trait was now typical what with the heavy consumption of breads, pies, cakes and baked goods in general. It was a mother's diet along with the perfume and not just Coleman's mother, but any mother.

Gert grabbed the telephone and called Win who was not at home. She tried him at school and he picked up. She told him she needed Coleman's phone number. Ten minutes later she was speaking to Coleman.

"Mr. Coleman, do you remember particular outstanding features of your mother's diet? Are there any foods she particularly likes?"

"Oh yeah, my mother's a freak for pasta and baked stuff. My whole life has been one great festival of bread, cake, or pie following enormous meals of spaghetti and things."

"Things?"

"Yeah you know, sausages, pepperoni, foods you layer on spaghetti."

"Right, okay. Now, one more thing. Do you know if your mother did anything to entice you to nurse when you were at that stage?"

"Did anything? I don't understand."

"I mean, did she wet your lips with something before hand? Did she do anything extra besides just sticking you onto her breast?"

"I don't know. I just found out the other day I was nursed. These aren't questions guys ask their moms."

"Well, I want you to do just that. Call your mother and ask her. Then get right back to me. Okay?"

There was silence. Then he asked, "This is important?"

"Yes it is. I think I have the answer to why you behaved as you did. Your mother's answer to that question will be the clincher."

"You want me to ask her if she did anything at all to get me to nurse... anything beyond just bringing a hungry kid in contact with a meal?"

"Right, that's it exactly. Call home now and then get back to me. Okay?"

"Sure. I'll call her and then call you back."

Gert gave him her number and said once again, to call immediately. He hung up and she added to her notes the elements she had found. At the end she added her guesses. While she waited, she had more wine and realized she had really enjoyed this little bit of detective work. Being able to solve a problem or answer a question with precise techniques of chemistry honed her appreciation for the field beyond her general high regard. While she was enjoying herself and the wine, the phone rang. It was Miss Merrill.

"Professor Lehman, I was wondering if you've finished with the perfume. If you are, I'd love to have it back."

"Are you planning to put Mr. Coleman through some more hoops?"

"I don't think I understand what you mean."

"I'm asking if you intend to wear it while he's around. You know, kind of push him into a similar reaction?"

"Oh, Paul and I are past that point. I don't need the perfume for that kind of reaction."

"Wow, you are a fast worker."

"I like him."

"I hope so." Gert smiled. "Anyway, I'm through with it and I think I found the answer to what happened."

"You did? That's amazing."

"Maybe, maybe not… just good chemistry, but you can have it back. I can bring it to school tomorrow. Would that be convenient?"

"Oh, yes. I'll stop by your office about noon?"

"Fine, see you then." Gert hung up and before she could get the wine glass to her lips the phone rang again.

"Professor Lehman, this is Paul Coleman."

"That was fast."

"Well, they weren't tough questions, and my mother thinks everyone in New York is crazy anyway, so she was only mildly surprised at them."

"That's nice. What did she say?"

"Well, she was a little embarrassed and wondered how come you knew."

"Knew what?"

"That she had to use a rose-water solution on her nipples to get me to nurse. It seems I was a reluctant feeder and had to be coaxed into nursing."

"A rose-water solution. That's what I thought. Did she, by chance, mention if she bought it or did she prepare it herself?"

"Boy, you really have a handle on this. As a matter of fact, she did say. The doctor gave her a recipe, and she and my father cooked it up. He still uses a small distillation kit to make perfume oils."

"He makes essential oils?" She asked with great surprise.

"Yeah, he always has. He's always taking flowers from our garden and reducing them to floral oils as he calls them. I guess you could call him an amateur perfume maker. He's done it as long as I can remember."

"That means he could have made a really potent solution."

"Oh, yeah, my mom's always loved roses and she said he made a strong solution. I guess that's why I also love roses. They're my favorite flower."

"That figures."

"What figures?"

"Well, best as I can put it together, you've been set up since you were a nursing baby to respond to roses. Since Miss Merrill's perfume was basically a rose perfume, that odor and other constituents in the perfume caused you to react as you did when she wore it."

"Other constituents?"

"Some additional elements were present."

"So that's what happened."

"Yes, that's what I think. So you aren't a serial rapist or the campus madman after all. And, what I'm calling the 'other constituents' explains why you reacted as you did. You and that perfume are linked in a very special way."

"Well, that makes my day. You don't know what this means to me. Thank you so much."

"It was fun working it out. I should thank you."

"Does Susan… I mean Miss Merrill know?"

"Nope, just you and me, and by the way, she called a while ago. She wants the perfume back. We're going to meet tomorrow, so I'd be on guard tomorrow night. If she puts some on you may be put to the test again."

"Hey, I'm glad you mentioned it, but I'm not going to tell her what you told me. I'd like this whole thing to go away."

"It's finished as far as I'm concerned. I think it's very interesting, but beyond that. I don't know. It's just interesting."

"Thank you so much, Professor Lehman you have no idea how great I feel. A full-scale disaster has turned into the exact opposite. Wow, this is all so great."

Gert laughed. "Your joy is catching Mr. Coleman and I'm happy for you. It's not hard to see that you and Miss Merrill have become a couple. I understand how you must feel." Gert almost said she envied him, but caught herself.

"Okay, Mr. Coleman good night and thank you for your help in all this."

"Oh, thank you Professor Lehman. Thank you. Bye."

He hung up and Gert stared at the phone. She did envy him especially that young girl. Pretty, slim—all the current requisites. If there had been a mirror in the lab, she would have looked at herself and been disgusted. But there was no mirror and there were none upstairs except in the bathroom. It made her life easier not to see herself.

Sadly, she finished the wine and cleaned all the varied apparatus she had used. An hour later, upstairs, she fell asleep listening to Prokofiev's Third Piano concerto.

CHAPTER 19

Susan Merrill knocked.

"Come." Gert announced. Opening the door slowly, Susan walked into the office. Smiling, Gert gestured to a chair, which Miss Merrill brought closer to the desk.

"You look bright and cheery today."

Susan smiled. "Well, I feel wonderful, the sun is shining and I see no disasters on the horizon, so I better feel good. There's no reason not to."

"Well, well, having a student not forecasting doom is refreshing. Usually, it's an exam, a paper or something that requires dark clouds."

"That may be so, but not for me. I think I have a boyfriend and a job and everything's looking up."

"A boyfriend and a job. Tell me about it."

"Well, the more I think of Paul, the more excited I get. I really like him and I'm sure he feels the same about me. The job stuff is only a possibility, but Lydia, Miss Cornell, well she thinks I have what it takes to be a model."

"Really?" Gert responded.

"Yes, we were talking the other day and she said she'd help me with photographs, introductions, everything."

"No kidding?" Gert asked, mildly surprised. "Well, well, it's been my observation that Lydia doesn't do anything without getting something in return. She isn't the type to do favors out of thin air."

"Well, I did promise I'd give her the perfume when you were through with it. I don't have anything else to offer."

"So Lydia wants the perfume. Did she say why?"

"All she said was that it might help with a new line of products from perfume to baby powder."

"Baby powder. Lydia?"

"That's right. She said she thought the perfume's fragrance might be nice for a line of baby powders in addition to everything else."

"Well, what do you know about that?"

"You sound a bit surprised."

"With Lydia it's always business and when she does anything, there's usually a more definite reason than a 'might be nice.'"

"Well, that may be so, but all I know is what she told me."

"Just another one of life's little mysteries, I guess. Maybe we'll all find out one day." Gert said, as she reached into her briefcase for the perfume. "Here's the magic elixir." She handed it to Susan who put it into her handbag.

"Are you sure you're through with it?"

"All finished. I did a complete analysis, noted everything and filed it all away. The conclusion I reached is interesting, and it could be a true mystery that remains an unknown, since not everything that happens has a nice cozy explanation. Mr. Coleman's reaction may never happen again."

"Well, I certainly hope so. Once was more than enough." She hesitated then asked, "Would you tell me what you concluded?"

"I could, but I think you'll have more fun if you get Paul to tell you. He may not even realize he knows, so if he's a bit reluctant just ask him to name his favorite flower. That should point you in the proper direction."

"His favorite flower?"

"Yup, and you might also ask him if he likes bread and baked goods."

A questioning look spread over Susan's face. "Okay, I'll do that, but I don't think I understand."

Enjoying being coy for a moment, Gert said, "Let me ask you this, when you smell that perfume does anything stand out? Do you sense one odor more than others?"

"The first time I opened the bottle I got a rush of flowers, and then it seemed to become kind of rosy, I guess. It's hard to talk about smells."

"You're right, but your senses are okay, since roses have a lot to do with everything, but I've said too much. Ask Paul when you're alone."

A bit befuddled by the conversation, Susan got up, thanked Gert and left to get to an afternoon of classes.

About six hours later, after a pair of Burgers de Luxe at Adolpho's Coffee Palace, Susan and Paul walked back to his dorm room. While they walked, Susan badgered him until he promised to tell her about the perfume. He said he would tell all once they got to his place. So arm in arm, they walked to the dorm, looking supremely at ease and satisfied. They were a good-looking couple and those who knew them saw that a match had been made. So often people on a date or just walking side by side, looked incredibly uncomfortable. Like they are certain the other has some communicable disease and a discreet distance is an appropriate safety measure. Susan and Paul were at the other end of that continuum. They looked like they were made to walk together.

When they got to the dorm, they went straight to his room. Being a graduate student, he was eligible for the single-room lottery, and only now did he fully appreciate his luck for winning a single room on the eleventh floor overlooking the park.

When they got to his room, she entered with the same hesitancy shown by a defuser of an unexploded bomb. But once inside, faced with the choice of the bed or a chair to sit on, she chose the bed and Paul's fantasies took wing. He sat beside her and put his arm around her. He would never forget the moment when she looked at him closed her eyes and leaned her face to his. All his thoughts vanished except his realization that he wanted to kiss her and hold her close. He wasn't thinking about would she or wouldn't she. He thought her beautiful and sweet and felt amazingly relaxed and honest about everything that had happened between them since they met.

He kissed her and she returned his kiss with a passion that matched his. They pressed against each other and then they slowly stretched out on the bed. Then, just as he was slipping his hand into her blouse, she stopped him and sat up.

"Okay, a promise is a promise. Tell me about the perfume."

He started to laugh and grabbed her.

"Oh, no, you said you'd tell me. Come on."

Seeing she was serious, he sat up and began. "Now, this is what I've put together from last night's phone conversation with Professor Lehman and thinking about what happened. She told me the perfume was a floral, primarily a rose fragrance, and that there were other things in it that amplified my reaction. But basically I reacted to the perfume because when I was a baby, my mother used a strong rosewater solution on her nipples to persuade me to nurse. It seemed I wouldn't nurse unless the rosewater was involved. I know it sounds crazy, but that's what my mother told me when I spoke to her."

He grabbed for Susan and they fell backward in a clinch. "Is that it?" she asked.

"Not exactly. Professor Lehman also asked me if my mother likes bread and baked stuff. Well, my mom's a freak for the bakery. Me too. My guess is that there's something to do with that involved in all this, but I don't know what." He paused. "So that's it. I was enticed to nurse with rosewater and your perfume is heavy with roses. Also, there's something to do with bread or baked stuff. I don't know. But anyway... that's the story."

Susan sat up. "Oh," she said. "I think I see. My father mixed my mother's breast milk in the perfume. He did it as a joke, but I bet the milk had something to do with the final result. You see, my mother is also a bakery nut. She loves cakes, pies, rolls, bagels, anything from the bakery. I bet the perfume has some kind of bread or yeast something or other in it with the roses and that combination is what turned you on."

"Wow, are you serious...breast milk in perfume? That's wild." He shook his head. "My god, this is like the movies. A magic formula comes to light with powers to turn young men into fierce and ferocious lovers."

She looked at him with a sly smile. "I wonder," she said. Then she jumped off the bed and grabbed her handbag. His heart sank because he thought she was going to leave, but she didn't. Instead, she groped in the bag and brought out the perfume bottle.

"Look what I have." she said, moving the bottle back and forth like a pendulum.

"My god, you have the magic potion. Quick, hide it before thieves come to steal it." They laughed as she sat down on the bed. Then quite deliberately, she put the perfume bottle down and slowly began to unbutton her blouse. He stared and started to say something, but caught himself. In silence, he watched as she stripped off her blouse and opened her bra and let it fall from her shoulders. He thought her breasts beautiful—incredibly white, her skin alabaster smooth. He stared at her nipples, amazed at their color. Contrasted against the whiteness of her skin, they looked like cherries on fresh snow. He wanted to reach out and touch them. Instead, he removed his shirt.

While he stared, she stood and unashamedly removed her jeans. This was not the moment for scintillating, witty and bright conversation. It wasn't the moment for any kind of conversation. He just watched. After removing her jeans, she stood alongside the bed looking at him. He knew it was his turn, so he jumped from the bed and removed his jeans. They faced each other, she in panties, he in boxer shorts. He reached for her and they kissed. She pressed in against him and he felt her breasts against his chest while she churned her hips against his ever-increasing hardness.

Placing her hands on his chest, she gently pushed him away enough for her to lean down and pick up the perfume. She backed away a step and then with unhurried movements, opened the bottle and poured it over herself.

Perfume cascaded down her shoulders onto her breasts and body. She rubbed it onto her face, her arms, her stomach, and her legs smoothing it over herself as if soaping in the shower.

The room instantly reflected the unleashed odor. If it had become visible, the cloud of essence would have been so thick sight would have been impossible. Though, at that moment, the visibility of scents mattered little to Paul, for he reached out for her when he realized what she was doing. She tossed the bottle to the floor and reached her arms out to him. Coming together, they fell onto the bed, hands groping, fingers grasping.

He felt as in a cloud. With his eyes closed, he kissed whatever part of her body was next to his lips. He didn't know what to do first. He kissed her neck and shoulders, her breasts, her stomach, her thighs. The waves of perfume drove him wild. He kept coming back to her breasts, sucking her nipples while she arched her back, pushing her breasts into his face.

After removing his shorts, he stretched out on his back and drew her onto him. She shifted her hips and when she was in exactly the perfect position, slowly, with tantalizingly ease, lowered herself. Deliberately, carefully, she started to move her hips, and in a few moments, it was bliss.

The alcohol in the perfume made her skin tingly and cold. She felt the wetness on her shoulders and breasts, as Paul's hands stroked her skin. The clouds of perfume surrounded her, enveloped her. It was like being in a forest mist. She arched her back and pressed down on him.

As if blind, her head was thrown back and her hands groped the air in front of her. Magically, they found his and their fingers locked. She leaned in against the resistance of his arms and used his strength to control her movements.

It was a study in slow motion with the sounds from the street below taking on an echoic effect. Time was stretched, elastic and damp. Then suddenly a convulsion ran through her body. Then there was another so strong she almost collapsed. A loud groan escaped her lips and she was surprised by the sound. Opening her eyes, she looked down at Paul. His eyes were closed and his teeth were clenched. He was arching his body upward and she realized the convulsions she felt were not hers alone. He moaned and raised his hips from the bed making her feel like she was on a swaying bridge of rope. Then his body arched and moments later she folded like a rag doll onto his chest.

Turning on his side, he wrapped his arms around her and they kissed softly but with great passion. Locked together, they rocked back and forth, unable to be still. After a while, they relaxed enough to look at each other and smile.

"That was wonderful." she said. "I knew it would be right."

"I was thinking the same." He touched her face with his fingers. "I knew it also."

Softly she asked, "Do you know what this means?"

"Not really, but I do know I want to stay here with you till this building falls down. I think everything's perfect."

"You're just saying that because I smell so good."

Shaking his head, he said, "This whole business with the perfume is nuts and I don't know whether it was the perfume or just seeing you naked that got me going. You really are beautiful."

"You really think so?"

"Are you kidding? Don't you see how people look at you?"

"I don't know. I don't look at them. I don't pay attention."

"If you did, you'd see people in the street stop and stare when you pass. You are truly beautiful."

He ran his hands down her face to her beasts. Slowly and gently he took a nipple in his mouth. A moment later, cupping her breasts in his hands, he stared at them saying, "It's your fault girls. You started everything. I was just minding my business and then the two of you came along. You both deserve a kiss for being so great... so wonderful!" He kissed each nipple and then kissed her mouth with a warmth and passion that was thrilling. She sighed and wrapped him in her arms.

"Oh, Paul, Paul, make love to me again."

Closing his eyes, he slowly ran his hands up and down her body and then he could stay apart from her no longer. He thought making love a second time would take longer, but to his amazement, it was exactly the opposite. He was so excited, so passion filled, he quickly came. She followed with almost no hesitation. Then they lay still, holding each other. Their eyes were closed and their breathing was even. They slept.

A loud bell was the first sound he heard. It was rapidly followed by a warbling siren. Hysterically, his eyes sprung open and he searched the room. The panic brought on by the noise abated when he realized it was a fire engine in the streets below. Taking a deep breath, he relaxed. It was dark and he couldn't see her, but he knew she was there, next to him. The warmth of her body and her smell were vivid realities. She rolled into him, kissed his chest and then slid her hands from his chest to his groin. Her hands caressed his testicles and penis.

"I love you guys. You're the best I've had in the last two days. I think you're great."

He sat up. "What do you mean the last two days?" He asked in a combination of real and mock surprise.

"Oh, my, my boys, he's jealous. Can you imagine that?" She gently squeezed his testicles.

Laughing, he said, "Woman there'll be no more experimenting with the native population. From now on you'll confine all empirical observations and explorations to the specific items you presently hold in your hands. Is that clear?"

"Oh, please dear sir, have pity on a youngster just arrived from the old country. I do not know your ways. Will you teach me?"

"Teaching you will be my pleasure. But you must understand, this is not a short course. At this school, we don't have two-week seminars or split sessions. When you enroll here, you're in for life."

Moving her hands to the sides of his face, she kissed him on the lips and then with her voice barely a whisper said, "I can handle that."

About ten minutes later, he got out of bed and switched on a small desk lamp. As he was getting back into the bed, she said, "Oh, shit!"

"What? What is it?"

"I just remembered. I was supposed to give the perfume to that Lydia Cornell."

He laughed. "That's not going to be easy."

"Damn. What'll I do?"

"Wait a minute, wait a minute. She never smelled it, did she?"

"No. No one has except you, me and Professor Lehman."

"No problem. Fill the bottle with anything. It won't matter. What difference would it make? What difference could it make?"

"That's right. You're right. Whatever I give her is it... right?"

"Exactly."

"I guess I could make her a present of your sheets. I think they'll smell like roses for a long time."

"Never will I part with them and never will I wash them. They're part of our history. They *are* history."

She looked at him and burst out laughing. "You're such a guy. Keeping the sheets would be very romantic, but never washing them...well...that's not romantic, that's criminal."

"All you dames get clean crazy the instant you settle down. Why is that?"

"I think you've been living alone too long… not enough social interaction. Not enough…" He leaned over and kissed her. She responded and they clung together in the middle of the bed. "Oh, Paul, Paul," she whispered in his ear. "I love you. I love you. I love you."

Holding her tightly, he said, "I never thought I'd find someone. So many others find each other, but I didn't think I would, but I have… I have. Oh, Susan, I love you so."

Like a wave sliding up a beach, the moment came to a peak and then ebbed away. They separated, but they sat looking into each other's eyes. He felt this must be what it is to be married to the right person. Once you've done it, there's no need to do it again. They smiled. The awareness was clear to both, from all the people in the entire world they managed to find each another. They managed to come together. A billion-to-one shot paid off. It was unbelievable, but wonderful.

The bathroom was across the corridor from his room. It made their shower together easy and convenient. Later they stood by the window, looking down at the action in the park below.

"Do you have any aftershave or cologne?"

"Sure I do. There." He pointed to a couple of bottles on the dresser. "The standard graduate student aromas, Old Spice because it's cheap and Obsession because I had a birthday."

"They won't do. They're too common. She'd know in a minute."

"What are you talking about?"

"I was thinking about how to get some perfume into that bottle so I can give it to Miss Cornell. I don't want to lose this chance she's offering me."

"What chance, a chance at what?"

She explained to him what Lydia had promised and the perfume was a sort of payment for the opportunities.

"Well, I agree with her about you being a model. You're prettier than a lot of the ones who are in the magazines. Some of them look like alien junkies… hooked on drugs from another planet. But you, god, you'd be great." He kissed her, and then asked, "Do you think she'd back out if you didn't give her the perfume?"

"I don't know. But I do know the perfume is important, that much came through to me."

"Okay then, she wants a perfume, we'll give her a perfume."

"What do you mean?"

"Look, let's get dressed and go down to Eighth Street. There are plenty of places where we can buy a couple of bottles of some cheap stuff which we'll mix together, so you can present it as the magic formula. Hell, it doesn't matter what you give her."

She looked at him with admiration. "That's right. She never smelled it and all she knows is what she's heard. Any perfume in that bottle will be *the* perfume. You're a genius."

"You sound like my mother."

Laughing, she got off the bed. "C'mon, get dressed and let's go buy a couple of bottles of Romance in the Harem or Thrill of Your Dick."

"I don't think they're selling the Dick stuff anymore... all gone...sold out."

"We can make some ourselves, later, okay?"

"My thoughts exactly. Now, let' go and see what's for sale."

They walked to Eighth Street joining the tourists. Their first stop was Yakimioto, a pseudo Japanese gift shop which sold everything from chopsticks to candles. They searched for something appropriate, but all the perfumes smelled spicy. Their second stop was the local ABC Pharmacy. Alongside the boxes of packaged chocolates and glycerin soaps was a large display of aftershave, toilet water, and perfumes... more than enough to choose from. After a sniff test, they bought two; Roses of Tralee and Peony Passion. The bill was $12.87.

Back in Paul's room, they combined the amber liquids in a plastic coffee cup and mixed it with what was left in Susan's bottle. To their surprise, the final product smelled pretty good. It was actively floral and seemed strong and substantial. So much so, that after a few minutes of mixing and pouring, their senses of smell were so overloaded that as Paul quipped, they would not have been able to tell dog pooh from spaghetti sauce. In addition, the sheets still reeked from Susan's perfume bath. There never was an occasion before or since, when a college dorm room smelled quite so pleasant.

When the bottle was filled to a level they both thought indicative of a used item, they stared at the remainder in the cup. It was obvious it would be tough to try to pour it back into one of the empty bottles and they could not bring themselves to throw out such a potentially worthwhile romantic accessory. So they decided to use it.

They undressed and leaped into bed. Then locked together in an embrace, Paul stretched an arm from the tangle and grabbed the cup. He threw it into the air above and they bathed in it as it splashed down.

The perfume mixing, the bottle filling, and the perfume-splash love-session, added to the abundant bouquet of the room, which by now had seeped into the corridor. Paul's room, the hallway, and the entire floor became so aromatic, the building's security personnel were firmly convinced that some adventurous student had created an illegal hallucinogen and was using perfume to cover his tracks.

CHAPTER 20

Entering Lydia's office, Susan noticed the furnishings were not typical items from an office supply house. Everything in it seemed personal, the desk, the wood pieces, the upholstery and even the accessories looked like her possessions rather than the choices of a hired decorator. Lydia didn't miss Susan's appreciative glances.

"You like it?" She asked, gesturing to the room at large.

"Oh, yes, everything fits so well. Did you do the selecting?"

"Yes, I did because I would never let some hack decorator choose what I have to live with every day. Where I work should reflect me, not somebody else."

"I couldn't agree more. That's one of the things I dislike about dorm living… the lack of space for the things I love. The things I've chosen as my own."

"Well, we think alike," Lydia said, as she led Susan to a small sofa in front of a large, sky-filled window. Susan sat and Lydia pulled up a small chair.

"In about ten minutes Dennis is going to come in and take you on a tour of the in-house art directors and let them consider you for placement in their campaigns."

"Dennis? Who is Dennis?" Susan asked hesitantly.

With a self-deprecating smile, Lydia said, "Now isn't that dumb. I'm talking to you as if you know about him. Dennis works here and does quite a few different things. He's a fill-in photographer and a sometimes personnel director and also acts as the go-between with the art directors group. When they need a specific person type, he's the guy who gets the body. He has a great eye and will place you in the hands of an account executive whose current job could best benefit from your looks and persona. I trust his judgment."

Susan nodded, not knowing what to say. Lydia moved to the edge of her chair and casually asked, "By the way, you didn't forget the perfume did you?"

"Oh, no, here it is." She reached into her bag, took out the bottle and handed it to Lydia who held it like it was filled with nitroglycerine. Glad to be rid of it, Susan breathed deeply and then asked, "When is this Mr. Dennis going to come by?"

"He's not Mr. Dennis....just Dennis. I don't even think he has a last name. As she said that, there was a curt double knock, the door instantly swung open and a dapper and slick-looking man strode in.

Lydia said, "Dennis, it'd be nice if you'd wait for a reply before barging in."

He smiled an oozing, leering smile. "I always burst in, babe, and you wouldn't believe what I've seen going on around here, people doing the kinkiest, sexiest things." He winked at Susan. "Were you two goin' to get it on? I'll come back later if you want time for a hot love session. That is, if privacy's your thing."

Upset, Lydia said, "Damn it, Dennis, we were talking business not planning a love-in."

"Sure you were, sure you were. Great lookin' dames like you two should be up on the desk doing the Vegas act, tongue in bung."

"Now don't get disgusting," Lydia hissed.

"Yeah, you're right... on the desk is gross, isn't it?" After a quick glance, he said, "You'd both fit on that little couch. That would work."

Susan almost laughed. This Dennis character was a large version of the high school gross boys she had learned to ignore, and he was not her problem. It was Lydia's office and he was her person. Let her deal with him. Susan wondered if she could, since she seemed lost for an appropriate rejoinder.

In that moment of heavy silence, Susan sized up Dennis. He was tall and sophisticatedly handsome and could have been a Hollywood super villain in a spy movie. He sported a permanent sneer that made him seem incredibly sure of himself—the high school tough grown up. She thought most women would find his reckless confidence attractive. He was the guy college virgins chose for their deflowering—a one-use, throw-away character. She figured that as long as he stayed in the appropriate milieu, he was unshakeable. But stick him in a setting where only brains mattered and he might not shine. But she guessed he was probably too smart to let that happen. Susan thought he would be the perfect gigolo.

Later that day, when she described the day's events to Paul, she referred to Dennis as a major leaguer compared to a Little League player. She guessed he was a guy who knew wine, danced well, was athletic, could make love like a champ, and was probably great fun to be with as long as that was all you wanted. Paul said he sounded like an Italian sports car with a cock. Laughing, she realized that description fit Dennis exactly.

Susan had learned in high school that trying to verbally match the tough guys was a losing proposition. Lydia evidently felt the same, for rather than respond, she strode to her desk and gently placed the perfume bottle in a drawer. Then looking up, she said, "Dennis, why don't you take Miss Merrill and do what I asked. Show her to the account guys and see who might be able to use her. I think she'd be a great picture. What do you think?"

He leaned back a step and looked at Susan as if she was a painting on a wall. "I think she'd be a great Playmate of the Year. I know I'd vote for her. Do you think she would get a kick out of posing naked for me?"

Susan blinked and wondered if he was joking.

"Damn, Dennis, shape up. For ten minutes get off it and be serious. I didn't bring her here to be the Queen of Beauty Parade. She has enough style to bring a good deal of class to any product and if we can use her, we should. Now stop screwing around and do what I asked you to do... okay?"

Dennis, taken back about half a millimeter, smiled a very professional smile and nodded. "Okay, okay, take it easy. Don't stretch your panty hose. I'll give her a look around this joint like she was going to buy it." He gestured to Susan to get up and follow him which she did. "Do you want me to bring her back here when we're done?"

"Yes, please... so we can have lunch. Will a couple of hours be sufficient?"

"No sweat." As he turned to the door, Lydia asked Susan. "You are free for lunch, aren't you? Mr. Charm barged in here before I could ask."

"I'm free. I have no class until tonight, and lunch would be great."

"Fine. Now, Dennis, go do your thing. I've got work to do and Miss Merrill's future awaits her."

He turned to the door and Susan followed. In the corridor, he asked her, "Okay, so you're a school girl, where do you go? I hope it ain't the church of the virgin."

"I go to NYU."

"Ohhhh, you live down in the Village with the dopers and weirdoes."

"You make it sound terrible. It isn't. Everybody there isn't a doper or strange."

"Those fucking people down there, they don't bathe. Why the hell don't you live uptown in the sixties on Madison or Park?"

"What do you mean, they don't bathe. I do. Everyone I know does."

"You want to take a bath with me? I'll scrub your back so good you'll never want to bathe alone again."

"Wow, you are something. No I do not want to take a bath with you. You got that?" She recognized the style and thought that maybe in this setting it's probably a good one. All you have to do is ask. A different girl or even the same girl at a different time might find the bath proposition hard to refuse. He has nothing to lose by asking. If he asks ten girls a day, he needs just one "yes" to have a fun bed-event.

"Hey, take it easy. All you have to do is say "no." I wasn't asking you to take part in a bank heist or a kidnapping… just a bath. You'd look great undressed."

"It isn't the bath. It's taking a bath with a stranger."

"Ohhh, I see. Well, by next week we may be old friends. I'll ask again." He stopped and turned to her. Leaning close and speaking in a low voice, he said, "Look, if I forget to ask next week, remind me, okay?" Susan smiled, realizing it would be hard to get upset and really angry with him. His style was as abrasive and crude as it was determined. Being around a character like him every day would be tough. He probably could wear down almost anyone.

Susan looked to her left and pointed to a door. "Is one of the people I'm supposed to see in there or maybe I should say, who's supposed to see me?"

"As a matter of fact, yes, but there's more than one joker in there. You'll see." He opened the door and ushered her in. The room was large with desks around a perimeter, like an empty courtyard. Taking Susan by the hand, he led her to the center of the open space.

Raising his voice, he called out, "Hey, you hot shots, pay attention. I have with me a golden girl, a beauty with a great bod who will make one of your ads the greatest. Now come and take a look. She can talk, so you can even ask questions." As Susan laughed, he took her hand and stretched her arm above her head, twirling her around. By the time she had spun two times, three people got up from their desks.

Back in her office, Lydia opened the drawer and grabbed the perfume. She twisted off the cap and passed the bottle under her nose. Her first reaction was pleasant. The perfume had a heavy floral quality and was easy to take. She rubbed some on her wrist. A moment later, she waved her wrist to her face. Very feminine, grown up and very old fashioned. It was definitely not a current item usable by both sexes. It was totally a woman's perfume.

Lydia wondered why that fellow Paul reacted as he did. There seemed to be nothing strange about the scent. It was quite straightforward, not at all subtle, and she could not detect any mystery ingredient that would make a man want to suckle. But, Lydia said to herself, I'm the wrong person to judge that. She replaced the cap and picked up the phone.

She called Mr. Dunn. "Hello, Tee. This is Lydia. I have the perfume. Dennis is right now escorting the girl who brought it to see if she'll fit into one of our photo campaigns." Dunn replied he was too busy at the moment, but would eventually get a chance to have a whiff. She hung up and dialed again. "Tom, this is Lydia. Would you please come to my office? I have the perfume and I want you to smell it." A few minutes later, he strode in.

"Okay babe, where's is it? Let me get a whiff and then watch out, I may come right across that desk with my Henry Jones waving in the air."

"Be serious. Here, smell." She placed her wrist under his nose. He closed his eyes and took several short sniffs. "Put some on your neck. It's hard to get a good feeling from your wrist." She did, and he came back around the desk, stood her up and took her in his arms. He pressed his body into hers and kissed her neck. The perfume was very apparent, but he didn't recognize anything different from his regular and standard horny behavior.

"If you let me, I'd love to get down on my knees and kiss you, but that's me talking my regular talk. It isn't the perfume. All I got is a nice smell of flowers. Truthfully, I like the smell, but I'm not turning into anything I wasn't before."

She put her hands on his chest and pushed him away. "I'll remember the offer, but are you sure you feel nothing different? No impulse for anything? No overpowering urges?"

"Well, holding you usually puts me into a heavy love mood, an urge that goes right to my Henry Jones."

"How do you feel now?" she asked, hoping for something other than his usual reaction.

"I have the feeling you'd like me to say I want to cuddle up on the couch, rip open your dress and nurse at your beautiful tits, but…"

"But, what?"

"But, what I'm feeling and what I'd like to do is not one bit different from what I'd normally like to do to you. I'd like to lay you out on that desk and create the orgasm of the week."

"You mean you don't feel anything different? Nothing?"

"Sorry, babe, the perfume smells sweet and all that, but it reminds me more of young girls working in the library than hookers working 43rd Street.

If you're going to use me as a sample, then I'd have to say the perfume is a bust. All it brings to mind is roses. That's it."

"Son of a bitch." Lydia blurted out. Her anger made it clear that her hopes had been high, but now, they were the same as the *Titanic* crewmen who had been getting ready for the return trip.

"I don't understand this." She said angrily. "This damn perfume was supposed to make you go wild, make you want to grab my breasts and start playing with them."

"I'll do that if it'll make you feel better," he said with a half smile.

"Oh, dammit Tom, this isn't funny. Don't you understand what this means? If the perfume is bullshit, then the entire idea for Complete Abandon goes out the window. There is no Complete Abandon if this damned shit doesn't work." As she said that, she picked up the bottle and looked at it.

"Are you sure it's the same?" he asked.

"What do you mean?"

"I don't know, I just thought that maybe what's in that bottle isn't the same as what started all this commotion."

"Damn, I never thought of that. But why would the kid switch it?"

"Now wait a minute. I'm not saying that. I don't know anything about switching anything. All I'm asking is how do you know what you got there is the same perfume?"

Lydia looked at the bottle. "You know, you're right. I don't know anything about anything. I just assumed the kid would bring it in as payment for me busting her into the model game. Maybe she's playing me?"

"What happened to the perfume before it got to you?"

Lydia stared at him. "Before... before it got to me?"

"Look, it started with the kid getting it from her mom, right? That's what you told me. The kid got it from home and used it and then this guy jumps her at school, right?"

"Yes, that's the story I got."

"Okay, what happened to the perfume since that day?"

"I don't think anything was done with it except..."

"Except, what?"

"Except she gave it to Gert, who owns the building where I live, the chemistry prof. at NYU, you know who I mean. I've told you about her" He nodded. "It was given to her so she could analyze it. In fact, the kid just got it back from her yesterday so she could bring it here today."

"How do you know the prof. didn't fuck around with it?"

"I don't, and Gert would be the one to screw around if anybody would. She's just the type."

"Well, I think you better talk to the kid and find out if she knows what's going on."

"Right now Dennis is dragging her around, showing her off to the art directors. I'll talk to her when he's finished." She walked to the window and looked down then turned back. "I'll find out what's going on. This is too goddamn important to let go to hell."

"Okay. I'm going back to my office. Keep me posted."

He headed for the door but stopped when she called out, "Tom, I need a favor from you. Please don't tell Dunn anything yet. Let me talk to the girl first. Maybe I can find out what's happened."

"What do you mean? Don't tell Dunn yet?"

"Oh, c'mon, don't be cute. I'm sure you're reporting to him."

"Why do you think that?"

With only slight annoyance in her voice, she said, "Jesus Christ, Tom, you guys must think I'm a real idiot. Maybe someday, A.T. Dunn would let me work on something like this alone, but that day isn't here yet. I would bet my bottom dollar he's told you to keep an eye on me so the operation doesn't get away from him. You're his spy, aren't you?"

He smiled wanly. "What the hell can I say? He's the boss."

"Hey, I understand. I'm sure it wasn't your idea."

"You're right about that."

She took a step toward him. "Will you hold off?"

With no hesitation, he said, "Sure babe, but do me a favor. Tell me what you find out from the girl. Okay?"

"Absolutely and thanks."

He turned to the door and said as he walked out, "I'll be in my office for the rest of the day."

She walked to the window and looked down at the cars and people in the street below as she wondered if Gert would fool with the perfume—alter it or change it completely, and if she did, why? Or maybe it was the kid maybe she's the one who changed it. And what would be the reason for that? In both cases, the possibility existed, but there seemed to be no reason for either of them to mess with it. Why? Why change anything?

For only a fleeting second Lydia considered the whole perfume reaction a hoax, that it was all bull. But she dismissed the thought as quickly as it had occurred to her because she believed the original story. Now she had to find out why things weren't going to plan.

About an hour later, when Dennis and Susan returned, Lydia looked at them and saw smugness on Dennis' face and joy on Susan's.

"Was it successful?" she asked.

"I'll say," Dennis replied. "Charley Ford is working on that leisure clothing line and when he saw her, he flipped. He wants to do a real college girl campaign and he wants Susan to be the big send-off. How do you like that?"

Lydia turned to Susan. "That's fantastic. I was hoping something like that would happen" She came out from behind the desk and sat next to Susan on the sofa. "Aren't you excited?"

"Excited?" Susan gasped. "That's not the right word. I'm dumbfounded. It's a fantastic dream come true. I can't wait to call home and tell my mom and dad. It's all so wonderful." She brought her hands to her face and started to sob.

Lydia turned slightly, "Dennis, why don't you leave us alone. I'd like to talk to her. You wouldn't mind, would you?"

"Nah, not at all, I'll find something to do." He started for the door, but turned when halfway. "Good luck, kid. And remember, When you're ready for some lovin', I'm always here." He waved and walked out.

Lydia took Susan to the ladies room to settle down and about ten minutes later, back in her office, they sat facing each other on the sofa.

"We'll have a lot of time to talk about modeling and working here, but right now I want to ask you about the perfume."

As Lydia said that a chill went through Susan. "What do you want to know?"

"Well, when you first wore it, I understand a young man reacted quite violently in an attempt to get to your breasts. Isn't that right?"

"Yes, that's what happened."

"Did you wear it again with him?"

"No, I… uh… why do you ask?"

"Well, I tried it to see if the same reaction would occur and it didn't. The man who smelled it on me didn't react at all."

Crestfallen, Susan said, "Oh, no reaction at all, huh?"

"That's right. The perfume smelled like nothing more than regular perfume. I was hoping you'd help me figure out what happened."

"How can I help?"

"Well, first of all, did the first reaction with the boy really happen?"

"Oh, yes, he went wild."

"Did you wear it again since that time?"

"I guess I did. I used some."

"Was it with a different guy?"

"No. It was the same guy and it had the same reaction."

"Then I don't understand" Lydia looked around the room trying to find the answer amongst the books and knick-knacks on the shelves and tables. She turned back to Susan. "So let me ask you this. When you got the perfume back from Professor Lehman, did it seem the same?"

"The same?"

"I mean, do you think Professor Lehman used it or changed it in some way?"

There are moments in everyone's life for choices to do something they've never done before and therefore, to become a different person. In her life, Susan had never before been confronted with the chance to lie and shift blame onto someone else. She instantly realized she could say the perfume did look different or smelled different when she got it back from Professor Lehman. If she did, it would be a question for Lydia and Professor Lehman to settle.

But she didn't. Whether it was her morality or more simply, her inability to effectively lie is beside the point, for what she told Lydia was that the perfume she got back from Professor Lehman seemed to be what she gave her, with only less in the bottle.

"Well then." Lydia said, "I don't understand."

It is a fact of human nature that reciprocity is normal currency. People try to repay in kind what another has provided. Send a greeting card, get a greeting card. Buy a round of drinks, get a drink. Invite them to dinner; they invite you to dinner. Regardless of the situation, when obligated, people are uncomfortable unless they can repay the existing "debt." The principle hit Susan hard and she was unable to resist. As much as she didn't want to tell Lydia what really happened, she was compelled to tell the truth.

"Lydia," she said softly, "I haven't been truthful with you. Let me tell you what really happened." Susan went on to tell her about getting the perfume back from Professor Lehman and how she and Paul used it up in their lovemaking. And how they bought and mixed together some ordinary perfume to refill the bottle.

Lydia listened to Susan's confession, and holding her anger in check, congratulated Susan for having the courage to tell the truth. Also, she said it was a testimonial to their friendship that Susan would not lie to her.

Then a thrill went through Lydia when she recalled that Gert had done a complete analysis of the perfume. "Susan, didn't you say that Professor Lehman made a set of notes when she analyzed the perfume?"

"Yes, that's what she told me. She said the notes were complete and filed away." It took only a moment for Susan to realize what Lydia was getting at. "Oh, I see what you mean. Professor Lehman's notes will tell exactly what was in the original perfume. You really don't need the perfume itself."

"That's right, Susan. The analysis will tell all."

"So all you have to do is ask Professor Lehman for the analysis and with that information, you can duplicate the formula, right?"

"Exactly. Once I have the analytic notes, I'll be able to re-create the fragrance."

About an hour after Susan had gone, Lydia called Tom and told him what she had learned. He asked, "Will the prof come across with the notes?"

"That's the big question and to be truthful, I don't know. We're not really friends and she's strange. She could just as easily say 'yes' as she could say 'no'."

"Well, honey, one thing is clear, without the analysis and notes, the entire project is up in smoke and you could be out the door."

"What do you mean? Are you saying Dunn would fire me?"

"He's a demanding guy. You got him all excited about this deal, and he's going to be pissed if it comes to zero. He's a real advertising man and when he sees a chance to push the public into buying anything they don't really need, he gets very up about it. So, if I were you, I'd bust my ass to get the analysis and the notes and whatever away from that dame. Without them, you'll be up the creek.

"Sonofabitch" Lydia muttered aloud, while thinking that one way or another, I have to get that goddamn analysis.

CHAPTER 21

Gert sat at the counter of the Chock Full O' Nuts coffee shop on the corner of University and Waverly. She had wanted a table, but there were only a few because the place had been designed for the in-and-out school crowd, not for lounging. Typical customers got off the subway, came up to the street and stepped in for a takeout before class. They must have moved ten coffees in containers to every one served to an in-house customer in their famous dark brown china cup.

When she had time to kill Gert sat and watched the lunch crew make and stack the cream cheese and date nut bread sandwiches. Aside from tasting great, those sandwiches had an interesting look and depending on her mood, the dark brown bread and the stark white cheese resembled either a vertical piano keyboard or a British crosswalk. Sometimes she would stare at the stack of sandwiches until her eyes watered and then the image would start to look like a fog-bound zebra.

As she sipped the hot coffee a tapping on the window behind her got her attention. Turning she saw Sol staring at her. She held up a hand to tell him to wait while she hurriedly took a last sip and slipped out.

"Isn't this your day off?" she asked him.

"What a good memory, remembering my day off." Taking her arm in his, he directed her toward the park. Arm in arm they walked looking like old lovers, old friends, or sister and brother. They looked good together.

"I was on my morning constitutional, a real walk around town. It's a way of limbering up and ready for an afternoon dance lesson. And, I must add, it's a real walk—not a cruise, mind you, just a legitimate walk."

"Sol, you don't have to say that to me. Your behavior or lifestyle, call it what you will, is entirely your business. My opinion is my business and I would never butt into your life unless I thought what you were doing was truly dangerous."

"I'm glad you think I have the appropriate judgment to regulate my own comportment?"

"Of course I do, but nonetheless, I still feel like a mother hen where you're concerned."

"I should think you would be more concerned with Winthrop. He needs some jolting, some sort of push into the mainstream."

"Yes, I agree. He's getting very close to the point of complete adjustment to the single life. We have to get him married or at least deeply involved with someone. And, don't think you're out of it; you aren't past my meddling."

"Oh Gert, please, my life is coming to a close. The best I can hope for and all I really want is a quiet exit."

She stopped and faced him. "Sol, what kind of bullshit talk is that?"

"I was just wondering about my end, about how I should or would go or what it would be like to fly off the roof over there onto a sidewalk. What do you think it's like?"

"Dying?"

"No, I mean hitting the ground. I'd guess you're aware of what's happening and can even see the ground coming at you and then, boom. There must be a noise. I bet you hear the noise."

"Well, I do not speak from authority, but I guess it's like what you hear from a pilot prior to a plane hitting the ground. There's talk and then, nothing. Say what you will, there's no pain. You hit, the lights go out and so do you."

"Doing it like that—well, at least there's no mess to be cleaned up in your place. I've known a few who shot themselves. That's a real disaster. Lots of blood, inside things." He shuddered. "Terrible...the roof is best. It may be awful for strollers, but for the doer - it's just boom and darkness." He took her arm and they continued to walk.

"Boom and darkness doesn't sound so bad." said Gert. "For me, I want it quick or better yet, I don't even want to know about it."

"Not know about it? What do you mean?"

"I mean dying in your sleep, which seems wonderful. You go to bed, listen to some good music, review the day's events, and maybe even make some decisions you'd probably forget if you did wake up and then close your eyes and never wake up. Sol, tell me if that doesn't sound great."

"It sounds okay to me." He looked at her and grinned broadly while extending his arm in a sweeping motion. "Do you realize we must be the only people traipsing along considering good and bad ways to die?"

Gert looked across the street at people sitting on benches and leaning against trees. "I don't know about that, Sol. Right now, over there, that kid could be a junky slipping into an overdose coma. We may be talking about death while someone there in the park might be doing it."

"Yes, yes, drugs are an awful problem."

They walked a bit more in silence until Gert said, "I think we'd be better off talking about Winthrop."

Sol smiled. "Yes, I think I'm a better Jewish mother than a professor of darkness. Anyway, how can we help the boy?" Before Gert could answer, Sol said, "I've even talked to Cyril about Winthrop. I thought one of Cyril's female gym pals might be an answer, but Cyril's so busy with his own muscles and his delightfully unsavory crowd, he's no help. But, wait a minute I thought Win and your tenant Lydia were a pair?"

"They're sort of on and off, but she's not for him. Winthrop may be unaware of it, but what he wants is a middle-class dream, a house in the suburbs, kids, dogs, all that. She wants limos, the Cote D'Azure, and most of all I think she's power hungry. Teaming up with a college professor would definitely not get her what she wants. She'd hate him in no time."

"They make a nice-looking couple."

"Oh yeah, you're right about that. They do look great together, but that's irrelevant. I would never say anything to him, but there have been many times she's gone on late dates after he's dropped her off. I think she uses him as a warm-up for those nights when other partners have more to offer."

"Ooooo, I love it when you're nosy. You're like me at heart, a real, a real, what's the word I'm looking for? It's a Yiddish word, a Jewish word, a butinsky, a busybody, a..."

"Yentah."

"Yes, yes, a yentah. What a wonderful word - yentah. I don't know how you create a plural in Yiddish, but that's what we are, yentahs. Ha!" He laughed aloud and skipped a little step, dragging her along. "A pair of yentahs," he shouted.

Gert laughed and they continued walking. For the next hour, they strolled and talked about nothing special until Sol asked about the perfume business.

"I'm done with it." She said. "I did the analysis, put my notes and the results in my lab file and I hope that's the last I hear about it. It was interesting for a while, like a nasty thunderstorm."

While they walked back the way they had come, they agreed to meet later at her place for an evening meal, and by promising to bring some good wine Sol begrudgingly got her to promise to tell him about the results of the perfume analysis and why what happened, happened. When they reached the science building, Sol left, for Gert had one more class.

He continued his stroll and thought about Gert's idea to get a girl for Winthrop though he didn't think he'd be much help in that department. It also occurred to him that Winthrop was not going to be so quick to let go of Lydia. He saw how he looked at her, and god, how he wished there was someone he could look at with the same passion. It was not going to be easy to get him off that scent. And certainly, it was clear to Sol from his own upside-down life that romantic involvements often occur with people who are the absolute worst possible choices. If that were true in this case Winthrop would resist any attempt to create a separation.

For a real cleft to take place, there would have to be a situation, something that would completely overshadow Win's feelings for Lydia whatever they were. As he walked, Sol tried to think of what might be done to create a problem that might bring about a separation between Lydia and Win, but he could not.

CHAPTER 22

Keep it simple, Lydia thought. Just ask for the analysis. Give Gert an easy choice of yes or no. If she agreed and handed over the notes, the problem was solved. Private chemists could synthesize the perfume and the campaign could be set in motion. But she didn't think Gert would agree.

Though there had never been any harsh words between them, Lydia knew that Gert didn't really like her and when presented with a choice, would choose not to help. The only "bad" behavior she could pin down was not faithfully watering the damned outdoor geraniums. Other than that, she had been a quiet tenant, respectful of the old girl's demands and always paid the rent exactly on time. In the end, she had no substantial grounds on which to base her negative estimation of Gert's feelings, but her intuition told her Gert was not a best friend.

But she also understood the other connection between them was Win and that could be the heart of the problem. Lydia liked him because he was a decent guy and almost always available. She liked him for his good looks and intelligence, but there were far too many negatives. He was bookish and kind of dull, even though he thought he was not. He lacked the driving ambition that turned her on. If he was more like Tom, she knew she would feel differently, but he wasn't and probably never would be. It always came back to ambition, to desire. He didn't want what Tom wanted. He was too careful, too tentative, while Tom was fearless.

And that was the major difference. It wasn't that Win was a coward, but he was anxious and nervous. He was too much the professor, too willing to consider what he labeled the ever-present alternatives. His world was colored gray while Tom lived in a black or white universe. For her, that difference was significant.

The more she thought about it, the more she believed her relationship with Win was the problem. For all she knew, Gert might fantasize a crush on him and resented the way she treated him. Or maybe Gert might imagine being younger and his lover. Anything was possible.

Women were smarter than men, and she knew her true feelings about Win were probably apparent to Gert. But maybe starting from a negative position could be helpful. Maybe she could work both sides of the street, be extra nice to Win so Gert would notice and maybe have a change of heart. Also, if she acted more loving toward him, he might help convince Gert to give up the analysis. But before she did anything, she knew she had to ask for the analysis. What happened after that would be based on Gert's response. Anything involving Win would wait until the outcome of her meeting with Gert.

Lydia knew when Gert got home, so she arranged to be in her place beforehand. Waiting behind her front door for Gert to arrive, Lydia timed the closing of the outside door so she could "casually" pop into the hallway as Gert was halfway up the stairs.

"Gert, hi… you have a moment?"

The older woman turned and looked down. "Sure, what is it?"

"I'd like to talk about that perfume, if I could."

"Sure, what's on your mind?"

"Well, if it's all the same, I'd rather not talk here in the hallway. Could I come up in about ten minutes?"

"That'd be no problem, but make it about fifteen, okay?"

"Great. See you in a bit."

Gert continued up the stairs and let herself into her apartment. She put the foodstuffs she bought for dinner with Sol in the fridge and then washed her face and hands. She was in the middle of getting out the salad stuff when Lydia rang the doorbell.

Gert offered her a seat at the counter. "Do you mind if I do some salad work? I've got someone coming for dinner."

"Oh, no, please go right ahead. I can talk as you do that."

"Okay, what do you want to know about the perfume?"

"I know that Susan Merrill got it back from you after you did the analysis of it. You may not know that Susan gave it to me when she came to my office to inquire about modeling."

"I know that. Susan filled me in when I gave it back to her."

"Maybe you don't know what happened next."

"What? What happened next? What do you mean?"

"Susan gave me the bottle of perfume as we agreed, but it wasn't the perfume you analyzed."

"It wasn't? Then what did she give you?"

"Well, it seems that she and her friend Paul had a love session the night before she came to see me, and during that event, they spilled most of the perfume on themselves."

Gert laughed. "They poured it on themselves?"

"That's right, and then to make sure I got what she promised, they bought some cheap stuff, mixed it together with what was left in the bottle and that's what she gave me the next day."

"So you got a bottle of what?"

"I got a bottle of cheap perfume, primarily some drug store special and it smells exactly that way, like a drug store special."

"Dammit, that's hysterical. Those kids are really something."

"Yeah, I admit it's kind of funny, but I was hoping to use that perfume as the basis for a new fragrance."

"The original stuff was just a cheap rose-based perfume. It's nothing special."

"I don't doubt what you're saying, but I would love to have had a chance to test it."

Gert straightened. "Oh, come on Lydia, I'm not a dummy. I know what you're after. You don't want to test it, you want to copy it, and hopefully, duplicate the reaction it had on that fellow, right?"

"Gert, don't be silly. How could you sell a product that caused men to want to nurse? Who would buy a thing like that?"

"Come on, Lydia, I don't think you want to start a breast-feeding binge, but I do think you would love to find out what was in that perfume so that with a little tinkering it could be made to produce a similarly intense reaction, not for breast feeding maybe, but for, well, I don't know, and I don't care. The last thing the public needs is some new advertised bullshit that makes them crazier than they already are"

As she spoke, Gert stopped slicing tomatoes but held the small gleaming knife in her hand and pointing it at Lydia, used it to punctuate her remarks as she spoke.

Staring at the blade, Lydia said, "Gert, I have no intention of producing a product to make the public crazy. Where do you get that idea? I'm not a manufacturer. I work in advertising and I have a chance with a big company to develop a new product from the ground up."

"The role you play is not important. I know you don't make anything, but you could supply that company's chemists with the perfume formula and they'd produce some junk with their only purpose being to make as much money as possible."

"Is that bad? That's what business is all about."

"Business is not bad I think the advertising business is bad. It creates desire where there is no need. And if your big company could, it would turn people into addicts and make them pay through the nose for whatever would satisfy those created cravings." She stopped, and then said in a louder voice clearly reflecting her anger, "Damn it Lydia, look at the tobacco companies. Look at what those vultures have done to thousands of people."

Trying to remain calm, Lydia said, "Gert, we're talking about perfume, aren't we?"

"Like hell we are. You're talking about creating some kind of perfume that will force people to act. You want to promote a reaction like the one that started this whole thing. That's what we're talking about here."

"Gert, you've got me marked down for something that just isn't so. I don't want to supply any company with anything and I certainly don't want to create addicts." Lydia stopped and took a deep breath, because remaining calm was very hard. But she willed herself to control her mounting anger. She knew the dumbest way to handle this was to get mad and try to match Gert argument for argument

"Gert, let me ask you a question, okay?"

"What is it?"

"If you were in my shoes and had heard about a perfume that caused the crazy reaction this one did, wouldn't you be curious about it? Wouldn't you love to take a whiff to find out what the hell the commotion was about?"

"That's two questions," Gert said.

Lydia smiled, leave it to a schoolteacher to go for that one. But before she could say anything, Gert continued. "Yes, okay, I see your point. Certainly I'd be curious. I think anyone would be."

"Okay, now add what you say is my normal curiosity to the fact that I'm sitting on a golden opportunity. I'm involved in a project that could lead to a major promotion and a way to make a name for myself. I'm like you, Gert. I don't follow the dumb rules for ladies and sit home while hubby makes the money so I can make the dinner. I want to do for me like you did for you."

She stopped and looked at Gert, who was listening. She had put down the knife and was leaning forward, listening.

"I'm sure you must have faced all sorts of crap," Lydia continued, "from all kinds of people, from men, when you decided to go into chemistry. You know, I can hear it now, 'a woman in science, well, I don't think it would be appropriate.' I can hear some old windbag telling you domestic science is a wiser choice than natural science. Well, dammit, Gert, we're in the same shoes. I want to take care of myself and not have to worry that the person I depend upon doesn't have a bug up his ass about something. We're the same. I'm after that perfume so I can work from a position of strength. I want to tell them what I want rather than take their orders about something they don't know a damn thing about." She stopped and sat down hard on one of the counter stools.

Gert looked at her wondering if she was sincere or if she was one of the smartest bitches she'd ever run across. How do I find the truth? She asked herself.

"I understand your curiosity, Lydia, and I certainly understand your position in business. What I confronted thirty years ago makes what's going on now look like nothing. Christ, it is nothing. When I was a kid, lady schoolteachers got fired for smoking in public. I was in school with assholes who thought a lady's eyelashes would get in the way when using a microscope."

Lydia watched Gert close her eyes and take a breath. In one motion she exhaled and reaching under the counter, brought out a bottle of wine. She pulled the cork and looked at Lydia with raised eyebrows. Lydia nodded and Gert grabbed two glasses and slowly poured the blood-red liquid.

"Here, let's take a drink and slow down." Gert handed a glass to Lydia who welcomed the pause. Trying to look as meek and innocent as she could, Lydia held the glass with both hands as she sipped the wine. She studied Gert over the rim of the glass and saw signs of unease and unhappiness on Gert's face. Maybe Lydia hoped, she was unhappy with herself.

Gert placed her glass on the countertop and much subdued said, "I don't want to be angry with you, Lydia, but I have a thing with advertising and I guess it rubs off on you. You're the handiest enemy around."

"I didn't think you had a problem with me. All I'm trying to do is protect my interests as best I can."

Now looking solemn and contrite, Gert muttered, "I know, I know."

"Gert, please don't think you're alone in your unhappiness with the advertising industry. I work in it and I know what goes on, but most of us in it are against the wall. It's like… it's like being a doctor and knowing there are unethical and incompetent colleagues killing people. You hate what they do, but you don't know how to stop them. I'm in the same boat you are."

"What do you mean?"

"Well, tell me, how many ignorant, unprepared, and plain dumb college teachers have you run across?"

"Quite a few unfortunately, but what's your point?"

"What did you do about them, Gert? Did you start a rumpus or did you just hope they would go someplace else, or maybe get hit by a car or by lightning? In other words, what did you do to cleanse incompetents from college teaching?" Gert stared at her, but said nothing.

"Right, well, that's exactly what I do when I run across the kind of industry people you're talking about. I know there are unethical and evil people involved, but I have no idea how to eliminate them." She took another sip of wine. "Gert, you have to understand the business. In every ad industry publication there are continual calls to be ethical, upright, and alert to any fraudulent or deceptive practice. We're all trying to be principled and moral, but it's a tough business. It isn't easy to do the right thing."

Gert was stymied. It had been easy to say "no" to Lydia before she sat here and asked. Complicating things even more was the truth of her comments. Gert was always after her colleagues to focus on the increasing number of poor teachers who not only couldn't teach but didn't even know their field. She realized they were as powerless to amend their situation as was Lydia and so many others in only slightly different situations. Nonetheless, as much as she understood Lydia's position and need, Gert remained suspicious.

"Look, Lydia, why don't you give me some time to think about this? Usually, I never give my analyses to anyone. They represent something special for me, like an artist's private output. They're personal and rarely, if ever, up for sharing."

"Ohhh," said Lydia, "I never thought, but if you want to be paid, I'm sure I could arrange that with my company."

"No Lydia, it isn't a matter of money. I don't need money, thank God. No, as I said I just need a little time… okay?"

"Of course. May I call you tomorrow?"

"Yeah, do that. Now scoot. I still have to make dinner."

Lydia thanked her for the wine and her time and went downstairs to gloat because she was certain Gert would agree and let her have the analysis. A short time later, while taking a shower, she was so pleased with her performance, she hugged herself. At about that same time Gert was finishing a dressing for the baked chicken she was preparing and as she painted the bird with the aromatic sauce, she decided to mention Lydia's request to Sol to see how he felt about it and hear what he had to say.

CHAPTER 23

Gert waited until he was deep into dessert before she mentioned Lydia's visit.

"Well, you're no dummy. Was she telling the truth or telling you a tale?"

"Honestly, Sol, I don't know. At first, I doubted her honesty, but as we talked I got the feeling she was sincere and not just using me."

He was thoughtful for a moment and then smiled. "Well, my dear, there is a way to play this game, if you want to be devious."

"You old devil, what... what idea is brewing in that skull of yours?"

"It's so simple." he said, smiling. "Just alter the analysis. Change the quantities of breast milk and carbohydrate contamination, a little less of this and a little more of that, then hand over the analysis and you're a good and caring person, and what she doesn't know she'll never miss."

Gert whooped. "Sol, you are incomparable. That's it. If she wants the analysis because she's going to try and duplicate the formula, she'll have private chemists create a product based on the formula."

"Do you know if she's aware of the addition of the breast milk?"

"I don't know and I don't care. If she knows, she knows. It makes no difference. Without the exact details, there's no way to guess the amounts of concentration, or the type of milk-fat molecules that would influence the mixture. And not only that, I suspect it wasn't just the breast milk that influenced everything it was the explicit milk from Susan Merrill's mother."

"Damn, doesn't it all sound unreal, like how could it actually happen?"

"You're damn right it all sounds unreal. It's a math professor's dream. The odds of those two kids coming together are beyond calculation." Gert took a swig of wine.

"And talk about probabilities. Consider what we're dealing with here. Coleman's mother entices him to nurse with rosewater on her nipples, so he's a sucker for anything roses, plus, his mother's a bakery freak so he's nursed with a rosewater appetizer and mother's milk loaded with carbs. The girl's mother is also a bakery nut, so her breast milk is loaded with similar carbohydrates. When her breast milk and the rose perfume got mixed, a booby trap specifically tailored for that boy was created. It reminds me of those unexploded bombs found in Europe after World War Two. Day after day, they remained where they were, then one day when some poor soul was walking by... boooom."

"How can you explain something like that?"

"You can't because we aren't equipped to handle the amount of involved variables or even actually recognize what those variables are."

"You mean, that maybe ten degrees colder and the perfume's a bust or the bomb doesn't explode?"

"Ten degrees? Come on. How about one half of a degree? Just try to imagine all the differences between any one moment in time and another moment in time. They're not quantifiable."

"That reminds me of some lectures I attended once given by Alfred Korzybski. Now there was a truly interesting fellow with novel ideas that smacked the status quo. He talked about the impossibility of accounting for everything that's actually going on at any moment because of our inadequate sense perception mechanisms – our failing eyesight, inadequate hearing, deadened taste buds, and so on. He coupled that with the myriad other things and events continually happening below our awareness threshold... things we can't see, or hear or smell, but nonetheless, are still there microscopically influencing everything around them."

"Hell, forget about microscopically. Just think about your own ears and eyes. When you're twenty, you see and hear a world that no longer exists when you're seventy-five. I clearly remember when my mother was in her seventies. She was always bitching about the blandness of food in restaurants. I tried to tell her that her taste buds and sense of smell were aging and didn't work that well anymore."

"Didn't work, huh?"

"Are you kidding? She never believed me. One of her pet theories was that salt packaged when she was a kid was saltier than what was presently available."

"It's all mystifying, Gert, and a giant pain in the ass." He finished the wine in his glass. "We forget the world we see out there is our world. No one else sees what we see."

"Yeah, tell me about it."

"You know, someday I'd like to get a mob of people together, like maybe in a ball park and give them a test. Can you all hear this? Can you all see this? Feed them and see if they all can taste the whatever-it-is that's in the food. When they realize that other people perceive what they don't, and vice versa, then maybe, just maybe, they'll stop trying to tell everyone what's going on and understand what they perceive is only going on in them."

"That's a noble idea, Sol, but I would put it in a drawer with the other idealistic notions you have. Our world is still governed by the loud mouth and the big lie and with TV it's gotten a lot easier to bullshit everyone at once."

He leaned back and laughed. "And now, my dear, on that wonderful note of societal bliss, I will take myself across the street and horizontalize my body until, I hope, tomorrow. That is, of course, if the tooth fairy doesn't claim me as I sleep."

"Very funny, very funny. Yes, you go home and let me prepare an alternate analysis for our dear Lydia." Gert laughed. "God, how I'd love to be there when they get a whiff of the stuff they'll make with it. I sure hope they like roses."

Sol paused at the door. "There is something bothering me about this perfume with its formulas and subterfuge and all that."

"What's buggin' you pal?"

"What if the formula you provide does evoke some sort of reaction in men who smell it—like it did for that Coleman fellow?"

"That would be very strange, since the formula I'll provide will have everything that was originally there, but in different quantities."

"Okay, but let's say that somehow, some chemist plays around with it and sticks in some breast milk, or cow piss, or whatever. What then?"

"The significant point... the key factor you shouldn't forget is that the original reaction with Paul Coleman happened because of him! If you smelled the stuff probably nothing would have happened, but you never know – stranger things have happened and will happen."

Sol remained in the doorway, a puzzled look still on his face. "But what if someone does add something to your formula and it does produce some weird reaction?"

"Oh, Sol, you've been reading too much science fiction."

"But..."

"Look, I'd be the last to say anything is impossible. If someone dumps something into the perfume and a real reaction occurs, then it's a shot from the heavens. It's a one-in-a-million event that would defy all known rules."

"But…"

"Okay, okay. Yes, something could happen and if it did, I would write it off as a strange event…magic, pure unadulterated magic. Okay?"

He smiled. "Yes, I feel better now. I hate to think of the world so obediently marching in step with all the rules. I'm for breaking the rules."

"Fine, now go home and go to sleep." He opened the door and jauntily stepped forward waving good-bye over his shoulder as he did so. Gert smiled and locked the door behind him.

CHAPTER 24

After smoking some truly exceptional pot given to him by a neighborhood friend, Win sat in his apartment's one comfortable chair and pretended he was reading. He was pretending because he was more deeply involved trying to figure when and why the words on the page had lost their symbolism. Even if he wanted to know when that cloak of obscurity had covered him, he knew there was no way to tell.

The words were no longer representatives of the writer's mind—the black marks that displayed that person's peculiar and specific way of seeing the world. Now they were merely a collection of inky wiggles on a white background.

They had become disconnected wiggles and squiggles, bereft of meaning, some larger than others, and some far more attractive than others. Concentrating mightily and staring hard at a page, his fuzzy intellect was able to register that some of the wiggles joined to form words. And that's when he realized he really liked words with *l* and more than one *m*. He liked the way "parallel" looked because he felt the double *l* showed exactly what the word meant. Another word that greatly satisfied him was "millennium." He was pleased that the same letter at its beginning and end provided an equilibrium that rested perfectly on the central pivots of the double *n*. Maybe someday, he thought, when he was more stoned than now, if that were possible, he would ask that word how it felt to be so precisely poised.

Glancing up from the page, he spied his image in the mirror and smiled. Being alone so much had robbed him of the simple pleasure of social contact and played havoc with his need to be nice to other people. When others were not available, he maintained a constant effort to ensure civility by being as nice as he could be to himself. He often thanked himself aloud for making and serving coffee and for cooking dinner, for getting the wash from the

Laundromat, and for making certain there was always enough toilet paper and napkins. He was pleased to be able to do things for himself, but truly wanted to do things for someone else.

Maybe he would ask Lydia to marry him and then she could come live in this, he looked around, in this filthy and strange apartment over a bar. He could picture her delight with music blasting through the floor at three in the morning. She would be happy to sing along with the tunes favored by the local drunks. He laughed. Only a nut would live in a place like this and quite obviously, he was fully qualified.

"What the fuck am I doing here?" he asked aloud. Looking in the mirror he saw himself shake his head. "Well," he said, "if you don't know, then how the hell would I know?"

He got up from his chair and walked to his tiny kitchen. As he was opening a cabinet to see if he had any spaghetti, there was a loud bang, then a millisecond later, another. He moved to the doorway of the room he had exited to see what had collapsed. A quick glance showed that nothing had collapsed, but there was plaster dust on his desk and on the chair he sat in moments before. He walked to the chair and saw little chips of paint and plaster on the seat. Glancing up he saw a hole in the ceiling. About a foot to the right of that hole was another, with sufficient dust on the floor directly under it to confirm it was not an old wound.

With his curiosity fired up he was ready to launch a comprehensive investigation to get to the bottom of this mystery, but before he could get going, there was another bang. This one was right under his feet and he felt the floor shudder with the noise. As more plaster dust came down, he saw the holes in the floor. Bullets, he realized, they were bullet holes! Some lunatic asshole in the bar below was playing Wild West and shooting a gun into the air. With his indignation soaring, he took a deep breath and ran down the stairs to the street and directly into the bar.

Pushing open the door he saw what he expected to see. In the middle of the room was a guy holding a gun pointed at the ceiling. The thirty or so people in the bar were frozen. No one was moving except the guy who was waving the gun around. Win swayed a bit himself as he watched the man and as he watched, he decided the guy had enormous nerve disturbing him while he was planning dinner. There was no question in his mind that the guy should be made aware of his indiscretion and how Win felt, so Win stepped up to the man with the gun.

"Hey, do you know I was upstairs reading and getting ready to eat when your bullets put holes in my floor and ceiling? Now I have plaster dust to clean up. What kind of shit is this? This is not the Fourth of July, and anyway, people don't celebrate the Fourth anymore with shooting. Why don't you get some illegal fireworks like everyone else and be satisfied with that? How the hell is a person supposed to prepare dinner if bullets keep coming through the floor?"

Win paused, took a breath, and then said, "Now, give me that gun and go to the bar and get another drink. Stop this bullshit and let me get back upstairs so I can cook my dinner."

As Win yelled, the man with the gun stared in his direction as if he were looking at a three-legged alien. His bloodshot and bleary eyes tried to focus but didn't quite succeed. If anything, he seemed to be fixated on Win's left ear, at least that's where his eyes were aimed.

Suddenly the guy blurted out, "Oh man, oh shit, oh man, I'm sorry, I didn't mean nothin'. I din wannu inetrup yer dinner. I'm sorry. I'm really sorry."

All the while the man spoke his gun was still pointing at the ceiling, but suddenly he brought his arm down and handed the gun to Win.

"Here, you take this. I'm sorry, I'm really, really sorry." he said, as Win took the gun from his hand and looked at it. It was a large and quite beautiful automatic pistol. Hefting it, Win was surprised at its weight. A Dirty Harry gun, he thought.

"It's okay," Win said as he put his arm on the man's shoulder and slowly steered him to the bar. "Charley, give this guy another drink on me, and put this thing away."

Win handed the gun to the bartender whose mouth had opened in surprise and terror at the first shot and was still open. It took a second or two for the bartender to regain himself enough to take the gun from Win and hand it to one of the uniformed cops standing to his right. Win glanced at the cops and noticed they had their guns drawn. He also noticed the bar was crowded with wide-eyed, silent people still in the same shocked state as had been the bartender.

One of the cops gingerly moved to the man who was now finishing someone's drink and in a quick move handcuffed him. The other cop holstered his own gun and with smooth, seamless skill, removed the magazine and the chambered cartridge from the drunk's automatic.

Then he walked to where Win was standing. "Hey, Johnny, that was the bravest thing I ever saw. No fear. No fear at all, just walked up to this drunken perp and talked him down. You should get some kind of award."

"Goddamn," the bartender said from behind the bar, echoing the sentiment. "Win, you're a goddamn hero."

Win looked around and saw many people he knew, the regulars, and an equal number he didn't know. Charley, the bartender, thrust a cold glass into his hand and Win drank it without looking to see what it was. Luckily, it was a glass of delicious imported ale—one of the few drinks Win had learned to appreciate.

Putting the glass down on the bar, Win protested. "Charley, please, I'm no hero. I just did what a man had to do." Then he paused, broadly smiled and laughed aloud. "Charley, did you hear that? Son of a bitch, I sounded just like John Wayne."

"You not only sounded like John Wayne," said a voice to his left, "you acted like John Wayne. That was the smoothest move I ever saw. In fact, if I didn't know better, I would have guessed it was a movie setup."

Win turned to his left and saw golden yellow hair, an enormous amount of glistening, shining hair. More golden yellow hair than any three females should or even could have. Then, leaning back an inch or two, he squinted and looked more closely. There was a face in the middle of all the hair. And it had green eyes in its middle, pink and glowing skin around those wonderful eyes, a straight nose with a few freckles and ample red-pink lips. It was the most beautiful face he had ever seen so close to his own. Looking at her he thought of oceans and surf and beaches and Malibu and Johnny Carson. This beautiful female person had just been crowned Model of the Year and was a guest on Carson's TV show. Then he looked over her head and saw he was still in the bar, so she couldn't be a guest on his show—maybe, it struck him, he was a guest on her show.

"God," he breathed out, "you're the most beautiful woman I have ever seen." He leaned closer, peered at her like a concerned dermatologist and said in a voice brimming with love and peace, "Death is wonderful. You're an angel and I'm in heaven where they have bars and imported ale. What a cool thing. Heaven is a bar in New York. Good God, that's wonderful."

Then she laughed and his heart filled with joy. The laugh matched the voice. The voice fit the face. She had to be an angel.

"You're not dead although you could have been. That was really brave, just talked the gun away like it was a toy."

"Who are you? Where have you come from?" He stared at her and then looked around once again to be certain he knew where he was. "Do you realize you are in a bar on the corner of Bank and Hudson? This is not heaven, you don't belong here." She laughed again and his heart melted for she also had beautiful teeth.

Everything around them came to a halt as the cops escorted the "drunk perp," as they dubbed him, to their patrol car. The instant they crossed the threshold to the street it was as if they had never been there. The drinkers returned to their glasses and the conversations picked up where they had stopped. Charley, all smiles and congratulations, came out from behind the bar, led Win to a table, and handed him another glass of ale. The girl followed him to the table, sat down and stared at Win who stared back.

Somewhere in the back of his mind, Win was trying to figure out the appropriate "thank-you" for the grass he had smoked. Since it was once a plant, he wondered if he should thank Mother Nature, God, the Devil, or maybe a Midwestern farmer who was supplementing his income, or a Mexican farmer who had no income at all. The "thank-you" list was endless, so he gave up and continued to stare at the yellow-haired beauty.

"Tell me," he asked. "What brings you here to Greenwich Village in New York City? I thought they keep beautiful California girls under guard so they can't leave and destroy the image."

"Number one, I'm not a California girl and I was there only once in my life. Number two, I came to New York from Minnesota, and number three, I work for a magazine and I'm going to do a story about you."

"My God, you look like that and you can write. Wow, and I now know you can count up to three, but writing a story, that's tough."

With a wonderful smile on her lips, she stared into his eyes smiled and said, "You're high."

"No, I'm not. I'm Winthrop." She laughed again.

He held up a finger. "Wait, I must be honest. I wasn't always Winthrop. That is really my middle name. My very real first name is Rex, but I have always preferred Winthrop."

"Middle names reverberate with parental obligations." she said. "Maybe a favorite uncle or a brother, but first names—they have special meanings. So tell me why were you named Rex? Where I come from that's what we call German Shepherds." Now he laughed.

"I know about that. Those dogs have the same name here. But to answer your question, my folks were big-time movie freaks and they were impressed with a particular actor so they named me after him."

For brief moment, her beautiful head tilted slightly to the left, before she said, "Well, I can think of two right off the bat, Rex Ingram and Rex Harrison, one of them?"

"Give the lady a seegar. Rex Ingram, and the movie was…"

"*Sahara*, right?"

Now Win was truly impressed. Ingram did not make many movies and he was probably best known for *Cabin in the Sky* rather than *Sahara*, but just knowing his name put her into a super-special category.

Win squinted at her and said, "You're right. It was *Sahara* and he played…?"

"Sergeant Tambul, the Sudanese corporal who found the well and later killed the German flyer played by…?"

"Kurt Kreuger," said Win, proudly.

In that neighborhood, during that week, the only other male-female success story was between two cocker spaniels involved in supplementing their breed. But since Win and the blonde girl were humans, they deserved the record book entry that dealt with the very best first "date." And now, both overwhelmed by the success of the moment, they stared into each other's eyes.

"What is your name?" Win asked.

"Guess."

"Guess? You're kidding. There are zillions of names. And, what's more, since you're from Minnesota, your name might be something I've never heard of, or your name might be John Deere or McCormick's Reaper or International Harvester. How can I guess?" Downing more of the ale, he muttered, "Not fair, not fair."

"Think movies." she said.

He leaned back in the chair trying to see as much of her as possible. Beautiful face; great hair; great neck; maroon and gold sweater; arms, yes; bustline, yes; watch, yes; wedding ring, no; blue jeans, yes; new-looking, sensible shoes, yes. Now, what movie would that add up to?

"So you want me to think movies, okay. I'll gamble big. The only time, I think, she was a blonde, and enormously elegant in a very simple way, like you, I'm thrilled to say, was Loretta Young in *The Farmer's Daughter*. But, she was blonde in that movie and never again, as far as I know. Now, since in Minnesota every girl is blonde, they took the name from that movie and named you Loretta. So, that's the movie and Loretta Young was the impetus, and since Young is a weird first name, I have to go with Loretta."

Smiling broadly, she cried out, "Right you are! I can't believe it."

Win closed his eyes tightly and kept them shut. He knew this was a dream and if he opened his eyes, it would all go away, vanish like his other fantasies.

"No one has ever gotten that right before." she said. "So, I'm going to continue the test. What is my last name?"

"Wait a minute, that's not possible. I've never read one page of the Minnesota phone book. That's asking too much."

"Oh, okay, if you want to play feeble. The last name is Anderson. Loretta Anderson is the entire tag, but I write under the name Lou Anders."

"A lady named Lou." he burst out. "That's Robert W. Service—you're from *Dangerous Dan McGrew*."

"Fantastic." she said, laughing. "You're like a stoned encyclopedia."

He rolled the words on his tongue. "Loretta Anderson... Lou Anders, I like that."

He was silent for a moment and then proclaimed, "My last name is David, after the king."

She laughed and he was thrilled. He wanted to make her laugh. He wanted to keep her laughing. He hoped she never stopped laughing.

"You're truly a funny man. Are you like this when you're not stoned?"

"I don't think so. I think I'm stuffy and kind of a book worm and busy trying to be more like I am right now."

"You mean funny and bold and not afraid to say exactly what you think?"

"Yes, that's it exactly."

"What are you afraid of?" She asked, drinking some of his ale.

"That's hard, I don't think I know. Maybe I was trained to be that way."

"Trained?"

"That's right." he said, finishing the ale. "My mother was a kid when she got to this county. In Russia her family survived the pogroms where Cossacks killed Jews because it was Tuesday or simply because they felt like it. As new guys, my folks were very nervous, so they tried as hard as they could to melt into the background. My mother learned how to avoid problems, to cross the street, to shut her mouth, to start no trouble, never make a fuss, to stay apart, all that stuff. And I learned it all from her like a good puppy."

She was silent and realized she would never again have to search for an example if someone asked her if ever she had a jovial conversation turn serious.

"Wait a minute, wait, how can you say you're afraid when a moment ago you talked a crazy man into giving up his gun?"

"I can't answer that. Maybe I'm generally afraid, but specifically brave. Does that make any sense?" He paused, looked up at the ceiling, and then leveled his stare at her. "But, what I am is not important. What *is* important, is you. What are you doing in this neighborhood? I'm around a lot and I never saw you before. Where have you come from?"

She laughed and signaled Charley for two ales which he hustled over. Win smiled at the atypical service. Normally, you had to wait until he got ready to serve you, but now, I'm a hero. He wondered how long that designation would last.

The grass was still making him smile so much he decided he would smoke more. A joint a day keeps the frowns away. Then he focused on the girl and realized she was staring at him. "Where did you go?" She asked.

"Regulating the internals, formulating plans for the betterment of mankind."

"Oh, I see. You know something? You're quite a character." Win leaned over and picked up her hand. Her skin was young and her hand was weightless.

"Never mind me, you, you. Tell me more about you."

"I moved into Two Horatio a month ago from a place on West 71st Street. I work for *MK* magazine. I was married, but I'm not anymore. I have no children, no car, no dog or cat, no bills, no major ailments and my teeth are in good shape."

Still holding her hand, Win floated. The sound of her voice and the beauty of her face lifted him from the seat. He closed his eyes. Was it entirely the grass? Never before had he been struck like this. He knew his tendency to be romantic, but this was amazing. Could you meet someone when you're high, flip out and still be bongoed when straight? We will find out, he said to himself. We will certainly find out.

"Tell me something," he asked. "I haven't thought about it till now, but I don't know what *MK* means. Are they initials of the publisher or editor, what? Help me!"

"The initials stand for *Make Known*. We are somewhat of an exposé magazine."

"I know that. I've read a few issues. But now I'll get a lifetime subscription. I won't ever miss a word you write."

"I may never write again."

Taken aback, he quickly asked, "Why? What do you mean?"

"I don't think I could handle my laptop with only one hand."

Win looked at her hand still firmly in his. "I think it is a beautiful hand," he said, "and you're going to have to learn to handle your machine with only one, because I don't intend to let go. I'm claiming it as my reward for an act, that by tomorrow will escalate into an adventure in which everyone in the neighborhood will swear was a bare-knuckled brawl with at least eight armed-to-the-teeth thugs."

"People around here tend to exaggerate. Is that what you're saying?"

With a wide grin, he said, "Let's just say that this neighborhood has a tendency to appreciate imagination and fantasy more than fact. I lean that way myself. How else could I explain your entry into my dreary existence?"

She gently and delicately wriggled her fingers from his and grabbed her glass before he could reclaim her hand. After she took a long drink, she said, "Okay… two things. One, I'm hungry. Where can we go to eat something? And two, tell me about you. I'm personally interested and I need info for the piece I'm going to write."

"Okay. One, we can eat here." She nodded.

He called out for Charley to bring menus. "Two, I'm single, never married. I live upstairs amidst books and dust, but you know that, but not about the books and dust. How could you know that? And now, some plaster and paint chips." He took a breath. "I'm an associate professor at NYU in the Communications Department. No cat, no dog, no fish, no TV, yes radio, yes CD, yes phonograph, yes cassette, yes computer."

Charley dropped two menus on the table and said in a low voice, "Win the food's on me. I owe you." As he walked back to the bar, Win called out, "I'll have a hundred and twenty-seven hamburgers, all medium well."

They both laughed at the look on Charley's face as he said, "Cute, very cute."

By the time the burgers did arrive, they were again holding hands, and they were delighted to be doing so. They ate and talked, drank more ale and talked. They didn't stop talking.

The regulars at the bar and other tables looked at them and with smirky smiles and nodding heads pointed them out to others. Win the hero and the new girl were the evening's topic. Everyone in the place acted smug like they had the inside info on a horse race, so certain were they of the outcome.

Later, Win walked her to her building and rode the elevator to her apartment. Gallantly, he escorted her inside and was impressed by the modernity of the furnishings and the overall neatness of everything.

"I know you don't have a maid. Well, I don't know that, but I'm assuming you don't, right?"

"You're right. I don't and I do clean the place myself."

"Promise me you'll never come to my place, at least not until the CDC certifies it fit for human habitation."

"It can't be that bad."

"It really isn't. It's just that I'm not overly concerned with dust and things like that. I don't feel I'm on a personal mission to keep the planet free of contaminants."

About an hour later when Win was saying good night, he asked if he could kiss her. Shyly, she agreed and he took her in his arms. Slowly, passionately, and with great reserve, he held and kissed her. He told himself there was no need to try for a leap into bed or for a tussle on the sofa. All that would come in good time. He knew that and was thrilled when he realized she did as well.

CHAPTER 25

When Gert handed her the chemical analysis, Lydia was brimming with delight. Having the analysis pleased her, but having Gert believe the story she concocted pleased her even more. Like every swindler, Lydia was overjoyed with a successful con. Putting it over on someone was blissful and that's why she was at home in the advertising business. So far, it had provided a rewarding and legal venue for her deceitful nature. Con artists of every stripe found a place in the advertising business so she was not alone. Reprehensible charlatans who would be fired from the worst carnival show were the vice presidents and senior account executives at major agencies. Like them and other tricksters, Lydia craved the feelings of power, the rewards, the control over the mark, the poor "suckers" who were the ever-constant victims.

Years before, when she established herself in the industry, she felt a bit sorry for the pool hustlers, race track touts, and card sharks who could work only a few suckers at a time. But mass advertising had given her an opportunity to put on hundreds of thousands of people. In all that time, she never felt the need to defend her actions. If people were stupid and willing to be duped, that was not her affair. Let them help themselves. If they couldn't, it was their problem, not hers. From her vantage point, Advertising was a great industry and she loved it.

After getting the analysis, she immediately called Tom, but he didn't share in her ebullience. He didn't seem overly thrilled and she could detect the sound of doubt in his voice, those subtle vocal variations between what is usual and what appears at other times.

"Are you sure you got the right analysis?" He asked.

"What do you mean the 'right analysis'?"

"Well, the way you described the old dame, I was wondering if she didn't pull a fast one and slip you a phony."

"Slip me a phony?!" she exclaimed in surprise. Then after a short silence, she asked, "But why would she do it? What's to be gained?"

"From our position, she has nothing to gain. But from hers, well, I don't know. Maybe just knowing she's screwing you around would please her."

Lydia considered what he was saying and had to reject it. "No, Tom, you're wrong. Gert and I have had differences in the past, but there's never been anything between us so awful or that created such animosity that she would deliberately try to screw me."

"Okay, then, congratulations, and let's get the damn thing to the chemists so we can find out what we got."

"Exactly, I'll take care of that and keep you posted."

What Gert had managed to accomplish in several hours, Apex Analytical Chemists did in two days. Considering their price was eight hundred dollars a day, the only real surprise was that it didn't take longer. Three days after Lydia handed the paperwork to a courier, a two-ounce bottle of the perfume sat on her desk. She stared at it as if she expected it to jump up and bounce around her office. The euphoric fantasies spawned by the amber liquid knew no bounds. She dreamily envisioned entry to the innermost circles of corporate power via Complete Abandon sales figures.

With no way to predict when that might happen, she often wondered why she wanted it so, why she so craved power. Trying to put a finger on any single specific cause was impossible, but she felt it grew from her relationship with her mother.

Like most children, she had neither control nor voice in the running of her life. She always followed orders from her mother, a woman whose sole concern was the way things looked. A happy family looked like one. A happy child looked like one. Everyone smiled. Everyone was polite. Reality never entered her mother's world. If everyone in the family looked right, the ever-present ill will didn't matter, for no outsider could see it. Simply put, her mother never saw what she didn't want to see. How their possessions looked and how the family members looked was all that ever mattered to her.

Lydia recalled the Sunday afternoon strolls through the park with the family nattily dressed as proof to the world that her mother ran an efficient household. For Lydia, merely going to the market for groceries was an event that paralleled the Easter Parade. There was never any moment for a relaxed form of dress. "What would the neighbors think?" was her mother's basic and enduring question. Lydia never thought of asking, of actually trying to find out what the neighbors thought. And now, when she thought about the neighbors she could recall, she laughed, since most of them were low-class, blue-collar loud mouths, who thought anything clean had to be new.

For several childhood years, she assumed she was constantly photographed. She was sure someone was taking pictures so her mother would know if she was deviating from long-standing rules. Pictorial evidence of digressions could prove her mother a failure. Lydia assumed that nothing else could explain her mother's zealous concern for appearance. She was always on guard against those she referred to as "them," the outsiders.

When Lydia went to the park, she had to stand by the bench as her mother talked to her cronies. It was Lydia's "job" to stay neat and clean while she painfully watched other kids her age run around, get filthy, and have fun. With sideward glances in store windows on their walk home, Lydia saw herself still pressed, still starched, still pleated. Upon reaching home her mother told her how happy she was as a result of Lydia obeying all the rules and still looking clean and neat.

Until she was twelve, she thought her mother the person who always knew the right way to do everything, but school conversations ended that thinking. Girl's bathroom talk gave her the will and the skill to decide for herself. She did not rebel as some girls did by running away. Rather, she learned how to do what she wanted and still present the picture her mother desired. By the time she was sixteen, Lydia was a master of guile. The success she had achieved in the business world was a bizarre testimonial to the effects of her mother's "training."

This Complete Abandon assignment would be no different from her previous successes. She thought it would be a smash and the sales would make her the envy of the agency and of Metro Brands. If all went as planned, a vice presidency at Metro would be the minimum she would take, and it all came down to the bottle in front of her.

Tom was in her office five minutes after her call and after she put some of the perfume on her neck and wrists. He smiled as she hugged him, thinking the embrace was not business related, but then he realized what was up.

"For a moment, I thought you were glad to see me."

"I am, but what do you feel?"

"Hug me again." She walked a step and put her arms around him. He breathed in the wonderful smell of her hair and then caught the perfume. He thought it wholesome and not unpleasant, but that was it. He sensed there was no compelling impetus for him to do anything but what he was already doing.

"I'm sorry, Lydia, but aside from the fact you smell very nice, that's the extent of it. There's nothing else happening."

He watched her as she moped to her desk and plopped into the chair which so engulfed her that she looked like a kindergarten kid at the teacher's desk.

"Son of a bitch," she muttered. "What the hell is going on?"

"Hey," he said, "this was always a possibility. All your money was on the perfume doing what you thought it would do. You never thought of anything else."

"I think something's fishy. Those kids did live through something. I saw them while it was still fresh. They were shook up, especially the guy. He did what they said he did. He attacked the girl in a crowded corridor and I heard him say he did it because he had *no choice*! He could not not attack her."

Tom watched her as her words gushed and he knew she still believed it all. "Okay, let's say you're right. There was a reaction. Then what happened? Where did it go?"

She stared at him, confusion clear on her face and then slowly a different look replaced it. Her eyes narrowed and her lips straightened. "You were right, damn it. That old bitch screwed with the formula and what we have here is nothing more than a pleasant perfume."

"Well, sorry to say, that leaves you up the creek."

"Like hell it does." she paused then said, "Wait a minute, just wait a minute." Tom watched as she opened an address book and then picked up the phone and dialed.

After a few moments, she spoke into the phone. "Susan, hi, this is Lydia Cornell. Yes, I'm fine and I hope you are also. Maybe you can help me with something. You see, I managed to get the perfume analysis from Gert, I mean Professor Lehman, and I was wondering if she mentioned what some of the ingredients were. There's an argument here at the agency whether there is an odor element in it besides attar of Rose."

Tom watched Lydia focus on the conversation, her face displaying the attention she was offering to every word. Then, suddenly, her face lit up and a broad smile appeared. He knew she had heard something important, for her demeanor changed completely. She hung up the phone and turned to him.

"Tom, you were right, that Gert is some piece of work. It seems that Greenwich Village's version of Madam Curie had a slight lapse and left out a major ingredient of the analysis. The kid just told me her father, as a joke, you got that, as a joke, mixed some of her mother's breast milk with the perfume. Breast milk! So it wasn't just the perfume smell that turned on that guy, it was the perfume and the smell or whatever the breast milk added to the concoction."

"Does breast milk have an odor?"

"How the hell do I know?"

Not sure what to do, they looked at each other. A minute passed before Lydia said, "Okay, this is the plan. I'm going to call a pediatrician and find out about breast milk. Then we'll have to figure a way to get the original analysis away from dear old Gert. Obviously, she doesn't want me to have it, so we'll have to take it."

"Take it, how?"

"I have no idea now, but I will. But first I'm going to find out about breast milk."

Tom nodded and turned toward the door. "Well, babe, this is all really strange. We started with a plan for a fragrance line and now it seems we're playing cops and robbers. I don't want to know about any of this, so I'm going back to my office. Give me a call if you need me, okay?"

Lydia nodded as she thumbed through the directory on her desk. Tom closed the door as she dialed.

"Hello, this is Lydia Cornell. I'm fine and you? As the personnel officer in charge of benefits, can you give me the name of a pediatrician some of the members have used? I need some medical advice. Sure, I'll hold."

In fifteen minutes Lydia had finished her call and learned from Doctor Harvey Green that breast milk does have a taste and does have an odor. Also, it is very rich in fats and so personal to each woman, that it totally reflects that woman's diet, lifestyle, and overall health. And most important, it would be exceedingly rare for any two samples to be the same.

As Lydia considered the information, she pulled out a pad and made notes.

1. Impossible to get breast milk that was in the original perfume.
2. Adding just any breast milk would make no sense, but...
3. As a test case, breast milk should be added to original perfume.
4. Where can I get breast milk?
5. The analysis Gert did does have details about the original stuff.
6. Is it possible to duplicate the original breast milk if the formula was available?
7. Must get the analysis from Gert!

She stared at the list for a time and then put in a call to Apex Analytical Chemists. They told her it would not be possible to exactly duplicate breast milk, but if a formula was available for it, they could come very, very close. Doctor Thatcher went on to say that it all depended upon the quality of the analysis. A good one would permit them to create material that reflected the chemical structure of the milk, but without the analysis, it would be impossible to know the constituent quantities. It depended, he emphasized, on the analysis from which they would be working.

She hung up and said aloud, "I must get that analysis."

An hour later, she and Tom were in a local café having lunch.

"I understand the pickle you're in," he said, biting into one. "But I'm no second-story artist, and I have no intention of taking anything or stealing anything from anyone. In fact, I strongly advise against it."

"I'm not asking you to do anything. All I want is the name of some trustworthy thug. Someone we can depend upon. I'm sure Gert has that analysis and it's just a matter of getting it."

"Where do you think it is, at her home or at her school office?"

"God," she said, raising her hands to the side of her head, "I never even thought of that." A moment passed, and then she said, "If I know Gert, she has it at home."

"Why? What gives you that clue?"

"Just a feeling I have about the first floor of her place. One time she complained about the inadequate school labs, that they're too public and not a place for detailed work. She also told me the sealed-off first floor of her house holds her private laboratory."

"What do you mean the first floor is sealed off?"

"Just what I said, if you count floors in her building, there are three. I live on the ground floor. She lives on the third floor. The middle floor is sealed. It's there, but you can't get to it from the outside or the inside. There's no visible inside door, at least none I ever saw."

"Then she has a special building. Who did it? I mean did she buy it like that?"

"No, she told me she had the entire building gutted and specially rebuilt."

"Then that's the way to find out. In this city, every nut and bolt has a plan and every plan has to be filed with the city. I'll bet the layout and the contractor's name are on file somewhere. All we have to do is locate the firm that did the construction and we'll know everything." Then glancing at the ashtray, he said, "You know something else? I can't believe there's no public access to that floor. If that's true, then that would seem to be a fire hazard—right?"

"Right!" she said smiling. "And I bet the local fire company also has some detailed info on that building."

Later, back at the office, Lydia spent hours on the telephone speaking to the fire department and city planning commission which confirmed what she thought to be true, that Gert had been the contractor for the entire project. Union officials in charge of the electrical, plumbing and carpentry work for private residences provided additional information. She learned the names of the manufacturers of the equipment that required special electrical connections. Eventually, the manufacturers told her what had been ordered, what specific alterations Gert had demanded, when the equipment was delivered and even which moving company delivered it to the 13th Street location. As much as it pleased her to get the information, Lydia was a bit surprised at the willingness of those with whom she spoke to divulge what they knew. There was no concern for privacy.

By the end of the day, she had learned the windows in the front of the building were essentially doors that were specially designed and hinged to open outward and she knew of the elevator from Gert's apartment to the lab. She also found out that she had to get into Gert's apartment and then take the elevator to the lab to get the analysis from her files. Since Gert's class schedule was available, the right time to break in would be easy to figure.

It seemed simple except for one major problem; the person who would break in and get the analysis. What she needed was a crook, a trustworthy crook. Were there such people? And then she thought about whom she knew who might know burglars. Not the drunken and desperate fools willing to take a chance for a couple of bucks, but professional thieves who could be hired and paid for a specific job. Thieves who could be employed just as you hire someone to change a tire or paint a house. She needed a Gangster Yellow Pages.

Planning a crime is not a problem the problem is who would know you're doing it? Who could prove you planned something? But, planning a crime that involved another person meant a fellow conspirator—a person who could incriminate her.

She was ironically amused because advertising is a business where lying and fraud are basic and she was having a problem coming up with a dishonest person. If she worked for the government or a defense contractor, there'd be a division of ex-military guys ready and willing for anything. That's why big companies were the best. They had everything you'd ever need. Being small, thinking small, or acting small would always be a problem. Fool one person, you're a bad apple. Fool a nation and you're a renowned politician, an elder statesman or maybe a corporate chief executive officer.

Not being stupid, she knew this required great care. It was too easy to end up like the dopes in the newspapers who are arrested when they try to hire a hit man and find out they've been talking to an undercover cop.

Sitting at her desk, she pondered her choices. As the minutes ticked by, one name kept reappearing in her mind. No question, he was the person who probably could come up with a name. She picked up the phone and dialed.

"Dennis? This is Lydia. Is it possible for you to come to my office for a minute or two? I'd like to ask you a question."

Ten minutes later he sat facing her, wearing his usual outfit and usual smirk. "Okay, what's the question?" he asked, leaning forward. "I hope it isn't about tonight. I'm all booked, but I can squeeze you in tomorrow, and, oh boy, how I'd love to squeeze you in."

She shook her head. "Don't you ever turn off?"

"I turn it all off when necessary. For instance, like when I have my weekly conference with Dunn."

She interrupted him. "You and Dunn, you have a weekly conference?"

With calm superiority, he said, "Lydia, you should be more discerning. Evidently, you're too easily taken in. Dunn and I are old pals, and my real role here would greatly surprise you, but that's not what you want to see me about, You want my bold act and my talk about being in a state of continual arousal and that I think you're dynamite and I make no bones about it and that I could love you forever and..."

"And what?" she asked, thinking this was not the usual Dennis.

"And, you know it because you dig me, and I know that."

"Well, let's put that aside for a moment. What I need from you right now is a thief. I need to hire a professional thief, and I thought maybe you might know one."

He smiled. "A professional thief... what the hell do you mean?"

"I need something stolen and I want to hire someone who can get it for me. That's it, pure and simple."

"Simple maybe, pure, well, I don't know. You understand we're talking dangerous shit here. Professional thieves are nasty people. They don't use lawyers or small claims court to settle problems. You can't mess with them. Just talking with them is dangerous, because blackmail is always possible."

"All I want to do is present the details about a job that must be done. They take it on, they get paid. If they refuse, then we go for a drink."

"When do you need to talk?"

"As soon as possible!"

His eyebrows went up. "What the hell is going on?"

"It doesn't concern you and you don't want to get involved. All I want from you is a name and a phone number."

"You gonna be home later?" When she nodded, he asked for her home number. "I'll call you later tonight," he said, and walked out of her office.

As she watched him leave, she reviewed what had just taken place. Good old Dennis dropped his mask and another person popped out. She wondered how many of him there were and if she should call him Sybil. And what was that about weekly conferences with Dunn? Obviously, she had missed something. Dennis was not the simple testosterone-filled playboy she had assumed him to be.

It had been a surprising day. First it was Gert who had given her a phony formula and, second, it was Dennis, who had another side she had never seen.

CHAPTER 26

Lydia sipped wine and looked up at the ceiling. Right up there, she thought. Right up there is the solution to my problem. On the other side of the ceiling is her lab and if I can get into it and get the analysis, I can write my own ticket. As she stared, she wondered if it would make sense to smash a hole in the ceiling, go up and take what she needed. Then she realized how stupid that was. There would be no way to explain a break-in through her apartment ceiling, and what's more, Gert would realize there was nothing of value in the lab to anyone except Lydia.

The original idea was better. Get a thief to break into the lab, take the formula and destroy everything. The more it looked like a neighborhood robbery and vandal trashing, the better. Yes, she thought, it should look like a bunch of crazies broke in, broke all the equipment and turned everything moveable upside down. Empty the files and burn every scarp. With a big enough fire no one, not even Gert could tell what was missing. It wouldn't be hard. It just depended on the burglar. Dennis had to provide a name. He had to come through on this.

She was too on edge to make dinner so she called the local Chinese takeout and as she waited for it, she recalled a recent meal she had with Win. She liked him, but it was clear from the day Gert introduced them that he wasn't for her. He was good looking, clever, and smart. In those ways he was fine. But he was proud to be a college professor and even if he wrote a great book, he might not get promoted. And if he did, he would probably make no more than eighty or ninety and she needed more than that, more than he would ever earn.

She thought about money and smiled. When this deal comes through, I'll have a personal assistant and pay her what Win is making now. Tom is more the right thing, but even he seems a little too satisfied following Dunn's orders. Tom's a great lieutenant, but I want a general. I want a guy who gives orders, but also, a guy who will happily take orders from me.

The food arrived and she was halfway through the soup when the phone rang. It was Dennis and he wanted to come over and talk. She told him that would be okay only if he had a name for her. He said he did. That excited Lydia tremendously and when Dennis did arrive a little while later, she was tingling.

When he came in, he looked different. He was wearing less formal clothing and the black slacks and shirt seemed to melt into each other under the gray jacket. His daytime dress was flashy; this outfit was the opposite. It looked regal and fit him so well she guessed it was custom made. But she dismissed that thinking he probably won the outfit in a poker game.

When he followed her downstairs to her apartment, he looked around admiringly and then plunked down on the couch across from her. She watched him take in all the details and didn't miss his eyes lingering on the takeout food containers.

"This is a really weird building. I've never seen a street-level apartment you had to walk down to get into. Why the hell has your outside entrance been closed off?"

Lydia laughed. "Gert, the woman who owns this place, lives on the second floor, or third, depending on your point of view. She redesigned it and had it built this way because she was concerned with security. The only way in is up the outside steps, through the front door, then up the inside staircase for her door or down a different staircase for mine."

"You mean there are no other ways to get in?"

"Well, you've got the backyard, but that's tough to get to without being seen. All these brownstones have active backyards and big windows so people can keep track of things. From the street side there's just one front door."

He nodded. "I guess it does make the place difficult for the walk-along break-in guys. You have to negotiate two doors to get in either place." He looked around again. "If your apartment was typical street level, you'd have to go through only one door." He laughed. "I guess the dame is not so dumb. She's right, limiting entrances certainly does make the place safer."

Slightly annoyed, Lydia said, "Look Dennis, I don't want to rush you along, but you said you had a name for me."

"Wait a minute, Lydia. I want to get things done also, but let's not move too fast. First, there are some things I need to know. You see, if I recommend a guy and he gets busted by the cops or private security..." He looked around and then asked, "There is no private security, is there?"

"Not that I've ever seen or heard."

"Well, you would have known if there was any, but to get back to what I was saying, if the grabber gets busted, I'd have to answer to his people and they have no sense of humor. So before I do anything, tell me what all this is about. I want a handle on things before I commit, okay?"

He eyed the food containers once again and then shifted his stare to her. "I know you're a tough lady and I like you for that. You know what you want and you aren't afraid. But being a tough tomato around the water cooler is one thing; setting up a job is another story altogether."

This wasn't in the plan she had considered. Making Dennis privy to the operation never occurred to her and she wondered if she should try to make up a story rather than tell him the truth. She realized it would be impossible to instantly create a plausible story. The hell with it then, she said to herself.

"What I'm going to tell you is private. You can't tell anyone else. Tom and Dunn already know, but that's it, okay?"

He stared at her. "You know, I should be insulted, but I expected this. You're always so busy thinking about yourself you've never really thought about me. You wrote me off as Mr. Eveready – a cock in a silk suit. Well, babe, you couldn't be more mistaken. I've been operating in that agency for years and I know everything. I know where every skeleton is buried, who buried it and why. I probably know most of the story about your perfume and that you need the complete analysis since the one you sent to Apex didn't do the job. Obviously, something is missing and information about that item is what you want stolen." He stopped and gloated. "Since you're not objecting, that's most of it, right?"

Reaching for one of the food containers, he looked inside, smiled and then grabbed a large shrimp. He looked at it for a moment, and then popped it into his mouth and ate it.

"My guess is there's a secret ingredient you need to know about. Thatcher at Apex told me you called asking about breast milk, so I'll guess that's the secret thing and what you have to know are exact proportions. Is that it?"

She stared at him with wide eyes. He did know everything and he was right about her. She had dismissed him as a wise guy who tried to screw every dame. It was like movie espionage. He was a spy using a playboy personality for cover. And it had worked, since she never thought of him in any other way.

She remembered telling Susan she didn't even know his last name, that maybe he didn't even have a last name. He was Dennis—just Dennis.

"Well, to say I've misjudged you would be true. You're right I never paid proper attention to you."

She reached over, took a shrimp from the container and bit a chunk out of it. Then holding what was left between her fingers, she started to fill him in. In the ten minutes they needed to finish the shrimps, she had told him everything.

"Okay, you now know it all now. So I want the burglar's name and I want to know about him. I want to make sure he or she can do this job."

"Fair enough. What do you want to know?"

"First, is he wanted by the police?"

"No, he's not wanted by the police and he's never been arrested. He's a successful thief who's laid off because there is no need to continue."

"You know him well? He's not some guy you met in a bar a month ago?"

"I know him very well and I've known him for a long, long time."

"Can you contact him?"

"I have."

"What did he say?"

"He was hesitant, since he's no fool, and also, he says he has to hear all the details before he agrees to work for you. Like many other successful people, he owes his success to careful planning. He never got involved in a caper he didn't plan and he firmly believes you must never leave your well-being in the hands of others."

"Well, since you know all the details, you can tell it all to him, but I want to meet him. I want to be able to judge him myself."

"Why? Do you think you're a good judge of people? You missed the mark with me and maybe you'd miss it with him. Maybe you'd think he was great and eventually find he's just a bum who never did more than steal bubble gum from the five and ten."

"Look, Dennis, I can't argue with you. You were right. I dismissed you and that was stupid. I try not to make mistakes, but with you, I made a big one, so it proves I can be as dumb as anyone else. And also, I don't think I could judge a burglar. But at least I'd like to meet him, to see him and be able to get a feeling about him."

"I've been waiting to hear you say that, Lydia. I've been waiting for you to say you aren't the smartest bitch who walks the earth. Humility is vital. The wise guys who think the police are stupid," he laughed. "They're the ones who get caught. Credit must always be given where it's due. Now that you've done that I can tell you the burglar's name."

She leaned forward, like the audience watching the movie scene when the detective unmasks the murderer. He stared at her, waited an appropriate moment and then said, "His name is Dennis, Dennis DeVito."

She almost asked about a rendezvous, but she never got the words out. It was the way he was looking at her. His eyes had narrowed slightly and there was a trace of smirk on his lips and after a moment she knew, he was Dennis DeVito. He had given her the name–his own name–and then she knew he would do it for her.

"I'm learning quite a bit tonight." she said.

He smiled. "Yes, you are, and so am I."

They stared at each other until she got up, and went for two plates so they could divide and eat what food remained. They ate in silence. He said little because he was hungry. She was reticent because she was embarrassed. He had pulled the rug from under her and left her with hundreds of questions, all she wanted to know about the agency's business. She also wondered if maybe A.T. Dunn was a figurehead and Dennis was the power behind the throne. Everything was upside down.

"You're staring," he said.

"Yes," she laughed. "You're the big surprise I never expected. So many things fall into place now that I know how deeply you are connected at the agency. You always manage to get things done. I've always thought it was your knack for handling things, little did I know how well you handled all of it."

"It's very easy to operate when you aren't hampered by standard office structure. All you have to know is who can do what you want and how to get them to do it."

"What if they don't want to do what you want?"

"That's when my unique powers of persuasion come in handy."

She did not know whether or not to laugh. "That sounded like a line from a movie," she said and then she did laugh. "That line is usually followed by one where a fat guy says, 'I personally deplore violence, but Bruno would take great pleasure breaking your fingers.'"

"Yeah, I've seen those movies and believe it or not, those lines came out of real life. The scriptwriters weren't the originators."

"Have you ever said anything like that?"

"Not really, but years ago, I was Bruno, the finger breaker. Now I'm the fat guy who owns several Brunos."

"I know we could talk for hours, but tell me, when can you get the analysis?"

"When is she going to be out for most of the day? You have her class schedule, right?"

"Yes, but I don't want to guess, let me make sure." Lydia went to her desk and got it. Holding it, she said, "Well, she teaches almost all day on Tuesdays. Leaves here to make a 9:00 class, has a one hour break, then three classes in a row. She's tied up from eleven to two. It's the exact same for Thursday. Wednesday's are different."

"That's great, next Tuesday seems best because I'll have time to prepare. Just make sure you have an alibi. You must be certain to have a rock-solid alibi for all day next Tuesday. Whatever it is make sure you're with other people and make sure they know you're around."

"Don't worry, I can always call a copy conference, an alibi is not going to be a problem."

"Okay, then, one last thing. Let me see the paperwork she did give you. I'm going to guess the original analysis looks very much like the one you got. I want to see the paper she used, the print format, the overall design of it. I want to be in and out in a hurry so I don't want to take the wrong thing."

As Lydia retrieved the analysis, she thought about what was going to happen and what had not been discussed. She walked back to the sofa and handed him the papers. "One thing…"

"What?" He asked, as he studied the sheets.

"We haven't discussed money for this business. My intention was to pay a burglar you were going to recommend. Things have changed, right?"

"Yes, they have. You won't have to pay me anything. The agency will make money on the product. You will make some money. I'll get mine along the way."

Lydia had no idea what he meant, but she was not going to make an issue of it. The important thing was to get the damned formula so Complete Abandon could get going. She shrugged her shoulders. "If you're satisfied with things as they are, then I'm satisfied."

"Great." He said, as he stood and headed to the stairs.

"I thought maybe you'd like to spend the night," she said hesitantly.

"That'll come in time. This is not my week for women."

She almost laughed. "What do you mean, 'not your week? Are you gay?"

"No. It's just that I like to experiment and as I said, this is not my week for women."

"Is this burglary thing also an experimental event?"

"Oh, no, I've done that before. You see, I like to take chances. The riskier something is the more of a charge I get from it."

He was one huge bundle of surprises, Lydia thought. Next thing he'll tell me is he's a cop and I'm under arrest for conspiracy. "Okay, I just thought I'd offer. I'm sure we would have a good time."

"Oh, I'm sure you're right, but there's no rush." As he spoke his face was expressionless; then he winked and smiled. A wink, a smile, the smile turning into a leer, that was the Dennis she recognized. That was the Dennis she thought she had learned to handle and disregard. That was the Dennis who vanished as this Dennis spoke. It was eerie. He was two people. For years she had been exposed to one and then tonight, in a matter of minutes, another was revealed.

He stared at her for a moment and then started up the stairs with her trailing. When they got upstairs to the entrance hallway, he looked at the staircase going up to Gert's and walked halfway up. Then he came down and said Gert's door locks and the lock on the street door were standard and could be opened in seconds. A moment later, she let him out the front door and watched him as he walked down the street

Walking back down the stairs, she reviewed what had taken place. It was still hard to believe. He was hard to believe. The entire situation was crazy, but, most important, it was going to happen. He would do it, break in, steal the analysis, and turn the lab upside down. By next week, she would have what she wanted. No more bullshit for her. The big time was waiting.

CHAPTER 27

At precisely half past ten, Sol started his morning constitutional. Traipsing around the Village was fun for him and incredibly invigorating. He loved to see what was new since his last walk and what new people he could meet—the outsiders, or as he thought of them, the off-islanders. In general, the same people hung on for years, but things were always changing and new folks were constantly appearing.

The building in which Sol lived had twenty-three floors with six apartments per floor and that represented at least 138 people if every apartment had only one person in it. Since there were some families in the building that meant there were more than 138 people in the building and he always wondered where they came from and what they did. He also wondered how he could meet more of them than he did in the short elevator ride to his third-floor place. He promised himself that if he ever were to move again, he would settle on a higher floor, so in that longer elevator ride he would be able to meet more people.

The sun was shining gloriously as he walked the twenty yards from his building's entrance on 13th Street to Seventh Avenue where he set out for 33rd Street. He knew that twenty city blocks were a rough equivalent to one mile, so his marching was guided by that figure. He intended to walk to 33rd Street for a healthy two-miler. The plan was to walk up the east side of Seventh and then cross over so he could do the downtown leg on the west side of the avenue. But when he reached 23rd Street, he remembered Gert's morning request to stop by her place and water the outside geraniums. She was highly pissed with Lydia for once again neglecting the plants and she had forgotten to water them herself.

He had turned a new leaf and was truly trying to be a decent and helpful friend, so Sol assured Gert he would go to her place, water the plants, and also give them a shot of her very own, specially formulated fertilizer. A few weeks before Gert had given him keys to her place, figuring that sooner or later, it would make sense for another person to have a way in. In return, Sol had given her the keys to his apartment. Neither would admit it, but they were aware of and worried about the looming disaster of old age and were smart enough to know help might be needed at any time. So, he changed his mind and started back when he reached 23rd Street. He figured he would get to Gert's in a little more than thirty minutes.

Dennis was all smiles at 10:45 as he turned the corner from 6th Avenue to 13th Street, acknowledging the three people who had nodded and smiled at him. The small corrugated cardboard package he carried under his arm was light and easy to handle because it held nothing more than two small pry bars, four cans of spray paint, and a glass jar of lighter fluid. In his other hand he carried the usual clipboard. He knew how to play this role and do what people expected him to do. No matter what part he played, no matter what character he impersonated, his performance was always calculated to match audience expectations. And, in this case, he had figured those expectations were generated by the way the character he was playing was depicted in numerous TV commercials.

Today he was a UPS delivery man. He wore the complete brown uniform and looked the part from his hat to his shoes. The glasses and the paste-on mustache made him look ordinary and eminently forgettable. But nonetheless, he presented a crisp, authentic manner and when people smiled at him as they did on TV, he smiled and winked back. To the outside world, he was just another well-mannered delivery man from United Parcel doing his best to carefully and quickly get precious merchandise safely delivered.

When he got to Gert's, he walked up the steps and faced the front doors so his body would shield his inserting one of the pry bars between them. He applied just enough pressure to spread them and free the latch from the striker plate. When the plate was clear, the door swung open and he was instantly inside the downstairs hallway. By not acting furtively and proceeding at the pace of a real UPS delivery man, no one would think him less than usual even if they did notice him. As was the case, he was seen by several people, but they dismissed him as a regular part of the cityscape and went about their business as they figured he was going about his.

Once inside, he crossed the small landing and quickly scaled the steps to Gert's door and after picking the lock was inside her apartment. Knowing the elevator's entrance was in a bedroom closet, it took him but a moment to find that closet. Using an elevator to descend one level seemed silly to him, but he got a kick out of Gert's extravagance. He knew no one who would expend so much money for something that was absolutely unnecessary. Walking down or up one flight of steps was not an obstacle worth the trouble involved to circumvent it, but why not? Why not spend the dough on a whim if you felt like it. He thought he would like Gert if he ever had a chance to meet her.

When the elevator door opened in the lab, he remained in the small car for a full minute, listening for any sound. He welcomed the silence, and when he was comfortable, stepped into the room lit a small penlight to find the light switches. Seeing them, he flipped them on. Under the bright fluorescents, he was able to easily scan the entire interior. Its neat compactness and lack of wasted space impressed him. Keen design was never an accident, and it was clear this work place represented a great deal of thought. Everything in it looked efficient and custom made to fit the available area. He had to hand it to Gert. If she designed this place, then she was really special.

The far wall held the window casings which he could see were intact but closed off to the outside by full wooden covers. There was no natural light coming in from anywhere. Looking around, he saw the file cabinet along the wall opposite the two large work tables. He moved to the file cabinet, and finding it unlocked opened the top drawer, in which he saw about eight inches of alphabetized yellow file folders. Even with the alphabetization, it was going to be tough to find the right one, but he had some hunches about how she would have filed it.

First he looked for "perfume" but found nothing. Then he went to the *A*'s for "analysis" and again found nothing. Then rather than trying to figure how her mind worked, he decided to go through them one by one. After three minutes of searching, he found what he was looking for. It was in a folder marked "Coleman/Merrill" and as soon as he checked it to be sure it held the original analysis, he pulled all the other files out and threw them on the floor.

Then he went to the cabinets, removed every glass container, and had an enjoyable time throwing them at the far wall. After smashing all the glassware, he deliberately set about breaking every item in the lab that was breakable. Everything exposed that could be broken he threw against the wall or smashed to the floor. After ten minutes of flinging and smashing, every fragile item was in pieces. Nothing breakable was left intact.

Satisfied with the damage, he took the spray cans from the box and began his art work. First, he sprayed "Kill the Jews" on one wall and added several large swastikas. Then, with red and green paint, he created nonsense graffiti that would look symbolically important to anyone searching for meaning. He then sprayed pentagrams and satanic symbols on the table tops and, by standing on one of them, was able to reach the ceiling, on which he sprayed, in black and green, "the devil loves all evil." On the wall across from his bait for the Jews, he wrote "don't fuck with poor people." For a moment he was tempted to substitute "Latinos" or "Blacks" for "poor people" but figured a nonspecific approach would prove more confusing. As he was spray painting these messages, he wondered if the current immigrant explosion would create an entirely new set of scapegoats for community misdeeds. In a few years, he figured new graffiti would spell out "don't fuck with the Pakistanis," but that time was not yet, so "poor folks" would have to do. He finished by spray painting everything he could reach.

After admiring his artwork, he walked back to the file cabinet and built a pile for burning with file folders, paper towels, some newspapers he found, and the cardboard box he carried in along with everything else that would burn. Wiping his fingerprints from the paint cans, he added them to the pile. Then carefully, he doused it all with lighter fluid and after smashing the jar against the wall, dropped a match onto the mess and watched it ignite with a whoosh of bright orange flame that slowly began to curl the papers to black ash. When he was certain everything was thoroughly engulfed, he headed for the elevator and was back in Gert's bedroom in less than twenty seconds. With the pry bars in his jacket pocket and the analysis safe on the clipboard, he headed for the front door.

Using the key Gert had given to him Sol entered the hallway and slowly proceeded up the stairs. At the top landing, he heard a noise he recognized. It was the sound made by Gert's elevator. She must be at home, he thought, since no one else was ever allowed in the lab and that's the only place the elevator went. Its movement would have to mean Gert was at home, but he knew that would be impossible because she was at school at this time.

Thoroughly confused, he opened the front door and slowly walked toward the bedroom to check on the noise he had heard when he saw a man dressed in a UPS outfit stepping from the elevator.

"Hey, what are you doing here and what were you doing in the lab?" Sol asked.

Dennis knew things could go wrong during any robbery and always planned to play out the hand that was dealt. So facing Sol, he said, "I was making a delivery."

Sol was momentarily befuddled, but he couldn't accept the fact that the delivery was made to the lab itself and not to the hallway where all packages and mail were usually delivered. "Where is Gert?" he asked.

Playing dumb, Dennis answered, "Gert? Oh, you mean the lady. She's stayed in the lab. The package I delivered was heavy so I followed her to the lab and after I put it on a table, she told me to leave."

It didn't seem right to Sol, so he loudly called out, "Gert, are you okay? Gert answer me if you're okay." There was no answer.

After a few seconds of staring at Dennis, Sol said, "I don't like this. Something is going on. I don't believe she's here. What are you doing here?"

"I delivered a package is all, now why don't you be a good guy and let me get back to my job."

"I didn't see any truck outside. I think you're a phony. What's going on?"

"Nothing that concerns you old man. But your being here now concerns me and that's bad news for you."

And before Sol could do anything, Dennis moved a step closer and punched him in the face. Reeling from the force of the blow, Sol tried to keep his balance but could not. Struggling to stay upright he stumbled backward into a wall and blindly reaching out, his hand touched a small vase on a side table. He clutched it and with all his strength, threw it at Dennis. As Dennis ducked the thrown vase, Sol grabbed the side table and threw that at Dennis and ran for the door. Easily ducking the thrown objects, Dennis ran after Sol who had reached the front door and pulled it open. Dennis caught him and forcibly spun Sol around. Then he punched him again as hard as he could.

Sol felt an enormous force and realized he was stumbling backwards. Although his brain was focused on his mouth and the searing pain, a portion of his awareness shifted to the back of his head as it rebounded from the wall behind him. He tried to see but there was nothing but blackness and flashes of light as he felt himself losing his balance. He felt his legs weren't holding him up so he tried to regain his equilibrium, but started to slip sideways. "I'll fall down the stairs if…" were the words he knew he was saying to himself as he did fall. Then his mind was filled with a jumble of words that made no sense. True to his life, he was trying to sort them out, trying to grasp what was happening. While he was straining for understanding, he heard a loud crunching noise and then he sensed nothing more as he was wrapped in thick darkness.

Sol had reeled backwards and after teetering on the top step for a moment he fell. The back of his head hit the top landing wall first and then his body twisted and somersaulted down the remaining steps. As he fell, his shoulders and head smashed into every step as his body twisted and turned its way down to the landing.

Dennis stood at the top of the staircase watching Sol fall. He watched the old man careen down the staircase, his body making no sound except for the muffled thumps as it hit each of the carpeted steps. There was an unreal silence enveloping everything until Dennis heard a sharp cracking noise that brought him back to the moment. He had no way of knowing that the cracking noise he heard came from Sol's neck as his head twisted at a sufficient angle to snap vertebrae.

After Sol's body came to rest, Dennis waited. Carefully watching for any movement and seeing none, he cautiously started down the stairs intending to hit Sol again if he was still conscious.

Intently watching Sol at the bottom of the stairs, Dennis tried hard to control himself as he made his way down the staircase. He reached the landing and peered at Sol's twisted body. Not really caring if the old man was unconscious or dead, he looked to see if there was a sign of pulse on the side of Sol's neck. Dennis watched for a full minute and seeing nothing that would indicate Sol being alive, he leaned down and grabbed Sol's wrist. Detecting no pulse, Dennis frowned but was absolutely unconcerned that he had killed the old man. Staring at Sol's body Dennis thought "a tough break for you old man" and stepped over him to reach the exterior door. Opening it, he carefully made his way to the outside steps. Unconcerned with what he had done, he casually walked down the outside staircase and still looking like the friendly UPS man, walked away from the brownstone.

CHAPTER 28

Gert's building on 13th Street was separated from a similar brownstone on 12th Street by two backyards. One was Gert's, the other belonged to the people opposite. While Gert rented one third of her place, the 12th Street people occupied the entire building. Owning a private house in New York City's Greenwich Village would be more than enough for most people, but the folks opposite Gert gilded their lily by taking enormous pride in their small backyard. Unlike Gert, they planted various items and cared for the plot of earth that was theirs. Possibly foolishly, Gert had left to Lydia the care of their few in-residence flowers, especially the out-front geraniums. Not caring for the botanical chores she had reluctantly inherited, Lydia dismissed the entire issue.

Because Gert's first-floor laboratory was quite effectively sealed off at both front and rear, no one over the fence heard a sound of Dennis' doings and Sol's undoing. But what they did become aware of was the smell of fire. In the outback between New York City and California there are an abundance of real fireplaces, wood-burning stoves, and the like, so the smell of burning is common and generally unnoticed. But in New York City, a fireplace is an uncommon and expensive proposition because wood has to be imported. The upshot was that most people with a working unit never bother with it because it is more trouble than its fantasy is worth. The people over the fence never used theirs and reserved their ancestral ceremonial need for fire by weekly offerings to their professional barbecue grill which was the size of a Volkswagen Beetle and had more chrome than a 1958 Oldsmobile.

About fifteen minutes after Dennis murdered Sol and disappeared into the crowds of Sixth Avenue, one of the over-the-fence-family members, reading the newspaper while stretched out in a hammock, sniffed the air and realized something was burning. The identification of what was being consumed became important. It was not the season for fireplaces and it was not the weekend, so barbecuing was ruled out, and that left the backyard sniffer with the frightful possibility that one of the nearby houses was on fire. To be certain it was one of the nearby homes and not his, a leap from the hammock and a hasty but complete tour of his premises certified it had to be a neighbor's misfortune.

Standing in his backyard and looking over the fence directly at Gert's, provided the witness with realization that smoke was coming through the cracks in the boarded-up second floor windows. Not wanting to be a fool, an alarmist or both, he waited until bright orange tongues of flame followed the smoke through the cracks. The dancing flashes of fire motivated his leap into action with a breathless call to 911.

While Dennis was walking up 13th Street to Sixth, the fire he started had crept across the floor and attacked walls, cabinets, and all else flammable. By the time the alarm was sounded, the fire had burned everything in the lab and was eating its way down to Lydia's and up to Gert's. The wall that separated the lab from the first floor interior hallway was the first to go, and when it did, the fire was free to rip upward. The outside walls, being fireproofed cement block forced the fire inward. In very little time, the entire interior was blazing.

Most folks encounter responding fire companies when they raucously go by. With sirens screaming, horns blaring, and lights flashing, the giant machines swoop into an intersection or come roaring down a street and then are gone. However, when they do stop, they are a sight to behold. With dexterity and coordination matching professional jugglers, the firefighters leap into action. One unit deploys hoses, attaches them to hydrants, and carefully directs the torrents. Other units break down doors and sidle into the inferno seeking to rescue any unfortunates. The first two men up the exterior steps of Gert's building and through the outside doors found Sol at the base of the blazing interior staircase. His body was quickly removed and a rapid search revealed no other occupants. Judging that all humans had been found and since no pets were known of, the fire teams poured water onto and into the burning building.

Officially, the fire was brought under control in less than forty minutes after the first alarm was called in, but in that time, most of the building's interior was destroyed. Since fire burns upward with greater ferocity than down, Gert's apartment was more damaged than Lydia's. But as anyone who has had a fire befall them knows, it makes little difference how much actual fire damage is involved. The stink of smoke and the tons of water create a problem few can live with after the fire is out. Essentially, the building was done in.

Since a dead body was found, the agencies to deal with it spring into action as did the others whose work involved the fiery death of a structure. The local precinct police, the coroner's office, the fire police, the Sanitation Department, building inspectors, utility company representatives, insurance agents, and last, but not least important by any means, French Cuff (Clean Up From Fire) arrives, it being an organization that boards up glassless windows and carts away debris city workers refuse to handle.

It would take a little less than three weeks for Gert to get the go-ahead to start the next step—rebuild or demolish her once-admired private home.

CHAPTER 29

That morning Gert was teaching a chemistry class when a campus security guard entered her classroom. The fellow who came in spoke just enough English to make clear it was important she call the phone number on the otherwise blank piece of paper he handed to her. While the students waited, Gert went to her office and made the call, to the Sixth Precinct it turned out. She calmly received the news that her house was on fire. Upon returning to the classroom and telling the students the class was canceled because her house was burning down, they thought it a joke, because she displayed no more emotion than what was usual when a quiz was returned.

Her usual leisurely walk home was hurried because when she hit Sixth Avenue the stretch from 8th to13th Street was covered in half the usual time as she grew increasingly anxious. Approaching her place she saw two large fire engines, a rescue truck, three police cars, an ambulance and lots of people everywhere. She pushed her way through the crowd and would have walked up the exterior steps if she wasn't stopped by a cop.

"Hey lady, where ya goin?" he asked her.

"Where am I going?" She responded, looking at him with confused eyes. "I'm going to my home. I live here." The cop moved closer and put his arm around her shoulders. Then, gently, but forcefully he walked her to the curb and stood her against a parked van.

"Lady, you ain't gonna be livin' in there for a while. Most of it was done in by the fire."

Gert knew the look on her face must be strange, because she understood the words he used but couldn't shake the feeling she was dreaming—that all she was seeing and hearing wasn't really happening.

"Wait right here and don't go anywhere," he said. "I'm gonna find some brass who need information." Gert nodded as the cop walked away. In what seemed like a moment, he was back with a uniformed fireman wearing a white helmet and a policeman with sergeant's chevrons. The cop wore a name tag—Murphy.

The fireman wearing the helmet asked, "Miss, the neighbors tell us the building is owned by Doctor Gertrude Lehman, a chemistry professor at NYU. Would that be you?"

"It's Gert and yes, that's me."

"Well, let me be the first to tell you how sorry we are that you have had this misfortune. My men will save what can be saved, have no fear." Gert nodded. The fireman went on. "Dr. Lehman, Sergeant Murphy here has some questions that have to be asked right now. Are you ready for that?" Again, Gert nodded.

Murphy swallowed and then asked, "Dr. Lehman was anyone stayin' at your place. Did you have any guests? Was someone else livin' in the house?"

Gert stared at the policeman not fully grasping what he was getting at. "No one lives with me. I live alone, but wait, I rent the basement apartment to a young woman. My God, was she hurt?"

"No ma'am, there was no young woman found anywhere. Was it possible your tenant had a guest or maybe her father stayin' with her?"

"No, she lived alone and had no guests I knew of. Why do you ask about a man?"

Both the fireman and the policemen removed their hats. "We did find a gentleman inside the building. An older man, over sixty, I'd say. A distinguished looking gentleman, white hair, glasses."

As soon as he said that, she knew it was Sol. "Earlier in the day," she slowly said, "I asked a friend to stop by and water the plants there." She pointed to the concrete planters by the steps. "Where is he? Was he hurt?"

Neither man said anything, their silence confirming what she feared. "Oh, my God." she exclaimed.

They stared at her for a moment, and then the policeman opened a small black notebook, looked at a page and asked, "Would your friend's name be Solomon Woodrow?"

"Oh my God," Gert exclaimed. "What happened?" She felt empty and didn't know what to do. She wanted to scream and cry and pound something, but all she could do was stand motionless as the two men stared at her.

"At this point, we don't know what happened to Mr. Woodrow. He was found at the base of the interior staircase. First reports, which are only speculative, indicate he may have fallen down the stairs. Possibly he was upstairs and when he smelled smoke, tried to rush outside and fell. We won't know much more than that until we get the coroner's report."

"He wasn't burned was he?"

"No, ma'am, it's an educated guess the fall was responsible, but as I said, we'll have to wait for the official announcement." The policeman wrote something in the notebook and closed it.

"Where is he? What's been done with him?

"He's been taken to the morgue, ma'am, and his body can't be released until the cause of death has been determined."

"I want to bury him. He was my friend, you know. He was my good friend, my closest friend."

She stared into space as the policeman said, "You'll be able to do that in time, ma'am, and we'll help as much as we can."

"It's so sad," Gert said. "He was a good person."

"I'm sure he was," the policeman said. "I'm sure he was."

The fireman hesitated as if making a decision and then asked, "If it's okay, I'd like to ask you about the building. Do you think you can answer some questions?" Gert nodded.

He asked her about the arrangement of the living quarters and about the laboratory that was on the middle floor. He apologized when he told her they had to break through a wall to get to the lab because they could find no immediate access to that space. Still concerned with the lab, his tension eased when she assured him there were no radioactive or toxic materials to be concerned about. Neither man would or could tell her much about how the fire started, but they reassured her that the fire police were extremely efficient and they would have conclusions in a short time. They asked her questions about the electric wiring, the equipment she had in the lab, whether she had any ongoing experiments cooking by themselves and if she had any idea how a fire might start. They talked for about half an hour and when they were finished, Gert asked if she could go through the house. They advised against that since the staircase had been burned and its stability had not been checked, but would be by tomorrow. After they asked if she had a place to stay for the night, and when she told them she did, they went back to their men to finish their work.

CHAPTER 30

They left Gert leaning against the van looking up at the building and thinking about Sol. What a way to die... falling down a flight of stairs seemed so ordinary, so foolish almost silly. She realized she would miss him terribly. He was like my anchor she thought. He may have thought I was his rock, his safe port in the storm, but it was the other way round. Oh, my good friend, she sobbed, I will miss you so.

Still staring at the house, her thoughts shifted to the building itself. Her face hardened a bit as she thought of how hard she had worked to make it into what she wanted. "I did it once, damn it, and I'll do it again!" She said aloud.

A voice at her side asked a question. "Gert, oh Gert, are you all right?"

She turned and saw her neighbor and reaching out clutched her arm, "Mildred, Sol is dead. They found his body inside. They think he fell down the stairs. This is so awful. I can't believe it. How can he be dead? It's ridiculous."

Gert raised a hand to her eyes and smeared her tears over her face. "Oh, Mildred isn't this terrible. My whole life got burned up. All I ever had is up in smoke. What'll I do? What am I going to do?"

"You're going to come inside with me right now and sit down. I know you can't relax, but at least you can sit down. I'll make some coffee."

The woman put her arm on Gert's shoulders and led her to a similar house next to her own. They walked up the steps and went inside. As she walked, Gert felt happy to get away from people staring at her and the firemen and policemen scurrying around like they were warding off an invasion.

As the coffee was dripping, Gert retreated to her neighbor's bathroom to splash water on her face. Looking in the mirror, she studied her face and saw the lines, the pouches, and the sagging skin that exposed her age. She didn't see the face of the relentless young woman who overcame obstacles and became a world-famous chemist. What she did see was the person the young woman had become. The face was old and battered, but there were no bruises like those on battered wives on the six o'clock news, for her bruises weren't red marks or bloodied cuts. They were loose folds of skin and brown liver spots. They were the disappointments, the hoped for successes that came slowly, the mate who didn't exist, and the companions who were slipping away. Now, added to those she could see, was a new one. There with the old was a new hurt, a new painful blotch. Now there was no more Sol to depend upon, to scold, to council, to look after, to get annoyed at, to saunter with. Sol was gone. Dead! A man's life comes to an end in a second or two. She recalled how they talked about dying and how he said he wanted it to be quick. It seems he got that.

Feeling a combination of sadness and disgust with the absolute dumbness of absolutely everything, she very slowly left the bathroom. Fully aware of her silent movements, she wondered if she was trying to be inconspicuous so Death would not find her also. Am I trying to be quiet so I'll blend into the background and be okay? She grunted a quick laugh and went to join her neighbor for that promised cup of coffee.

Sitting with her neighbor Mildred helped, because she was able to sort out her next moves. Never before had Gert no place to go with everything that had been familiar maybe permanently out of reach. She felt like she was dropped on a strange planet with no luggage and no way to change underwear. Realizing everything would have to be bought new staggered her.

The first phone call she made was to Lydia who reacted as if she was joking when Gert told her what had happened. When Lydia asked about her belongings, Gert related what she had been told, that the next day was the day for inspections. For no reason she could pinpoint, she sensed Lydia wasn't terribly shocked or broken up at the news. To Gert's inner ear, Lydia sounded casual and distant.

But before Lydia could hang up Gert said, "There's some additional bad news, very bad news." There was a pause and an intake of breath. "What… What else?" Lydia asked.

"It's Sol."

"What about Sol?"

"He's dead." She hesitated. "The police are guessing he died falling down the stairs."

"What's that you say? Sol… Sol is dead? What was he doing there? How did he get involved?"

"I don't know, but I'm guessing he was doing me a favor. I asked him earlier today if he would water the outside plants, and the only reason he would be inside was to get the water and fertilizer. He had keys."

There was a long silence before Lydia said, "The outside plants. He was watering the outside plants?" After another long pause, she said, "Oh my god, he would be alive if I had watered them. My god, it's my fault."

"Lydia, don't be stupid. Sol didn't die because you're lazy about watering plants. His life was more important than that and anyway God doesn't play such stupid games."

After another long silence, Lydia asked, "What are you going to do?"

"I'm not sure, but you better make arrangements for yourself, maybe rent a hotel room or go to a friend's place."

"Don't worry about me, I'll be okay. I'm worried about you."

"Don't worry about me. I can handle this." Maybe needing to reassure herself, Gert repeated, "Don't worry, I can handle this." Then nodding, she added, "Maybe I'll run into you tomorrow, but before you come over, I think you'd better call the Sixth Precinct to see if it's safe. Ask for Sergeant Murphy. He should know something by then."

"Are you sure you're going to be okay?"

"Don't worry. I'll see you tomorrow."

Gert hung up and called Win, but got no answer. Being momentarily stymied, she finished the coffee and then got a bright idea.

"Mildred, I'm going out for a while. Can I call you if I need a place to sleep?"

"Oh, Gert, don't be silly, of course. I'm always up late. Just come and ring the doorbell."

"Thanks, that's a load off. I'll call you later, one way or the other."

Getting up, Gert grabbed her briefcase and handbag and left. There was a uniformed cop in front of her house and she could see flashlights moving around inside. At least they're looking, she thought as she crossed the street. While talking to Mildred, she remembered Sol had given her a set of his keys when she gave him hers. It occurred to her there would never be a better time to use Sol's apartment.

CHAPTER 31

As she approached Sol's building she had an eerie, haunting feeling that she should not go in, but her practical side won out and she did, nodding at the doorman as she got on the elevator.

Like his mind, Sol's place was neat and orderly with fitted bookcases, small tables and chairs, traditional upholstery, and ample lighting where it had to be. She found his phone book and went through it identifying the names she heard him refer to as friends. She called each and broke the news. Cyril, in particular, was very emotional when he heard what had happened and Gert could hear his voice change from sadness to anger and then back to sadness when he regained his composure and insisted on handling all the funeral arrangements. Lastly, she called Win, but again got no answer.

Sitting there in Sol's apartment amidst the things he had accumulated was ghostly. There was no way to avoid what she saw and not recall what Sol had told her about each item. She looked at a small metal sculpture on a piece of marble or alabaster and she could hear his voice boasting about getting the whatever-it-was for a great price in Mexico. As she stared at his things, she started to cry and in an effort to control her grief, threw herself on the sofa. But that made her cry all the more.

She lost track of how long she cried, but she was just getting herself under control when the phone rang. With almost no hesitation she got up from the sofa and was about to lift the phone when she realized where she was. "Do I dare?" she asked herself. She hoped the caller would give up and make things easy, but the phone kept ringing. Finally, she gave in.

"Hello."

"Hello." There was a pause, then "Gert is that you? Where's Sol?"

"Win, I've been trying to reach you. Where are you?"

"What's the matter? Is something wrong? Your voice sounds funny. What's the matter? Where's Sol?"

"Win, are you home?"

"No. I'm down the block. I'm at Two Horatio."

"Come over to Sol's, something's happened."

"I'll be right there. Are you okay?"

She hesitated and then said, "Can you just come over, please?"

"Okay, five minutes."

It took less than that for him to be banging on the door. With him was a stunning young woman who Gert had never before seen.

Win took Gert's arm and walked her to the sofa. "What happened?"

"Oh, Win, I don't' know how to tell you. Sol's gone. There was a fire in my place and it seems he was trying to get out and oh, I don't know what happened, but the cops think he fell down the stairs because they found him at the bottom."

As he stared at her, Gert saw his face change. He looked like he had eaten spoiled food and needed to spit it out. "Son of a bitch, I don't believe it. How can he be dead?"

He looked across the room to where the girl sat, and Gert could see her face reflecting the pain he was feeling. "Oh, Lou, you never even met him." She got up and came to his side and when she put her hand on his shoulder, he reached up and put an arm around her waist. "I'm sorry," she said, as he pulled her a bit closer.

"Win," Gert asked, "you want to introduce me?"

He looked at her and then at the girl at his side. "Oh, god, I forgot, forgive me." Shaking his head like he was trying to clear it, he said, "Gert Lehman this is Loretta Anderson." They nodded at each other.

Gert smiled at the girl who looked like a television shampoo ad with those elegant, innocent and beautiful young women who had flowing and glistening hair. "Please drag over a chair," Gert said to her, and Loretta picked up one of Sol's tall dining chairs and brought it closer to the sofa.

"Gert, tell me what happened. Tell me about the fire. What happened? How did it start?"

"Win, I wish I could tell you something that made sense, but all I can tell you is what I know." As Gert spoke, Loretta reached over and took Gert's hand in hers and Gert smiled at her, thinking it a very sweet gesture.

"Win, less than two hours ago I was in class and a guy from security comes in and tells me to call the Sixth Precinct. I go back to my office, call and they tell me my house is on fire. So I cancel the class, rush back to my house and find the street filled with fire trucks, cop cars, ambulances, you name it." She took a breath. "By then, the fire is out and my place looks like 1945 Berlin. The cops and the fire guys question me about my lab and tell me they had to break through a wall to get to the lab and then they tell me they found a body and it's Sol. They took him away to the coroner and will let us know the cause of death when they determine it. That's it. Aside from having a cup of coffee with my neighbor and coming over here to make some calls, that's it. You got it all."

He stared at her. "That's crazy. How the hell does a fire start and burn down the whole place?"

"I don't know, but I'm very suspicious about it. My wiring and heating system were basically new and in great shape. I don't believe this was an act of God event. There's something fishy here."

Loretta broke in. "You mean arson?"

"Look, I don't know, but I just can't believe it started by itself."

Win hesitated. "Do you think maybe Sol started the fire?"

"No… I doubt it. There'd be no reason for him to start a fire. It's warm out and… no, that can't be. Of all the things that make no sense, Sol starting a fire would be number one."

"Are the fire investigators looking into it?" Win asked.

"Oh yeah, when I was coming over here, I saw them poking around inside. I don't know what they'll find, but I hope they find something. I don't want this thing written off as one of those mysterious and unaccountable events."

"They're pretty good at their job. I did a piece on them a year ago and they know the score. If something isn't kosher they'll find it."

Gert asked Loretta, "You're a writer?"

"I work for *MK* magazine; write under the name of 'Lou Anders.'"

"Lou Anders." Gert hesitated, then said, "Wait a minute, that magazine piece involved a fire in the Bronx, the one with Roman Candles on the roof?"

"That's right."

Win broke in. "Gert, this is the most wonderful female I have ever met. I'm so sorry Sol isn't here to meet her." He paused. "God, I can't believe he's gone. This is so crazy."

"No, Win. It's what life really is. Everyone expects enough time to do all the things they hope and dream about, but there isn't any time. You're here and then boom, you're not."

"I know, I know. Everyone says that all the time, but how do you get it under your belt? How do you understand what that means?"

"I wish I could answer that." She stopped and looked at Loretta. "What I can tell you is that I still see myself like you see yourself. I feel young. I think young. My mind is young even though I know I'm not. I know my hands are old and my feet are old. All my parts are old and any second one of them might fail and bingo, it's over. It's so weird, when I look in the mirror I see what is and also what isn't there. The mirror is a friend, but somehow it lies to me."

They sat in silence and Loretta looked around the apartment rather than say anything. She noticed the touches that made it personal. "I would have liked to have met him. Judging from his taste, I think I would have liked him."

"There's no question," Win said as Gert nodded.

"Hey," said Gert, "you know, I'm hungry. I haven't eaten anything since this morning. Why don't we go out?"

"Good idea, good idea. But before we do that, I want to know where you're going to sleep tonight."

"Well, my neighbor Mildred invited me so I can sleep in her place, but," she looked around. "I think I'm going to sleep here. I feel comfortable and relaxed here. Maybe it's a way to say good-bye. Does that bother you?"

"Hell, no." Win said. "There is no right thing to do"

Gert nodded. "But what do we do now?"

As Gert and Win stared at each other, Loretta said, "Look, our lives haven't ended, so we just go on and do what we usually do. I think that's the answer."

Gert nodded. "You're right, and you know what? I'm even hungrier now. How about you two? Are you hungry?"

Win smiled. "That sounds good to me," he said.

Looking better than they had only minutes before, they got up, and after Gert used the bathroom and called Mildred, they went to the Spanish place on Greenwich and had a meal Sol would have loved.

CHAPTER 32

Something wasn't right, maybe a noise or an odor. She didn't know what it was, but it registered and it scared her. There! A noise, it was something mechanical and electric. It hummed. *Did I leave a machine on in the lab?* Chiding herself for possibly leaving something running, she was ready to throw back the covers to go and check.

Wait a minute, she said to herself, wait. That noise. It was an elevator. *Mine?* Then she rubbed the blanket between her fingers. It was flannel, her blanket wasn't flannel. She strained to see, but there was nothing but blackness.

Suddenly, the straining to see paid off. Seeing became easier. The sky brightened. She could see a little. She was in a boat, a small boat and it was gently rocking. She was holding an oar. Glancing to her right, she saw Sol. They were seated side by side in the boat, a rowboat on a lake. She pulled at the oar, dug it deeply into the water and hauled the handle to her chest. The boat surged as it reacted to her force, but they got nowhere because he wasn't rowing. They were going in circles because he wasn't rowing.

She could only see Sol in profile, because she could only glance sideways, but she could see he looked tired. "Row, Sol, row," she cried, but he didn't move. His hands were locked on the oar, its paddle dragging in the water. "Sol, you have to row. We're going in circles. Sol, row, row!"

As she dragged at the oar she looked down and saw their feet. Hers strained against the decking for leverage, but Sol's weren't moving. He wasn't moving. *Why isn't he moving?* She wondered. Instantly, the question struck her. Was he holding the oar in the water or was the oar holding him in the seat?

It grew brighter and she could see more clearly. She pushed her body sideways as far as she could from his because there was no other way to see him. She saw that his eyes were closed and he was pale. "Sol, Sol," she cried and pushed at his shoulder with her own. He moved. Finally, she thought, finally. His body pushed forward and she thought to gather strength for a rearward pull on the oar, but he didn't move back. He slumped forward and collapsed on the oar. Then slowly, like he was a wisp of smoke, he slid under the oar to the bottom of the boat. Then the oar he had leaned on silently slipped into the water. She watched it float away.

She let go of her oar and grabbed for him. Her fingers closed on his jacket and she pulled, but he was too heavy. She couldn't get him back up beside her. Frustrated, and angry, she tried again. Leaning over, she grabbed at him at the same time her oar slipped into the water. She let go of him and tried to grab the oar, but it was too late, it was gone.

The boat straightened slowly. They were no longer moving in a circle. Crumpled in the bottom of the boat, Sol was motionless. Everything was still. She leaned forward trying to reach him, but he moved away from her. She saw water in the boat. There was water touching her shoes. Sol was dissolving in the water. The bottom of the boat was melting and he was melting. She reached into the water for him, but there was nothing to hold onto. He and the water had become one and when she looked again, he was gone. There was only water. He was no longer there.

"Sol," she cried. "Where are you? Where have you gone?"

Then she looked up and peered into the light which was getting brighter, but there was still nothing to see. She reached to the light and felt cloth. Cloth? How could there be cloth where there is light? But it was cloth and she touched it and clenched it between her fingers. It felt like flannel, soft, nappy and warm. She flung it away and a brighter light flooded into her eyes. It was the sun. Sunlight! She bolted upright in the bed, blinded by the sunlight streaming through the window. Shielding her eyes, she turned from the light and saw Sol's apartment spread out around her. It all came back in a rush, everything came back and she flopped back on the bed as tears filled her eyes.

Three hours later she was walking across the street, feeling competent for arranging everything that needed arranging. She had managed to locate a qualified substitute who would cover her classes until things got settled. She had also spoken to Sol's building manager and he agreed to let her use the apartment for as long as she needed it. His only concern was that the utility bills got paid when they were due.

She had called the local precinct, and Murphy told her he would meet her at her place because there were questions in need of answers. He also said they would be meeting the assigned fire police investigator, who also had questions. Her insurance agent said his actions were governed by the ongoing investigations, but she needn't worry, because everything was up to date and the company would have no reason to delay payment unless arson was involved which might create a delay.

CHAPTER 33

Walking to the house, she saw Murphy speaking to a guy in a hard hat who held a clipboard. When she was about fifty feet away they separated and the guy with the hard hat got into a double parked van with city markings, which promptly sped away. As Murphy turned and saw her, a uniformed fireman came down her front steps.

"Good morning to you, ma'am, how are ya doin' today?"

"Good morning to you, Sergeant Murphy. I'm doing as well as can be expected. What's going on?"

"Well, ma'am the city inspector just left, and he said there's no danger of anything collapsing and that the building is still in good shape and can be easily rebuilt. Just the interior got it and it all looks a lot worse than it really is. I guess that's kinda good news, right?"

"Better than I thought, but it's still a sonofabitch."

He smiled. "Now that's the truth."

The fireman joined them and after introductions, Murphy waited outside while the fireman and Gert went inside. As they went up steps into the burned-out house, Gert blurted out, "God damn!" The fireman with her, named Conroy, looked at her and said, "You may not believe it, but this is not bad. It may look awful, but everything's still solid."

Gert was staring at an enormous hole in the wall that exposed the interior of the laboratory. "How the hell did that happen? Was there an explosion?"

"Nope," said Conroy. "The boys did that to get in there. You really didn't think they were going to be getting on the bedroom elevator and calmly riding downstairs to get to your laboratory?"

"But did they have to make such a big hole?"

He half smiled when he said, "Ma'am, when they made that hole this place was the inside of a barbeque. They weren't overly concerned with the interior decoration or desecration."

"Okay, okay, don't rub it in." She paused and then asked, "Tell me, Fireman Conroy, do you like your work?"

He laughed. "First of all, it's Lieutenant Conroy, and second, I love this job. I took it when I was rejected by the FBI because I smoked pot in college and third, this was the best job I could find where I would be paid for solving puzzles."

"You were rejected by the FBI for smoking pot in college?"

"That's right. They have their rules, you know."

"What assholes."

They walked through the hole in the wall into the lab. As soon as Gert entered she saw the just barely discernible words, "Kill the Jews" on the opposite wall. "What the hell is that? Who wrote that?" she yelled out.

"We were hoping you might have an answer," Conroy said, as he walked to the wall. "Have you ever been bothered by neighborhood vandals or by anyone who might hold a grudge? Was there ever a student who got a bee up their bottom about you? Is there anything you can think of that might explain this?"

"Sonofabitch, goddamn sonofabitch," she said, as she walked to the wall and looked at the words and the remnants of the swastikas. "I don't believe this shit. Is this Munich in 1939?"

"Doctor Lehman, for a moment, let's try to get past what you see, 'cause at times things aren't what they seem. Please try to be cool about this."

He crossed over to her. "Consider this. Sometimes vandals do things like that because they're nasty and they mean it. Other times, things like this get done to divert attention. It's very easy to ignite passions and have us wasting our energy running after phantoms."

Gert looked at him. "You're a cool character, Lieutenant. That's very smooth thinking."

Smiling, he took a little bow. "Now, to business. Was there anything in this lab or in the house worth taking, worth stealing, that could be covered up with a little fire, a convenient track covering fire?"

That's a good question Gert thought. Then out loud, she mused, "Now, what do I have, what did I have worth taking? There was a little cash, no antiques, some jewelry, but nothing of great value. My lab equipment was standard, nothing custom or rare. My patents are in my bank vault. There was nothing of value here, nothing that would warrant this."

As she swept her arm in an arc, a fleeting thought pushed into her brain. Everything in the lab had been around for a while. The perfume analysis was the only item that was newly done, but she dismissed that as ridiculous. "No." she repeated. "There was nothing."

"Then it really could have been vandals, just screwing around?" he asked.

"Hell, I don't know." She looked at the burned-out tables, the smashed glassware, and the broken equipment. "Tell me, Lieutenant, do you have any idea how it started?"

"Yes, I do."

"Well okay, goddamn it. Let's hear it."

He walked to the file cabinet. "As you can see, this cabinet is empty and that means someone emptied it. I wondered why it was emptied and the conclusion I came to is that something was taken from it and by emptying and burning what remained, it'd be impossible to know what was taken."

As he spoke, Gert again thought of the analysis which was the only item in the cabinet that was worth taking. All the rest was old and essentially worthless.

Conroy continued. "If the fire had started by accident, say from a wiring problem, then the contents would still be inside. Burned or not, it wouldn't be empty. Since the fire trail, which you can see on the floor, started in front of the cabinet, I'd say someone emptied it, poured an accelerant on the papers and boom."

She looked at the floor and saw that it was possible to follow the charred path from that point. "How do you know an accelerant was used?"

"I tested for it and found traces of thinned petroleum distillate—lighter fluid."

"Conroy, don't forget you're talking to a chemist." He smiled at her. "And, you're telling me this fire was not an accident and the motive could be vandalism or cover for a robbery?"

"Exactly, and I've spoken to your neighbors on both sides and in the back, and no one heard a thing. Not one sound. It's possible, but there aren't too many cases of silent vandals. Now, aside from that, no one saw any youngish people on the street yesterday morning and we have never had any reports of vandalism in this neighborhood except for some graffiti"

"So you're ruling out vandalism?"

"Oh, no, I can't rule it out, but I don't think there's enough evidence to pin that tale on the donkey. For my money, I'd say a disguised robbery 80 percent with vandalism at 20 percent. There's just no way to be certain."

"I follow, but now can we go upstairs? I want to see what's left of my prized possessions."

They walked out through the hole in the wall and up the steps, water squishing under their shoes from the still-wet carpets. The door to the apartment was open with the keys she had given to Sol still in the lock. Looking inside, her heart sank when she saw the extent of the damage. Her chairs, tables, the sofa, the plywood countertop she built, paintings, everything in the living room and kitchen, which was over the lab, was gone. A small table that held a small vase was on the other side of the room. She stared at it wondering how it got there.

"I see you looking at that broken table. Why does it interest you?"

"Well, it used to be over here by the door and it held a small vase. The vase is in pieces over there," she pointed. "And the table is not here, but there. Do you think your guys moved it?"

"That's hard to say, a hose has enough pressure to bounce a table like that all around this room, so it's a tough question to answer, but I'll try to find out if that table was moved."

Continuing their inspection, they moved to the bedroom and bath which were in better shape. The farther back in the house, the better things were.

"Well," she said looking around, "this is a pleasant surprise. Aside from the stink, there's not much damage."

"Yeah, you were lucky. The fire was pretty well contained to the lab and the room above it."

He took a step closer to her. "Will you do a favor for me and check your valuables to see if anything's missing?"

Gert went to her dresser and managed to tug open the top drawer. She removed her jewelry box, opened it and held it for him to see. There were gold rings, bracelets and earrings, all her valuables were still there.

"Did you have any cash money around?"

"As a matter of fact, I did. Wait a minute." She went into the bathroom and brought out a flower pot filled with bills. They weren't burned and they weren't wet. She took the money, counted it, and put it in her bag. "That was two hundred bucks in plain sight."

"Well, Doc, in light of that, I'd say my estimates were off. I'd revise now. Since your jewels and money were not taken and the file cabinet's contents indicate a cover-up for a possible theft, I'd say vandalism is now around 5 percent, and a poorly covered-up robbery at 95 percent. I can't see neighborhood nuts leaving the gold and the cash. Normally, they'd come in just for the valuables with a fire a fun thing to celebrate the victory of making a score. Here, there seems to be no score, so why the victory celebration?"

"So it's a robbery, you're telling me."

"That's the way my report's gonna read. I can't see it any other way."

"Okay," she said. "Now what about my friend, Professor Woodrow? What ideas do you have about that?"

"Well, first let me say I'm very, very sorry you lost a friend."

"I appreciate that, but I'm really pissed off and angry that he died. Particularly now that you're telling me this might have been a robbery and to me, that means there's a strong possibility he was murdered and didn't die in a fall."

"I think you're jumping the gun there, Professor. He could've come up the stairs without knowing the lab was on fire, and since the lab was closed off to the stairs, he wouldn't have known anything until he opened the apartment door. Then he might have seen the fire or become aware of it, panicked and in rushing to get out, fell."

"What you say makes sense, Conroy, but wouldn't he have smelled smoke?"

"I can't say, but if he did, then coming upstairs would not have been too bright. I'm going to assume he didn't have an inkling of the fire until he got up to this level."

"Okay, so there are two choices. One, my friend died in the fall trying to get out of here. Or two, in some way he was killed by the bastard who took something and then started the fire, right?"

"There is a third choice that he had a heart attack because of fright and then your two choices wouldn't count." He shook his head. "I think it's best to wait to see what the medical examiner has to say. With that information, we can rule out possibilities and get a better handle on actual events."

Gert wiped a tear from her eye with a handkerchief. "Let me tell you this, Conroy. If it turns out there's a chance he was murdered, I'm going to figure out who did it and settle the score."

"Don't you trust the cops?"

"It's not that I don't trust them, I'll feel better if I get justice my way. I don't dismiss the courts and the system, but they're slow and I'm not young, this has to come to an end before I do."

"Yeah," he said. "I know what you mean. Very often I'd like to kick some butt to get things moving, but that's our system. It's slow and often wrong, but you know, others are worse."

"I know, I know, but I don't care. I'm going to settle this. I'll find out who did all this and save the state some dough. He was my friend."

"Doc, I'm getting the impression you're no soft touch when it comes to students with a sob story."

"Conroy, most of my students think I'm one tough cookie, and they are 100 percent right. So far, I've lived my life guided by what I thought was right. I haven't gone wrong yet and this situation is no different. I respect you and I respect the cops, but I'll do it the way I want."

"Doc, you sound like that TV commercial; 'I'll do it my way.'"

"That was my line before they stole it."

They took a quick look at the back terrace, and if not for some burned rubble on the ground below, there was no way to tell there had been a fire.

She took another look around, flipped through some clothes in the closet and was thrilled to find them untouched although they all smelled from smoke. Then, with Conroy leading the way, she followed him downstairs. When they got to the entrance hall and faced the hole in the wall, Gert said, "I'd like to take a look downstairs, if you don't mind." He nodded agreement and they walked to the doorway that led to Lydia's apartment. The door itself was propped against the wall at the head of the stairs with the remains of its hinges hanging limply on the charred wood.

As they walked down, Gert asked, "Was there much fire damage here?"

"Not that much, really," he answered, "mostly water damage."

She could see he was right. The furniture wasn't burned, but everything had a grimy look to it. Wherever she touched, her fingers left a whitish spot, as the soot that had been there was transferred. A good deal of water was on the floor even though most of it had probably drained to the basement and there was no way she wanted to look down there.

"I hope your tenant has renter's insurance."

"Oh, I'm pretty sure she does. Miss Cornell is too smart to miss that."

"It's amazing how many people don't have that insurance."

"Yeah, you don't take care of yourself you're up a tree, simple as that."

He looked around and she followed his eyes. The fire damaged the ceiling, but little more. The rest of the place was messed up by the water.

"Had enough?" He asked.

"Yeah, I guess she was very lucky." He nodded and they headed for the stairs.

When they got outside, Lydia, who was talking to Murphy, turned and saw them coming down the steps. She put up a hand as if to call a halt to her conversation, ran to Gert, and threw her arms around her. "Oh, Gert, isn't this terrible?"

"You can say that again."

"Sergeant Murphy was telling me what he knows about the fire and poor Sol. I can't believe it. It's unreal."

Gert freed herself from Lydia's embrace and wondered if she gave a damn or was just acting. Then she scolded herself for being harsh and decided to accept Lydia's concern as real.

"Have you checked your place yet?" Gert asked in a soft voice.

"No. I just got here and Sergeant Murphy said I should wait for Lieutenant Conroy before I did that."

"Good idea. He knows his stuff and he'll keep you from disturbing evidence or hurting yourself."

Lydia looked a little startled. "Evidence?" she asked.

"Damn right, evidence." Gert grunted. "This fire looks like a crude attempt to cover up a robbery."

Conroy quickly jumped in. "Wait a minute, please. We have no solid conclusive proof one way or the other. I think it's a bit hasty to conclude it was a robbery with the fire as an added attraction."

"Well, there may not be enough proof for you, but there's enough for me," said Gert.

The three of them stared at her. Then Murphy said, "Professor, I'd like to ask you some questions, if you wouldn't mind. This may be a good time, if you're up to it."

"Am I up to it? Are you kidding?" She turned to Conroy and said with authority, "Lieutenant, take Miss Cornell to see what's left of her stuff. I want to hear what Sergeant Murphy has to ask."

Conroy smiled and saluted, then gestured for Lydia to follow him up the steps. A soon as they were out of sight, Gert turned to Murphy. "Let's have your questions, Sergeant. I want to get to the bottom of this as quickly as possible."

"We all do, Professor Lehman. Believe me, we all do." He looked at the clipboard he carried and then asked, "Professor Lehman, by now you must realize we have our doubts about the reason for this fire. I talked to Conroy and he feels as I do."

"And how do you feel, Sergeant?"

"Well, generally, the idea that this fire was started by vandals who were just having some perverted fun just doesn't wash, even though the wall writing and such gives that indication, I doubt it. Vandals would have had a party in your apartment and also in Miss Cornell's place. Everything in the lab was smashed, but nothing in either apartment. Typical, red-blooded, Greenwich Village thugs would have broken everything they could reach, and since they got into the laboratory, they could have gotten into either apartment. They didn't do that. They confined themselves to the lab and all the damage was in that space. It seems the lab was the major concern of whoever broke in."

"Yes, I thought about that. The only way into the lab was through the elevator in my bedroom. To get to it, they had to go through my bedroom and nothing was broken in there. My jewelry was not touched and cash in the john was not taken. So, whoever it was knew where they were going and what they wanted to do."

"Right you are, Doctor. You have a mind like a policeman."

"The cops don't own logic, Sergeant."

His eyebrows raised as he said, "Right!" Then after a hesitation, he continued. "Now, let's consider this. Let's consider that there was something in the lab someone wanted and they broke in and did what they did, just to get it, whatever it was. Now, can you think of anything in the lab that was valuable enough to justify all this?"

Gert couldn't get the thought of the perfume analysis out of her mind, but she said, "Not really, Sergeant, there is not one thing I can think of that would be worth a fire and a death. But, let me ask you a question."

"Let's say there was a final exam in my files and some students wanted it so they broke in to get it. How could you prove it was taken and didn't burn in the fire?"

"You couldn't. The pile of ash in front of the file cabinet is burned too completely. There's no way to tell if something was taken before the fire."

"Well, let's say I give that final and found people who would not normally get 'A's got great marks. That would prove to me they took it."

"But that's not proof. There could be any number of reasons why bad students improve. Stealing the exam is but one of many possible reasons; you'd need better proof than that."

"Such as?"

"Well, first, a confession, but that doesn't seem likely. Second, an answer or something turns up that could only have come from the stolen exam, but that still doesn't mean it couldn't have come from dumb luck. Nah, if it was a specific object you would be looking for, then all you gotta do is find it—but something on paper, something that could be guessed, how could you prove the students didn't just get lucky and guess right?"

"I see what you're saying. As long as there's a chance the answers could come from luck or from some other way, you can't say those who have them, stole them."

"That's right. It's like two people working on some science project in different parts of the world. They both may come up with the same or right answer at the same time and neither one stole anything. They just got to the same place at the same time."

"It happens all the time."

"I know, Professor and certainly you know that better than me."

"So, even though I may have a gut feeling about what happened and could really be right, I could never prove it."

"I don't see how." he said.

Gert closed her eyes and nodded. "I don't see how either."

Then he asked her if she had something in the lab that didn't belong to her that someone might have wanted. He also asked about the gas supply and the electric wiring. He said Conroy had already told him there was no propane or kerosene. He asked about threats, strange phone calls, or outlandish letters at home or at school. It was all a blank.

Eventually, Conroy and Lydia emerged from the building. She looked relieved and he looked like he wanted to ask for a date, but other plans were made. Lydia said she would return the next morning to gather what she could and that she was staying with a friend. Murphy said the precinct would provide a guard until the place was secured and its status as a possible crime scene was lifted.

He and Gert arranged to meet the next day so Gert could formally identify Sol, and he promised to go over the coroner's report with her when it became available. He told Gert to stay away from the house that afternoon because the detectives would come by and also that he felt certain all police business would be finished by the next morning, so whatever was going to be done could start at that time.

Before they parted, Gert got the name of a good clean-up company from Conroy. French Cuff, he said, would not only take away debris, but would also repair doors, windows, and do whatever was necessary to secure the place. She planned to call them from Sol's and the sooner they started the better. With nothing more for them to discuss they separated with promises to keep in phone contact.

CHAPTER 34

The cab ride to the agency was hellish for Lydia. She was nervous and frightened. Dennis' stealing the formula and setting a fire did not upset her, but a dead person, a murder of someone she knew, that was a different matter. She was proud of her toughness and her ability to stay calm, but Sol's death was not in the plan she had envisioned.

All she had wanted was the correct analysis, but maybe Dennis didn't get it. Was it possible the place burned and Sol died and Dennis didn't get the analysis? That was an outcome she didn't want to deal with, but she could not push it away.

Sol's death truly bothered her, but not because of any emotional attachment. Rather, she knew murder was not something the cops forget. Murder means detectives, investigations, questions, and, worse yet, it could lead back to her. As the cab bounced along the broken streets, she created a wishful-thinking scenario that ended with Sol dead and Dennis not involved. But how could Dennis not be involved? How could he not be guilty? If he was caught, he would certainly implicate her. Dennis was not a guy to take the blame. He'd probably seek immunity and say she forced him into it. There was no way she could shield herself. Even if she managed to get rid of Dennis, how could she be sure he didn't protect himself in a way that would incriminate her?

She kept asking herself what had happened. What was Sol doing there? Was he there to water the stupid plants? Why did he have to die? How did he die? She hoped for the possibility that the robbery and Sol's death were not connected, but she realized she was thinking nonsensical thoughts just to make herself feel better. She knew that every element of the ugly mess was part of the same package.

Dennis killing Sol had to be the dumb move of the decade. Stealing a piece of paper is one thing, but killing. "Damn!" she said aloud. The cabby thought she was commenting on his driving and turned his head as much as he could.

"Lady, gimme a break, the roads are all busted up and the traffic is a bitch."

She gave him a dirty look. "Hey, just drive the goddamn cab and mind your own business." He watched her in the rearview mirror and figured answering wouldn't be smart, so he said nothing for the remainder of the trip. When they arrived, he accepted the fare and her tip without looking at her.

Her anger was spilling over and those she passed in the lobby saw it would be better to let her go by without a word. When she got to her office, she sat at her desk and fought to keep control. Tears of anger and frustration seemed ready to gush, but she would not let that happen. Let me get him in here, she said to herself. Let me get him in here and find out what happened. When I know the worst, then I'll be able to figure the next move. But until then, let's not be stupid. "Let's stay under control." she said aloud.

She dialed his extension and he answered with his cheerfully snide attitude sticking way out. "Good morning to you, you lucky person, you've reached Dennis."

"Would you do me the favor of coming in here and giving me the glorious details of yesterday's little adventure?"

"Lydia, doll, don't you even say hello? Being abrupt with your coworkers is not what the management gurus tell us is the way to maintain a favorable corporate atmosphere."

"Dennis, you… goddamn it, will you get in here and fill me in. I just came from the house and there are problems, monstrous problems."

"Baby of mine, did you say 'fill me in' or 'fill me up'? I'd much rather fill you up than in, but as I said, that will come and a guy can't be too pushy, can he?"

"Dennis, please. I'm in no mood for it. From where I'm sitting, I think we're looking at jail time, serious jail time, so get in here and tell me I'm wrong. Okay?"

"Nervous Nellie, I'm coming. I'm coming. Hang on."

She hung up and stared out the window wondering if the grief was worth it. A few minutes later, he knocked on her door, came in, walked to the desk, picked up a side chair on the way, and dragged it dead center opposite from her. He sat and with a feigned serious expression on his face, stared at her. She stared back, amazed at his casual attitude.

"Jesus Christ, Dennis, this is not the time for bullshit. We have real troubles. Why the hell did you have to kill that old man?"

His body stiffened and his face drained of expression. "Kill what old man?"

"Don't you know what happened?"

"What the hell are you talking about?"

"They found a man, someone I happened to know, by the way. They found him at the bottom of the inside stairs. What the hell happened?"

"Sonofabitch!" he exclaimed and looked past her, first to the window and then to the ceiling. With his eyes half closed and his head slowly shaking, he muttered, "God damn it."

With apprehension clear in her voice, she asked again, "What happened?"

"Hey, take it easy, take it easy." Setting his feet on the floor, he sat back in the chair. "I found the analysis, emptied the file cabinet and started the fire. When it was burning, I went upstairs in that dinky elevator to leave and there he was, standing there. He asks me some dumb-ass question and I smacked him right on the button. I figured I knocked him out and when he came to, he'd remember a UPS guy with glasses and a mustache. Anyway, he wasn't out of it and he threw some crap at me and tried to get out, so I had to hit him again."

He shook his head, got up and then slowly walked to the window where he stood motionless. A few moments later, he turned and she noticed the expression on his face. He looked like a driver who had run over a dog. His face bore a glint of "sorry," but it was offset by the more visible shrug of "what's done is done."

He took a breath and then said, "After I hit him the second time, he fell down the stairs and when I got to him, he looked unconscious so I just stepped over him and out. Believe me, I didn't want to kill anybody, but right now, that's booze out of the bottle."

"Did you leave any clues?"

"Don't be stupid. There's not a fingerprint or anything. And anybody who was paying attention would remember a UPS guy going in and coming out. Anyway, nobody pays attention to them and nobody could pick me out of a lineup, if that's what you're thinking."

"I'm upset because not for a moment did I think somebody could get killed. And also, I'm scared. Stealing is one thing. But murder…"

"What murder? There was no murder. Look, all they got is an old guy dead at the bottom of the stairs and the first thing anyone's gonna think is that the guy was rushing to get out of the house to get away from the fire and he fell. In his rush, he tripped and fell. That happens all the time with old people. They're always falling down stairs. Shit, they fall everywhere."

She understood what he was saying and it sounded okay and also, judging from what had been said at the house, there was no murder investigation under way. And maybe Sol's death would be seen as accidental, since it seems to be the first thing everyone is considering. Even the fire police guy wasn't sure what happened. So, if the worst happened and they decided the fire was an attempt to cover a robbery, they'll never know what was taken. Gert couldn't prove someone stole the analysis or anything else. As Lydia ran it over in her mind, she realized her breathing was more even, steadier, and less frantic. She felt better.

"You're right, Dennis, old people are always falling down."

He smiled at her and she could see the cockiness returning as he sat down. Leaning back in the chair, he said, "The last thing I want, babe, is for us to no longer see eye to eye on this. We can really do a number here, but we've got to pull together, right?"

"You're right." she said and meant it. They looked at each other, neither knowing what to say. She asked herself, what now?

It took a moment for her to answer her own question. "Okay," she said with her tone indicating acceptance and a readiness to move on. "Where is the analysis?"

Dennis smiled like he hit the Lotto. "Right here, babe," he said, and, reaching into his jacket, he removed an envelope and handed it to her. She took it from him the way an alcoholic takes a drink from a bartender. Opening it, she removed the sheets of paper on which Gert's handwriting was instantly recognizable. Then, laying the sheets on the desk, she took the analysis Gert had given her from a drawer. Dennis came around the desk and together they compared the pages.

"See," she said, pointing to a formula on the second page. Written in black ink on the stolen analysis was a line of chemical symbols almost twice as long as the same line on the first analysis. "You see the difference? Everything seems to be the same, but that is definitely different. There's much more to that line of symbols and that must be the difference. That's what all this is about."

"Let's hope that's the difference, if it's not, then what do we do?"

"I don't want to consider that," she said. "We have what we have, so we'll go with it."

"You want me to call Thatcher?" he asked.

"Yes. No, no. Let's go there. I want to keep this as private as we can."

Placing both analyses in the envelope and putting it in her briefcase, they left the office.

Going to Apex was not easy during rush hour, but they got there before Thatcher left. They were ushered into his office and told to wait while a technician located him. Ten minutes later he came in and apologized, saying he had been in the middle of a sequence and couldn't walk away.

"Never mind that," said Lydia, "we have another version of that analysis and want you to compare them." The papers were laid out side by side and Thatcher immediately recognized the difference.

"You see this set of symbols?" he said, pointing to the same line Lydia and Dennis had noticed. "These are for a constituent not present in the first analysis. Now that I have quantities and a complete chemical description, I should have no trouble duplicating the solution, but it will not be an exact duplicate of the original."

"How long will it take you to do that?" asked Lydia, the note of urgency clear in her voice.

"I could have a few ounces for you quite quickly, but there may be some delay getting the breast milk. But let me worry about that. I have a friend who is a pediatrician. I'll get some from his office. There are always nursing mothers around."

"Do you think it would matter who the donor is?" Dennis asked.

"Well, this has been discussed, and as I told Miss Cornell, each woman's milk supply is person-specific and unlike any other. While the nutrient supply and overall makeup are generally similar, the specifics depend up the woman's lifestyle. So you must realize the chemical breakdown of the milk in the original formula can *never* be duplicated. We can create a match that is close, but no more than that, so an exact reaction to this formula's perfume should not be expected."

"Well," Lydia said, "I think we'll cross that bridge whenever. Right now, let's get some of it made up so we can assess the reactions. I feel good about this, and if we hit it right we will all benefit. You follow my thinking, Doctor Thatcher?"

The creepy smile that covered Thatcher's face matched the silent movie villain who had just captured the heroine. "I follow it very well, and you can count on me to help in every way. I want to be a part of this. You have brought to me a welcome change from the day-to-day. You have brought me an adventure."

Dennis and Lydia looked at each other and smiled. "Doc, with this one, we're all on an adventure," said Dennis.

Arrangements were made for Thatcher to call when the sample was ready and then Dennis and Lydia went back to the agency. The remainder of their afternoon was spent considering the rationale and the campaign theme for Complete Abandon.

At 6:30 Lydia put in a call to Win, and after a long talk about Sol, she asked if she could spend the night with him. Never thinking he would refuse, she was amazed when he did. He told her they should have a talk about their relationship, since he felt things had changed. It took her a moment to realize she had been very gently dumped.

Not being fazed for more than a moment, she called Tom, who graciously invited her to dinner before they would head to his place for the night. As she prepared to leave, she wondered why she hadn't asked Dennis. The best answer she had was that Dennis was a bit too sharp, a bit too hard to handle at this point. Win and Tom were easy and she felt in charge with both of them. But Dennis was another matter, since he was unpredictable and not easy to read. Flicking off her office lights, she knew it would be only a matter of time before she could flick his switches with the same ease and control she had with the others. Now smiling and filled with cheer, she headed for the elevators and the meeting with Tom. Her exit was a far cry from her entrance several hours before.

CHAPTER 35

Gert sat in Sol's apartment looking through the books in his library. There were many fine editions, a treasure trove of texts and fiction that probably could not be found anywhere else. Realizing that most would be impossible to buy, she felt it would be criminally foolish to let them disappear as old books do, or let them be turned into recycling waste. So she made a vow that when she had her place rebuilt she would do two things in Sol's memory. First, she would take all his books and include them in her collection, which was already promised to the NYU library. In that way they would continue to be of benefit. And second, she would establish a scholarship for promising students in his field. That would be the least she could do.

His memory should not die as so many others did. She felt it odd that at an academic institution, a place continually engaging the past, faculty members no longer actively teaching were forgotten as quickly as last week's cafeteria specials. The old saying, "out of sight, out of mind" was unfortunate and absolutely true.

But why was it so true? She hoped she would not forget Sol even though it seemed common for the living to forget the dead. No, she realized, the living don't forget the dead; it's simply that the dead do not figure in the usual activities of the living. They can't participate. They can't advise. They aren't around so their contributions are limited to what they offered while they were alive. So, their endowment depends on the memories of the people who knew them. If those memories are flimsy or vague, then they are forgotten.

Still not satisfied with her thoughts, she wondered why it was so common for the living to forget the dead. Why is "out of sight, out of mind" so damn true and what does it mean? Is "sight" referring to visual elements? If it is, then is that saying true for blind people? In their case, would it be, "no longer heard, gone from thought"? Did the blind forget as fast as the sighted? Is there a difference for them?

How stupid we are, she thought. We march around liked puffed-up toy soldiers, getting comfort from the silly little things we have trained ourselves to do and regard as meaningful. But it's all so dumb. We're here and then we're not, and what we accomplished while we were here is wiped away as bugs on a summer windshield.

She knew she was getting maudlin, but she missed Sol and was not sure how to mourn him. Standing by his graveside crying her eyes out was not her style. She would cry here, in private. There was no need to present a sorrowful face to the world. There was no need to play sob sister for those who would attend his funeral. Better she should stay angry and pissed off so she could get even with the bastard who killed him. If she could do that, then everyone who knew Sol would recognize that revenge was the only and proper way to mourn—to make the killer pay.

The telephone interrupted her thinking, and she answered as if she were back in her place. Then she realized she wasn't. She hoped the caller already knew about Sol. It was Winthrop and he wanted to talk, so they agreed to meet at La Hambra, the place on Greenwich around the block from Lou's. It would be nice to have dinner with them, since it would give her a chance to talk about Sol and learn about the girl Winthrop found. She had not yet heard the story about that happening, and knowing him, there had to be a story. That aside, a girl who looks like that and has a brain in her head to boot, must be special. So, looking forward to a pleasant evening, Gert cleaned herself up in Sol's tiny bathroom and walked to the restaurant.

La Hambra, was typical Greenwich Village in that it underwent a weekend transformation. From Friday to Sunday, it became a tourist place with a flamenco guitarist and customers from the boroughs who wanted to make believe they were in Spain. But during the week it was different; there was piped in music—Sinatra from the sixties and Spanish music the waiters liked. Gert, Sol, and Win were weekday regulars and enjoyed the complete lack of pretense which, of course, was exactly the atmosphere every weekender wanted.

When she entered, her eye was immediately attracted to Lou, whose hair stood out in the forty-watt darkness with a shine like a lighthouse on a dark coast. She and Win were in the booth Pablo, the owner, had assigned to Gert, Win, and Sol. Pablo always tried to protect his regulars from anything new. He wanted them to feel at home, so he insisted they sit in exactly the same place whenever they came in. It was never any use arguing about his decision, since he insisted he knew what was best for his customers, and also what was best for, as he put it, the "ambulance" of the dining room.

As she sat, Pablo swooshed to the table, and, placing his right hand on his heart, he looked at Gert with a basset hound's expression.

"Professor Gert… I just heard the sad news about Professor Sol. To say I cannot believe it is to say what is in my brain. You know how I feel about him. I love him like I love you and Professor Win." He stopped, took a breath, swallowed, and said, "My words are gone because I am so sad." With that, he spun on his heels and disappeared through the kitchen's swinging doors.

Not looking directly at Win and Lou, Gert said, "I wonder if Sol had any inkling how much people loved him. The last few weeks he'd been feeling sorry for himself and wondering about his life. It never seemed to dawn on him that people really liked him."

"You know," said Lou, "it's possible to be so upset with yourself that you can't understand how anyone could like you, let alone feel real affection."

"I think that was it exactly, but how would you know that? Were you ever in that position?" Gert asked.

Nodding, Lou said, "I think we've all been in that position. So many people know us only from our day-to-day lives and think we're really okay. But, we know ourselves and we know all the skeletons. The displeasure we feel about ourselves may be hard for others to understand. Did you ever try to tell a person who says 'I'm worthless' that they aren't?"

"Right," said Win. "That happens to me all the time. I'm forever telling good students they're good students, but they think they're just run of the mill."

"You're not alone there," said Gert. "That was Sol up to his ears. He was so busy thinking about how he didn't measure up, that he never spent much time thinking about how he did."

Lou's eyes lit up. "You know that would be a wonderful piece for the magazine. There are so many people besides me, Sol, and Win's students who need to be reminded that they're not as awful as they think."

"Make sure you add one other element," said Gert. "Make sure you include that some people who are totally convinced they are wonderful, usually aren't."

"Are you saying that the normal way to be is to think less of yourself than you actually are?" Win asked.

"No, I'm not, but Win, the last thing I know is what's normal. I only know that really good people in every field I can think of—the really first-class good ones are modest and never boastful. It's the phonies and the clowns who puff up and tell you they're great."

"Are you talking about any group or people in particular?"

"No, Win and I don't want to point a finger. Every calling has their own. Just look at our place. Did you ever see such a bunch of smug, self-satisfied people?"

"I had teachers like that," said Lou. "And I had editors like that." She laughed dryly. "You're right, Gert. No field is free of them."

"Sol was the other end of that continuum. He was far more modest than he should have been. It's sad he'll never know how people felt about him." Their conversation lapsed as they stared at each other not sure what next to say.

Breaking the silence, Gert said, "Okay, let's change the subject. Let me get to you two. What exactly is going on? Last week, you two were strangers on the planet, now you seem to be Siamese twins. How did you meet?" Before either could answer, Pablo appeared carrying a bottle of red wine and three glasses.

"This is for you with my compliments." He placed the glasses and poured an inch into each. "If you don't mind, I would suggest the Shrimp special, everything super fresh." Not hesitating a moment, they nodded and he swept back into the kitchen.

Win picked up his glass. "To Sol," he said raising his glass as did Lou and Gert a moment later. They touched their raised glasses and drank. When Win and Lou placed their glasses on the table, Gert said, "Okay, Winthrop, let's have it."

"Well, what happened was like this. I was in my place feeling lonely so I smoked some pot and then tried to read. Downstairs, some asshole in the bar decided to punctuate his remarks with gunshots into the ceiling. Just angry enough at the interruption and high enough to be brave, I went downstairs and confronted the guy, got his gun, and let the cops take him." He refilled his glass and continued. "Lou was in the place checking out the neighborhood. We started to talk and bingo."

Gert looked at Lou. "Was that the way it was?"

"Not quite. He's being exceptionally modest. The guy with the gun had the entire bar at a standstill for over an hour. He had all of us locked in our seats. It was terrifying. Two cops were there but couldn't do anything. We were all frozen. This guy was waving a giant gun around, ranting about nothing that made any sense. But when he fired into the ceiling, Superman flew in."

She sipped some wine and continued. "Gert, it was Mr. Brave to the rescue. He burst into the bar looking real angry, you know the look, pissed off and in the right. Well, he walked up to this guy as if he held a pencil instead of a big gun and yelled at him for disturbing his reading, messing up his floor, and ruining his evening meal. All that time, the guy was staring at Win like he was his mother telling him to clean his room. Anyway, Win talked to him some more and like it was a rehearsed scene, the guy gently handed him the gun."

She looked at Win and smiled. "It was absolutely bold. I've been in quite a few bars and I've seen some tough characters, but Mr. Cute here, he takes the prize. High or not, what he did was heroic."

Win was blushing and staring at the tablecloth while Lou was talking and Gert thought that was cute. "So that was the meeting?"

"Gert," Win said, "our eyes met, and for me at least, it was wonderful. My heart jumped. It was like seeing water in the desert."

"Now isn't that a romantic way to describe a relationship." Gert shook her head and then smiled. Looking at Lou, she asked, "Do you mind mister hero talking for you? Are you a pair?"

Win burst in. "Don't bother to ask her. I know the truth. She felt it as much as I did. She may try to be cool now and make believe she's choosy and standoffish, but that wasn't the case. Our eyes met and there were sparks, and not just from me. The lady was just as smitten as I was."

Lou laughed. "What do you do with a character like this. But he's right. It has to be genetic. We were meant to be."

"Well," said Gert. "That's wonderful. I wish you both as many sparks as you can handle." She raised her glass and they touched them together once again. As they were setting them down, the waiter arrived with their food.

Shrimp a La Hambra looked very much like Paella, but no one was in the mood to argue about names, since it also looked delicious. They ate everything, and afterward they sipped brandy and tried to figure out what led to Sol's death.

"You have to understand," insisted Gert, "there was nothing taken from my apartment or I guess, from Lydia's, so that leaves the lab. The only damage was in the lab. The only graffiti was in the lab."

"Wait," said Win, "What graffiti?"

"On the wall, across from the elevator door, was 'Kill the Jews,' and there were swastikas sprinkled here and there."

"Really? 'Kill the Jews'? Are you serious?"

Gert looked at him the way she looked at students. "No, I'm not. I'm making it up to color our conversation. Of course, I'm serious."

"But who would do such a thing in your lab? I can see that on a building wall, but inside a residence? That doesn't make sense."

"Well, how about if you want to point a finger in the wrong direction?"

They stared at her for a moment and then reacted as if they had figured the final clue for the *Times* crossword.

"Oh," said Lou, "you mean by doing that they would throw the investigators off track and have them looking for neo-Nazis vandals or the like."

"That's right, and I fell for it. When I went through the place with Conroy, I reacted like a trained seal. But he was cool. He pointed out the silliness of doing that and not doing the rest of the vandal thing."

"The rest?" Win asked.

"Yeah, a complete bashing—clothing torn up, food everywhere, furniture smashed, graffiti all over, money and jewels taken, you know, a real trashing of everything." She took a sip of wine and sighed. "But the only damage was in the lab, so Conroy thinks it could be a cover-up for something else."

"Who's Conroy?" asked Lou.

"Lieutenant Conroy is a Fire Department investigator."

"So what you're saying," Lou said quietly, "is that the fire was a phony to cover up something else." She stared at Gert. "But what's the something else?"

"That's the big question. I had no equipment or materials you couldn't buy at any supply house in the city. The only irreplaceable items would have to be my records, my files."

"Were they taken?" asked Win.

"Nope, they were burned. Whoever did this emptied the file cabinet and set fire to all the paperwork."

"And that started the fire?"

"Right."

"So, Sol's death," Win said, "could be because he was running from the fire or he was killed by whoever started the fire." He hesitated, then asked, "When is the coroner's report going to be ready?"

"I have an appointment with the cops tomorrow. I'll know something by the afternoon."

After a moment, Lou looked at Gert and said, "I know I'm an outsider in all this, but there seems to be one crucial question. What was in your files valuable enough for someone to want, something worth all the trouble?"

"Well, I think there was only one item." She took a drink. "Has Win told you about the situation in school involving perfume and a guy attacking a girl?"

"Yes, he did."

"Well, I didn't want Lydia to have the exact formula for that perfume because I was sure she'd somehow turn it into a product that would screw people up even more than they already are. So, Sol gave me the idea of giving her the perfume analysis minus the major ingredient. I did that, but I told the young girl who was involved that I had the complete analysis in my lab. I'm sure that information got back to Lydia and when she found the perfume that was made from the analysis I gave her didn't do anything, she must have made arrangements to have my analysis stolen, and that's why the fire and that's why Sol's death."

There was a moment's silence and then Win excitedly whispered, "But Gert that means you're saying that Lydia was behind Sol's death."

"I'm afraid you're right. That's exactly what I'm saying."

"You can't think Lydia set fire to the lab and killed Sol."

"No, I don't think she personally did it, but I would not put anything past her. I'd bet she hired someone to do it, someone not too bright. *They* set fire to the lab and killed Sol, but Lydia is as involved as they are."

Win ran his hand over the top of his head. "I can't believe this. Lydia is ambitious and cunning, but murder?"

"Do you have any proof?" Lou asked.

"Nope, not one shred. But it makes sense and it all fits."

"Have you told the cops?"

"No, but I may. It depends on the findings with Sol. If the cops think his death was an accident, there's no way I could convince them there was a robbery and a murder. They'd just pat me on the head, tell me not to read so many mystery stories and send me home."

"What would you do then?"

"Well, I've been thinking about that, and I guess I'd have to settle the score myself."

Win lurched backward against his seat as surprise registered on his face. "What do you mean you'd settle the score yourself? What are you going to do?"

"I'm not sure at the moment, but I'll tell you this, no one is going to get away with killing Sol and then dance off into the sunset. That's not going to happen."

Lou and Win looked at each other and then looked at Gert who had picked up her glass to drain the last of her wine.

They realized she was serious

CHAPTER 36

Sergeant Murphy read the coroner's report. What it said was that in general, there was nothing inconsistent with a fall down a staircase. The deceased had a significant contusion of the left anterior mandible with several teeth chipped at that point; there was an additional, but trivial cranial contusion. There was bruising on his face and he had a broken nose that may have come from a beating, but it is all consistent with a fall. In addition, there was moderate bruising of the torso which was also totally consistent with such a fall.

The direct cause of death was an acute transverse cord lesion at C-4. That was consistent with respiratory paralysis as well as the loss of all sensation and reflex activity as well as other autonomic functions. Essentially, death was instantaneous. The remainder of the report covered stomach contents and such, items to which Murphy paid scant attention, since he was still in the process of savoring his first-of- the-day coffee and an accompanying buttered roll.

He was hoping he would be left alone long enough to finish his morning pleasure. Too often the phone would ring or someone would stop by to gab, and the pleasure of finishing the roll with the last slurps of coffee would be lost. It was totally impossible to explain how important it was to him to be able to finish the coffee and roll together—the last bite of roll washed down with the last of the coffee.

He once tried to explain and was immediately regarded as a nutcase, since everyone knew the coffee pot was never empty and a fresh cup or refill was always obtainable. His argument about the roll was almost understood, since he referred to its odor, its fresh taste, and oven warmth. People listened politely but walked away shaking their heads.

He knew sitting at his desk with coffee and roll was foolish, because if he had to talk to someone, the coffee would be cold by the time he got back to it and the roll would lose the crispness he really liked. So he buried his face in the report and tried to make the last two inches of coffee and piece of roll vanish at precisely the proper moment. He lost the battle, however, when Detective Lieutenant Randolph plopped himself on the edge of the desk.

"You got the coroner's report?"

"Yeah, I got it right here," he said, as he slowly, sadly, and carefully put the plastic cup down next to the fragment of roll that was resting in the middle of an ocean of crumbs and poppy seeds. Murphy looked at the remains of the roll with the full realization that by the time he was able to finish that last piece, his brain-stomach coalition would be totally disconnected from what had already been eaten. His brain would not understand that the last piece of roll was the end, the last of what had come before. That final bite of roll would send a signal to his brain as if it was the first mouthful of a brand-new roll. When that happened, and he knew it would, for it had happened before, he would be faced with the awful task of trying to explain to his stomach and brain that there was no more roll. He also hated the additional weight a second roll would add to his expanding frame, but he was helpless in the face of these incontestably superior forces.

He handed the report to Randolph who quickly glanced at it and asked, "You satisfied it was an accident?"

Murphy shrugged. "Damn, I don't know. How the hell can you prove otherwise? Some of the facial bruising stands out, but all the rest is what happens when someone goes down a flight of stairs."

"Okay," he said, handing it back. "Don't lose sight of the other cases that need immediate attention, but let me know if you get a feeling there's more involved here."

"Right, I'm going to talk to the lady in whose house this happened and if she gives me something to go on, I'll let you know. Otherwise, case closed."

"It looks that way to me." He got up from the desk and sauntered back to his office.

Murphy watched Randolph walk away and then shifted his gaze to the coffee cup and the piece of roll knowing that he was once again on the short end of that stick. After a moment of deliberate consideration, he folded the waxy paper over the remains of the roll and balled it in his hands. Then he stuffed it all into the cup. He figured by not finishing either, that case certainly remained open and would be available for lunchtime consideration.

He picked up the phone and dialed the number Gert had given him. She picked up after the third ring. "What?" she asked.

Murphy stared at the handset, recalling he hadn't heard that sort of hello in a long time, not since the military when everyone was too busy and every call was an interruption.

"Professor Lehman, this is Sergeant Murphy. Is this a bad time?"

"No. What gives you that idea?"

He frowned. "Nothing, nothing, I'm calling to give you details of the coroner's report, what there is of it."

"What do you mean?"

"Well, there's nothing in the report to offer credence to the idea of anything but an accidental death. Professor Woodrow's injuries were generally consistent with a fall down the stairs. There's nothing out of the ordinary. No real reason to suspect foul play."

"Specifically, what killed him?" she hesitantly asked.

"He died as a result of a broken neck."

"That's it. Kaput! He had a broken neck and you wash your hands of it. In your world murder only happens when there are holes in people with blood leaking out?"

"Of course not and Professor you know better than that. There's just nothing to consider."

"What if I would tell you there was something of value in the lab and it was probably the reason for everything that happened?"

"Do you have any proof of that? Before the department is going to start an investigation, we would need more proof than a 'probably the reason for everything.' When we talked before you said there was nothing of value in the lab."

"Well, I've reconsidered because I didn't want to be accusatory, but now I'm sure that a chemical analysis was taken and it was the reason for the break-in, the robbery, and the fire."

"Wait a minute, what robbery, break-in, arson? So far, all I can see is a case for the arson squad, since the fire doesn't seem to be something that happened by itself. But we're going to need proof that the fire was connected to a robbery. And, a good deal more proof that the whole shebang was connected to Professor Woodrow's death."

"Goddamn it, it's obvious."

"Now wait a minute. Look, let's say we have a fire that did not start by itself. Okay. Now, beyond the fire, your jewelry and money wasn't touched or taken and neither was Ms. Cornell's. So I can agree that the lab was the target. Now, what was in the lab? Before you said there was nothing of value."

"Now I'm telling you there was something of value. And also, how do you casually explain away the ease the thief had in getting to the lab? I had a private hidden elevator from my bedroom to the lab and very few people even knew about it. How the hell did the thief know about it?"

"Okay, what you say is true. Considering the elevator, it looks like someone knew about it and that's important. Also, what was this item of value?"

"It was a chemical analysis I had done of a perfume. It was in my file cabinet and it was taken. It was the reason for everything."

"How do we know it was taken? Everything in that cabinet was burned. How do you know the analysis wasn't burned along with everything else?"

"I know! Dammit. I know!"

He waited a moment, and then asked. "What proof do you have?"

After a moment, Gert said, "What if a line of perfume is produced that is identifiable as quite similar to the perfume I analyzed? I know they're going to use my analysis to produce the perfume. I know they are."

"Okay, first, who is or are they?"

"I don't think I can say right now."

He stared at the pigeons fluttering on the window ledge, and as a gray one took off and let go a white bomb to the street below, he said, "Okay, you don't want to say right now, okay, some other time." The gray pigeon or one that looked like it landed on the ledge. Probably a miss down below so another bombing run was called for.

"So putting 'they' aside for now," he said, "let's say a perfume is produced and it smells like the perfume you analyzed. How could you prove it isn't a concoction somebody else dreamed up? What makes it special?"

"Well, let's say it produces an effect never before produced, how about that?"

"But now we're back where we started, Professor. Unless you can prove the perfume, the effect, the whole thing was absolutely tied to the analysis, and the perfume could not have been mixed, made, created, whatever, by somebody else, if you can prove no one else could have made it then maybe we've got a case. Could you prove that?"

Gert could see where the conversation was headed. She realized it as soon as he told her the cause of death was completely attributable to a fall down the stairs.

"No I could not prove it even though I know it's the truth. I just know it the same way I know that the robber pushed Sol down the stairs and killed him."

He paused considering whether he should meet with her and talk this out, but he sensed a monumental resistance. It was obvious she was convinced it happened as she thought it did, and she wasn't going to pay much attention to contrary ideas.

"Professor Lehman, I have real sympathy for you. A good friend has died in mysterious circumstances and I understand your need to explain it. Without an explanation, there's no closure. I really understand that. We have hundreds of cases in our files that are never going to be resolved. Everybody who is connected and involved with those cases is frustrated because there's no end. But that's the way they go."

"Look, Sergeant Murphy, I know that on many cases you've had a feeling that things weren't what they seemed, right?"

"Sure, it happens all the time."

"Well, that's where I'm at. I can accept that Sol died of a broken neck, but I can't buy the idea that he fell down the stairs trying to get out of a burning house. I know in my bones there was a break-in and the bastard who broke in killed him."

"Professor, I can understand that. I know those feelings and I have to agree that there was a break-in and yes, a fire was set, but there is no proof that whoever did that also took the chemical analysis you speak of and also killed your friend. What or who do we look for aside from going after the person who broke in?"

"The perfume. You have to seek that out."

"Okay, so let's say a perfume is produced. How…"

"Wait," she interrupted him. "If the perfume is produced then I know my tenant, Lydia Cornell was somehow involved. She wanted the perfume formula and she certainly knew all about the lab and the private elevator. But right now, I don't know how anything can be proved one way or the other, but that's your job."

He hated it when somebody was absolutely sure of something he doubted. So many people said things as if they were 100 percent certain only to be proved wrong later. Until they're shown to be wrong, they speak like the word of God. They speak like there is no possible way for them to be off base. She was like that. No doubts even though she could be totally wrong. Was that confidence? Was it stubbornness or an inability to recognize someone else's truth? If that is it, then it's ego and nothing more. Then it's strictly personality. Are professors like that? He asked himself.

"Hello? Sergeant, are you still there?"

"Yes, yes, I'm sorry. I was lost in thought." He let out a breath. "Look, before I label this an accidental death and no more, I want to look into what you said. You said your tenant wanted the perfume formula and she knew all about your apartment. Based on that, I want to question her to at least get her alibi for the time of the fire. As far as the perfume is concerned, on that point we'll have to wait to see what comes out."

Gert liked what she heard. "I'm pleased to hear that you take me seriously and are not so quick to bury the affair."

"I'll contact you if I find out anything pertinent. Okay?"

"Fine."

"Professor, for the time being, I'm going to label this an accidental death so you'll be able to claim the body for burial. Okay? All you got to do is call the morgue." He gave her the number which she wrote down so she could forward it to Cyril.

"Now," she said, "what the hell can I say?" She was silent for a long moment. Then she said, "Let me ask you. Is there an appeal situation here? Can I speak to someone else about this?"

"Sure, I don't want to cut you loose. You're free to speak to my immediate superior, Lieutenant Randolph. You can call him or see him, up to you."

"I'm going to call him. Okay?"

"Please, Professor Lehman, do what you think necessary because the last thing I want is for you to be up in the air, but as I said, there are so many cases never resolved. After a while you learn to live with books that have no last chapters."

"Okay, Sergeant. I thank you for your concern and I hope we will meet again."

"That goes double for me."

He gave her Randolph's number and hung up the phone. What a call that was, he thought, as he watched the squadron of pigeons gather themselves for another bombing attack on the street below. When they took off, he walked to Randolph's office and leaned into the doorway.

"I just spoke to the professor whose house burned. She's convinced her friend was murdered by a robber who set the fire. It was all done, she thinks, to cover the robbery of a chemical analysis she did of a perfume that has, I gathered, very special qualities. She's unhappy with the accidental death tag, because she thinks it's a murder. Also, she said, her tenant, a Miss Lydia Cornell, wanted the chemical analysis which, the professor says, was the reason for the break-in and fire. I'm gonna look into that, but she's gonna call you and talk it over."

"Do you think her position has merit?" Randolph asked.

"Hell, I don't know. First she said there was nothing worth taking in the lab. Now she's saying the chemical analysis was the reason for everything. I guess it boils down to proving the analysis she's talking about wasn't in that pile of burned papers. The lab guys said the burn was so complete, there's no way to tell what was burned or what wasn't. So, she's got no actual proof, but she's a real tough dame and she's convinced she's got a handle on the whole mess."

"Is she gonna call today?"

"That's the impression I got."

"Okay, I'll keep you posted."

As Murphy walked back toward his desk he caught sight of the wall clock. It was ten-thirty, a good time for a coffee break with a seeded roll thrown in. He changed his direction and headed for the stairs and the coffee shop a block away.

Gert waited fifteen minutes and then called Lieutenant Randolph. She went through exactly what she told Murphy and listened as Randolph told her Murphy was going to continue with the investigation even though there was insufficient proof indicating foul play in Woodrow's death, because it could be attributed to the normal and natural fear of fire. And that was what caused his hasty exit and fall. Finally, he told her the fire would be pursued by the arson squad and Murphy would continue his inquiries.

The information about the perfume intrigued him, but since there was no way to know if the analysis was taken and not burned. He did, however, tell her to contact him if a perfume with specific special qualities did hit the market. He said even though there may not be clear proof that a new fragrance product was based on the analysis she believes was stolen, it still provided an opportunity for inquiries. His promise of future action was the best she could get.

After hanging up, she stared at the phone. What a bitch this is, she thought. Without proof, how do you prove something to be true? Over and over she searched her mind for a piece of information she had left out. Was there something unique about that perfume, about the analysis? As she listened to herself she realized she sounded like the typical graduate student stuck on a thesis problem. They're sure they know the answer and what they know may actually be true, but that's not the way it goes.

She told herself what she told them when they reached this point, science demands more than intuition. A reliance on feelings may be comfortable, but it isn't good science. In the search for truth and accuracy, a hunch may be meaningful, but it must lead to solid ground. You can't use hunches as the sole bases for truth. Procedures must be supported and answers must be supported. The inability to replicate a procedure or an outcome leads to a science that is inconsistent. It becomes nothing more than maybe you can do it today or maybe you can't. Now she knew exactly how those students felt.

Sergeant Murphy's take on open cases bothered her. She couldn't imagine what it must be like to have questions never to be answered. Even if there was only one case crying out for some sort of settlement, she would go nuts not attending to it. This situation was enough to drive her crazy. How does he handle it? How do they all handle it? She realized being a detective was not the job for a full blown compulsive like herself. Knowing some bastard is guilty and having no way to prove it must be really hard to take. Playing by the rules creates a game that was not for her.

As she sat in the familiar yet unfamiliar apartment, looking at Sol's things, she made two promises to herself. First, to support the opposing idea, she would honestly try to find proof to counter what she believed to be true. And second, if she didn't find any proof to the contrary, she would not be bound by the rules Murphy had to follow. She would settle everything herself and even the score for Sol.

CHAPTER 37

Once again Lydia sat at her desk staring at the small bottle of perfume sent by Apex. Unlike the other, this one had a note from Thatcher. He assured her the sample included the specified amount of breast milk, and that he was able to locate a milk source he guessed resembled the chemical breakdown of the milk in the original. She noted his doubts, but at this point, who could be sure of anything? Whatever the case, he had done his job. Now it was a matter of trying it out.

As before, she opened the bottle and applied it as she would any other perfume, a touch below each ear, at each wrist, and between her breasts. The rose odor was clear and seemed to remind her of the other one, but now it was time to see if all that had been done was worth the effort. With preparations ready, she called Tom and asked him to come in for the second test.

Some moments later, there was a soft knock and he strolled into the room. He saw the small bottle on her desk and a sly smile spread across his face.

"Well, well, here we go again."

"Don't say anything more, Tom, just come here and hug me."

She stood as he came around the desk and took her in his arms. For just a moment she sensed the muscular tenseness of his body and waited for the clinch to become more strenuous and steamy as it always did, but it didn't. Instantly, she sensed this was not Tom's typical embrace, which started out hot and proceeded to hotter. Now, she felt his muscles relax and she felt him press against her. He held her with gentle certainty and a tenderness he usually displayed only after their lovemaking. Something was very different. Her glee was almost impossible to contain, but she did control herself, for she wanted him to realize there was a difference. He had to be able to describe what he felt.

She started to pull away and ask him what he was experiencing, but he did not give her the opportunity. He stood quietly, holding her in his arms with soft, melodious murmurs coming from his throat. Later, she would say he was purring. To the same degree he was relaxed, she was joyful. Even with no confirmation from him, she knew the perfume had worked. The way he was holding her and his mumbling engendered a warm, protective feeling for her. The gentler he became, the more tenderness she experienced and offered. That surprised her, for she did not expect her reactions to be involved, but they were. His peaceful pleasure electrified her and she bathed in tranquility.

But there was something more. Along with the sensation of control, she felt a responsibility, an emotional sensitivity, a sensation of caring as well as pure affection. It was wonderful to be held. All tension and apprehension flowed out of her. It was like an emotional sauna providing relaxation and serenity. Amity and calm swept over her and she wanted nothing more than the feelings to continue.

Finally, with real effort, she pushed at his shoulders and their bodies separated. He was reluctant to let her go, but she managed to free herself, get to her desk and sit.

"Tom, please sit down on the sofa." The authority in her voice was plain and he backed up a few steps, sat, and then leaned back into the thick cushions, his face a clear mirror of the luxurious sensations he was still experiencing.

He looked at her with awe. "That was fucking wonderful. I haven't felt like that since the first time I got laid." He smiled. "Man, it was like…" He opened his hands palms up. "Hell, I don't know what it was like, but it was wonderful." He was smiling at her like a kid who finally got the present he always wanted. "What about you?" He asked. "Did you feel anything like that?"

"Yes." She answered. "I did and I'm still feeling something, but not what you are. There's nothing sexual in what I'm sensing. I feel relaxed, fulfilled, motherly."

"Motherly? Is that what we want to sell?"

"Don't be stupid. Think about what happened. Did you ever have an experience like that? Well, we did. Now we have a fair idea of what that guy felt when he passed that girl in the school corridor."

"No we don't," he said. "He didn't have a wonderful reaction at all. He got violent and ripped her blouse to get at her breast to suckle or whatever. What I felt was nothing like that. There's a major difference here. It's not the same."

She hesitated then said, "Sure, your reaction wasn't like his, but it was something. The perfume brought about something. You didn't just appreciate the smell. Don't lose sight of what happened. I put on some perfume, you hugged me, and we were transported."

He nodded. "Yeah, it was weird. I've never been hypnotized, but I guess that's what it's like. I just let myself go and the sensation overpowered me."

Wide eyed, she cried out, "Oh, yes, yes, that's it. I love it. I let myself go and the sensation overpowered me. I let myself be overpowered. I surrendered and was overpowered. Those ideas, they're going to be the footholds for the Complete Abandon theme." She grabbed a pad and made quick notes. Then, she looked up at him and asked, "Tell me, were you afraid? Was it fearful to be taken over?"

"No." he said, hesitating. "At first I think I was a bit nervous, but then I felt safe, secure, very relaxed." He stopped and she thought he was thinking of how to make the point, how to tell her. She was right for what he said next was clear to her and would be equally clear to anyone else.

"I don't know if it's the same for women, but when a guy's got to take a leak and can't find a place he gets jammed up. Every muscle from ankle to waist, they're all doing nothing but holding it in. Then, when he finds a place and lets it go, that's the feeling I had. It was a physical sensation of pleasure, of opening up."

She stared at him. "You are such a dope. Of course it's the same for women. When a woman is in that situation and can't find a place, women don't even have to sit down. As soon as they begin to squat, they start to pee. It's like being in a safe place and okay to let go." She made additional notes on the pad and then looked up at him. "Oh, my god, Tom, this is fantastic, absolutely fantastic."

Ever since high school he felt he had a handle on things. He thought himself able to manage the events he confronted, but this was a new experience. He remembered his reaction when Lydia first told him about the guy and the girl in NYU hallway. He thought it all bullshit but wanted to meet the guy and congratulate him for coming up with a phenomenal way to score with a girl. But now things were different.

He wanted to be able to explain what happened, but was at a loss for comparisons. "Lydia, that was amazing." His eyes glowed with the admiration he felt for her. "When this started I wondered if you had lost your marbles, but now, well, you haven't lost anything. You're on top of the world." He laughed. "Like Cagney, Lydia, 'top of the world, Ma,' top of the world."

She felt buoyant. All her dreams had come true. He was right, top of the world. But thrilled as she was, she knew she needed additional confirmation. She trusted him, but he could be putting her on and merely acting out a reaction.

"I'd like to try it on Dunn. What do you think? That a good idea?"

He shrugged. "I don't know. If you want to, I guess. I was going to tell him, but trying it on him?" He scratched his head. "Oh, what the hell, he'll probably enjoy it."

With a broad smile on his face, Tom went back to his office as Lydia called A.T. Dunn and asked if he was free. He told her he would make time if she had good news. She reapplied the perfume and headed for his office.

Once inside, she went through the usual formalities and then marched up to the desk where he sat, and said, "Hug me!" He stared at her.

"I see you doubt my success," she said. "Come on, then, be brave, and give it a try. Get up, put your arms around me and breathe deeply."

Very slowly, he got up and did what she asked. His arms tightened around her and then they relaxed. He held her loosely with no real passion, but she realized he wasn't letting go. And then after a moment or two, he placed his head alongside hers as if to start dancing, but he did not move. They stood motionless.

She whispered in his ear, "Well, what about that?"

He dropped his arms and took a step back. "It's all very interesting, for I was getting great pleasure just holding you. The perfume is noticeable and I was instantly aware of it, but as I was considering it, I suddenly felt this other thing, this other feeling. I felt I just wanted to hold you and be close."

"Has anything like that ever happened before?"

"Not that I can recall."

Lydia's eyes were flashing and she never felt more powerful. "I promised you success and we have it. We have a perfume that produces emotional physical reactions in men. They can no longer remain passive. We have them!"

Dunn stared at her the way a fair number of Hitler's henchmen must have stared at him, enthralled with his vision but unsure of the future.

"Tom's response was more passionate than yours, but I don't think degree matters. He thoroughly enjoyed it."

"How many others have you sampled?" She was surprised by his question, but instantly realized he was right, for additional testing would be necessary to discover the perfume's true parameters.

As he stepped back to his desk chair, she noticed he was moving much more slowly than usual and she wondered if he was ill. In fact, she thought he looked a little pale.

Once seated, he looked up at her. "Two reactions, no matter how positive, cannot be the basis for a national advertising campaign. We will immediately assign this to Research and Sampling and have an appropriate statistical package developed. When they're satisfied we have a winner, then the ball can get rolling."

He picked up his phone and dialed, waited a moment, and then said, "Please come in. There is a situation in need of your expertise."

A few moments later, after a knock, Theodore Hicks, the resident super-intellectual loped into the room. After a nod and a smile to Lydia, he stood, almost at attention, in front of Dunn's desk

"Ted, two things. First, I want you to hug Lydia."

She laughed aloud. "You're not serious?"

"Of course I am. He's a man. Let's see his reaction."

Hicks, eyes bulging, turned to look at Lydia. She nodded and took a step closer to him. Nervously, Hicks looked back to Dunn who nodded and mouthed the words, "Go on." Then Hicks turned back to Lydia and, looking at her as if she was holding a gun, stepped closer and put his arms around her. Instantly, she realized that never before had she been held as Hicks now held her. In trying to find a comparison she settled on how a person would hold a long dead fish found in their car trunk. It took only a moment, but she knew the perfume had absolutely no effect.

"Okay, Ted," Dunn asked, "What do you think?"

"What do I think about what... about hugging Miss Cornell?" Dunn nodded.

"Well, sir, I know who Miss Cornell is, but I don't think we are at the hugging stage in our relationship."

"Right." said Dunn. "Was your reaction to hugging Miss Cornell different in any way from the reactions you normally have?"

"Sir, I do think Miss Cornell is very pretty and I like her perfume, but we are strangers so I cannot be as relaxed as I would like to be."

"Okay. Now for the second thing I want." Hicks immediately turned away from Lydia and stepped back to face Dunn's desk. "Miss Cornell has a perfume in her office that produces a very strong physical and emotional reaction in *some* men. So far it's been tested on three subjects. Mr. Randall, myself and you. Both Mr. Randall and I had reactions; you did not."

"Wait, wait," injected Hicks. "I think I would have reacted differently if I knew Miss Cornell better. I was not relaxed and I would guess you and Mr. Randall were. My usual state of up-tightness might have something to do with my lack of reaction."

"I cannot say you're wrong, Ted. So I want you to take that into consideration when you test the perfume. Vary the testing so strangers and non-strangers are involved." Hicks nodded and Dunn continued. "Now, I want you to get the perfume from Lydia and run a series of tests so we can determine with good certainty how the perfume would work in the general population. I want a statistical breakdown so we know what we have in our hands. Don't skimp on the testing. Clear?"

"Absolutely, I can have it ready in about two weeks."

"Go to it." Then turning to Lydia, Dunn said, "I want you to presume we have a meaningful product ready for the market in need of copy. Get the premise and rationale worked out. Both you and Tom work on this."

She smiled and nodded. Then, waving a "come along" to Hicks, who followed her, she returned to her office and handed him the small bottle.

"Take care of that stuff, honey. It's going to be worth a fortune."

He looked at the bottle. "Can you tell me why it worked on them and not on me?"

"Hicks, let me be honest. No one understands or knows why it does what it does. Every chemist I've spoken to says it shouldn't do anything except smell nice."

With eyes shining he said, "So you're saying it's magic?"

"It certainly seems that way, and I don't give a damn if it violates chemistry rules or defies explanations. All I care about is that the perfume does something."

Half smiling, he said, "You know, Miss Cornell, Lydia, I might do better if you gave me another chance to hug you." She laughed, thinking you can't blame a guy for trying.

"I'd bet you'd do better, but right now, it's time for work."

With that, he put the bottle in his shirt pocket and sort of bounced out of the office.

Sighing, she sat at her desk and made some notes.

1. Two weeks for Hicks to prepare a demographic analysis.
2. Call Gert. Get my clothes to a dry cleaner.
3. Move in with Tom.
4. Call Win. Wish him well. No need for him to be an enemy.
5. Tom & I start work on the copy.
6. Dennis? What do I do about Dennis?
7. Dunn seems less than his usual self. Is he okay?

CHAPTER 38

When the doorbell rang, Gert yelled, "Come!" and continued to pour water into the teapot. She heard the door open and footsteps on the wooden floor. Poking her head out of Sol's small kitchen she saw what seemed to be a burst of color. Then focusing more carefully, she saw a man who was probably Cyril standing in the hallway. He glistened and radiated as if he had an inner source of light, but with a closer look she realized it was his clothing doing the broadcasting.

In his left hand was a powder blue hat that matched his sport jacket. Their colors were not complements. They perfectly matched each other as did his stark white shoes and white trousers. Under his jacket he wore a navy blue dress shirt that served as appropriate backdrop for the yellow silk tie.

It took a moment for her to register all of him. The white shoes matched the white trousers. The jacket and hat formed a powder blue duet. He was a truly amazing sight.

But his clothes offset the ruddy redness of his face, which boasted of steam rooms and saunas and in an unavoidable and sweeping self-appraisal, Gert thought compared to him, she looked like a Welsh coal miner coming off shift. If there was any aspect pointing to her buoyancy, she would have clutched at it, but his hair sunk her straight away. There was quite a bit of it and not one single blond strand was out of place.

She wondered how he could wear a hat and not mess the coif. Then she realized he didn't wear it, he carried it, and, by doing so, demonstrated he knew how to complete his outfit. The hat in his left hand was balanced by a walking stick delicately held by three fingers of his right hand. It was a pip, a regulation Fred Astaire walking stick. Gert believed she had never seen one except in a movie and here was the real thing gently tapping on the waxed hardwood floor. As he stepped toward her, he switched the stick to this left hand and extended his right which she shook.

"I am delighted we are able to meet. There was never a time when Sol did not speak of you in warm and flattering terms. He considered you a close and valuable friend. I will do the same."

When he had called to arrange this meeting, Gert did not perceive the richness of his voice, which was lost on the telephone. As a result, she incorrectly imagined him smaller and certainly less flamboyant. Now, hearing him in person, she enjoyed his radio announcer-like timbre and judged it masculine and forceful.

Anyone seeing him would probably figure his dialect to be either cultured French or Royal British or possibly one that was unidentifiably European, but no one would expect him to speak the American-English he did. Only those with exceptional awareness of American dialects would recognize the slight English flavor to his speech reflecting the upper-class regionalisms of Boston's Brahman dialect.

When he turned to survey the apartment, Gert could see his hair was as complicated and neatly arranged at the rear as it was in front. In a second, she knew no one could do their own hair like that, so someone must do it for him or it was a wig.

As a woman, Gert knew she didn't match the current idealized females with their abundance of height and lack of flesh. She wrote that off to genes and felt little remorse, but here was a man who outweighed her by a good fifty pounds and stood just a bit taller. Comparing herself to a fashion model and coming up short was explainable and manageable, but losing the "How do I look?" contest to a man was really a blow. She wondered how it was possible for him to be more feminine than she and still be a man. The answer to that question thoroughly depressed her.

When he finished his look around, he focused his light blue eyes on her and she saw their color matched his hat and jacket. Could he have contact lenses to match his outfits?

Then, in a soft voice, he said, "I am pleased to have this chance to meet, for it is important we speak. It is most difficult for me to be here and not see Sol. In fact, this is the first time I have been here and not seen him. To say I am crushed by his death is a mild statement. He was a gentle, intelligent, and kind man, a model for many of us."

"What do you mean by 'model'?" Gert asked.

"It is not easy to explain that term to one who is not a member of the community, but let me say that Sol managed to live his circumstances with great and unending dignity. Never did one see or hear him bemoan his situation. He displayed and possessed far more strength than he suspected and those who knew him admired him more than he admired himself."

He moved to the sofa, sat, and crossing his legs at the ankles, displayed blue socks that matched his hat, jacket, and eyes. Gert flashed to her past and her childish delight when she first saw Technicolor movies. She remembered every color was separate and stood out in spectacular brightness. He looked like those films.

Still speaking softly, he said, "Sol always spoke of you." Then, suddenly, he got up from the sofa and crossed to the large window that looked down at the backyards of the adjacent townhouses. After staring out the window for a moment or two, he abruptly turned to face her. "I want you to tell me everything. I want to know how he died and I want to know why he died."

"Why he died?" Gert asked with surprise.

"Yes, I want to know 'why.' I cannot believe he would have fallen down a flight of stairs. Sol always carried himself well and he was not clumsy. His dancing lessons proved that. I am annoyed and bothered when the facts I know seem to be contradicted by facts I do not know. So, if you can, please explain everything."

Gert paid scant attention to his remark about dancing lessons, for she sensed an ally. "I'm also upset about what happened and I've got some ideas about it."

"Tell me. I want to know everything you know and also, most important, I want to know what you suspect—if you have suspicions."

So Gert told him. She related everything she knew and everything questionable starting with the reaction Paul Coleman had to the perfume and finishing with what Sergeant Murphy told her about the coroner's report.

"Just as I suspected," he said. "Not for a moment did I think Sol would tumble and break his neck." Gert watched his jaw muscles tighten and his eyes narrow. The ruddiness that before had given him a cheerful appearance vanished, replaced now with the hard, dark crimson of anger.

When he sat on the sofa, he had rested his hat next to him, but he held onto the ebony stick. While she told him what she knew, he had remained standing as still as a store mannequin. But now, suddenly, his hands stirred. He twisted the dark rod and to Gert's surprise it came apart. In an instant, one hand held the black wood shaft, in the other was what had been secreted inside—a gleaming blade of silvery metal.

With a relaxed but firm grip on what appeared to be a foot-long scalpel, he looked at Gert. Then calmly and in a very soft voice, said "I do not want to give you the impression I am a clown on a rerun of some TV variety show." As he spoke, he held the gleaming mini-sword in front of him and flexed it like a dueling foil.

She was transfixed and stared at the glistening blade wondering if he had actually stuck anyone with it.

"Wow, is that legal?" she asked.

"I am not concerned with its legality. I carry it for its usefulness. In the past when I have unsheathed this weapon, I have used it and there are a number of loud and foul mouthed fools here in the Village who can attest to that."

Gert was only mildly surprised, for she wondered what it must be like for a man like Cyril to merely walk the Village streets. In no way could he escape the stupid and the ignorant. To be him, one had to be ready to deal with the numerous challenges that would certainly occur.

"If the opportunity arises," he said, "I will use this on the person or persons responsible for Sol's death. It would give me pleasure to inflict as much pain on them as Sol's death has brought to us." Then with a liquid quick movement, he brought the two parts of the stick together and the lethal blade vanished in the wooden shaft.

With the weapon hidden, his demeanor changed and as if they had been talking about afternoon tea, he asked, "Does my desire to help rectify this situation give you reason for alarm?" Gert emphatically shook her head. "Good," he said. "I want to help in any and every way."

He walked back to the sofa and leaned the formidable stick against an arm. "But," he said, "First things must be first. Since the police are apparently satisfied with a decision of accidental death even though they say they will question the Miss Lydia Cornell you mentioned. And, if she is as clever as you imply, she will have a proper alibi and provide them with zero. Be that as it may, the medical examiner's office will undoubtedly release Sol's body quite soon. Please allow me to take care of everything relating to his funeral."

"Will you have a problem with the financial end of things? I have ample funds, you see, and—"

"Finances will not be a problem," he said curtly. "I own and operate several funeral homes here in the Village, and I have others throughout the city. Funerals are what I do."

Then, a second later, and in a softer voice he said, "This is my promise to you here in his home. His warmth and humanity will not merely float away and be forgotten. Those who destroyed his life will pay. He will be avenged!"

Gert shivered and thought, how stupid and how wrong is the stereotyping we bring to bear on people in our society. So many would take one look at Cyril and write him off as a cotton puff incapable of tough, determined action. She wondered if his entire self-presentation was calculated and deliberate so people would underestimate him.

He picked up his hat and stood. "I have taken up more of your time than I anticipated. I'm sorry if I have kept you from your work."

"You haven't kept me from anything. I was looking forward to our meeting and would love to serve some tea, unless you have to leave."

He put his hat and the ebony stick back on the sofa and followed Gert to a small dining table Sol had placed against the wall that separated the small kitchen from the living room. From the kitchen she brought out a tray with the tea and some small, rich cakes. They sat and talked about Gert's idea for getting even and wondered if they would be able to bring it off. She had worked it out in her mind and had no guilty second thoughts with any part of what she planned. The only real problem was identifying Lydia's accomplice. Finding out who had been in the house and had actually killed Sol was going to be difficult. He agreed there would be no quick solution. Any satisfaction would have to be delayed.

Their conversation was interrupted by the telephone which Gert answered. After a moment she came back to the table. "That was Winthrop David, another friend."

"Oh, I know Win, Sol introduced us about a year ago. Is he coming over?"

"Yes, I told him to come up, since I wanted him to meet you. I didn't know you had met, and also to tell him to get things started with Coleman and the girl, Susan Merrill."

"Do you think she will be able to find out anything at Miss Cornell's advertising agency?"

"I don't know what she might find out, but I do feel the agency is involved. If Miss Merrill hears talk about a new product called Complete Abandon, then we can be sure Lydia and someone else are up to their necks in this thing."

For the next moments they were lost in the magnificence of the Pistachio Mousse tarts Gert bought at Joan Claude, a new bakery on Sixth, lost until the buzz of the lobby intercom jolted them from the tarts. As Gert rang back, Cyril picked up the empty foil cup the tart had been in.

"Where did you get this?" He waved the cup. "Wherever it is from, the place has to be new and it has to be a patisserie. No mere bakery I know did it. And I know all of them in the Village and not one can make a wonderful, authentic mousse tart like this."

Gert really got a kick out of him. Ten minutes ago, he would have run his sword into and out of some poor bastard and now he's waxing ecstatic about tarts. The doorbell rang and Gert got up to let Win in. When he walked in and saw Cyril, he said, "Hey, hey, two of my favorite people."

Gert leaned toward Cyril. "He's mister joyful these days. Found a new girl and is convinced he has the happiness market cornered."

"You're right. She's just great and she loves me as much as I love her."

"Are you sure?"

"Cyril, what kind of thing is that to say? I can only operate at face value. She tells me she loves me and I believe her."

"Good. Take advantage of every moment. Like poor Sol, our days are numbered."

Win sat down and Gert poured a cup of tea for him. "Yeah, Cyril, I know what you mean. I am still so pissed off about Sol I don't know what to say."

Gert leaned forward. "Winthrop, Cyril and I have been talking about plans to avenge Sol and believe me, we will. But first we will have a funeral for our friend. In the meantime, I want you to do me a favor."

"Anything at all."

"Good. I want you to contact Paul Coleman and meet with him and Susan Merrill. From what I gathered, the girl has managed to get a modeling job at Lydia's agency. She'll be in a perfect spot to tell us about what goes on there and especially, who is close to Lydia."

"I already know Lydia's very close to a guy named Tom Randall. In fact, I think she's moving in with him until she can get settled. She wanted to move in with me, but I told her I found a new girl so that was out."

"I know that Randall guy," said Gert. I met him a couple of times when she had him over. He seemed decent to me."

"Hey, don't misunderstand me. I'm not saying he's not okay. He's the guy she's running around with now, that's all." Win sipped some tea. "If I know

Lydia, Tom is just the moment's choice. She's not ready to hook up with any guy for too long. She's playing a game where there's only one winner—her."

"She sounds like a real cutie." Cyril said.

"You have no idea. We had a nice thing for a while, but I always got the impression I was like an umbrella. You know, convenient to have around, but easy to live without."

"Well," said Gert, "as far as I'm concerned, she's responsible for Sol's death and, believe me she will pay for it." Her tone was so grave that both men were silenced. Then Cyril took her hand in his. "Don't you worry the people or person responsible for Sol will not walk away."

"Oh, I have no doubt about that, Cyril."

"Gert," Win asked, "do you think the Merrill girl will refuse to be a spy, for that's what I'm going to be asking her to become."

"I don't know, Winthrop. She may be reluctant to get involved and I guess I wouldn't blame her. She's not really connected to any of this and she may feel loyalty to Lydia since she got her the agency job."

"Don't worry, I'll talk to her and if I have to I'll lay it all out for her."

"Listen, if you think she'll balk, bring her to me. I'll tell her what I think happened to Sol and when she hears it, she'll help. I think she's a good kid who is gonna be pissed off when she hears the whole story."

"You know," said Cyril, "there is the possibility this girl will tell Lydia what we want her to do if, as you say, she is loyal to her."

"You have a point," said Gert nodding, "but I don't think she's stupid and probably figured out Lydia's intentions right from the start. All Lydia ever wanted from her was the perfume. The modeling job was just a bribe."

"Look," said Win, "I'll talk to her and judge whether snooping is repugnant to her. I don't think she'd have any reason to try and hide her true feelings."

"Yeah, I would agree with you." said Gert.

"Very well," said Cyril as he stood. "I'll start the arrangements for the funeral and when I have information, I will call and tell you what has been arranged.

Cyril offered his hand to Gert and Win and then retrieved his hat and walking stick and exited the apartment like he was leaving a royal audience with the queen.

They looked at each other for a moment, and then Win said, "That is quite an original character."

"You can say that again, pal, and be sure you don't ever make him your enemy. I don't think I want him pissed off at me."

"What do you mean?"

Gert told Win about Cyril as they shared a fresh pot of tea and a pistachio tart she had stashed. Win spent an hour more with Gert because he sensed she wanted to talk about old times and especially Sol, and also because he thought she was lonely.

CHAPTER 39

At 7:30, before he left Gert's, Win called Lou to say he would pick her up at her place at 8:30, and then he went to his apartment. There, he called Paul Coleman and told him it was important he speak to Susan that night. It was agreed that Paul would bring her to the Riviera Bar.

At 9:00 Lou and Win sat side by side in a booth nursing two beers. "Do you think she'll be willing to go along with what you'll ask of her?"

"Hell, I don't know, but right from the start she seemed decent and open, and I have a hunch she's a lot smarter than any of us think."

"Why do you say that?"

"I just have a feeling from my years in the classroom. Eventually, you get a hunch about certain students. The bright ones give off signals. Their eyes shine, their posture is prideful, and their work shows a sense of humor. I don't know for sure and yet I do. You know what I mean?"

"Sure, it's the same with people I interview. Sometimes it's like talking to a fence post; it's different other times. I think most people can tell if someone else is on the ball."

"What is it we see? What gives the clue?"

"Well, it's like you said, it's in the eyes and the way they carry themselves. It's also, whether they follow your line of thought so you don't have to spell everything out."

"That's what I saw when I looked at you."

She pulled back a bit to see more of him. "What do you mean?"

"Well," he took a sip of beer. "When I first saw you I thought your face was an angel's face. Your skin and eyes were so alive and, and besides being beautiful, you looked vital, aware, like you were ready to live life. You looked thrilled to be alive and ready for whatever came along. You looked eager and enthusiastic. Oh hell, I don't know what word to use. All I know is when I looked into your face, I saw fireworks."

She snuggled up against him. "You were stoned out of your mind," she said. He laughed. "While that may be true, it isn't true now and it wasn't true yesterday. Whenever I see you, when I talk to you, when I'm with you are moments I'll never forget. Damn, I love you so."

"It's the same with me; I love you too." They turned to each other and kissed.

"Remind me," he whispered in her ear a moment later.

"Remind you about what?"

"That the next time I ask you to marry me, we won't be sitting side by side. It makes the clinches difficult."

She closed her eyes. "Please say that again. I want to be sure I heard what I heard."

He pulled back, turned to her as much as the booth would allow, and touched a hand to her face. "Loretta Anderson I want you to marry me because I love you more than any man has ever loved you or will ever love you. If you say 'yes' you will prove to the world I am worthy of you, and that's all I could ever ask to be. And, if you want, I'll call your father in Minnesota to ask for your hand."

She started to softly sob, "Oh, Win how could I say no to all that? Since we met, my life has been wonderful, you make me feel so alive, so..."

He leaned to her and straining against the table top, they kissed again.

"Would it be better if you two tried to dance on the dance floor?"

They separated and turned to see the waitress staring at them with her head cocked to one side "If we were in Mexico, France, or some other free-thinking place, there would be rooms upstairs. But we ain't. We're here in Greenwich Village, New Yawk City, so I'm asking if you want more beer."

Her face glistening with tears, Lou said, "We just got engaged. He asked me to marry him."

The waitress cocked her head to the other side and furrowed her forehead in question. Lou wiped away a tear, "I said 'yes.'"

"Now, ain't that grand? You want me to bring champagne?"

They laughed and Win cried out, "Yes! Bring champagne. Bring a good bottle and four glasses."

The waitress glanced at the empty seats. "It's a small engagement party, ain't it?"

"Not at all, here come some guests."

The waitress and Lou looked to the entrance and saw a couple come through the door, scan the crowd, and then walk to the table when they saw Win, who was now furiously waving at them.

Since Lou had never met Paul or Susan, there were introductions and then congratulations when the big news was spilled. Win got a real kick to see Lou acting like she was Susan's age. They were giggling and whispering and after a few minutes of sipping champagne, the two of them scooted off to the ladies room, hand in hand like sorority sisters.

While they were away from the table, Win asked Paul whether Susan was still modeling at Lydia's agency. Paul told him she was and that the agency was very pleased with her and had offered her more work than she could fit into her class schedule.

When the girls got back, Win told Susan and Paul about the fire and Sol's death

"You mean that sweet old man I met at Professor Lehman's? He was killed?" asked Susan. Before Win could answer, Paul said, "Ohhhh, I heard a faculty member had died. So it was him."

"Yes, I'm afraid so and unfortunately, they may write it off as accidental."

"When you say 'unfortunately' you're saying you don't think it was an accident, right?"

"That's right Paul, I don't. And let me tell you why I think it was not an accident." Win told them about the fire and the trashing of the lab and nothing else. He tried hard to be fair and not directly accuse Lydia, but Susan caught on immediately.

"Wait a minute. All this has to do with the perfume my mother sent to me, right? When I gave Lydia the phony perfume, she realized she would need Professor Lehman's analysis of the original if she was going to duplicate the effect. I knew Professor Lehman had the analysis in her laboratory because she told me."

"That's right," Win said. "But first, Gert . . . Professor Lehman . . . gave Lydia an analysis that did not include the breast milk."

"Oh," Susan exclaimed. "That's why she called me." Like practiced conspirators, they leaned over the table toward her as she spoke. "Lydia called me to ask about the original perfume and I told her about my father's joke with the breast milk and that Professor Lehman said she had a complete analysis of the perfume which included the breast milk. After that Lydia was as sweet as could be."

"I see, so that's how she found out Gert had done a complete analysis," said Win.

Susan drew her hand to her mouth. "My god, she found out from me, and when they went to get the complete analysis, they killed Professor Woodrow."

"Now wait a minute, wait a minute. No one knows if that's true." Win said.

"Well, you may not know if it's true, but it certainly makes sense to me." First she looked at Paul and then at Win. "What is it you want me to do?"

Win smiled. "I was hoping you'd understand. You see, if Lydia is behind all this, she didn't do it herself. Somehow she got someone to act for her. It had to be someone she knows and trusts. Someone, I think, who might even benefit from having it or why would they be involved?"

"Well, I guess you could say there are three men she's sort of involved with. There's Tom Randall, who I think is her boyfriend. There's A.T. Dunn who runs the place, but I don't think he's the type, and then there's Dennis. I don't know his last name, but if I had to pick a thief from the three, it would be him."

"Isn't he the guy you told me about?" Paul asked.

"Yes. He's the guy who put the make on me the instant he saw me. He's a real wise guy. When I told Paul about him, he said he sounded like an Italian sports car with a cock, and that's perfect." She paused. "If I had to pick a stinker from that crowd, I'd pick Dennis, no question."

"Okay," said Win. "Then here's what I'd like you to do. Just try to find out where the perfume business is at, where it's up to. If you get a chance to speak to that Dennis or the other two, see if they'll talk about it. Don't start asking direct questions and don't take any chances. Just see if you can find out anything about the perfume. If I remember correctly, Lydia wanted to call it Complete Abandon."

"Don't you worry about me, I'll find out what's going on."

Win sat back and took a breath. "Remember," he said, "just ask innocent questions. You mustn't get anyone suspicious. If we're figuring this right, one of them is a killer and he'll protect himself, so you must be careful and avoid any kind of confrontation. Okay?"

"Don't worry. I know my way around men. I always have."

Leaning forward, Paul asked, "Now what does that mean?"

She turned to him and smiled. When she did that, her face changed and Win realized what it was the agency saw in her. She could 'speak' with her face. Aside from her good looks, she knew how to raise an eyebrow, how to tilt her head, how to hold her lip so you know exactly what was on her mind. Her face was like a billboard sending messages.

"Hey," said Paul. "I guess that was a silly question, wasn't it?"

When Susan turned back to Win she saw how serious he looked.

"Look Susan, whether you know your way around men or not isn't the point. If Dennis is the guilty party, he's a dangerous man. And if he suspects you are fishing for what is not your business, he may become dangerous to you. I'm worried about this even though I want you to do it."

"Believe me I wouldn't volunteer if I were the slightest bit nervous about it. I can handle this. You'll see."

CHAPTER 40

In the short time Susan had worked at the agency, the staff photographers used her for different clients. Her appeal was a combination of extreme good looks and a visibly cheerful disposition. She was unlike the majority of models, because they were quirky and quick to display their neurotic baggage. Far more than half of them truly did not understand what people meant when they congratulated them for being so beautiful, so lovely; so up to the minute. For those girls, their faces and underfed bodies that the photographers and clients ogled, were nothing more than the "them" they had seen in mirrors every previous day of their lives. They saw their blemishes, their lack of physical balance, and their flat, featureless physiques. Most of their abundant anxieties were attributable to their inability to see the perfection they were supposed to symbolize.

To be complimented for something you do not clearly notice can lead to a skeptical regard for those who express those compliments. It becomes hard to believe people who tell you you're not what you think you are. The upshot is a lack of trust not only in what those people say, but also in those people as well.

Fortunately, Susan avoided those feelings. It wasn't that she didn't believe she was pretty. She did believe that. She recognized the symmetry of her features and her ability to project an expression that easily transferred to photographs. As all people do, she compared herself with those around her, but rather than quake for what she didn't possess, she shrugged off the differences and accepted what she was and how she looked. In short, she was healthy and represented such a significant variation from the norm that the majority of staff photographers clamored for her.

Today's work was called an irrelevancy—a cheesecake photograph that has absolutely nothing to do with the product in the advertisement. Susan got a kick from these sessions because she often didn't know what the product was and guessing became a game. So, as she stood in front of a rear-projection beach scene, wearing a skimpy bikini and holding a large red beach ball, she tried to figure out the client's product. She figured it should have something to do with vacations, swimming, Caribbean travel, suntan lotion, beaches, summertime, something that made sense with her outfit and the prop.

"C'mon Frank, give me a hint."

"Don't move. Don't talk. Let me get a few more shots and I'll tell you the whole truth. Just stand still."

As the camera's automatic drive snapped away, she thought about the number of shots. When she was a kid, she had a cheap camera and used it for "say cheese" pictures at the zoo, the ball game, or at a party. One event usually meant one, two or at most, three pictures. But here, they took pictures by the dozens and drove themselves crazy trying to decide which was best. She told them to take two and make a decision by tossing a coin. They laughed at her.

"Okay, that was great. You can ease up," Frank said.

"Tell me," she said, kicking the beach ball at him. He ducked as it sailed over his head. "Well," he said, "believe it or not, this series is for a stock brokerage firm."

She stared at him and then laughed. "That's crazy. Buying stock is serious stuff and I would think those firms would want to stress their smarts. What the heck does a picture of me in a bikini have to do with anything?"

"Well, my best guess is the creative team thinks a pretty girl in a bathing suit will put the potential customers in the right frame of mind."

"That's exactly what they think, Frank. You got it 100 percent." Both Frank and Susan turned to the dimly lit back of the studio and saw Dennis. He continued to talk as he walked into the light.

"When the typical reader of the business section—older, married, solid, gets a look at Miss Hot Stuff here, they'll think of the days gone by and how sweet it would be to recapture them. The ad will be screaming at them, invest with us and you'll get rich, rich enough to dump the wife, rich enough to say 'fuck you' to the pain-in-the-ass kids, rich enough to find a great piece of ass like sweetie-pie here, rich enough to run off to the sunshine for a life of sucky and fucky."

Susan laughed. "I don't know if you're wrong or right, Dennis, but I wonder how your answer would rate on an exam in an advertising class."

"It should get a fucking A, because it's right on the money. But I bet some asshole who spends every day bullshitting about advertising would probably think it's a little gross, huh?"

"You could be right about that," she said, as she grabbed a robe from the back of a chair. "You should go for a job as a lecturer in the night school setup. Maybe they could use someone with your grasp of the business."

"Hey, that's not a bad idea," he said, as he came up to her, stopping about a foot away and then in a softer voice said, "I know another good idea. Why don't we go into the dressing room and you can model for me, a little private show." He stepped in front of her, slipped one hand into the robe, and, pushing up the bikini top, grasped her naked breast. His other hand darted between her legs to squeeze her crotch. "I would love to taste instead of touch," he said, grinning.

As she backed up feeling like some grotesque insect had crawled on her skin, she grabbed his wrists and pulled his hands away. Then with more disgust than anger, she said, "Dennis, why don't you grow up and stop acting like you were fourteen sneaking feels on the subway?"

Frank, who saw what happened, started to approach them. Dennis turned to him and said, "Hey Frank, mind your own business. This has nothing to do with you."

"Jesus Christ, Dennis, you can't treat everyone like shit."

"You're right, Frank. I am a crude son of a bitch and if you want to keep your job, mind your business and butt out." And then turning back to Susan, he asked, "Hey, you love it, don't you?"

"Right, Dennis, about as much as I love leprosy." She pulled the robe tightly about herself. "Frank," she asked "are we finished?"

"Yeah, we're all done." He looked at Dennis as he asked her, "You gonna be okay?"

"Don't worry about me. Dennis dahhhhhling likes his women upset. I think anger turns him on."

"You turn me on, babe. You know that. You get me all hot."

"Speaking of hot, Dennis, why don't you wait here while I get dressed and then you can take me for some coffee. Will that calm your overeager libido?"

He stared at her while wetting his lips with his tongue. "You're really hot shit. There's just one thing that's gonna calm my libido and you know what it is."

"Right, I think you made that clear. But I'd rather have coffee, so why don't you wait for me to get dressed. Okay?" He smiled, but said nothing as she walked into the dressing room.

About twenty minutes later, they sat facing each other in the building's café.

"You know, Dennis you'd do a lot better with women if you'd stop being so gross. You're an attractive guy."

"Shit, don't tell me how to handle women. You're a kid, a damn good-looking kid, but still a kid." He gulped some coffee. "Lots of women say what you say, but they really want a nasty fucker who treats them like crap."

"Do you think women are so down on themselves that they all want to be treated that way?"

"I don't know or care what they think about themselves. All I know is I've always treated them like shit and they've always come back for more."

"Not all," she said, as she took a bite of muffin.

"Of course, not all, but enough. Enough to keep me very satisfied."

She had to admire the way he played his hand. Confidence oozed out of him and he was about as audacious as any man she had ever come across.

"You're so sure of yourself. Wouldn't it be great if somebody could put your confidence into a bottle?"

"What do you mean?"

"Well, I don't know, but say something like a love potion. You put it on and the opposite sex does whatever you want."

He shook his head. "No, that wouldn't work for both sexes, just one."

"Just one?"

"Yeah, men would cream over that. Like when you're with that special babe, smear some crap on yourself and the chick drops her clothes and opens her legs. Goddamn, men would freak for that."

"You don't think women would want something like that?"

"Shit no, no way. Women want to control guys. If there was a love potion that got men ready to go in an instant, women would be raped all over the place. No, women want control. They want some crap that would guarantee them bein' able to just snuggle with guys. So, if they feel like screwin' 'em, it would be their idea, not the idea of some hyped-up hero with a giant erection."

"Okay, then someone should create a love potion that makes you snuggle, you know, gets the action started."

"That's on the way, baby."

"What do you mean, 'that's on the way'? Is there such a thing?"

"Hey, baby, before you know it, you'll be able to go into a store and buy a perfume that will do exactly that. Women will put it on, and men will act like puppies."

She laughed. "C'mon Dennis, be serious. There's no such thing."

"Not yet, there isn't, but very soon you're going to be able to buy a perfume that will do exactly that." He sat back looking like the kid who got 100 on the spelling test. "It's gonna come out of this agency, right here, A.T. Dunn is gonna be the big pusher, and yours truly played a major hand in getting it to go."

"That's fantastic, and you say you played a role in its development?"

"Damn right I did, kid. You could say that without me, there wouldn't be any love potion."

"Now you've got me interested. I'd love to get my hands on something like that."

"Why would you want it? If you want some action, I'll give you enough orgasms to keep you happy for a month. I would just love to suck on your clit." He leaned against the table almost knocking over the coffee cups.

"Jesus, Dennis, control yourself."

"You see, 'control yourself.' That's what I'm talking about. You want to control me. All women want control. Men, Shit. All men want to do is get sucked and fucked all day and night."

She looked at him in awe. He was one of a kind—at least she'd never met anyone like him. Was it true, she wondered, that all men thought as he did, but only a few, had the courage, stupidity, the whatever, to act as he did and say what he said?

"You know something," she said. "You have a real magic with language. Have you ever considered writing copy?"

"Very funny, very funny," he said, as he finished the last of the English muffin and coffee in one bite and one swallow. With his mouth half filled, he said, "Babe, I could do whatever I want at this agency, and when this new product comes out, I'll be able to decide exactly what I want to do. I will write my own ticket. All you're gonna have to do is tell me what you want and be nice to me, and you'll have it."

"And be nice to you."

"Hey, don't be a kid." He stared at her. "Look, you're probably giving it away now and giving some to me isn't going to be the end of the world. Lots of women think I'm not the worst thing in their lives."

"I'm sure they're right, but I have other plans. I want to marry a nice guy, have some kids and live in a small house upstate."

"Jesus Christ, you sound like you got some fatal fucking disease. 'Live in a small house upstate.' Are you kidding me? You got looks, babe. You should be here in the Apple where things are happening. 'Upstate,' that's what they used to say about guys going to Sing Sing."

"That was 'up the river."

"No difference, no difference at all." When he said that she noticed he was looking at her in a different way. Now he didn't seem so eager to fling himself at her. Evidently, she was becoming distasteful, no longer registering as the party girl he wanted.

"Dennis, I think we can be friends. I think you need a woman as a friend, a woman who can help you straighten out your life."

"Hey, babe," he sneered. "You are startin' to sound like the nuns at the parochial school. The last thing I need is a woman for a friend. Women are for loving and for sex and for having good times with. Women are not for friends."

Trying once again to turn the conversation to the perfume, she said, "I suppose that's what you meant when you said men don't want a love potion to do what women want, that men want to have sex and then go to a baseball game. Women want something different."

"Hey, I like that, baby. Men want to have sex and then go to a ball game, that's it exactly. Ha!"

He lit a cigarette. "What women want, shit, they want little boys suckin' at their tits. Women want babies and like I said before, they want control!"

He suddenly stood, stretched and then leaned down to her. "You wait for the perfume to come out. When it does, a lot of guys will be goo-gooing at mommy's tits. It's going to be a breast-feeding bonanza."

Smirking, like he had beat out someone for a parking spot, he reached into his pocket, pulled out some bills and tossed them on the table. "I'll see you later, okay?"

She smiled back. "I won't be around this afternoon. I have classes. Remember, I'm still in school."

He looked down at her the way you look at a person in a restaurant who has had an entire meal dropped on them by a clumsy waiter. Then sneering, he gave her a perfunctory nod and headed for the door.

Susan remained at the table trying to get straight in her mind what he had said, and when she felt the information was secure, she went upstairs and checked with Frank, who reminded her to be very careful around Dennis, and that she was free to go. She immediately left and headed downtown eager to tell Win what she had found out. To her, it was obvious that Lydia's agency was going to bring out a product that would replicate the effect of the perfume her mother had sent to her.

Unfortunately, the bus ride down Fifth was not enjoyable because of the exhaust fumes from the surrounding traffic that crept back into the bus. Needing some fresher air, she got off a few blocks north of Washington Square and made it just in time for class.

As she waited for it to start, she thought about what Dennis had said. Even if he was merely boasting and only trying to act the big shot, it was clear he was involved in the theft of the analysis from Professor Lehman. She shivered when she remembered his hands on her flesh, maybe the same hands that had to do with killing Professor Woodrow. It was difficult for her to understand how one person could kill another, yet she realized how strongly she felt about revenge. If it was true and Dennis did indeed kill that old man, then he should receive the exact same punishment. That seemed fair to her. That balance seemed fair.

After class, Susan sat in Win's office and related to him, as best as she could recall, what Dennis had said.

"He actually said, 'without me,' there wouldn't be any love potion?"

"That's right, Professor."

"Please call me Win. I think we're way beyond titles."

She looked at him in what he thought was a funny way and then said, "You know, so many professors here seem to regard the title 'professor' as critical. I remember when I called one mister by mistake it was like I cursed his mother. He freaked."

"Susan, you have to understand what's involved. It takes an awful lot of work and time to earn that title, and also, for some it's a description of their life and not merely a job title."

"Oh, I understand that. But I think it has more to do with keeping a distance and pointing out who is more and who is less important."

"Sure, that's right, but don't forget some people are more secure, others less. Anyway, please call me Win, not Winthrop as Professor Lehman sometimes does."

"Fine." she said with a smile. "Now to get back to what Dennis said. Aside from, 'without me there wouldn't be any love potion,' he also said, 'women will put it on and men will act like puppies."

"Fantastic. What could be clearer?"

"That is what you wanted to know, right?"

"Absolutely, but there's one more favor."

"What?"

"I want you to tell Professor Lehman exactly what you told me. Is that okay?"

"Sure, when?"

"Well, if you can wait a few minutes, I'll call her and we'll arrange a time."

She nodded and he picked up the telephone. Gert was not in her office so he called Sol's and she picked up on the third ring.

"What?"

"Gert, it's me, Win. We're in luck. Susan Merrill is here in my office and she just told me about a conversation she had with a guy at Lydia's agency. I want you to hear it, so I'm asking if we can get together tonight."

"Absolutely!" She said. "Any time is good for me, so let her pick what's convenient for her." The emotion in her voice was clear.

Pointing at the phone Susan said, "I heard what she said; her voice carries. If it's okay, I could meet at eight."

"Win, I heard what she said. Eight is okay, and don't forget to tell her where I am. And I want you and Lou to come also."

"Can I bring Paul?" Susan asked.

Win was about to tell Gert what Susan asked. Instead, he laughed and handed her the phone. "I don't think you need me as a middleman."

Taking the phone, Susan said, "Professor Lehman this is Susan. I was just going to ask if it's okay for me to bring my boyfriend Paul?"

"Susan, honey, for what you've done, you could bring the Fifth Armored Division and I'd bake cookies for all of them. You probably have the information I've been seeking."

As far as Susan was concerned, all she did was have a short conversation with a wiseass guy, but, if it turned out that Dennis was the one who killed Professor Woodrow then he deserved whatever he got. Feeling righteous, she handed the phone back to Win, who assured Gert they'd be there at eight.

CHAPTER 41

Later that night, Win, Lou and Gert sat in Sol's apartment waiting for Susan and Paul to arrive. Gert was overjoyed when Win told her that he and Lou were going to be married.

"Oh, that's great. Too many people in academia wind up alone because it can be hard to find someone who'll not be intimidated by a lot of formal education."

"I know what you mean," said Lou. "My ex couldn't deal with me having a master's degree and making a living as a writer."

"Was he an educated man?"

"Yes, Gert, he was. He had a bachelor's degree and was a commissioned Air Force officer."

"Oh, he was military. That's important. That life is unlike the business world and it screws up their perceptions. There aren't enough women in the military and too many of those guys are so testosteroned, they can't understand women doing anything but screwing and serving drinks."

"That sounds like my ex."

"Did he resent your work?"

"No question. I would be working on a story, on the phone, or out running down facts. To him, none of that mattered. He wanted me around when he was around. The importance of my work was never real for him. He once called my career a diversion. How about that?"

"I understand that," said Win. "And I sincerely hope you don't intend to keep on working after we're married, do you?"

Lou looked at Gert, smiled, and then turning to Win, said very slowly, "Oh, no, dear, I won't be able to work after we're married. I'll be far too busy tending to you. A man in a wheelchair requires so much attention."

Win laughed and grabbed her hand.

Gert looked at them, "You're a lucky man, Win. Just don't forget that old Chinese saying and you'll be okay."

"What saying is that?"

"It translates to 'only a complete idiot screws up a good deal.'"

"Oh, that one." They laughed, as Gert went to get coffee and snacks. While she was pouring, the doorbell rang. It was Paul and Susan. They came in, sat and joined in the pastry and coffee.

When they finished, Gert said, "Susan, I want you to tell me everything that went on in this conversation you had. But first, who did you talk to? I know Tom and I have heard of Dunn, the big cheese. You talked to someone else, right?"

"Yes, Professor Lehman."

"Gert, please call me Gert."

Susan looked over at Paul with an 'I told you so' expression and continued. "Well, Gert, I talked to a guy named Dennis. I don't know his last name, but I could find out. Anyway, he's a guy who's always around the place, and as far as I know, he doesn't have a specific job. He's everywhere sticking his nose into everything. Like today, the photographer who was taking pictures of me seemed ready to defend me when Dennis got fresh. In fact, when Frank, the photographer, asked if I needed help, Dennis told him to mind his own business or he'd be out of a job. And Frank backed off, like Dennis could deliver on his threat. So obviously he's got power in the organization, but I don't know what it is. When I first got there, he was the one who showed me around."

"Did you see Lydia today?"

"No. I rarely see her. I go to the studio area and she's in the executive section."

"But Dennis was in the studio area?"

"Yes, but I think he was waiting for me. The photo schedules aren't private."

"You know," Paul broke in. "I don't think I like this guy very much. What did you mean before when you said he got fresh?"

"Oh, nothing. He felt me up that's all."

Paul's face turned red. "He felt you up? Is that nothing?"

She looked at him. "Paul you have to understand this kind of a guy. He's gross and squeezing someone's flesh means nothing at all to him. And you can't let it mean anything to you. He stops when he gets no reaction. It becomes a big deal only if you let it."

"Well, I want to know if he bugs you again."

"I don't think he will. After today he thinks I'm nothing but a silly little schoolgirl and that's not for him."

Gert, who had been listening intently interrupted. "He sounds like a real creep. But that's not the issue. What did he say about the perfume?"

"Well, I'll try to cover our conversation as it happened. First, we were talking about his overconfidence and I said it would be great if it could be bottled so either sex could use it. He said men want sex and women want to control men, and then I said it would be great if there was a love potion that would make men snuggle. He said such a thing was on the way—that you'd be able to buy a perfume that will do exactly that. Women will put it on and men will be like puppies."

"He said that? He said 'buy a perfume'?"

"Yes, he did and when I said there's no such thing, he said wait a month or two and there'll be a perfume that will do it. In fact, he said it twice. Then a little later when we were talking about the difference between what men and women want, he said women want control and If I wait for the perfume to come out, I'll see half the guys in America goo-gooing at mommy's tits, and that it's going to be a breast-feeding bonanza."

Gert burst out, "A breast-feeding bonanza? He said that? He said 'breast feeding?' He actually used those words?"

"Yes, he did, and I realized he was talking about the reaction Paul had to my mom's perfume, the start of all this."

"You're goddamn right that's what he was talking about." Gert exhaled and looked up at the ceiling. "Well, I'll be a son of a bitch. What I thought happened really did happen. They have the analysis that included the breast milk. They have the original analysis."

"Do you think this guy Dennis stole it?" Paul asked.

Gert shook her head. "I don't know and I don't have any idea how we could prove it even if it is true, but at least I know it *was* taken, and I feel pretty certain the fire was a cover-up and… whoever started that fire killed Sol."

"Oh," exclaimed Susan. "How horrible."

They sat in silence looking at each other and not knowing what to do or even what to say. Lou looked from one to the other. "You know I'm at a disadvantage here because you all knew Sol or at least met him, and I never had that chance. I feel sad because I know something awful happened but I, well, I never knew him, and yet…"

"Don't say it, Lou. There's no need. Sol was a good person, a good friend who didn't deserve to die, and believe me I'm going to do my best to see the appropriate justice is done." After saying that, Gert crossed to where Paul and Susan sat.

"I want you two to go. Susan, what you have done was very important and there is no way I can tell you how much I appreciate it. But, from here on out, I'm going to be planning things and doing things and I don't want either of you involved. Whatever I do, I want it on me, not anyone else. Neither of you should be part of this anymore. Do you understand what I'm saying?"

They looked at each other and then at Lou and Win who had listened to Gert as carefully as they did.

"What do you mean doings things?"

"Susan, right now I don't know, but whatever happens, you two have a full life ahead of you, as do you two."

She turned to Win and Lou. "So you must all go. I will handle this now. If there's going to be trouble, I'll take care of it. A good friend of Sol will help me do whatever has to be done."

"Gert, Sol was my friend also."

"I know that Winthrop, but you're going to be married." She turned back to Susan and Paul. "And you two might, so it wouldn't be fair to get any of you involved."

"Can't we be the judge of that?"

"No Win, you cannot. I'll be the judge."

"Wait a—" interrupted Paul, but Gert cut him off.

"Never mind the gallantry, Paul. This isn't the movies or some off-Broadway play. This may get serious and maybe dangerous. I could not live with myself if any of you got hurt, or, well, it doesn't matter. This is my affair to settle and I will."

"But damn it, Gert," Win almost shouted. "I want to help."

"I do too" said Lou.

Susan looked at Paul and a moment later said, "So do we."

Gert's eyes shifted from one pair to the other. "I thank you for that and I'll take up your offers if I need help, but I want you to understand me. I said I would settle this score and I will."

Lou stood and slowly picked up the dishes to take to the kitchen. When she came back in, she stood alongside Win until he stood. A moment later, Susan and Paul got up.

"Gert," asked Win, "Are you sure you want us to leave?"

She looked up and nodded. "Yes, I'm going to call a friend and tell him what we've learned. From now on, this business is going to be our business."

She slowly escorted them to the door. "I promise though, that I'll certainly ask for your help if we need it."

Then with pleading eyes, she asked, "Do you really understand why you must go?"

They nodded and left.

CHAPTER 42

Cyril answered the phone with a long, drawn-out "Hellllooooo." In the background Gert could hear music loud enough to illustrate Cyril's reluctance to mourn in a traditional way.

Gert listened for a moment and then guessed. "Mozart, right?"

"Wrong, my dahling, it is Cyril. And what musical genius is this?"

"It's Gert."

"Forgive me, my dear I thought you were one of my neighbors calling to tell me my music player was functioning. They are so very helpful. They assume I wouldn't notice it is working beautifully, but you did not call to say my music is overly loud. Therefore, you must have some news."

"That I do. I definitely know the analysis was stolen and did not burn up with my other papers."

"That is fantastic news, and who took it?"

"Well, I know who has it, but I'm not certain who took it. Right now, though, I feel about 90 percent positive who did, but—"

"My dear," he interrupted, "these days, being 90 percent certain is as good as you'll get, so give me a name and I will make certain he or she never sees the light of another day. There are coffins continually leaving for burial from one of my places and it would be easy to stick the bastard in a box, with company, and put an end to all this."

"Wait, wait …'with company?' What is that?"

"Dahling, most coffins have ample room for a guest or a pet or just about anything. You couldn't guess the things people want to be buried with. I've heard it's nice to have company on a long trip, but anyway, there's always room for a guest in the bottom of the box."

"Yes, company is always nice, but… what I know is his first name, where he works, that information, but…"

"Do I hear in your voice an aversion to immediate action until you are absolutely confident you have the right person?"

"Right. A mistake would serve no purpose."

"Reluctantly, I must say you are probably right, since eliminating the wrong person would keep me up past my bedtime. You see, dear Gert, my fellow man has never sufficiently endeared himself to me to warrant significant concern."

"Stop playing such a tough guy."

"Oh, dear Gert, but I am. I am as much a contradiction as any straight. I am a big softy and also as nasty as can be. Sometimes I do not know what I am. You see, being several people at once is very confusing."

Gert laughed. "Cyril, you're funny...I get a kick out of you."

"Cole Porter, 1934...a wonderful song. Did you know him, by chance?"

"Who? Cole Porter?"

"Yes, of course. Isn't he who we are talking about?"

"Oh, Cyril, please stop playing around. This is serious business."

"Gert, dear Gert, you must learn about life. Look at dear Sol. Walked around with the weight of the world on his shoulders, very concerned, very involved, very much a sad man. Do not mimic him. Believe me, we will deal with the scum who killed him and they will wish they had not. It is as simple as that. Mark my words. Their shortcomings will not drag us down to their level of insignificance."

"But Cyril, life *is* serious."

"Gert, please, life is nothing. It is our view of it that makes it what we think it is. If one sees it is as serious, it is. If one sees it as a moment of complete lunacy, it is that. By itself it is nothing. We are the manufacturers of its meaning and Sol made his about 80 percent serious. That is why he was so often morose."

"He must have caught it from me."

"Oh no, you are far less melancholic than he. In fact, I suspect you could be a lot of fun. Maybe it is simply that you too often forget."

"Forget what?"

"That we will all end as Sol. Gert, honey, remember I know death. It is what I do. I know we will end up on a dirty sheet, in a dirty box, waiting to be stuck into a dirty hole and rather quickly forgotten. That's the truth, my dear, and it is high time you digested it. You must stop thinking of life as a mission with medals and trumpets at its conclusion. Life is a completely absurd situation that, fortunately, we can make more interesting if we put in the time."

She was struck silent for a moment. "I don't know what to say."

"Good. Then your mission tonight is to think about the fleeting moments left to you and whether you want to spend those moments smiling, laughing, enjoying yourself, or sitting in the library looking up the etymology of the word 'comatose.'"

Gert wondered how Sol could have been so sullen when he was running around with Cyril. "Why didn't Sol pick up more of your attitude? I find it irresistible."

"My dear, merely think of the people you know. Just imagine their faces in your mind. If you are good at imagining, you will find some faces are frowning while others are smiling. Those who are frowners are reflecting their essential nature. That is what they are. That was it from birth and that is how they live. The smilers, on the other hand, are reflecting their innate nature. Can't you recognize that?"

She paused for several seconds, and then said, "Yes, I think I can."

"Wonderful. It is an explicit duty in your life to extricate yourself from any relationship with frowners and associate exclusively with smilers. If you hang with the frowners, they'll give you the downers. That rhyme is mine, but the choice is yours."

"In other words, walk on the sunny side of the street."

He was silent. She waited, but he didn't speak. "Aren't you going to tell me?" she finally asked.

"Oh, I was being polite I thought you were going to supply the information."

"No, I was setting you up."

"Oh, well, okay, that was Dorothy Fields and Jimmy McHugh. 1930. I believe."

"I'll check and let you know."

"Don't bother. I am correct."

She laughed. "It's hard to frown while talking to you."

"That is the point, my dear." He paused. "Now, tell me how are we going to proceed?"

"Well, the guy we're interested in works at an advertising agency on Madison. The girl who got the information from him also works there. I guess we have to figure a way to get a confession from him without endangering the girl or anyone else."

"I completely understand and I will think on it tonight. We must meet tomorrow so I may tell you of the plans for Sol's funeral. When we have discussed that subject we can return to this one. I want you to think of a ruse, a ploy, some sort of trick we can play on this fellow, so he will think it is in his best interest to tell us what we need to know."

"That might be a problem, for if he confesses, he'll essentially be telling us he killed Sol."

"Yes, that is a problem. So, we must conceive a way to make him think he will suffer greater damage by not telling us. We must present him with alternatives so that the best choice for him will be self-incrimination in a murder."

"Would anybody be that stupid?"

"It depends on the choices he is offered, does it not?"

She sensed where his mind was at and realized he was right. There certainly are worse things to happen to a person than being branded a killer. "Yes," she said. "It does indeed depend on that." She paused a moment and then added, "Cyril, you're my kind of guy. You've got imagination."

"That was Johnny Burke and Jimmy Van Heusen, 1940."

Laughing, Gert said, "I'll call you tomorrow morning to set a time and place for a meet."

She heard him say, "Not too early, darling," as she lowered the phone.

CHAPTER 43

Gert was waiting at table for Cyril in the main dining room of the Greenwich Plaza Hotel figuring it was exactly the place Cyril would choose. Taking inventory, she could see almost the same number of blue-haired, white-gloved ladies you'd see at Schraft's, but here they were with sleek, handsome, well-dressed young men. Gert also noticed there were as many men escorted by men as there were women escorted by men. Not at all like the Village bistros she knew, where almost everyone but her wore bib overalls and sat alone.

"Do you like what you see?"

She looked up to see Cyril dressed as elegantly as any one person could manage. The cut of his suit and the colors of his coordinated outfit made her wonder if in her entire life she had ever been adequately dressed. She shook her head.

As he sat, he asked, "What does the head shake mean? What are you thinking about?"

"To be honest, I was admitting to myself that no matter what I wear and no matter what you wear I think I'll always feel I'm covered in mud."

"Gert, don't let my expertly tailored clothes disturb you. For it should be obvious that even if I was totally nude, you'd see I am clearly a superior person."

"With a great sense of humor."

"Mais oui, mon cher, mais oui."

Gert laughed. "Damn it, Cyril, you make me feel like I'm always playing catch-up ball."

He smiled. "My dear, let us order, let us eat, and then we will discuss the plans I have made for the funeral."

Gert let Cyril order and he did it very well. They started with date nut bread squares, followed by Greek lemon soup with hot phyllo triangles filled with a mix of spinach and feta, and then mocha mousse for dessert.

After their meal and while waiting for dessert, he told her of the funeral arrangements. "First, it is unfortunate no funereal establishment in the Village, not even one of mine, is large enough to hold the number of people who will attend. Therefore, the ceremony will be in the main ballroom of this hotel. Furthermore, to put your mind at rest, I can vouch for the on-site staff. Good taste will prevail. Second, dear Sol will be cremated and his spirit as well as his ashes will join us for the service. Third, a great number of people have requested the opportunity to publicly say their good-bye and I see no reason to limit them as to time or subject matter."

The waiter brought demitasse and each a mocha mousse. Neither spoke while they ate, but before she had half finished hers, Gert signaled the waiter to bring her another. With amusement in his eyes, Cyril asked, "Are you not worried about your caloric intake?"

"What you said last night about frowning and smiling really struck me. So much so, that I will no longer concern myself with the consequences of my actions. I intend to enjoy what time I have left."

"Well, super good for you, but let me continue. Since we are going to serve food and beverages, those speakers who bore or entertain the assemblage will have to deal with actual reactions, so have no fear about windbags seeking a place in rhetorical history. The audience will be quickly drunk and any orator who does not deserve their time will be rapidly whooshed away."

Surprise evident in her voice, Gert said, "Food and drinks, drunks? Cyril this is a funeral."

"I am well aware of that, my dear, and I am also aware of what Sol would have requested if there had been time. We shall remember him as a great friend, a real person, and certainly, an avid believer in the great need for good times."

"I've never been to a funeral that wasn't, well, a funeral."

"Yes, I too have been to and arranged scores of those typical events, and I have also arranged many quite unlike the typical. And one more thing, one way or another, I'd like the fellow you suspect as Sol's killer to attend the affair."

She stared at him. "How can we arrange that? I don't know him and all we do know is that he works at the same place as Lydia. And, also, what do you mean, 'one way or another'?"

"Just that. It'd be nice if he attended regardless of his physical condition. You follow?"

She thought she understood him but decided not to pursue it. "You know, connecting with him could be a problem"

"Is it possible he might be lured into our hands by the young girl who managed to secure the information about the stolen formula? Could she, would she, offer herself to him and suggest they meet here, in a room upstairs? Do you think she would agree to that?"

"I have no idea. I'd have to ask. But let's say she agrees and he comes, then what?"

"You leave that to me. I have very loyal friends well equipped to handle such a person and let me assure you, when we get our hands on him, he will answer any question we ask." He laughed softly. "I am sure he will even answer questions we do not ask."

Gert stared at him. "Torture?"

"No, not at all, not at all. As I said last night, we present choices. Give this person a choice of this or that and allow him to select whichever suits him." He smiled. "Gert, it is very much like the old *Let's Make a Deal* TV program. Monty would ask door number one or door number two? You remember. He provided choices. People selected. And a one-legged guy got a bicycle while a person living in the desert got a boat."

Gert laughed and regretted it had taken Sol's death to bring her into contact with Cyril. It would have been greater fun if Sol were with them.

CHAPTER 44

Theodore Hicks stumbled into Lydia's office carrying two very large ring binders and an assortment of file folders trapped against his chest by his forearms. He looked like a Jerry Lewis movie.

"I have the test results," he announced.

"Why don't you put them there on the credenza and tell us what you found out."

"Whatever you say, Mr. Dunn."

While Hicks untangled himself from the reams of paper, Lydia looked at Dunn who was casually staring at the sky through the large window. "Doesn't this get you excited?" she asked him.

"It certainly does. Why would you think otherwise?"

"I'm not sure, but I guess it's because you look so matter of fact. Like all this is just another day at the office, and if I may say, you haven't been looking well. Are you okay?"

"I'm fine, Lydia. But this is, after all, just another day at the office."

"Well, maybe for you it is, but for me, this is a big day."

Hicks theatrically cleared his throat. "Ahemmm, what is it you want to know?"

Lydia looked at him as if he were crazy. "Theodore, just tell us how the stuff tested out, okay?"

"Well, in a nutshell, it seems to work 42 percent of the time."

Hesitantly, Lydia asked, "Would you say that again, slowly?"

"I said it works less than 50 per cent of the time. In other words, if there were 10 men it would probably work on 4 of them."

She stared at him.

Sensing her discomfort, he said, "You have to understand, Miss Cornell, most likely we are dealing with some sort of inexplicable genetic aberration.

The perfume will work on some men, but not all men will experience the hug effect."

He snickered. "I named it that, but whatever we'll call it the perfume will produce the hug effect in approximately 4 of every 10 men."

Lydia's eyes darted to Dunn. "Well, how's that? Good enough for you?"

"Oh, yes. I was planning for us to go ahead if it worked even a bit less than half as it has. This may not be a sure thing therefore the copy has to be perfect. We have to phrase the promises just right."

"You leave that to me," she said. "I have the essence all worked out. In less than a week I'll be able to present the basic framework for the campaign."

"I'm glad this has worked out as it did, Lydia. It will be a major step in your career, and it will also mean something good for the entire agency." He smiled and walked to the door. "Ted," he said, turning back, "come with me. I think Lydia wants to be alone just now."

Hicks managed to grab the binders and folders and while smiling at Lydia, waddled out with Dunn.

Silently, she thanked Dunn because she did want to be alone. She sat at her desk and breathed deeply, enjoying the glorious warmth of the moment.

After a while a smile played across her face and she picked up the phone and dialed. She heard one ring, then two, then, "Hello?"

"Dennis, it's me, Lydia. I was wondering if you would come to my office."

"Sure, babe, I'll be right along." It took him about a minute and a half to come swaggering through the door.

"What can I do for you, babe?"

She got up from her desk and stood alongside it. "I want you to sit down there." She said, pointing to the sofa. Dennis raised an eyebrow and tilted his head in question, but did what she asked. He walked to the sofa and sat.

"Now what?" he asked.

In answer to his question, Lydia walked to her office door, locked it, and came back to the sofa and sat alongside him.

"What's all this?" he asked, leering at her.

Looking at him, she said, "I realized I never really thanked you, and I want to do that now."

He smiled. "Is this full or partial payment? Not that I won't appreciate whatever it is, but I was certainly hoping for—"

"Oh, Dennis, just shut up and kiss me, okay?"

He did what she asked and then ran his hands over her body. As they kissed, he cupped her breasts and then smoothed her thighs as he pressed down on her. He reached under her dress and gently massaged her crotch. Then he opened her dress and freed her breasts. After staring at them for a moment he leaned to her and grasped a nipple with his lips.

They looked like teenagers in the backseat of a car at the drive-in, but they were not kids on a date. There was no hesitating nor were there moments of decision or doubt. They both knew what they wanted and how to get it.

She knew that, with Dennis, it wouldn't take long. Some men need coaxing to enter into the physical, but not men like him. He was always one heartbeat away from an erection and two beats away from an orgasm. By now she was equally aroused and wanted him as much as he wanted her, so she slowly leaned back and drew him on top of her. Several minutes later, they sat alongside each other on the small sofa. He looked around and then laughed aloud.

"What's funny?"

"Well, the way we're sitting here, like in a waiting room of a train station or even a bus station. I tell you, if it was a bus station, I think it would be a place for the best fucking bus ride ever." Then he said, "And Lydia, you got to be the best fucking driver, ever!"

Now she laughed. "Is this where we start complimenting each other?"

"Hey, come on. I may not be Mister Great, but you don't want your money back, do you?"

"I didn't pay anything."

"Well, then you certainly got your money's worth."

Eventually, she told him about the findings Hicks had presented and that the entire project would rapidly move ahead. When he asked about the remainder of the evening, she told him she had to meet Tom Randall for a dinner appointment and that also, now that she was living with him, it would be strange if she had a date.

Saying he understood, he unlocked her office door and left her sitting on the sofa. Feeling relaxed, she sat there for about five minutes until she had to get up to answer the phone. The operator told her a Police Sergeant Murphy wanted to speak to her.

After a few clicks, she heard, "Miss Cornell, this is Sergeant Murphy, we met at the time of Professor Lehman's house fire."

"Yes, I remember you," she said. "What can I do for you?"

"Well, we will have to meet to discuss your whereabouts that day and also, for me to learn more about your desire for a certain chemical analysis Professor Lehman said you wanted."

She froze. Would it be possible for the police to tie her to the robbery and worse, to Sol's death? Reluctant to think that could happen, she brazenly said, "Of course, Sergeant, when and where shall we meet?"

"I will let you know about the time and place. In the mean time, if you have an alibi for that time of day, please bring the information with you."

"Certainly, you'll call me?"

"Yes. Goodbye."

She hung up, stared at the phone and then dialed Dennis. When he answered, she said, "Dennis, the police just called me. They want to see me about the fire and about the analysis."

"Hey, don't sweat the cops. They're always screwing up. You said you would have a good alibi and there is no way they can prove anything about the analysis. Don't let them bullshit you. They always talk big, but they're nothing but a pain in the ass. And look, if it comes to it, I know some very good lawyers who deal in criminal matters all the time. We're free of any charges. Don't get nervous."

"But I am very nervous."

"Relax, you weren't there and the idea for the perfume that we got from the college kids was enough for us to get started trying to create a perfume with the ingredients we knew about. We're in the clear so I wouldn't sweat this. Meet with them and play tough. They have nothing."

"God, I hope you're right. I can't get the idea of the murder out of my mind."

CHAPTER 45

"He was such a doll. He helped me remove most of my clothing from the apartment."

Staring at her he asked, "What did you offer him?"

"Oh, come on, Tom. I'm willing to thank people who help me. But you make it sound like I'd flop on my back for the guy who delivers the newspaper."

Briefly, he looked at the floor and then at her. "You're right, I'm sorry. That was nasty. I guess I'm pissed about sharing you."

"What do you mean, 'sharing me'?" she asked sharply.

"Well, it's just that I have this feeling you use sex like it's a tool, like a hammer to a carpenter. You use it on the job."

"That's exactly right. I'll do what I have to do to get what I want. Don't you?"

He hesitated. "I don't know. Maybe I have no basis for complaining, few men do, but it seems different when women play that game."

"I think your morality is screwed up. Are you saying I can't have sex when it benefits me, but guys can fuck whenever it suits them for any reason they deem worthy?"

"Is my middle-class upbringing showing?"

"It isn't your middle-class anything. It's just the stupid basic idea that men and women can't act the same way or do the same things. It's just the usual American hypocrisy."

"It's different in other places?"

"You know as well as I do that in some countries religious lunatics kill a woman for looking at another man, while in others they aren't hung up on gender like we are. If men do something and its okay, then women can do the same thing."

Aside from knowing there was no reason to argue with her, he also knew she would always do what she wanted no matter what he or anyone thought. He stared at her, admiring her beauty, hoping she'd change her attitude, but sensing there was little chance of that. So, like most of the pivotal moments in his life, he decided he would just let things happen, realizing that in six months or so, she would be in his life or out.

He sipped some wine, and then asked, "What about your furniture, you know the soft pieces you had in there?"

"There's none of it worth anything. I told Lieutenant Conroy his guys could take what they want, but he declined. So I'm going to leave it all there for Gert, the Salvation Army, or the guys she'll get to rebuild the place."

"When is that going to happen?"

"Best as I can tell, she's waiting until after that guy Woodrow's funeral. When that's over, she'll oversee the rebuilding."

He got up and taking the empty wine bottle with him, went into the kitchen.

"Do you want more wine?"

"I'd love some." He came back with two bottles. "I have a red and a white. Which does it for you?"

"Let's have some red… time to build some passion." He smiled and opened the bottle. A moment later, they sampled the wine.

"Hey," she said, "this is good. What is it?"

"Chianti."

"Really… to me, Chianti always meant a wicker-covered bottle, a candle stuck in it, a red and white table cloth and pizza. It was the cheap wine of college."

"Yeah, a lot of people think that way, but when you spend some bucks and buy a quality Chianti, an expensive one, then it's a different story."

She smiled and took another sip. "You know I'm glad you let me move in. I really appreciate it. Staying here makes me feel my life is almost normal."

"We can be good for each other."

Reluctant to pursue what he meant by his remark, she changed the subject.

"I've been thinking about Dennis. Tell me about him. What's his status at the agency? Is he half owner with Dunn?"

"I know what you mean and I'll tell you right out, I know little about their relationship. But as far as I can tell, I think he and Dunn do own everything.

But I get the feeling every now and then that Dennis owns everything and Dunn is merely a figurehead. To me, Dennis has always been a puzzle."

"Is it possible he's Mr. Big at A.T. Dunn?"

"Could be. There are plenty of agencies bought by people who prefer to stay in the shadows. Their usual game is to hire waspy ivy leaguers to run the show."

"It's amazing how crude he is sometimes. He's so like the movies. I wonder if he's involved in organized crime."

"I don't know and that question is never one to ask. At A.T. Dunn, I do my job and get well paid for doing it. Believe me you'll do a whole lot better when that perfume takes off."

"I'm sure of that." She took another drink and then, after a slight hesitation, said, "You know something Tom? Dennis was the one who got the real analysis."

He sat up and moved to the edge of the chair. "You mean, you mean he's the one who set the fire and—"

"That's right. He set the fire and killed that guy. Our Mr. Dennis is a murderer. How does that one sit?"

He stared at her. "Wow. I had the feeling he lived by his own rules, but killing."

"He scares me and I get the feeling killing means about as much to him as swatting a fly. If it matters, though, he said the killing was an accident."

"That doesn't matter. If he was robbing the place, it's felony murder. He may not have intended to hurt anyone, but he did, and the law couldn't care less if he meant it or not."

She shivered a bit as she said, "I don't know what to do."

His eyes narrowed. "Why are you upset?"

"Well, he robbed the place for me. I told him about the analysis and how important it was and, I'm involved, I guess."

Nodding, he said, "Yeah, you're probably an accomplice before the fact." After a pause, he added, "Jesus Christ, Lydia, Dennis holds the key to your future."

"Well, I'm not going to sweat it. If the law gets involved, I'll just deny everything and then it would be his word against mine. I'd just deny I said anything about anything."

He smiled. "And you're a sweet young thing while he's a nasty bad man." Lifting his glass, he toasted her and drank.

"You nailed it. He's a trashy thug and I'm pure as the driven snow, right?" She lifted her glass and drank.

He stood and raised his right hand. "Of course, your honor, Miss Cornell is as fine and upstanding a woman as I know or have ever known. And, if she'll come to bed with me right now, I'll swear she has a map of New York tattooed on her stomach."

Lydia laughed, stood and extended her hand. "Come on sweets," she said, "it's time for a snack on Long Island's south shore." They were both laughing as they walked into his bedroom.

CHAPTER 46

When Gert arrived at the Burger and Bun, she could see that Frankie had put Susan Merrill and Paul Coleman at the window table. Inside, trying to make her way to them through the crowd bunched around the "wait to be seated" sign, she slowly inched toward their table.

"Well, well, look who's here. Since you ain't been in lately I was beginin' to wonder if you wuz eatin' at some other joint. Are you?"

Gert looked at Frankie, but all she could see was that awful bug tattoo creeping up his neck. She shifted her gaze so she could look straight into his eyes.

"How are you, Frankie... everything under control?"

"We are doin' okay, and how's it been with you?" Gert nodded and started to say something, but Frankie cut her off.

"You got no idea how happy I am you came in. Some of them students have been drivin' me nuts."

"What's the problem?"

"Well, you know most of these kids think I'm a weird guy, but that's okay. The problem is I got a trivia head and I know and remember lots of whacko things and they all know that, so lately, they've been after me to help solve a riddle."

"So?"

"Well, it's your pal, the old professor. He dropped a riddle on a class and took off without givin' the answer and they've been after me and everybody else tryin' to figure it out."

Gert stared at him. "I guess you didn't hear the news about Professor Woodrow."

His expressionless eyes made it clear he had not. "The old professor, as you call him, was Solomon Woodrow and," she cleared her throat. "and... well, Professor Woodrow, he was killed a couple of weeks ago."

"Oh. He's the one. I heard a prof had checked out, but I didn't know who. So it was him. Shit. I really liked him. He was fun. What happened? Heart?"

"Oh, no, he was killed, murdered."

"What? Murdered! God damn, son of a bitch, it's the freakin' movies. What the fuck? That's awful. Did they catch the doer?"

"What do you think?"

Nodding, he said, "Yeah, fat chance." He looked really sad and Gert was moved. She reached out and touched his arm and he patted her hand. After a moment, he asked, "You gonna eat?"

"Yes, I'm meeting those two at the window table."

When he saw where she pointed, he said, "Oh, them. Yeah. I gave them that table 'cause she's a great looker. He's ordinary, but nobody's gonna notice him anyway. I didn't know you was joining them. They didn't say anything if they had I woulda given them your usual table."

"It doesn't matter. If I could just get over there." Gert swept her arm at the mob between them and the window table.

With that, Frankie rose to his full height and screamed at the crowd blocking their path. "One side, here, one fucking side, move over, make room. Let a civilized person get through here."

He pushed forward like a tug boat in the bay and Gert followed him the same way she followed the little old umbrella ladies in the subway. As lumps of people parted for those determined females, this crowd likewise melted sideways.

When they reached the table, Paul stood, but Gert waved him back down as Frankie pulled out the chair for her and then moved it back in when she sat. Anyone watching must have thought she was the owner, since no one ever got that service from him or for that matter, from anyone who worked there.

He stood above them and spoke directly to Gert. "Prof, permit me to say, I am deeply saddened by the news you bring and if you do not object, there will be no check. That gesture is the least I can do at this moment. I really liked that old man."

He closed his eyes for a moment and then opened them as he dropped three menus on the table. "I'll be back," he said, as he pushed his way through the crowd which absorbed him like white pants claim black ink.

Gert watched him walk away and smiled. As crazy as he seems, that's a decent guy, she thought. Then turning to the two beside her, she said, "I want to thank you both for coming. I've got an important matter to talk about with you."

"What is it?" Paul asked.

"Well," said Gert, "let's order first, since the meal is on the house and from what's going on in here, if we order now, we might get served by Thanksgiving."

"I know what I want," Susan said. Paul nodded and Gert looked for Frankie, who at that moment materialized with three glasses of iced and lemoned water.

"Okay, what'll it be?" A few moments later he repeated, "One veggie burger, one turkey burger, and for the prof, one beef cheese monster. Three sides of fries, one small plate of coleslaw and potato salad, plenty of pickles, and three vanilla cokes, right?" They nodded and he merged into the pulsing group in the middle of the place.

"What is it you want to talk about?" Susan asked.

"Well, Susan, after what you found out at the agency about that Dennis, it's pretty clear he's the guilty party. It would be impossible to go to the cops and tell them what you say he said, since he would deny ever saying anything. So we're left with a killer and no way to deal with him."

"You really think the cops would have no chance with what Susan found out?"

"Paul, if you were him and the police asked about the situation, what would you say?"

He nodded. "Yeah, I see what you mean. We have to assume he has some kind of alibi and when Susan tells her story, he says to the cops, 'what are you talking about? I never said any of that. I was in China having my portrait painted on a piece of rice'... right?"

"Exactly, I'm afraid the police can't help us. We have to help ourselves."

"Help ourselves? What do you mean?" Susan asked.

"Well, a gentleman, Professor Woodrow's long-time partner, is prepared to deal with Dennis."

They looked puzzled and Paul asked, "Partner...deal with him. What does that mean?"

Gert exhaled. "How do I tell you what I mean by partner? Well, Sol was a homosexual."

She stopped, waiting for them to react, but they didn't. Good for them, she thought. Then taking a drink of water, she continued. "Many people in that community are very upset and angry that his killer may get away with it. So, as to what 'deal with him' means, I've been told if we can get Dennis to a certain location, the problem will be solved."

"The problem?" Susan asked.

"Dennis."

"Ohhhh," they said, almost simultaneously.

"Solved... but how?" Paul asked.

"I don't know and I don't want to know. All I want is the score to be settled. That son of a bitch shouldn't get away with what he did."

As Susan and Paul thought about what Gert had said, the food arrived. Nothing much was said for the next fifteen minutes as they devoured their burgers. Gert watched the young people eat their "safe" food - their veggie and turkey burgers. Normally, that's what she would have had, but after Cyril's speech, she decided to do what she pleased for whatever time was left for her. As she ate, the bloody drippings from her beef cheese monster pooled in the plate and formed a vegetarian's river of sin, but Gert loved every bite.

Later, after dessert and coffee, Susan asked Gert, "What do you want me to do?"

Gert looked at her with true admiration. "Susan, you're a very smart young woman. I was hoping I wouldn't have to spell things out."

"You aren't going to ask her to do anything dangerous, are you?"

"Please, Paul, give me more credit than that." Turning to Susan, Gert said, "Right now, the plan is for you to make a phone call and wait in a room."

"Make a phone call and wait?"

"That's right. If you're willing to do it, you call Dennis and tell him you are in a specific room in a particular hotel here in the Village."

"Would I have to meet him?"

"Not directly. Maybe you'd have to answer the phone if he called. But that would be it. The 'community' I mentioned before—they'll meet him."

"Then what happens?"

"Nothing that concerns you. You leave. What happens after that is not your affair."

Paul hesitated then asked, "Do you think they'll kill him?"

"I don't know what they'll do, and I don't care what they do. That man killed my best friend. He took away a person who was very important not only to me, but also to the school and to his many friends. What that man did cannot go unpunished."

Susan nodded as Gert sipped some coffee. "You know something," Gert said, "If I was as young as you two, I'd have time for developing new friendships, but I don't have that time. Compared to you both, I may have ten minutes left and that really matters to me. For me, losing Sol was like losing an arm or leg…a part of my body. I miss him very much and I always will."

Susan straightened up and squared her shoulders. Gert thought she looked like John Wayne going into battle. "I'll call him." she said. "You just tell me where and when."

Gert reached out and patted her hand. "Thank you, Susan. Thank you."

Suddenly Frankie appeared. "Prof, I'm sorry, but I gotta have that riddle answer. Do you know it, the one that's drivin' everybody nuts?"

"Which riddle is it?"

"The one about the three monks and three pears and each takes one and—"

Gert cut him off. "Frankie, one monk's name is Each. Got it?"

He stared at her blankly for a moment and then his eyes lit up and a mile-wide smile covered his face. Yelling, "I love it. I love it." he turned and reentered the mob.

CHAPTER 47

"Okay, here's the main theme." Randall held up a craft-board card and placed it on the easel. Dunn looked at it and slowly read the copy out loud.

FEAR – THE THIEF
To the Woman Who Is Afraid to Let Her Dreams Come True
Maybe it was yesterday, maybe years ago—you heard of a woman who
found the man of her dreams—and a dream formed in *your* mind.
"Some day, when I'm no longer afraid, I'm going to find my man."
Will you? Or will you always be afraid?
Will your dream stay just a dream forever?

"Now that's the main theme, right?" Dunn asked.

"Yes. We play to their dread, to their timidity, to their overall apprehension and psychological terror. We stress the ideas that life is short and whatever you want will never be acquired if you are fearful."

"Tom, show him another," Lydia said. He picked up another card and placed it on the easel in front of the first.

Complete Abandon
will help you get the man of your dreams.
Wear **Complete Abandon** and your man will behave as **you** want…
He will be captivated, controlled, enraptured, entranced… by **YOU!**
Are you brave enough?
You can control a mesmerized and spellbound man…**how?**
Wear Complete Abandon

Dunn slowly read the card, his face impassive. Neither Lydia nor Tom could guess how he felt about any of it. As she watched him, Lydia thought he was probably a champion poker player and you would never know whether his hand was a winner. There was no tell, nothing showed, but he didn't look well. He was pale and seemed thinner. He hadn't looked well for a while and she wondered if he could be sick.

"Is there another?" he asked.

"Yes," said Tom, as he picked up another card and placed it on the easel.

Wouldn't It Be Fantastic and Exhilarating to Safely Tempt a Man?
To drive him crazy with passion and remain secure.
To kindle fervent, blazing ardor and still command the moment.
Nothing would happen unless **you** wanted it to happen!
Wouldn't **power** like that be wonderful?
Complete Abandon will give you that strength.
Complete Abandon will give you the power you have always wanted.
Wear another perfume, who knows what might happen.
Wear Complete Abandon and what happens is up to you!!

"Okay," he said. "I get the drift and I like your take on it. Like just about everyone, women are cowards bathing in indecision and vacillation. Complete Abandon will allow them to take a chance and remain safe and secure." He paused. "Damn, I like that."

Dunn stood and turning to face them, said, "I can remember how I was before therapy. In college I was a play-it-safe guy, always afraid, nervous about this, nervous about that. Then one day I'm in a bar and the resident drunk asked me what I was afraid of, and before I knew it, I was pouring out all my shit. I was afraid of my mother, my father, of not being accepted, of being considered a jerk. Damn, I was even afraid to admit I was afraid."

"The drunk listened and tells me to see a shrink. He says there is no reason to be that afraid, that we're all gonna die and what the hell difference does it make when or how or where. The damned show's over when it's over. Now no one had ever said anything like that to me before and being half drunk myself, I promised the guy I would see a shrink and I did. Two years with the campus guy and then a few more years afterward and now, I don't give a fuck about things that worry most of the people in the world." He smiled at them and walked back to the chair and sat.

"Those ideas are great. I was hoping you'd understand how to deal with our public's neurotic tendencies. It is such an old story. Find a weakness and punch away. With the big pharmaceutical boys playing up every fear that already exists and creating new ones every day, we can join what they've started and promise the same crap they promise." He paused, and then said, "I can't wait to get after the widows and the spinsters."

He laughed and Lydia felt she was walking on air. She knew the copy made sense and hoped he'd like it, but this reaction was more than she expected.

Looking satisfied, Dunn said, "I'm going to speak to Metro this afternoon and set up a meeting. I'll let you know the time when it's set. Now, Lydia, would you be willing to give a little demonstration, like the one you did with Hicks?"

"Certainly if you think it's in good taste. But don't forget, we can bring in hookers and give the boys from Metro a real lunchtime treat."

Looking thoughtful, Dunn said, "No, I've considered that. But I want to play it straight. This is too important for the usual bullshit, lots of money involved, and since we own the formula, I'm hoping we can license it to them. And if they agree to that, we can look forward to big bucks all around."

"Do you think they'd go for a percentage of sales? Something like that?"

"I don't see why not. They're as greedy as we are." He paused, and then asked to see the main theme card one more time. Tom fished it out from under the others and positioned it.

Dunn stared at it and smiled. "Fear the thief. Oh, I like that. I do like that. Think of all the little shop-girls and the screwball women in the city. God! If we take space on the afternoon soaps, we will sell perfume by the tanker truck."

"Do you think Metro will go for the budget? Tom asked.

"Hey, those bastards are interested in one thing and one thing only." Then, turning to Lydia, "That stuff better work the way it should."

"I see no reason to think it won't. I go by what Hicks proved out. Maybe two out of five guys will have the predictable reaction and offer the appropriate response."

"Okay, okay." Then he said, "I'm going to insist at least five Metro people come to the meeting. I don't want to take a chance and have only one come and that guy would be the one on whom the stuff doesn't work. That would be the ultimate disaster."

"Right," said Lydia, "that's smart."

Dunn reached into his jacket and brought out a small notepad which he opened to a page covered with writing. He looked at it, nodded and said, "Okay, now, two more things. First, how do you intend to set up the ad page?"

Lydia looked at Tom and then said, "Let me." He nodded and she said, "The basic plan is a full page, all white. The bottle shape will be faintly visible, you know, like a watermark. That image will cover the entire page and all word copy will be in black. By the way, that's how I see the entire campaign, straightforward, black and white. I see the page in thirds with the top third devoted to the main theme material. That stays the same in every ad. The bottom two-thirds of the page will carry the specifics like loneliness, or control, like any of the three we showed you." She motioned to the easel. "And we have quite a few more brewing."

"Okay," he said. "I have no problem with that. What about the container, a bottle?"

She picked up a sketch book from a chair, opened it, and showed it to him.

"Now, we see a bottle. In fact, we never considered anything else, but our roadblock is the bottle's shape. We've gone around in circles with that."

Slowly turning other pages of the sketch pad so Dunn could see the pictures as she mentioned them, she said, "We thought a bottle shaped like a cock, a bullet, something to indicate power and—"

Dunn interrupted her. "What about a chain?" he said.

"A chain?"

"Yes, Tom. A bottle shaped like a chain, say three or four links, each about an inch tall and the top link or the middle link is broken. My idea is freedom, letting go, opening up. That's the idea."

"Okay, said Lydia. "I follow. How about a solid bottle with the links sort of carved on it or layered on top. That might be cheaper."

"You're probably right, but I don't know if we should be concerned with expense at this point. Let's try to get the idea straight. Can you think of anything that indicates Complete Abandon better than a broken chain?"

"Open handcuffs?" asked Tom.

"A large, thick, glass skeleton key?" said Dunn.

"Maybe a single link," said Lydia. "Or a glass circle, a circle of glass that is obviously broken, a circle that is clearly and obviously opened." She paused and paced, then said, "Wait, wait, how about a glass bottle in the shape of an open or broken circle?"

"I like that," said Tom, as Dunn slowly nodded in agreement.

Beaming, Lydia said, "Okay, I'll check and find out how that would work out, the cost, production time, and so forth. I'll have some figures by tomorrow."

CHAPTER 48

Four days later, promptly at three, five Metro guys walked into the conference room A.T. Dunn used for the hard sales-pitches. It had a wall of windows on one side covered with expensive drapes, while on the opposite wall sat two credenzas holding trays of small sandwiches, fruit, urns of coffee, tea, bottles of water and soft drinks. The credenzas were flanked by cabinets holding electronic components. The short walls held a projection screen and a large freestanding blackboard. The center of the room was covered by a massive brown mahogany conference table at which Lydia, Tom and Dunn manned one side with the five executives from Metro facing them.

For most of his pitches, Dunn usually began with a talk about language and how it changed over time. His prime example was the blackboard, which he pointed out had become a chalkboard, which, as if by magic, had become, he stopped at this point and spun the blackboard to show a large whiteboard, whose days are numbered, he said, since it now had become a dry-erase board.

After his self-satisfying speech about language, Dunn stood at the head of the table where he could use the projection screen as a backdrop and stared at the five from Metro for approximately one minute. Then he said, "Gentlemen, today we are going to make history. The five of you are in a position to begin the greatest merchandising renaissance since the automobile. When Henry Ford recognized the seemingly inherent laziness of human beings and gave them an automobile to use instead of their God-Given legs, he ushered in the new order of manufacturing and selling, one that used the physical functioning of people as a basis for the well-considered attack on their wallets. We are going to do the same! We are going to use the customers themselves as our prime selling tool."

The group from Metro, looking puzzled, stared at each other and then back at Dunn who had pulled a lectern from the side of the room and now stood behind it like a lecturing professor. As is the case in every session of this type, the five Metro men were unequal in the areas of status, rank, and finances. The big man of the group could be easily recognized by his clothing, which was far more Hollywood than Harvard, and by his gold jewelry, which was sufficient to keep a Moroccan bazaar in business. And furthermore, since the four men of lesser rank with him knew it would be foolish for one of them to ask the first question, they relaxed and let him pose it.

"Dunn, what the hell are you talking about?"

Smiling like a just-fed dolphin, Dunn said, "Mr. Malone that is a discerning and appropriate question, because I realize you may find it a bit hard to follow my basic point. So let me ask three questions."

Dunn stepped out from behind the lectern and moved to a spot directly across the table from Malone. He raised one finger in the air and said,

"Number one, what is it that every woman craves? Number two, what is it that makes them want children and to guide those children through childhood into adulthood? And, number three, what is it that they most regret losing when their children leave the fold?"

Malone, staring at Dunn for a long moment and figuring he would look terribly stupid trying to answer Dunn's questions, turned to his left and singled out one of his group, the youngest looking one. "Riley, I'd like to hear from you since this is your first meeting as one of my assistants and it's time to get your feet wet. Let's see if you have the answers Mr. Dunn seeks."

The fellow Malone singled out was tall, young, and good looking. He stood and said, "Well, Mr. Malone, Mr. Dunn asked three questions and my answer changed after each one. The first one dealing with a woman's craving led me to think of love and romance. But the second question dealt with children, and while love and romance are still involved, I think we now have to consider a woman's basic maternal instinct—the need to be a mother. The third question threw me off a bit because it dealt with loss, and women do not want to lose love and romance and they probably never lose their maternal instinct, so what we are looking for is something every woman wants, that is as basic to her as maternal feelings and something she often loses."

He turned to face Dunn and said, "It is control, Mr. Dunn, that's the answer to your questions, right?"

Nodding vigorously, Dunn shouted, "You're right, young man, control is the key. That's what we all want, but women want it in spades, control!"

Malone was visibly confused and looked like he had been asked the final Jeopardy question in a strange language, but Dunn, Lydia and Tom were smiling. The other three Metro men were shaking their heads, not knowing whether they had witnessed greatness or the moment their coworker had committed job suicide.

"Mr. Riley, is it?" The young man nodded and smiled as Dunn continued. "Mr. Riley, you are one smart son of a bitch and have a mind that should be working for me. I threw out those questions figuring no one but me and my people even had an idea of what the hell I was talking about, but you, you jumped on the wagon and grabbed the reins."

Now, also smiling, Malone asked, "Mr. Dunn, do you think I surround myself with fools?" He looked like an owner whose horse had just won the Derby.

"No sir, Mr. Malone, I sincerely hoped you would surround yourself with boy geniuses like you obviously do. A man who is just smart may not be able to grasp what we are going to present to you now. To fully understand what we are going to show you, a person needs brains, foresight, vision, call it what you will. We are talking about a revolution in the fragrance industry. Months and months ago you told us to get a new fragrance product line ready. Well we've done that. Miss Lydia Cornell here," Dunn pointed at her. "She has worked a miracle for you and your company. The product we are calling Complete Abandon will not only make you a fortune of money, it will also make your company famous."

He walked to the lectern and continued. "Gentlemen, I'm going to let Miss Cornell fill you in on the rest of our presentation and, let me add, we are going to prove everything we say. If Miss Cornell says something is true, we are going to prove it to you so you'll have absolutely no doubts." He gestured for Lydia to come to the lectern and very slowly walked back to his seat.

Lydia got up and as the Metro men gaped at her, she slowly walked to the front of the room. That day she took full advantage of her sex appeal by wearing a very simple, understated, man-tailored shirtdress in a dark purple silk. The dress was so very plain no one would think of it as a sexy item, but it was. Its complete lack of fussy trim and straight lines forced the men's awareness to her lean, but shapely figure and her cat-like grace.

She smiled at them as they mentally undressed her. "Good afternoon, gentlemen. Now that we've established a woman desires control, the question becomes—how do we give it to her? Because quite obviously, any product that could give her control would be an important product for all women, wouldn't it? Well, wouldn't it be wonderful if we had a perfume that would prompt men to act in a docile and loving manner, and in no way become unmanageable? Wouldn't that be great? How safe and secure a woman would feel. The nagging worry of unwanted sexuality, of a man forcing himself on her, would be removed. She could relax and act as she pleased. Wouldn't it be wonderful if I, for instance, could put on a perfume and when you hugged me you would have no choice but to act gently and delicately? Please note, gentlemen, I did not say you *might* act that way. I said you would *have no choice but to act that way.* If that were true, I would relish the control and I would absolutely love the product that gave it to me."

Looking determined and serious, Lydia walked back to her place at the table and picked up her handbag. She reached inside and removed from it a small, unlabeled bottle of amber liquid. "There it is gentlemen." Pointing to the bottle, she very slowly said, "This is Complete Abandon, a secret formula that A.T. Dunn owns and which we will provide to you for the fragrance line we promised."

"Wait a minute, wait a minute, Malone burst out. "Are you telling me that the stuff in that bottle is a magic formula that can make me and my guys behave in a particular way?"

"That is exactly what I'm saying, Mr. Malone, that is exactly it."

"Well, normally I would laugh at you, but I know Dunn and he's not an idiot, so I have to imagine there's some truth to all this, but, you said or somebody said, they could prove it."

"We can." Dunn said.

"Then you go ahead and prove it."

Lydia opened the bottle. "Before I do this I want to make sure you understand one important point."

"What is that?" Malone asked.

"According to our statistical research, this product will work about two out of five times. That is why we wanted five of you here today. The odds are it will work on some of you if not all, but we'll see. Now, I'm going to put this perfume on as I would normally put on any perfume. Then I want each of you to hug me, just hug me. I know this is strange for you and I hope you won't be embarrassed. This is too important for that. So just hug me and we'll see what happens."

The five men looked at her and then at each other trying hard to hold back their tendency to roll their eyes in disbelief. Then they watched Lydia apply the perfume to her wrists, the crook of each elbow, both sides of her neck, and between her breasts. She then motioned to the men and Malone immediately said, "Riley, go give her a try."

The tall, young man got up from his seat and walked up to Lydia. He reached down and put his arms around her, crushing her to his chest. After a short time, he lowered his head and let it come to rest alongside hers while his shoulders visibly relaxed. He stood in front of the room with his arms around her as minutes ticked by. The only noise in the room was breathing and some street sounds drifting in from below. Finally, Malone saw Lydia's hands pushing on Riley's chest.

"What's the matter with you Riley? Let her go."

Turning to face him, he said, "Mr. Malone, I couldn't."

"You couldn't, you couldn't what?"

"I couldn't let her go. Holding her was wonderful, so peaceful and calm. God, was that the perfume?" he asked, as he turned to Lydia.

She nodded and motioned to one of the other men and as he stood, she replenished the perfume. The second had the same reaction as the first, the third felt it somewhat, so he said, but the fourth did not.

The third and fourth young men looked like they had been caught with hands in the cookie jar, a combination of "why me?" and "damn!" One managed to stammer he had liked the smell of the perfume, but felt nothing more. Lydia immediately jumped in and said their reactions were exactly what their statistics predicted. Not every man would react.

Dunn stared at Malone and said, "How about you, want to give it a try?"

Malone hesitated, but he did stand and walk to the front of the room where he hugged Lydia. About a minute went by before he reluctantly freed himself, and turning to Dunn said, "Son of a bitch, that was something."

Ten minutes later, after some food was eaten, they were once again seated at the table, but now they were talking business.

"Dunn, that's the greatest stuff I've ever confronted. I can tell my grandchildren I was in the room when the first product of this kind was unveiled." He stopped and looking thoughtful asked, "What kind of product is this? What the hell do you call it?"

"That's a good question, Mr. Malone and I really don't know what to call it. I refer to it as 'Bio-Det.' standing for the response most of you experienced, which, I think, is biologically determined. Since there's never been anything like it, I don't know what else to call it. Do you have any idea?"

Malone smiled. "God damn! Me, I'm going to call it gold, pure gold."

"Mr. Malone, may I?" Riley asked.

"Say whatever you want Riley." Malone bellowed. "Goddamn it, you're part of history also."

Riley turned to Dunn. "Mr. Dunn, I think 'Bio-Det' is a great name for a class of products that can create physical experiences. And, if I may, do you have additional ones? Is this it or are there more?"

Dunn looked at Lydia and Tom, then back at Riley. "At this point, we have this one finished, but you can be assured we are diligently at work perfecting others."

"Will Metro be in the running for the others?" Malone asked.

"Of course, as long as we can work out a proper deal for Complete Abandon, there should be no reason not to let your company handle all the additional products."

"Could you give us an idea about the others? What are they like? What do they do?"

Dunn smiled. "Mr. Malone, at this time, it would be premature to speak about other Bio-Det items, but I will say that as soon as they are finished, you'll have first crack at all of them."

"All of them?"

"Take my word, every one!" said Dunn, with an air of positive finality that turned the page on that subject.

Two hours later, Lydia and Tom sat in Dunn's office discussing the arrangements that had been made with Metro. "With the amount of money this account is going to bring into the firm, we're going to need a different setup, a different organizational grouping," Dunn said, while seated.

"Knowing you, I'm sure you have something in mind, right?"

"Well, Tom, this is how I see it. The three of us split the rights to the formula for the perfume. We share the royalties equally. That alone should bring each of us an enormous amount of money. I will continue overseeing the agency, since that's how it's been. Now for the changes I see." Looking at Lydia, he said, "I would like you to handle the Metro account. You'd be in charge of the perfume, toilet water, all the direct offshoots, and everything else, the soaps, talcum, other cosmetic products. And Tom, I want you to take the idea of 'Bio-Dets' and run with it. I'd like to see you turn that idea into the greatest revolution in retailing since time payments."

He inhaled deeply and sat back in his chair, closed his eyes, and let out a deep breath. "Now, how does that sound?"

Almost immediately Lydia said, "About the royalty split, we'll have to draw up an agreement, a contract and it should be completely specific and legal." They nodded.

"And concerning the 'Bio-Det' products," she continued, "I would like us to also share equally in whatever comes from that idea. Okay?"

Dunn looked at Tom and again they both nodded. Then Tom said, "I'm glad we are able to deal with all this in a sophisticated way. It would be a pity if we got greedy."

"You're right," said Dunn. "If we were stupid we could kill the goose that's going to lay a very golden egg."

"So it's agreed?" Lydia asked.

"Sure," said Tom. "I'll go along with the deal as you both specified." He paused. "Never in my wildest dreams would I, could I, have dreamt all this up. I still don't know if I believe it."

Dunn looked up at them. "Yesterday, shit, this morning, we were in the advertising business. Now damn it, we are the advertising business." He picked up the phone and said, "I'll get the legal staff to draw up three-way agreements, okay?"

Then Dunn looked at Lydia and hung up the phone. "What's wrong?"

"Well, I'm sorry, but I can't get Dennis out of my mind."

"Dennis?" Dunn asked. "Why are you concerned with Dennis?"

"Well, he was instrumental in helping get the perfume formula and I'd bet he'd want to be included. At least that's what I'd guess. I don't see him sitting on the outside looking in as the three of us play in a sandbox filled with cash."

Dunn shook his head. "Don't you worry about Dennis; he's my concern. The arrangement we have is between the two of us and concerns no one else."

They were silent for a moment until Lydia asked, "You know, sometimes I get the feeling he runs the place, not you."

Dunn stared at her. "As I said, Dennis and I have a special arrangement and most things are never the way they seem. Dennis is living proof of the old advertising idea of selling the sizzle not the steak."

Tom glanced at Lydia and was pleased to see she looked as confused as he was. But before either of them could ask Dunn what he meant, he said, "Look, like I said, don't either of you worry about Dennis. He's my affair. I'll take care of Dennis."

"Well, that's a relief." she said.

Dunn again picked up the phone and said, "Look, you two go out for food. I'll call legal and in a few days we'll sign for our future, how's that?"

When they were gone, he crossed his arms on the desk and slowly laid his head on them. A minute or two later, with significant effort, he reached into a drawer to take out a prescription bottle. Opening it, he slowly took two pills from it, stared at them for a moment and then with visible strain, swallowed them. Then, closing his eyes he once again gently rested his head on his arms.

CHAPTER 49

At his desk in the executive area of the agency, Dennis was reading about the Knicks' game the night before when at half past three his phone rang.

"What is it? Can you make it short? I'm busy."

"Dennis, this is Susan, and I have been trying to reach you. You know, you're a hard guy to pin down."

"Susan? What Susan is that?" He asked brusquely.

"Boy, you must really get around. Just two weeks ago, you wanted to help me out of my bathing suit. Now you forgot who I am. That's just great for my ego."

"Oh, you, that Susan, hey, babe, I haven't forgotten you. I just figured you'd be knee deep studying the times table or something like that."

"Hey, come on, I'm a bit past multiplication, but I have been studying and I need a break."

"Well, that's really nice, but why are you calling me?"

"To tell you the truth, I'm not a hundred percent sure why, but you fascinate me. You're such a hot guy, so always ready for, well, what can I say? You excite me."

"No kiddin'? You think I'm hot stuff, huh? Well, how come when I asked you for some action, you turned me down flat? Huh, answer me that."

"I don't know what to say, but you scare me. You come on so strong and forceful. I guess I'm afraid of you."

Leaning back in his chair and stretching, he gloated. "Hey, I'm a pussy cat. There's nothing to be afraid of. All I want to do is have some fun is all."

"I was hoping you'd say that because I want to have some fun also. I need a break and I think it would be great if we could get together."

"You mean you want a date? Like we should go to the movies and have ice cream sodas after?"

"No. I don't want an ice cream soda, but the movies sound good. Only I don't want to go to any theater."

"Well, where do you wanna go? You wanna go to Hollywood?"

"No, I was thinking of a hotel here in the Village. I just had to get out of the dorm, 'cause the other kids were getting me nuts. So I took a room at the Greenwich Plaza to study, and when I saw the rooms have triple X-rated movies, I thought of you."

"Hey, baby, that's a real compliment, triple X-rated. That's wild. You know, I was almost in one a few years ago?"

"Really?"

"Oh, sure. I'm big in that department, ha, ha!"

"I'd love to see just how big you are."

"Well, babe, why don't I come over so you can do a hands-on investigation?"

"You mean you'd really come to see me?"

"I'd be crazy not to. You're okay. But, when I'm through with you, you're gonna be better"

"Oh, you're so bad. But I bet you're good at being bad."

"You got no idea how bad I am."

"That's great. I'm in room 417."

"Are you there now?"

"No. I'm calling from the dorm. But I'm going to get a bite and then go over. I'll be there after six."

"Room 417, you said?"

"That's right."

"Great. I'll see you after six and get yourself ready for some high-class action."

"I can't wait."

He hung up and smiled like a lottery winner. Then he laughed as he leaned back as far as the chair would permit. He reached down and closed his hand over his privates. "Boys," he said aloud, "you are gonna get a workout tonight." Then he brought the chair back to its regular position and picked up the phone. He dialed Manhattan information and got the number for the Greenwich Plaza Hotel.

Feeling smug, he asked, "May I have the front desk, please?" It took a moment. "Maybe you can help me." He said. "I'm supposed to meet my cousin there and I forgot her room number. Her name is Susan Merrill, she is registered, isn't she?

A smooth voice responded, "Yes, sir. Miss Merrill is registered in a suite, room 417. Shall I ring her, sir?"

"No. That won't be necessary. I'll be stopping by as we arranged. There's no need to disturb her."

"Will there be anything else, sir?"

"No."

"Well then, thank you for calling the Greenwich Plaza Hotel."

"My pleasure, I assure you." He said as he very confidently hung up.

After she gently replaced the hand piece in its cradle, Susan looked at Gert and Cyril. "Was that okay?"

"Darling," said Cyril. "That was spectacular, splendid. It was perfect."

"What do you want me to do now?" she asked.

"If you would, we'd like you to stay till he gets here," said Gert.

"Okay, that's no problem."

"Good. Then let's get some food. I'm hungry."

Cyril grabbed the room service menu, noted what they wanted, and by four thirty, they were deep into sandwiches and salads. Nothing was said about the events that would unfold, and Susan, reconciled to her role, felt no guilt. However, at first she feared Dennis would retaliate in some way if the plan backfired, because she was luring him to the meeting, but as time passed and she grew more aware of the anger and determination of both Cyril and Gert, she knew she would be safe and, maybe more important, she knew Dennis was not going to smugly strut away from the crime he committed.

When this event or situation began, she doubted being able to carry out her role with no concern for Dennis' fate. But when circumstances force a confrontation that compels action, like now, she realized people discover unsuspected strengths and weaknesses. By agreeing to be part of the plan, she realized she was no different from others who knew little or nothing about their ability to act in ways different from their typical behaviors. Now she was not upset by her lack of regard for Dennis, rather, she was surprised and impressed by her strong convictions and moral strength and also the calm she was able to muster.

In justifying her actions, she thought of news reports describing acts of bravery in which soldiers and civilians felt what they did was not brave but was the right thing to do at that moment. They acted with no regard for personal safety, whether dragging a buddy to safety or saving someone's life. That was how she felt, that she was doing the right thing at the right moment.

At five thirty, there was a knock on the door and the three of them froze. Cyril motioned for Susan to respond. She asked, "Who is it?"

A resonant male voice responded. "It's Frank. I'm here to meet Cyril."

Gert and Susan both turned to look at Cyril when they heard his name and when he visibly relaxed, they exhaled. Getting up, he opened the door and a man entered the room. After introductions, Susan realized the man, who looked like a football player, was a member of Cyril's "community." With no discussion, the man called Frank sat on the sofa and silently opened a canvas bag and removed several lengths of rope and two large rolls of tape. Then they waited.

At ten minutes after six, the phone rang and Cyril motioned Susan to answer.

"Hello."

"Hey, babe, this is lover boy. I'm downstairs and I'm comin' up. You ready for me?"

"I can't wait for you to walk through the door. I'm so nervous."

"Relax, baby, tomorrow you'll be able to look back on tonight and remember what a great time you had."

"Hurry." she said, her voice husky with intimacy.

"God damn, you are ready for me. I can tell."

Cyril turned off the main lights leaving on only two small lamps, and then he and Frank took up positions alongside the door. Susan sat in a chair that had been positioned about ten feet into the room directly in front of the entrance.

Cyril told Susan to sit in the chair and cross her legs. "When he knocks just say 'come in.' the door will be unlocked so you won't have to get up. When he gets into the room, stay in the chair. We'll take care of things from that point." Very calmly, he walked back to stand beside the entrance door.

There was silence in the room and in the corridor until Susan heard the elevator doors open. A few moments later, she saw a shadow in the space under the front door. Then there was a knock.

"Dennis?" she asked.

"You bet, baby."

"Come in." The door swung inward and he filled the lighted space. As he stood in the doorway, looking at her, she uncrossed her legs, and after placing her hand on her knees, slowly spread them. As he moved to enter the room she could see his eyes glued to the space between her legs.

CHAPTER 50

When Dennis had taken three steps into the room, Susan heard a strange sound a second before he collapsed to the floor. The sound was hard to describe, but it sounded like "bonk." She instantly realized that either Frank or Cyril had hit Dennis on his head and the sound surprised her. She thought that would make a dull sound, like a thud, but it sounded more like a baseball hitting a bat.

Almost simultaneously with Dennis collapsing, the door was closed and Gert switched on the lights. Frank immediately put tape over Dennis' mouth and then tied his ankles and wrists. When that was done, Cyril approached Susan.

"You are going to leave now. Will you be okay?"

She nodded.

"Frank will take you to the lobby where Paul is waiting. Are you sure you're okay?"

"I'm fine and Paul is waiting?" She asked with surprise. When Cyril nodded, she said, "That's great."

Then she offered a thin smile. "You know, Cyril, I'm really okay and I think I'm better at this cloak and dagger stuff than any of us thought. I have no problem with this." As she spoke she glanced at Dennis on the floor, thinking he looked like a piece of lost luggage at the airport.

Gert brought her jacket and Frank took her by the arm and walked her to the door. A few moments later she was with him on the elevator heading to the lobby.

Cyril and Gert managed to place Dennis in a straight-backed chair. Then they removed the ropes, taped his ankles to the chair's legs and his wrists to the chair's arms and then replaced the ropes across his chest and around his neck. A lamp was placed so that its light would shine directly into his face, and when Gert turned off the overhead lights it looked like they had recreated a scene from a 1950 noir film. When Frank returned, they waited for Dennis to regain consciousness.

About five minutes later, Dennis moaned, and a moment or two after that, his eyes popped open and then shut when the full force of the lamp light hit him. When Frank drew a stiletto from his pocket and snapped open the blade, Dennis' eyes flashed open. He stared at the long, thin blade following the weapon's movement until it disappeared under his chin. He was motionless until he winced when he felt the blade press against his throat. With just a bit of pressure, the knife point pierced his skin, and when there was a drop of blood on the blade, Frank moved it so Dennis could see the bright drop glistening in the intense light. As Dennis stared at the drop of his blood, a soft moan indicated he understood what he was being shown.

Very softly, Cyril said, "I'm going to take the tape from your mouth. If you call out, the knife will cut your jugular and that scream will be the last sound you will ever hear and the last you'll ever make. Do you understand?"

Hesitantly, Dennis nodded, and Cyril slowly started to pull the tape away. When Dennis' mouth was free, he looked around the room trying to see outside the blast of light hitting him. But after a moment he stopped looking and started talking.

"Hey, where is that little bitch? When I get my hands on her she won't be so damn pretty."

Almost whispering, Cyril said, "I don't think you're in any position to make threats. If I were you I'd start saying my prayers."

Straining to see who was talking, Dennis smirked. "Look guys, let's get something straight. I don't think you know who I am and how I'm connected. Mess with me and you're in trouble. My pals will be after your asses. Best be smart and untie me. If I walk outta here, we'll forget the whole thing."

Gert looked at him with disgust thinking he was just a damned gangster, nothing more than a big mouth, wiseass thug. When she spoke he was visibly startled.

"Dennis, you have this figured all wrong. This is not the stuff you usually play at." He twisted his head and strained to see her, but was defeated by the light.

"Forget that girl. We're dealing with a different event. The score we're settling concerns the man you murdered when you set that fire and stole the analysis."

"Hey lady, you got it all wrong. I didn't kill anybody and I didn't set any fire. You got the wrong guy."

Frank knife pushed the knife point a bit more and the blade tip entered flesh.

"Hey," Dennis called out. "What the hell are you doin'? Stop that, you're gonna hurt me."

"That's the idea you dumb shit," hissed Gert. "You don't tell us what happened, you're gonna get very hurt. Now, why did you kill that old man?"

He was straining against the tape, and when he tried to move, the ropes around his throat and chest tightened. He was pinned into the chair and after a few futile attempts to move, he knew it. "Look, I'm tellin' you, you got the wrong guy. I didn't kill nobody."

He was starting to sweat, but his front stayed up. "Hey, lady, what happened? Somebody knock off your old man and you think I did it? Believe me, I didn't. I didn't kill anyone."

When Frank closed the knife Dennis heard the click of the closing and figured there was no longer an immediate threat, so he relaxed a bit. "You guys are finally getting smart. Look, I'm tellin' you. I didn't kill anyone. You got the wrong guy."

Cyril stepped behind him, placed another piece of tape across his mouth and leaned in close to Dennis' ear. He whispered, "We have the right man. We know that, but we want you to tell us exactly what you did, so we are going to apply more pressure, and when you are ready to tell us, just nod and we will talk. Understand?"

Dennis began to shake and streaks of sweat began to inch down his face, dripping onto his shirt. His clothes quickly took on the look of outfits southerners wore prior to air conditioning. In an instant his fancy suit became a formless lump of cloth.

Frank picked up the canvas bag and took out a pair of chrome-plated pliers with yellow rubber handles. Then he took another straight- back chair, placed it directly in front of Dennis and sat.

Sitting with their knees almost touching, Frank looked at Dennis. "I bet you think we're fooling around and this is all some silly game. Well, pal, it isn't, and I'm going to prove that to you right now."

He reached out, took hold of the fingers of Dennis' left hand and roughly pulled them to him. At that Dennis flinched and murmured something made unintelligible by the tape on his mouth. No one was sure, but they thought it sounded like "ow" or "hey." Then Frank released all the fingers except the pinky. Holding it straight, he very gently moved the pliers alongside it. Softly and slowly, he said, "Dennis, I have two choices for starters. I can break the finger or pull the fingernail, which do you prefer?"

Dennis' reaction was immediate. He tried to talk, but the tape reduced his speech to a series of incomprehensible sounds which he quickly realized were making no sense, so he started to shake his head from side to side.

"Can't make up your mind? Well, then I'll decide." With a gentleness that was surprising, considering the circumstance, Frank placed the jaws directly behind the fingernail and clamped down. Then he slowly bent the end of the finger back toward the wrist. With that, Dennis started to whine. As the end of the little finger was bent backward, Dennis's whine grew and peaked when the finger bone audibly snapped.

After a moment, Frank slowly removed the pliers from the broken finger as Dennis' whine lowered in volume and intensity to a soft sobbing.

Cyril leaned close and said, "I'm going to remove the tape so you can tell us what you did to our friend." Reaching down, Cyril pulled the tape from Dennis' mouth and waited for his sobbing to lessen.

With tears and sweat running down his face Dennis stared at his broken finger. Then he looked up. "You people are crazy. Why are you doing this? I didn't kill your friend and you fuckers know it. Is torturing someone your idea of a joke?"

"Tell us what you did. Tell us why you killed the old man."

"I didn't kill nobody, but I will get you guys. Me and my pals will kill every one of you for fucking up my finger."

"Stop your denials, you idiot, you're in no position to tell us what you're going to do. Right now, what you should do, and fast, is tell us why you killed the old man."

Shaking his head and trying to see the faces behind the light, Dennis said, "I don't know what you're talking about. I didn't kill any old man."

Cyril waited a moment before he put the tape back on Dennis' mouth. "Have it your way."

Frank leaned to the side and brought the small bag onto his lap. Reaching into it, he took out a small propane torch and a pair of powder blue examination gloves.

Making sure he was in Dennis' view, he slowly put on the exam gloves and when he was satisfied with the fit, he reached forward and unzipped Dennis' pants. Even with half his face covered with tape, it was easy to see Dennis' level of terror increase. A continuous groan rasped from his throat when Frank reached in and pulled out his penis.

Dennis's eyes bulged when the torch was activated and a thin blue flame hissed out. As Frank lowered the torch toward his penis, Dennis' moan rose in pitch. Then Cyril repeated what he had said before. "Remember to nod your head when you are ready to talk."

With bulging sweat filled eyes, Dennis stared at the pointed blue flame and whimpered as the hissing torch was moved closer. If eye movements are an indicator of tension, then Dennis was at a peak. His eyes darted up, down, and in every direction, trying to see past the light, but all he accomplished was squinting into its brightness. Gert had no doubt about what he was trying to say or what he would say if the tape was removed. His pleading was very obvious.

The torch's flame was moved yet closer and when near enough to brighten the area of Dennis's crotch, Gert wondered when he would feel the heat. Her thought was answered when his moan became a higher pitched squeal. She wondered what he was thinking now that his usual bravado was meaningless. He was helpless and he knew it, so she figured he would very quickly begin trying to save himself from what was to come.

With his eyes swelling in their sockets and his rasping breath coming in gulps, he started to rapidly nod. The torch, which was near enough to singe his suit fabric, was moved back, and then Cyril whispered, "You want to tell us what happened?"

Dennis was nodding continuously and Cyril had to hold his head still as he removed the tape from his mouth. "Tell us what you did."

With his eyes blinking in an attempt to clear the sweat that had been running into them, Dennis took a breath and then wet his lips. "Look, you gotta understand. I didn't do anything on my own. I was ordered to go there. I was told to get the analysis and start a fire to cover my tracks. It wasn't my idea."

"Whose idea was it?" Gert asked.

"It was Lydia. You know Lydia? She told me to do it. She had to have that analysis. She ordered me. She told me to do it."

"She didn't tell you to kill the old man."

"Hey, come on, you gotta understand. All I did was break into the house, get into the lab, find the analysis, and leave."

"Wait a minute, wise guy, if you did just what you say, then who broke all the glassware and wrote that idiotic stuff all over the walls. If you didn't, then who did?"

"Oh, yeah, yeah, well, look, ya gotta understand. I was tryin' to point a finger at local crazies. I thought if I broke up a lotta stuff everybody would think the whole bit was nothin' but a break-in and trashing by weirdo kids."

"So you broke things and wrote things?"

"Yeah." he said.

As crazy as it seemed, Gert got the impression he was proud of what he had done. The almost boastful tone of his voice and the way he spoke made him sound like a kid who had earned a merit badge and was now telling his scout buddies how he did it.

"After I broke all the stuff I could, I found the analysis and then emptied everything in the file cabinet and started the fire. I—"

"Wait a minute," interrupted Gert. "The analysis. How did you know what to take? How did you identify it?"

"Before I did the job, Lydia showed me another analysis she had. She said I should take paperwork that would look just like what she showed me." Gert knew he was talking about the first analysis.

"So I started the fire, waited until I knew it would really burn and then I went upstairs to leave and there's this guy standin' there. I almost shit. But when I see it's an old guy and since I was wearin' a disguise—"

"What disguise?"

"I was wearin' a UPS uniform and I had on glasses and a phony mustache." He waited, but there were no more questions.

"I knew the guy would never ID me, so I figured if I knocked him out, I could just walk away. So, I whacked him a couple a times, and he fell backward. Then he threw some stuff at me and I hit him some more and he bounced against the wall and then down the stairs. I walked down the stairs step over him and left. That's it. That's everything. I never killed that guy. All I did was punch him and he fell. I didn't kill him."

"Well," Cyril said, "true, you didn't stick a knife into him or shoot him, but the fall down the stairs broke his neck and he was just as dead as if you had stabbed him."

"But I didn't mean it. You gotta understand. I didn't mean it." He started to cry, and Gert felt a momentary pang of remorse which was just as quickly swept away by a burst of anger.

"Stop your crying, you piece of shit." she hissed at him. "You've probably been worming your way out of trouble since you were old enough to talk. Well, those days are over."

He looked up, trying to make eye contact. "What are you gonna do?" he asked, the tears stopping as quickly as they had started. Then his voice took on a new sound and Gert sensed something different was on his mind. He had told them the whole story and now that he had, his concern turned to what would happen next.

"What're you gonna do?" he asked again. There was silence.

"Hey, hey, let's take it easy here. What's goin' on? Look, like I said I didn't mean to hurt that guy. All I wanted was to get away. I didn't mean to hurt him."

Cyril replaced the tape on Dennis's mouth and then turned to Gert. She had planned the next moments carefully and knew exactly what she would do. She got her handbag and removed from it a small metal case. Dennis strained to see what was happening but couldn't, and his moaning increased, Gert guessed he knew they had arrived at a significant moment, and she never knew if he heard her open the case and remove the hypodermic syringe. Calmly and slowly, she came up behind the moaning man and with no ceremony or words pierced his neck about an inch above his collar. Saying good-bye to Sol in her mind, she quickly and efficiently emptied the syringe's contents into Dennis and felt good doing it.

Since she was behind him, he had no idea what was going to happen until he felt the jab of the needle and then, realizing he had been injected, he began to squeal and squirm. For less than two minutes, they watched his movements diminish as the thiopental sodium solution knocked him out.

CHAPTER 51

"How long will he be unconscious?" Cyril asked.

Replacing the syringe, Gert said, "I gave him a short-acting barbiturate so he should be out for at least three hours, maybe a bit more, long enough."

"That's fine." said Cyril, as he turned to Frank, "Are we clear on the next move?"

Frank nodded. "No problem at all. We leave here, march through the lobby with our friend, who quite obviously had far too much to drink, the naughty boy, load him in the car and take him, right?"

Cyril nodded. "Let's do it."

They made short work of replacing the furniture and untying Dennis, and in less than five minutes were heading for the elevator. The walk through the lobby went exactly as planned, with no one paying attention to the "drunk" being supported by two of his buddies. In step with them, Gert marched along as if she was the school nurse accompanying the sixth grade on their trip to the museum.

Outside, as Cyril supported Dennis, Frank opened the rear door of their car and got in. Cyril pushed Dennis in and then got in after Frank had Dennis seated. Gert got behind the wheel and when they were settled, pulled into traffic.

"Shall we go?" Cyril asked.

"Love to." she answered.

Even though it was rush hour, they arrived at Cyril's newly acquired undertaking venture in less than ten minutes. Lo Spirito Fugace, the funeral parlor to which they went, offered a service that was becoming increasingly popular because of the escalating cost of an actual in-ground burial.

New Jersey had at one time the vacant land everyone turned to when a cemetery was needed. But, eternal resting places, as they were often called, became so increasingly necessary, with so great a number of people buying and using the available plots, that very little space was presently vacant or available. The demand was so great for relief that a very old business became a new business.

Cyril being a rather reserved traditionalist was not overly familiar with this step away from previous practice, so he bought a funeral parlor that had the new facilities and he also hired from a competitor a Signore Emilio Rossi, the very necessary specialist, who was now managing the new business Cyril had renamed The Fleeting Spirit.

When they arrived, they pulled the car to rear entrance, where Signore Rossi waited with a wheeled cart. Cyril greeted him and asked, "When do we begin?"

Signore Rossi offered a distinctive Italian wave of his hand, which freely translated into English stood for, "That is up to you." Cyril then asked him, "How long will it take?"

"Two hours."

"Very good. Let us begin."

Signore Rossi nodded and moved to help Frank and Cyril load Dennis onto the gurney-like cart, which Gert saw had steel rollers as its surface. Signore Rossi then led the way into the building and in and out of several rooms, each one becoming less ornate and more functional. When they came to a steel door marked "Danger-Private," Rossi stepped aside and gestured for them to enter. Cyril turned the knob and pushed open the heavy door.

For a fleeting moment Gert wondered just what she had put into action. Was all this correct? Was it sufficient? She knew nothing would bring Sol back and Dennis' elimination might satisfy her desire for vengeance, but what would be the long-range cost?

Just as she would balance out a chemical equation, she tried to see both sides. She tried to imagine the world the next day. Sol was gone, but would the world be a better place without Dennis? She decided it would be.

Cyril was looking at her and read her expression. "Having second thoughts?"

"I had them. Nothing has changed."

"Fine." He then turned and nodded to Rossi who gestured for them to follow. Moving ahead of them, he put on a pair of thick gloves and led them to a waist-high metal door set in a brick wall at the other end of the room. With no fanfare and with surprising ease, Rossi opened the doors to the fires of hell.

The room lit bright orange as the blast of heat and light burst through the opening. Rossi turned to them and pointed to a series of rollers inside the furnace that matched the height of the rollers on the cart. They pushed the cart to the brick wall where it stopped. Then they shifted their hands to Dennis and pushed him onto the furnace rollers. There was a slight downward tilt to the furnace's interior rollers, for once his body was inside it kept on moving. Gert watched the flames leaping up as it gently came to rest. Rossi waited long enough for them to see Dennis' clothing start to burn, then he slammed shut the metal doors. Removing the thick, heavy gloves, he turned to Cyril, "Two hours."

Cyril nodded. "Marvelous. We have finished our task." Then without missing a beat, he said. "What about we all go for dinner? How does that sound? Gert, are you hungry?"

"Yes, I am. I'm hungry enough to eat for at least two hours."

They were laughing as they strode from the room.

CHAPTER 52

The main ballroom of the Greenwich Plaza Hotel was a large room that was continually converted to suit the demands of the party planners who had paid the required fees for their specific catered affair. It had been used for countless weddings, dances, Bar Mitzvahs, sweet sixteen parties, testimonial dinners and quite recently, a divorce party, but never before had it held a catered funeral

The hotel's catering director was an imaginative set designer who never got the chance to do a full-fledged Broadway show, but he had come close, so he was more than ready when the word came that this ballroom booking was to resemble, but not match, a regulation funeral.

He rightly assumed any group planning a catered funeral party and supplying their own kitchen staff would not sit still for a very ordinary black-crepe-on-everything spectacle. He checked to be sure and when told "black was out," decided to create a funeral that would be remembered more for the set decoration than for the departed person. As a result, the ballroom was covered in white and gold.

Wherever they could be hung, strung, or stood, there were white flowers. They adorned the twenty round tables, each set for ten, with gold-plated flatware and customer-supplied tableware of navy blue and gold. The centerpieces were white orchids, which came close to matching the white and gold brocade slipcases covering every chair.

The result was a room that at first glance, looked antiseptic and lifeless. However, after that first look, its elegance became clear. The only danger foreseen by the director was the likelihood that the attendees would wear black. Then he found out who the "honoree" was along with who was footing the bill and his worries were put to rest. Knowing Cyril Wilson was involved meant a room filled with people who would dress as flamboyantly as they lived. The exquisite white and gold creation would be the backdrop for a kaleidoscopic rainbow so brilliant that only the spectacularly sculpted urn of ashes would remind all of the true purpose of the evening.

Approximately two hundred people had been invited, but word had spread so there was no way to exactly know how many would show up. Extra tables, chairs, and appropriate paraphernalia were available and would be placed, if needed, as was additional food and extra help – much like reinforcements in check prior to a major battle.

Risers had been added to the ballroom floor, thereby adding two levels at the front of the room. The first level held two long tables and a small podium. On the second level, which was clearly visible from every part of the ballroom, was a white bier constructed of metal and plastic. It had been designed to resemble a plant with thick entwined branches that held four large artificial white flowers. Between the flowers, in the center of the arrangement, was Sol's urn, which was cast to resemble a brilliant, blooming blossom. Behind everything at the front of the room were floor-to- ceiling white drapes that had midway gatherings created by circles of gold metal. Overall, it had the look of ceremonial solemnity from a past civilization completely enamored with romance.

Gert gasped when she entered, since she had never seen a room bedecked as this one and never had she imagined anyone could arrange a funeral memorial to look like what she was seeing. She knew the room's decoration was in response to Cyril's demand that "black was out," so to do her part, she had bought a red pants suit because Sol had often said she looked good in red. Her outfit was a tribute to his taste, even though she told Win she thought she looked like a small fire engine.

"Win, look at it all," Gert said. "It's so beautiful it could be Princess Grace's wedding"

Both Win and Lou were equally transfixed, but when they heard her say "wedding," they turned and faced each other. To develop complete communication without words takes some couples years; for others, it never happens. But Win and Lou had managed to accomplish it in months. They knew as their eyes met how their wedding would look. To seal the bargain they had silently made, they embraced and kissed. Gert watched them.

"Hey, this is a funeral. Did you forget?"

It took a moment for them to separate. "Gert," Lou said, "We're getting married."

"I know that. I know you're engaged."

"No, no, I mean we're getting married here. This is so beautiful. This is what we want."

"Hey, is a thirty-second scan all you need?"

"We know it's hurried, but it's what we want."

Gert poked Win in the arm. "I don't want to screw up your plans, but in this city you need a license, a blood test, you know the foolish formalities."

"We know. We'll do that later. If there's a preacher, a reverend, a rabbi, or even a money-grubbing TV ecclesiastic here tonight, we'll get that son of a bitch to say a few proper words. We'll do the legal stuff later this week."

"I think I would ask Cyril before you do anything like that. Don't forget that this is Sol's funeral."

Just at that moment a large group of people strode in with Cyril in the lead looking like a majorette fronting a marching band. As Gert expected, he was dressed in white from head to foot, but the color limitation did not prevent him from fulfilling his love for style. He wore a gold vest and in his lapel was a black button about the size of a nickel. With the vest melting into the white of the tuxedo, the black button jumped out like Aunt Jemima at a KKK rally.

Gert flashed back years to a painting in NYU's School of Commerce lounge. It was big—probably fifteen feet by twenty and took up most of the wall where it was hung. The artist had named it "White on White," because it was a totally white canvas with a basketball-sized slightly less white circle near its center. It was absolutely boring and pointless until some wise student put a red circle about the size of a dime in the center of the white circle. Now viewers had something to look at. After that slight addition, the painting was a great sight. Cyril was in that league, because the small black button visually jumped to be about the size of a car tire as it rested on his lapel. There was no question in her mind some people have a real fashion sense while some do not and never will.

Seeing Gert, Cyril strode toward her. He was followed by a man in a totally maroon outfit: tuxedo, shirt, tie, shoes, totally maroon. It was Frank, the fellow who helped at the hotel.

"Gert, my dear," said Cyril. "I'm glad you are here, and, if I may, I must say you look rested and quite well."

"I'm fine and from what I can see, you made good your promise for this to be an over-the-top funeral. It looks like we will pay off the other half of our debt."

Cyril smiled warmly as Win asked, "What debt, Gert? What do you mean?"

"Nothing Win, just something between Cyril and me."

"Ah, Win, my boy, so good to see you once again," Cyril said, extending his hand, "I will never lose sight of the fact that Sol always spoke of you in the highest and warmest terms." They shook hands and Win introduced Lou.

"Tell me, Cyril," Win asked. "Would you think there's going to be an official clergyman here tonight, someone who could marry us?" As he spoke, he put his arm around Lou's waist and drew her close.

"You want to get married here, tonight?"

"Sure, why not? Sol and I often spoke about me getting married, and as many times as we talked, I told him I didn't think it would happen. Then I met Lou and my mind was changed, but good. I could think of no better place to get married than here at Sol's funeral. I'm sure his spirit would appreciate it."

They all smiled, and Gert said, "Damn, that sounds good to me. How about it Cyril? Do you think there'll be somebody here to do the job?"

"Oh, I should think so. We will have quite a few full-fledged and legal members of the cloth here tonight. You will have your pick. All you need do is let me know when."

"Cyril," Frank jumped in, "I think their ceremony will fit better after the showing rather than before?"

"You are right. I should think before. There may be too much noise afterward."

Win, Lou and Gert all did almost simultaneous double takes, first at each other and then at Cyril. "Showing," Gert asked. "What showing?"

"Oh, damn, I was hoping to keep it a surprise from you." He hesitated for a moment, and then said, "And I will. You will find out when everyone else does. And, believe me, you will appreciate it."

Smiling, Gert said, "Cyril, since you're involved, I have no doubts that I will."

He moved forward and took Gert's arm. Together they looked like a rolling slice of strawberry shortcake.

"Let me escort you to the seating-card table and we will find out where the gremlins have placed us all." Everyone followed Cyril and Gert as they strode forward to the table. As it turned out, Gert, Win, Lou, and the NYU faculty and administration people were seated at one of the long tables on the first riser.

People coming in alone or in groups converged first at the place-card table and then drifted to their assigned seats. Quite quickly it became clear to Gert that the "gremlins," as Cyril called them, had not been cowards and separated Sol's friends into two worlds—the gay and the straight. Rather, the opposite was the case, allowing Gert the strange pleasure of peering at the crowd, trying to figure who was in which camp. Some made her guessing easy, since those wearing a combination of Mardi Gras and Island voodoo outfits self-declared themselves. While those wearing quieter clothes made an opposite statement.

Little by little the tables filled, and Gert, greatly amused, watched the guests adjust to each other. It didn't take long for the subdued, but nonetheless, very festive air to take hold. She glanced at the other long table on the riser and recognized many school colleagues and close friends. When Cyril sat beside her, he asked, "Well, what do you think? Would Sol have approved?"

"As I said before, you're an amazing man. He would have loved it."

When the room seemed full, the fellow Gert knew as Frank stepped to the podium and switched on the microphone. When he was noticed by the crowd, the standees took their seats, others stopped fidgeting, and then they all offered their attention.

"Ladies and Gentlemen, Madame's et Monsieur's, Signoras et Signors, Guys and Dolls, boys and girls, I will begin our tribute to Professor Solomon Woodrow by quoting an anonymous poet.

'He thanks you for the love that you have shown,
But now it is time he traveled on alone.
Though you can't see or touch him, he will be near,
And if you listen with your heart, you'll hear
All his love around you soft and clear.'"

He paused and looked up from the cards he held to scan the silent group. Then slowly and evenly, he continued. "I know many of you have lost your love and yearn for the time past when all was well, but that is not as life is. When I speak of love, I refer to the opposite of what some are thinking. I do not mean love as Casanova practiced it. I do not say 'love' and mean seduction, courtship and sexual gratification. If that is love, then it ends with the sexual act. It can be repeated with the same lover or with others, but it exhausts itself in the realm of ecstasy. When that moment is reached, that lover must start all over again and again and again until at last the rhythm is so stale that it is a weariness to start."

He reached for a glass and after a drink, continued. His voice, now more resonant than before, was rich, deep, and captivating.

"The love to which I refer is that which makes the two energized and victorious. They walk better, they think more clearly, their secret worries drop away, their world is now more fresh and interesting, and they can do more than they dreamed they could. Love of this sort can grow. It is not like youth, a moment that comes and is gone, remaining only as a memory of something that cannot be recovered. Love like this can grow because it has something to grow upon; it is not contracted and stale because it has for its object, not the mere relief of physical tension, but all the objects with which the lovers are connected."

He stopped, stared, almost glared at the audience, then said, "Those of us who knew Solomon Woodrow knew him to be generous and wise, comforting at times and aggravating at others. He was smart and silly, fastidious and foolish. He was all things a person should be. I loved him most when he made mistakes for it was at that time his humanity was displayed. He was a famous teacher, professor, scholar, an author of repute, and he knew he wasn't supposed to make mistakes. But he did, and then he laughed at himself, and particularly, at the foolish world that expected him to never be wrong. He knew what he was and because he knew, he laughed, certainly not all the time, but enough, he laughed enough."

Then he looked up into the audience. "Is there anyone with something to say? I don't want to be the only person to speak."

A man at a table on the right side stood. "I want to speak." And he did so from where he was. "I knew Sol for more than twenty years and I want to quote the bible." He paused, took a breath and said,

"Happy is the man who finds wisdom.
The man who attains understanding,
Her value in trade is better than silver,
Her yield, greater than gold.
She is more precious than rubies;
All of your goods cannot equal her.
In her right hand is length of days,
In her left riches and honor.
Her ways are pleasant ways,
All her paths, peaceful.
She is a tree of life to those who grasp her,
And whoever holds on to her is happy."

That man sat and another stood. He talked about Sol's love of food and how what was served at scholarly conventions was usually more important to him than what was said. As he spoke about Sol's being able to detail the complete menu of past conventions, scores of people smiled and nodded. Then Cyril stood and said that he had one of Sol's private journals. And in that one Sol had written about and rated every meal served at every convention, restaurant, and catered affair he had ever attended.

People randomly rose and had their say. Win stood and talked about the emptiness Sol's death had brought to his life and the incredible luck of finding love at almost the same time he had lost a true friend. Gert stood and talked about her relationship with Sol and that they saw each other every day. She talked about the way Sol had died—trying to protect her belongings and how she lamented his death.

Speaker after speaker rose to offer what their hearts enabled them to say and then as abruptly as the outpouring started, it stopped. After about a minute of silence, Cyril walked to the podium and announced it seemed time for dinner to be served. He went on to say the meal had been planned from the pages of Sol's journal and emphasized before he sat, that to some, the meal might not seem coherent, but that was because it was a series of dishes Sol loved and not a menu meant to be logical or consistent.

A grand piano was rolled out and music was played as waiters carrying the courses appeared. Each table received the same dishes one after the other and the diners were hard put to make choices since everything looked, smelled and eventually tasted wonderful. The starters were: miniature cheese quiches, stuffed mushrooms, lamb kebabs, spicy shrimp, and new potatoes with black caviar. That was followed by three soups: carrot and orange, scallop bisque or blue cheese with bacon.

Then, three pasta dishes: green lasagna, spaghetti with oil and garlic or pasta carbonara. The main dishes were raspberry chicken, pork chops with black currant preserves, roast shoulder of veal, or lamb chops. The main dishes were accompanied by an abundance of vegetables, salads, breads, potatoes, rice, and beans. Finishing it all were cakes, pies, ice creams and cookies. And for those diners who were fussy, there was, on either side of the room, a complete outdoor frankfurter stand and a table with carvers ready to serve up kosher deli sandwiches for the beef tongue, pastrami, and corned beef lovers in the crowd.

The meal took four hours and during that time other speakers came to the podium to offer words of praise and sorrow. Finally, when the moment for coffee and brandy was reached, Cyril moved to the podium.

"Ladies and gentlemen, good friends, not so good friends, and people I do not like at all: Welcome! It is with great pleasure I say 'welcome,' and I hope you will remember tonight and remember Sol, who was a loving good friend to us all. When I learned that most unfortunate fact that Sol had died, my heart filled with sorrow. It is still heavy, but my sorrow is mixed with joy."

He paused and dabbed at the corner of his eye with a golden silk handkerchief he took from an inside pocket. Then, clutching the silk in his hand, he went on. "If I had never known Sol, I would not feel the remorse I do. But, frankly speaking, I am pleased to feel the sorrow, for it reflects my love for him. I do not avoid the anguish, the grief, the distress. Those feelings mean I miss him now and will always miss him."

He stopped and lowered his head. The audience was silent except for the few who sobbed. Maybe a minute passed, maybe two. Then he looked up. "Is there a clergyman in the house this evening?"

Several hands went up from different places in the room. "Would you all come forward?" Four men in black came to the podium. Anyone entering the ballroom at that moment would have judged what they saw as a quartet getting ready to sing.

"Gentlemen," Cyril said. "Sitting right here," he pointed at Win and Lou, "we have a couple that wants to get married. Winthrop was a close and long-time friend of Sol and getting married now, here, would have pleased Sol's sense of humor. So what I am asking you to do is bless their union. It will not be a legal ceremony. They know that, and I can assure everyone, they met before this evening" He stared at the audience waiting for the snickers to die out.

"Their legal wedding will take place after the usual formalities have been dealt with, but now, now is a wonderful time for words of alliance. What better way for us to imprint this night in our memories? In the future when we hear about or read about or maybe even think about a wedding, you will think of this one, and you will also remember Sol. You will remember the union that begins this night, the night we have come to honor our friend." He gestured for Win and Lou to join him at the podium.

Lou, looking more embarrassed than Win, walked with him to stand alongside Cyril who was between them and the four clergymen who had come forward. There was a strained silence until one of the clergymen asked Win a question, but since the podium's microphone was designed to pick up only the speaker, it did not properly register sounds off to the side. Only those closest to the standing group heard the short conversation that consisted of each of the clergy offering wedding appropriate sayings and Win and Lou stating they did want to be married to each other.

Then, when all went silent, a man in the middle of the ballroom stood and yelled out, "Hey, Win, how much do you really love her?" All eyes focused on the fellow who looked like the "Bouncer of the Year." Then, the entire ballroom inhaled as the man slipped his hand inside his jacket and pulled out a large, black gun. With no hesitation, Win jumped in front of Lou.

Seeing Win move, the man with the gun smiled broadly, slowly replaced the weapon, and called out, "You see, pal, I couldn't hear what was said, so I thought I'd test your love my way. A lot of guys would have ducked and run. You didn't, so as far as I'm concerned, you passed the test. I'd say you do love her."

Then the man started to applaud. The crowd, now collectively exhaling, joined in and Lou spun Win around. "You got in front of me. You really are a hero and, my God, I love you so." She threw her arms around his neck and they kissed as the crowd whistled and applauded.

When the crowd had once again settled into their seats, Cyril, now alone at the podium, signaled for quiet. After a moment, he said, "I must tell you that Riley, there," he pointed to the guy who pulled the gun, "Riley, is one of New York's Finest and is legally allowed to carry that artillery piece with him."

Then, after bowing in Riley's direction, Cyril looked out to the audience. It was easy to see he truly enjoyed being the center of attention. Not a drop of nervousness or any sort of self-consciousness showed. After a minute of soaking up the dividends of celebrity, he said, "Now, my friends, we are ready for the evening's pièce de resistance. We are going to have a showing."

He waited for the collective murmuring to stop. "Few of you knew of one of Sol's loves, something he always longed to do well. It was his very well-concealed hobby and one of his life-long pursuits. In his memory, I thought it appropriate to show what Sol so admired and enjoyed." He looked to the side, nodded and three men pushed an enormous flat screen TV into the space between the long tables.

"What we are going to see now is Sol doing one of the things he loved."

The ballroom lights were dimmed and the set was turned on. Gradually, Sol's image appeared on the screen. He was tuxedoed, held an ebony straight-shafted, silver-tipped walking stick, wore a straw hat, and stared straight into the camera. He didn't move until an off-screen pianist started playing "Tea for Two" and then he slowly began a soft-shoe dance routine.

Everyone was enthralled because Sol was good. The grace he displayed was fluid and rhythmic and he really could dance. He didn't move with the awkward clumsiness amateurs display – even those who know the moves but lack a necessary internal rhythm. Sol danced like a full-fledged well-trained professional.

When "Tea for Two" finished, a similar song was played and all told, three separate tunes were played and Sol danced his way through each. It was a treat no one expected and everyone loved.

As were most, Gert was astounded. Often Sol would say to her, "Time for my dance lesson," and leave. He never said more and she always thought he was being cryptic about a romantic tryst. The well-kept secret surprised her as did Sol's real talent. He had copied a great many of Fred Astaire's moves, since Fred Astaire was the archetype of class, grace, and ability. Also, tap dancing meant something different to men and women. Women enjoyed it and understood how difficult it was. But men, to them it was an expression of freedom, and all dance lovers knew that the better you were, the easier you made everything look.

Cyril enjoyed it all so much, that he demanded the tape be run a second time and at the end, the crowd was standing, whistling, and applauding.

Cyril then raised his arms and said, "Now we are going to have a tap dancing contest. We are going to offer a prize for the best dancing and there are the judges." he said, pointing to Gert's table. "They will pick the winner." Gert smiled even though she wanted to cry. This is so wonderful, she thought. If Sol were here, he would have loved the craziness of it.

When quiet was restored, Cyril held up a box that had "Lo Spirito Fugace" and "The Fleeting Spirit" printed on its side. Holding it he stepped to the microphone and said, "As you know, a proper soft shoe routine needs sand or some abrasive material on the floor so the dancer can achieve the desired effect. Fortunately, some ash-like material has come into my possession that will be perfect. Sol once told me that ashes make a better sound than sand and we found the perfect ashes for the Solomon Woodrow Dance Contest. If Sol was here, he would really enjoy dancing on *these* ashes."

He looked at Gert and smiled broadly. His smile made it clear. She knew whose ashes they were.

"One more thing," he said. "I have to limit the contest winner to an amateur. No professionals allowed, okay?" The crowd applauded.

Gert watched and then slowly got up from her seat and walked to where Cyril stood. "Please Cyril, I want to spread those ashes."

He nodded and handed her the box. The three men who brought out the TV moved it out of the way and then brought out several sections of wooden dance floor which they placed between the long tables. Gert slowly opened the box, looked inside and smiled. Then she walked around the wooden floor, sprinkling the box's contents. When the box was empty, she handed it back to Cyril. "Thank you, my friend. Thank you for everything," she said, wiping away tears.

A trio had set up and was playing as Gert walked back to her seat. It took only a minute or two for the first dancer to walk to the dance floor, spread the ashes with his toe, and began his version of "Tea for Two." When he finished, another came on and so it went. At one point, emboldened by Gert and Lou, Win gave it a whirl by swaying in time to the music.

Eventually a winner was selected and he received as his prize the same large TV they had watched before. The other winning dancers received bottles of champagne, with a case going to one of the clergymen who came in a close second to the winner. Ultimately, almost everyone in the ballroom tried to do a soft shoe dance and a delighted Gert watched from her seat as the "special" ashes were ground into a dust that almost totally disappeared. It was a phenomenal finish to an amazing evening.

CHAPTER 53

A very neatly dressed fat man flanked by three men, one very large and two thin, walked into the executive office area of A.T. Dunn. The fat man told the receptionist he was an old friend and wanted to see Mr. Dunn.

Looking at the fat man and wondering if his clothing was custom tailored, she smiled. The fat man returned her smile and she instantly thought of an uncle on her mother's side as fat as this man. So fat, in fact, that he had to order custom-made clothes. She had no idea who these men were, but she could recognize the fat man's good clothing when she saw it. He wore a dark gray, probably custom suit, a grayish shirt and a maroon tie. A nice combination, she thought, so still smiling, she asked "Do you have an appointment, sir?"

One of the three men, a thin one, moved swiftly toward the girl but stopped dead like he hit a wall when the fat man raised his hand. "Relax," he said, and the man did, even backing up a few steps. Then the fat man turned back to the receptionist.

"Miss, just tell Mr. Dunn that Mr. Smith is here. He will see me."

The girl was sharp enough to now realize these four were not typical visitors. She didn't think they might be manufacturers seeking an agency for a new or old product, nor did they seem like competitive ad men dropping in for a schmoozy lunch and a few drinks. To her eye, supremely and wonderfully trained by television and film, they looked like gangsters. But not the smash and grab hooligans hanging on street corners. These four looked like a better breed of gangsters.

The receptionist's mother, who desperately wanted her to stay in Queens, marry an Italian boy, and avoid Manhattan, had relentlessly told her to always avoid any guys who looked like gangsters no matter how they dressed and no matter where she was. She, being a good daughter, in that one specific respect, calmly picked up the intercom phone, told Mr. Dunn, when he answered, that there was a Mr. Smith to see him. Then she quickly got up from her desk, grabbed her handbag, said she needed the lady's room, excused herself, and beat it.

As she left the reception area, Mr. Smith motioned to one of the men to open the door to Dunn's office, which he did, allowing Smith and his entourage to stroll in.

Dunn, seated at his desk, was surprised when the door opened and the four entered. Looking at them, he thought the first man, the fat one, looked familiar, but he did not recognize the others. Trying unsuccessfully to recall where he had met the fat man, he rose from his seat and extended his hand. "My name is Alexander Dunn, may I help you?"

The fat man walked to the chair in front of Dunn's desk and sat.

"Yes, you may." he said, "My name is Mr. Smith, Mr. John Smith. I'm here at the request of Mr. Salvatore DeVito. He requires information."

Dunn's wondering who these men were ended when he heard Salvatore DeVito's name. That name registered because Dunn knew the name and now he knew these men.

"What does he want to know?" Dunn asked as he sat down.

"Mr. Dunn, Mr. DeVito told me to make it simple, so I will. He, and me too, we want to know where's Dennis? That's it."

At that moment, Dunn realized he had been expecting this visit, for Dennis was the connection to DeVito, and now with Dennis missing, the connection was not as it was supposed to be. An unavailable Dennis presented a problem.

Shaking his head, Dunn said, "I don't know where he is. He hasn't been around for over a week. I don't keep track of him, you know. He comes and goes as he pleases. I'm sure you understand that."

"All we understand is that he ain't been to see us, as is our arrangement. The last we hear is that he is workin' on a big deal. A big deal here, I should add, that's supposed to involve a fair amount of money. So, what we got is a big deal, a lot of dough, and no Dennis."

"Mr. Smith, I can appreciate your concern. When he didn't show up for a few days I called him, but all I got was his answering machine. I've left messages, but he never called back. I didn't know who else to call."

Frowning, Smith said, "You could have tried to get in touch with Mr. DeVito."

Nodding, Dunn said, "I did, several times, but the one number I have got me nothing but an operator saying the party was unlisted."

In response, Smith silently stared at Dunn. The three men stared at Smith. Dunn returned Smith's stare and then said, "Since you're here asking about Dennis means you don't know where he is either." Dunn got out of his seat and was going to move to the window, but two of Smith's men closed in from either side, so he sat back down.

Visibly nervous now, he said, "Now look here, Mr. Smith, Dennis has gone off before and never told me anything at all. Christ, last year he went to Vegas and stayed three weeks. He never called or wrote. I had no idea where he was."

"I remember that, yeah, I remember." Smith said. "Well, it never mattered if he didn't tell you, we knew where he was. As long as we knew, everything was okay."

Visibly puzzled, Dunn asked, "Well, what do we do now?"

"We are going to check some more, and then we'll be back in touch. Don't go anywhere."

"Don't go anywhere. What do you mean, don't go anywhere? I have a big business to run. And another thing, I will probably have to go out of town for an important medical appointment."

Looking concerned, Smith asked, "Whatsamatter, you sick?"

Dunn slowly nodded and Smith said, "Well, I hope it ain't serious. And I know you got a business to run. Maybe so, but, it'd be best if you hung around."

He got up and started to walk to the door. Then he stopped and turned. "Dunn, we heard the messages you left on Dennis' answerin' machine, so I think you're playin' it straight. Your messages started comin' right away so it seems you were lookin' for him right from the beginnin'."

Dunn stood up. "Look, I want you to tell Mr. DeVito that I don't know where Dennis is and if I did, I'd tell you. There's no reason not to tell you. Dennis and I get along. We aren't best of friends, but we always get along."

"Look, Mr. DeVito knows you and Dennis were okay together, and he knows you were trying to find him, so I don't think you got anything to worry about, but you never know, pal. So, like I said, hang around." He turned to the door which was held open by one of his men and walked out.

Dunn flopped back into the chair and a moment later opened a drawer in the desk. He took out a bottle of whiskey and a small towel. Wiping the sweat from his face and taking a deep breath relaxed him enough to slowly open the bottle. He put it to his lips and after two large swallows, closed it and put it back in the drawer.

It was the 'You never know, pal,' from Smith that got him worried. "Smith," he thought. What is that? That guy is as much Smith as I'm Goldberg. He got up, walked to the window, and looking down at the street, thought about DeVito and his people who let him run the business. In the past, they had never come to the agency. All the other meetings were at country clubs, beach clubs, golf clubs, night clubs, race tracks, baseball stadiums, but never before at the office. This could be dangerous, Dunn thought. Salvatore DeVito was not a man who needlessly got involved.

Dunn flashed back to his early days and the bankruptcy of Smithson and Gallagher where he had started, and when that firm went bust, how he was out on the street. That was when DeVito sent for him. Having no idea who DeVito was and thinking he was just another agency owner Dunn went and got a super surprise. DeVito knew all about him. He told him "they" thought he was a good organizer and a good businessman and that "they" liked the way he conducted his affairs. He told him 'they' had watched him at Smith and Gal and liked what "they" saw and that "they" would take a chance on him. Dunn never found out who "they" were, but was flattered when DeVito said he would bankroll an agency and wanted him to run it. "They" made him front man and even named the agency after him.

When he was given free reign, he realized it didn't matter if the agency made or lost money. Such brazen freedom appealed to him, so he took chances he would never have taken if he had to answer to a board of directors or if the money was his own. As it turned out, his gambles paid off and A.T. Dunn became a legitimate, money-making agency, with millions in billings. To this day, he still didn't know if the agency was a place for laundering money, for hiding money, or an actual investment with making money as its goal.

So Dunn ran the agency and DeVito and "they" made a lot of money. Then one day, several years back, DeVito showed his appreciation by having his nephew Dennis work there.

At a Yankees game, DeVito told Dunn, bringing Dennis in so he could learn the business was a gesture of affection, but Dunn never quite saw it that way. DeVito asked him if he would send his own son or nephew to work in an inefficient or stupid place, and Dunn answered, "No." "Well," Dunn recalled him saying, "I feel the same way. So I'm sending my nephew to work with you. You'll teach him the business and guide his education and maybe someday, when you want to retire, Dennis can take over."

That had been seven years ago, and since that time Dennis had learned what he wanted to learn. Unfortunately, most of his learning had been done with his pants around his ankles and when Dunn brought that up, DeVito had laughed. At that moment, Dunn realized it didn't matter what Dennis did. Very possibly, the agency had gotten DeVito's backing just so Dennis would have a place to go in the morning, if he decided to get out of bed. Dunn remembered he had shrugged and also laughed aloud, but he was thinking that if the agency failed, DeVito would have probably found or bankrolled another business for Dennis to learn.

But now, Dennis was missing and Dunn knew it might become his problem. The last thing he wanted was to get stuck in the middle of anything that resembled a feud or old-world vendetta, or worse, some kind of territorial dispute between rival family factions.

He picked up the phone and called Tom who said he had not seen Dennis in over a week. He called Lydia, who said the same. Dunn could tell from their voices they were not sad Dennis was not hanging around, but if DeVito got upset and wanted answers they didn't have, no one would be happy for very long.

CHAPTER 54

The next day, Lydia was visited by Mr. Smith and his three guys. She was in her office trying to phrase some copy for Complete Abandon when they marched in.

"Hey," she cried out. "I'm working here. Who the hell are you guys?"

Smith marched up to her desk, waited a moment and then sat in a chair one of his cronies brought to a spot directly in front of Lydia's desk.

"Miss Cornell, my name is Smith and I'm here to talk to you about Dennis. First, let me ask, do you know where he is?"

"Dennis? No, I don't know where he is. I don't keep track of him." After a moment, she said, "Dunn called me about Dennis. Did you visit him yesterday?"

"Yes, we did. He knows nothing and now you know nothing. Is that the way to run a business?"

"Wait a minute. Just wait a minute. I don't know you and I don't think I want to know you. So, why don't you just get your ass out of here."

Broadly smiling, Smith looked at one of his guys. "See, Dennis said she was a tough bitch. I guess he was right." They all laughed.

Lydia was growing uneasy having the four men in her office, so she got up. "Where are you going?" Smith asked.

"I have to go to the bathroom."

Smith looked up at the ceiling. "This is some strange place. Every lady we meet has to go to the bathroom." Then he asked, "You got a kidney problem?"

"What the hell are you talking about?"

Now looking less friendly, he said, "Sit down and listen. When I'm finished, maybe then you really will have to go to the john."

Lydia sat and picked up the phone. "Who you calling?" he asked.

"I'm calling Security so they can escort you guys out. I think maybe you got in the wrong place. There's a pool room across the street."

Smith smiled again and nodded at one of his guys who came to the desk, gently took the phone from her hand, and placed it back on the cradle.

"Hey," she said.

"Look, Miss Cornell, we ain't gonna leave, so forget that. I want you to listen to what I have to say, and when I'm finished, and not before, we'll leave. Okay?"

Lydia answered him by leaning back in her chair.

"Okay, now. I'm looking for Dennis. You might say I am his uncle and I am concerned for his welfare. He calls every Friday to tell me what's happening here at the agency, at his home, and in his life. Well, we didn't hear from him last week and we didn't hear from him this week. He is not in his place. He is not here. We cannot find him and that arouses grave feelings of concern."

"Look, I told you. I don't know where he is. We aren't living together, you know."

"Yes, I know you aren't. I also know you were involved in a little deal in the recent past. He did something for you and we know your method of payment. I might add, now that I see you, I think you must be a very popular bill payer."

Lydia, growing angry, reddened. "Does that son of a bitch tell you when he goes to the bathroom?"

"No. He does not, but he would if I wanted him to." Pausing, he reached into his jacket and took out a large, gold cigarette case. He opened it and removed a long, thin brown cigarette. She was watching him closely. "Care for one?" he asked. "Custom made."

"No, don't smoke. I think it's a dumb habit."

"Yeah, a lot of people feel that way. Me, I like it."

He lit up and leaned back in the chair. "Last I heard this deal of yours is a beauty and going to make everybody a lot of money. And that you will score big with the Metro arrangement. That's good, a deal like that makes everybody happy. The money angle is set so everyone gets plenty, there's going to be dough for all four of you. But now that Dennis has vanished, it looks to me maybe one of you guys thought you'd get more if he wasn't around to get his share of the pie. So, maybe one of you wiseasses decided to make the pie bigger by cutting down on the people at the table, right?"

"Don't be ridiculous. Dunn said he'd take care of Dennis as far as money was concerned, so the split for that deal was always in thirds. There was no fourth hand."

Smith sat up. "Are you tellin' me the deal you guys made was a three way split? That Dennis was not figured in for a whole cut?"

"That's right. After we worked out the deal with Metro, Dunn proposed a three-way cut and specifically said that he would take care of Dennis. I wasn't going to complain; that arrangement meant a bigger cut for me."

"This is all very interesting. The way I heard everything from Dennis, he did the tough part getting the paper from the dame's place while you guys sat on your asses and watched him take chances."

"Hey, I give it to you that Dennis had a tough job, but nobody twisted his arm. When I talked to him about getting the analysis, he volunteered. I didn't put a gun to his head."

"Yeah, he told me. He said he even enjoyed doin' the job."

"Look, nobody from here did anything to Dennis. If he's missing it's a problem that came from his life outside."

"Yeah, you may be right. No matter though. We'll find out. One way or another we always do."

Smith had a way of leaving people with exit lines they could ponder for the rest of their days. And as it often turned out, some people he talked to had a long time to mull over his remarks, while others had only brief moments to consider what he meant.

Leaving Lydia's office, he strolled into the main corridor considering another visit to Dunn, but felt he would do better checking on what she said with a visit to Randall. Like he owned every inch of the building, Smith and his entourage calmly strolled past Randall's secretary and walked into his office.

"Hey," Randall said, getting up from his desk, "Who the hell are you guys?"

"I have some questions." Smith said, walking to the desk.

"Questions? What the hell are you talking about?"

"Look, Randall, I represent the man who is Dunn's silent partner. I talked to Dunn, I talked to that Cornell dame, and now I want to talk to you."

Randall had always suspected a silent partner, because he knew Dunn was on the street after Smithson and Gallagher went bust. And he knew that when an executive from a bankrupt outfit suddenly has the dough to start a legit agency, there had to be a big money man in the mix somewhere.

Smith sat in front of Randall's desk and introduced himself. When Randall asked about the other men, Smith told him to pay them no mind. Then, without mincing his words, Smith said, "Now, we know that yesterday you got a call from Dunn asking if you knew where Dennis was, right?"

"Is that what this is all about? Dennis?"

"That's right, it's about Dennis. Now, as I said a moment ago, Dunn called you to see if you knew where Dennis is, right?"

"How do you know that?"

"Well, yesterday we saw Dunn. Today we saw Miss Cornell, and she got a call from Dunn asking about Dennis. I figure if he called her, he also called you, right?"

Tom looked at the fat man and felt he was back in a college play, trying desperately to escape the predictable lines and the predictable outcome. "Yeah, he called me and I told him what I'm gonna tell you. Dennis is his own man. I have no idea where he is, where he goes, or what he does when he gets there. I don't even know where he lives, for Christ's sake."

"For your information, he's got a place in the Village, a loft near Kenmare Street and a regular apartment uptown. He ain't in either of them and he ain't here. Why don't you know where he is?"

Randall stared at the fat man thinking it was hard to understand why it was so hard for him to understand. "Look, maybe I haven't made myself clear. Dennis and I go out for drinks now and then and we go on double dates and have good times, but I don't keep track of him. He does what he pleases. Even around here, he does what he pleases. He doesn't have any responsibilities."

"What do you mean?"

"When I come here in the morning, I have things to do. I plan copy. I write copy. I consult with others in the firm about the psychology of the campaigns we're running or planning. I have all sorts of responsibilities. Dennis doesn't do anything. Most of the time he hangs out with the photographers, trying to con one of their models into an afternoon fuck."

"No shit. That's hot stuff." Smith glanced up at one of the three men. "You see, I told you Dennis was havin' a good time here. You thought it was all pencils and bullshit. You see, you were wrong."

The other man shrugged and smiled. Then, turning back to Randall, Smith said, "I've been led to believe that Dunn and you guys decided on a four-way split for the money from the Metro account. You, Dunn, the Cornell dame, and Dennis was each gonna get a full quarter, right?"

Randal shook his head. "No, that's not right. Dunn told us the money was going to be split in thirds and he was going to deal with Dennis from his end. It was and is a three-way split."

"Oh, really? Do you think that's fair? Dennis did the work to get it all going."

"That's right. I can't argue with that, but I can't tell Dunn how to split the money. He told us how it was to be and I was happy to hear it. When Dunn said he'd take care of Dennis, I thought he had worked out a deal with him."

Smith looked up at the ceiling, took out his cigarette case, picked out a custom-made cigarette, and lit it. "So you're telling me that Dunn said he'd take care of Dennis?"

"Yes, that's what he said."

Suddenly Randall thought he was back in that college play. "Wait a minute, wait a minute. Are you thinking that when Dunn said 'he'd take care of Dennis' he meant like on a bad TV show, that 'take care of him' meant he's gonna kill him? Is that what you're thinking?"

"Well, it crossed my mind."

"That's crazy. Dunn and Dennis were like father and son. They really got along."

"Well, I know how it used to be, but things change. Hey, my old man and me were tight pals till I was about ten and then he thought I changed into a punchin' bag. Needless to say, our relationship was not smooth after that. It took him a while and a lot of black and blue, but eventually he realized I was no punchin' bag."

"I'm sorry to hear you and your dad didn't get along, but that's not the way it was with Dennis and Dunn. They did get along."

"So what you're tellin' me is that there's no reason here that we can say is a good reason for Dennis' vanishing act?"

"That's right. If Dennis is not around, it's not because of what's going on here."

"Well, you may be right, but I still gotta talk to Dunn about the money split. It don't feel kosher to me."

Randall's mind was working overtime, and he realized this fat man was the point guy for the heavy money and it might just be possible that if they forced Dunn out, the possibility of him taking over was not so absolutely crazy. The money people might look at him the way they had looked at Dunn when they began this operation.

"Well," he said, "it's certainly possible; people can change. To my eye, Dunn and Dennis always got along, but there's always a part of the story nobody knows. I have no idea about how they really got along. It always seemed okay, but…" He let it trail off so Smith's already suspicious feelings might be pushed a little more.

"Yeah, things ain't always what they seem. That's the truth." He leaned over and crushed out his cigarette in an ashtray.

"Okay," he said as he stood. "I think it's time for me to have another talk with Dunn. I want to get this money business straightened out. It ain't like Dennis to let cash slip by, especially big cash."

Randall stood up and offered his hand, but Smith either didn't see it or chose to ignore it. He turned to the door which one of his men already held open. Outside, he stopped at Randall's secretary's desk.

"Miss, why don't you go for coffee, I need to use your phone."

One of Smith's men burst out, "Hey, they don't take coffee breaks here, they take bathroom breaks." Then he laughed. The girl looked first at Smith, then at the laughing man, and with no hesitation, got up and scurried away.

"I think you're right, Carlo. She looked like she needed the john more than a cup of Joe." Smith was also laughing as he picked up the phone.

Ten minutes later the four of them marched into Dunn's office. At his desk, Dunn looked up saw them, and turned pale.

"What is it? What do you want now?"

"I don't want anything. It's what Mr. DeVito wants. He wants you to come and have a talk. I am going to bring you to him, now."

"But I have business to do. I have a meeting."

"Tell that guy Randall to go and take notes. Okay?" The three men surrounded Dunn at his desk as he called Randall.

A short while later they strolled out of the lobby into the street, like a group setting out for an early lunch. The people who noticed them were more impressed by the size of the limousine they entered than anything else. However, it would have been plain to any observant person that one of the five was nervous and had an ashen look to his skin even though it seemed tanned. That particular man walked with two men alongside and a very big and hulking man behind. They all followed a fat man who marched along like he was leading a band.

To the observers, the two thin men, the large man and the fat man looked like typical city guys, not tanned, but not pale, just the usual pallor. It was that fifth man who stood out. He didn't look well at all.

CHAPTER 55

Seconds after the limousine's doors closed and locked, the car nosed into the heavy traffic. Trying to take his mind from the moment, Dunn wondered where DeVito lived but was reluctant to ask, for he knew they would not tell him. Everything was secret until by some unexplained logic, you were admitted into the fold. And that could be accomplished by a hand wave or a nodding of a head. With no knowledge of DeVito's location, Dunn assumed the ride would be long enough for him to snatch a bit of a nap, so he closed his eyes and leaned back into the leather seat.

As Dunn managed to peacefully fall asleep, Lydia was wide awake and upset since working out an appropriate campaign for Complete Abandon had become complicated, while, simultaneously, it was thought to be uncomplicated. To Lydia, it proved a pain because she wasn't satisfied with what was referred to as "standard techniques." She was on a quest for "something different," but no one at the agency could offer a technique that was "something different."

The standard media advertisements in the usual outlets were acceptable, statistically workable, and typically productive, but all had been done before, and she wanted an approach that was as dynamic and new as the product she was pushing.

She sat in her office and stared at the sky through the window, thinking about how to get at what she wanted. She knew those who had been assigned to come up with a new technique were working hard to develop an approach that was new, but they seemed to have hit a wall. They constantly told her there just didn't seem to be the something new she wanted. Slightly fed up, she got up from her desk and grabbed her coat figuring a walk around the block might help.

On the street the usual numbers of people were marching. Some walked alone and some strolled in groups of two or three. Most were gabbing away. She watched them as she walked and wondered how she could break into their conversations. How could she fix it so they would talk about what she wanted them to talk about?

That could be managed, she realized, if she could break into their conversation and change whatever was their subject. If I could get them to listen to a spiel pushing Complete Abandon that would be great, but how to do that? As she walked she forced herself to think from a different perspective and look at advertising in a new way.

She walked and thought. She walked and looked at what was happening around her. There were people in front of her and people behind her. She could clearly see those in front, but those behind her were essentially invisible. She knew they were there, but because she couldn't see them, they essentially vanished.

Then she had an idea. The people on the street she could see were just like the ads running in newspapers, magazines, and on TV and radio. They were visible. They were the standard media carrying the standard message.

But the people behind her or on a different street were invisible. She knew they were there, but because she couldn't see them, they didn't exist in the same way the visible people did.

The public was sophisticated enough to recognize advertisements for products and knew those ads were in specific media for delivery of their specific message. That was the way things have always been done. She realized she needed another media, another way… a way that was different from the way things were now done.

So how about a nonstandard technique? How about a concealed approach? An approach that would be unlike the usual but might work better than what is typical?

She knew word-of-mouth advertising was very strong, particularly when it came from others who are known and maybe trusted. How about if I hire actresses capable of "real" sincerity and have them follow a script that has them pitch Complete Abandon to selected groups of consumers?

In that way I could break into any conversation that exists as long as the actresses I hired were able to direct the talk to a push for the product.

Her imagination started to soar and she could see a typical Waspy female in a country club during a golf tournament or tennis match. She is part of the crowd and she fits in. She is talking to women around her, and what she is saying is the script she has memorized. That script, which we will prepare, extols the benefits of our product. She is like a spy spreading a properly prepared piece of propaganda. It tells of the incredible benefits of Complete Abandon, but not the way those benefits were stated in our print ads. Rather, she is telling those around her how she personally benefits in her marriage or with her boyfriend.

The hired actress is herself an advertising medium. She is in a conversation as a simultaneous advertisement and participant. She is an unrecognized secret ad. To her listeners she is merely one of them honestly passing on some words about a product she uses and loves.

Lydia stopped and took a deep breath realizing she had it—that was the new technique. Elation blossomed within her because she knew she had hit on a technique that was invisible, but still functioned as a medium carrying a prepared message. "I'm going to call it our clandestine approach," she said aloud, and headed back to her office.

Seated at her desk, she took a tape recorder from a drawer and turned it on. What she intended to do was act out what she envisioned to be a typical encounter with a potential customer. Staring at the recording machine, she started to speak.

"Okay, let's say we have two women who are watching a tennis match at a local club. They're in their middle thirties and similar, save that one is blonde while the other is a brunette. The blonde takes a bottle of cologne from her purse, applies a bit to her neck, and then leans toward the other woman.

"Have you tried this yet?" she asks.

The other woman responds, "Oh, I'm sorry, I was watching the match and didn't catch what you said."

"I asked if you had tried this yet."

"Tried, tried what?"

"This." She shows her the bottle. "It's Complete Abandon and it's fabulous. This is the cologne, but I also have the perfume. It's just amazing."

The other woman says, "I saw an ad for it or I heard something about it." The woman looks at the bottle. "If I remember, the ad said, use it and have some kind of control over men." She laughs. "Does it work? Do you have guys panting and clawing to get their hands on you?"

"Oh, you've got it all wrong." The blonde says. "It does work, but it does the exact opposite."

"What do you mean the exact opposite?" the surprised brunette asks.

Leaning closer, the blonde says, "The usual perfume ads always say their stuff will drive men crazy. If that were true, they'd be all over us."

"Just what I need," the brunette says with a trace of disgust in her voice.

The blonde smiles. "I know what you mean. Thank God those ads are all crap. But this stuff, this stuff doesn't promise that. Complete Abandon offers control. It turns men on, but *not* hot and heavy. All they will want to do is cuddle."

"Cuddle? G'wan." She flips her hand dismissively.

"No. That's the truth. It turns them into puppies. All they want is to be held and rubbed. My guy, sometimes he's a monster, but this stuff turns him into a kid who wants mommy to hold him."

"Have mommy hold him? You're kidding." The brunette has now turned her full attention to what the blonde is saying.

"Honest truth. I put on the perfume, he hugs me and that's where it stops."

"Stops?"

"That's right. More happens only if I want more to happen."

"God, if that were true, I'd bathe in it. I love my guy, but sometimes he's such a pig. There are times I don't mind that. But lots of times it's the wrong moment."

"Yeah, I know what you mean," she says. "I was in the same boat, but no more. When I want action, I put on anything. When I don't, it's Complete Abandon and nuzzle time."

"God, that sounds too good to be true." She laughed. "But what's to lose? Is it at the mall?"

"Of course, it's in all the stores."

"I'll get some," She looked back to the court. "and tell the girls. A perfume that makes them nuzzle, that's fantastic."

The blonde woman stands up.

"Are you leaving, the brunette asks?"

"'I'm afraid so, another appointment. But I'll be back. I'll see you again."

The brunette says, "Okay, and thanks for the advice."

Then the blonde goes to her car in the club's parking lot and, while sitting in it, crosses the tennis club's name from her list. "Three more to go this afternoon," she says to herself and heads out.

Lydia reached out to turn off the recorder. That would work, she thought. That would work perfectly. Extremely satisfied, she began to imagine where and how else this invisible advertising would work. She closed her eyes and thought for several minutes.

Then, in a burst of energy, she opened her eyes and grabbed for a pencil and a pad, where she wrote across the top of the page,

Additional locations and additional situations.

At every mall with a beauty salon an actress starts a conversation and pushes the product.

At every meeting of bowling clubs, ambulance corps, nurses gatherings.

In the entire Greater Metropolitan Area, hundreds of ladies will hear about the wonders of *Complete Abandon*.

Actresses will be hired to fan out into the female population and spread the word.

Every financial chat room catering to females will have an authorized female whose job it is to simultaneously push Complete Abandon as well as call for the purchase of Metro stock

Complete Abandon will be pushed over the Internet, via personal phone calls and live conversations. All social media sites will be used to hawk the product.

The product will be advanced wherever women congregate: beauty salons, sports facilities, schools, hospitals, nursing homes, dance academies, soccer games, PTA meetings, gyms and the like.

Then she put the pencil down and imagined the clandestine approach in full effect, with its focus on women in their traditional meeting places. Since women in those places were less likely to reject messages that had the earmarks of friendly and useful advice, the realization of it all being an ad would be well hidden. And while the traditional ads were often rejected, these cunning and unapparent ads should be accepted and acted upon.

Leaving little to chance, Lydia was also planning a full-fledged standard approach for the complete product line. She foresaw accelerated sales at a level no one anticipated. She hoped there would be gleeful and greed-full smiles at both A.T. Dunn and Metro with her contribution recognized with promotions, acclaim, and significant benefits, both financial and social.

CHAPTER 56

Dunn woke up and after glancing at his watch realized they had been driving for almost an hour and were probably someplace in Westchester County or out on Long Island. He saw the bricks giving way to trees and the trees morphing into fields of cared-for lawns. As Dunn stared from the car window, he thought how living and working in Manhattan had eliminated a car from his life. As he looked at the football-field lawns, he tried to remember the last time he actually had driven a car. He used taxis, but he recalled that he had once told himself he would buy a car if he got married and had children. Since he never married, and now, never would, a car was as much out of his life as a family.

They left the highway and traveled a maze of country roads with large estates on both sides. Eventually, the car slowed and they pulled between two gates to a long, serpentine entrance road. When they arrived at the house, the three men escorted Dunn from the car, and they followed Smith as they walked on the loose white gravel of Salvatore DeVito's driveway. Approaching the house, Dunn looked at it and thought its immense size was typical for a well connected "businessman."

They entered through a pair of well-polished wooden doors into a vast marble-floored main hall. Glancing left, then right, Dunn figured the rest of the house would be equally enormous and filled with a great number of appropriately decorated rooms. The upholstered furniture and wood pieces he could see looked exquisitely real, but simultaneously false. They looked a bit too new to bear the label of antiquity.

"Nice place, huh?" Smith asked.

"Isn't it sort of big?"

Smith looked puzzled. "Sure it's big, but what would you expect for a man of Mr. DeVito's stature?"

"I'm just trying to say that it looks like there are a lot of rooms for, well, how many people in Mr. DeVito's family?"

"Which family?"

"The immediate family, you know, mother, father, wife, sons, daughters, that family."

"Oh, I see, well, maybe you should ask him, and if he wants, he can tell you. That's his business." Smith raised a hand and everyone stopped.

"Boys," he said, "wait here with Mr. Dunn till I find out where Mr. DeVito is and when he wants to meet." Smith walked into an adjoining room as one of the men pointed to a low bench by the staircase. Dunn sat. They stood. Everyone waited.

While they waited, Dunn turned his attention back to what he could see. The staircase behind him had white marble treads and risers with black wood for the balusters and for the hand rail, which was more than six inches wide. Big enough, Dunn thought, for any size rear end to slide down.

He shifted his gaze to everything in view and it all looked very expensive and of fine workmanship. The walls around this central hall were painted to resemble an Italian Renaissance palazzo and Dunn guessed what to expect before he looked up at the ceiling and inwardly smiled when he saw it was painted to somewhat resemble the Sistine Chapel. It wasn't a copy of the chapel's ceiling, but had a very religious theme. It was clear to Dunn from what he could see that Mr. Salvatore DeVito was a very, very rich man.

He had not kept track of the time, but he figured about thirty minutes had passed since he sat on the bench. He knew better than to complain or even say anything to the men who waited with him. They had been told to wait and that's what they would do until they were told to do something else. Dunn wondered if the stone statuary he could see had started out as people waiting for an audience with Salvatore DeVito.

He told one of the men he had to use the bathroom and the man walked a few paces and pointed to an almost invisible door under the staircase. Dunn followed and went into a small room finished in green marble. He relieved himself and then looked in the mirror. Even though he felt pretty good and was not experiencing any pain, his eyes were puffy and he was sweating. When he opened the door Smith was standing with the other men.

"You okay?" he asked.

"Yes. Will I have to wait much longer?"

"No. He's ready to see you now. Follow me."

Smith turned and walked through the doorway he had used before. Dunn walked beside him. The three men walked behind, the large man in the middle, the thin men beside him. They trooped down a long corridor that had windows on one side, while the other wall held a succession of paintings, each about three by four feet. The arrangement was reminiscent of the family portrait galleries in the passageways of European palaces. This series began with a painting of an old man and ended with a modern-looking portrait of another man Dunn thought looked like DeVito as he remembered him, but was probably his father or grandfather.

When they emerged from the hallway, they entered another passageway with a wall of floor-to-ceiling windows that faced a garden, so sculpted and organized, that it looked false. Dunn wondered if it held fake butterflies and stuffed birds. Suddenly, Smith walked directly toward the plantings. Dunn looked ahead and saw a large furniture-filled room, with DeVito sitting at an ornate desk. For a moment Dunn couldn't tell if DeVito was indoors or out until he saw tinted glass behind him and realized where DeVito sat was actually indoors. About fifteen feet from DeVito's desk, the three men stopped at the edge of a carpet that had been woven to resemble a Paul Klee painting. Dunn hesitated, but Smith motioned for him to walk with him to DeVito's desk.

"Mr. Dunn, it's good to see you again." DeVito came from behind the desk and shook Dunn's hand with great energy, then motioned for him to sit.

"Come, sit here beside me" As Dunn sat, Smith backed away to join the men at the carpet's edge.

DeVito sat and asked, "What do you think of my garden? Good plan?"

"I've never seen anything like it. You must love flowers and things that grow."

"Ah, yes, flowers are nature's payment to us for not completely ruining the earth. As long as we treat it well, we will have flowers. But if we poison the air, the flowers will vanish."

"I don't think the government will let things get that bad."

"Ha! The government does whatever the highest bidder tells it to do. I've always hoped the very fat-cat-crowd likes flowers."

Dunn studied DeVito, trying to figure what was coming next, but the man offered no hints. He was about sixty, maybe a bit more, and very elegantly dressed in a custom-made suit that was slimming where a person should be slim and broad across the chest and shoulders. The gray streaks at his temples matched his mustache, and his shirt matched his healthy-looking tanned skin. Dunn had the feeling of being in a movie where nothing was real, but nonetheless, looked wonderful.

"Have you made a mistake? Mr. Dunn?"

"Pardon me?"

"I asked if you had made a mistake, an error that will cost you."

"Look, Mr. DeVito, I'm not stupid and I know why I'm here. Your man Smith probably thinks I'm behind Dennis' disappearance and maybe even thinks I've gotten rid of him. I hope you understand that's completely ridiculous."

"Well, Mr. Dunn, Dennis has vanished and the last we know is that the deal with Metro money doesn't sit right. Dennis does the work and he gets none of the money. That's not right. Do you think that's right?"

"Of course that would not be right. I intend to give him my share. That's why I set it up as a three-way split. I wanted him to have more than a fourth."

DeVito stood, but did not step away from the desk. "You want me to believe you were going to give your share to Dennis and take nothing for yourself?"

"That's right. That's how I planned it."

DeVito sat down. "Now, I want you to tell me why you are so willing to give away so much money. Please understand, Mr. Dunn, it isn't that I don't believe you, but in my experience I have never found anyone willing to give anything away. People make trades and certainly make deals, but outright gifts, well, if what you say is true, it will be a first for me."

Dunn exhaled loudly and leaned forward from the waist as his chin sagged against his chest. He brought his hand to his temples and a moment later he began to sob.

"Mr. Dunn, are you okay. Are you sick?"

Dunn slowly lifted his head and wiped his eyes, and then he spoke slowly and carefully. "Mr. DeVito, I have only months to live and I wanted to make a gesture. I wanted to provide for Dennis. I knew he couldn't take over the agency's operations and I thought a good deal of money would help him get by."

DeVito was visibly stunned. Leaning forward, he asked, "You have only months to live? What do you mean?"

"I've got pancreatic cancer, and it's spreading. I'm shot, finished."

After a long moment, DeVito said, "I'm sorry to hear that, Mr. Dunn. Is there anything I can do?"

"I appreciate your asking, but I've been seen by many doctors and they all agree. I don't have much time, but who knows, mistakes have been made before. Maybe I'm a mistake."

"We'll get back to your problem in a moment, but let's see if we can settle this business about Dennis first. Why do you think he could not take over the agency? Why do you think he could not do well?"

"He could do well, but I don't think he would want to run the agency. He wants to have fun, go to Vegas, screw the models, stay out all night, and party. He puts in time at the agency, but he's not the kind of guy to run it. He's not ambitious that way."

DeVito stared at him. "I would agree with you about Dennis. He is, as you describe him, not overly concerned with day-to-day business affairs. I know that, but he is my nephew, my brother's son. He's family and I have to provide for him."

"Try to understand, Mr. DeVito, you and Dennis having the same last name led me to figure he was connected to you, but I didn't know how he was connected and I never asked about it. During the years he's been with me, it was easy to see he wasn't interested in running the agency. Nevertheless, I wanted to give him something." Dunn stopped talking and took a deep breath.

"Mr. Dunn, can I get you anything? Do you need a doctor? I can have one here quickly?"

Dunn muttered, "No, thanks."

"Okay, but please tell me if there is anything you do need or want."

Dunn nodded and continued. "Mr. DeVito, the last time we saw each other was years ago. I knew you were important then, but things change and I didn't know of Dennis's relation to you. So I thought I would provide for Dennis while I was able. The Metro money will come to a significant and continuous amount. With a three-way split, the people involved will never again have to worry about money. I wanted to do that for Dennis."

DeVito was motionless and it was obvious to Smith and the other men that he was deeply, deeply touched. He stood and moved to the side of Dunn's chair. "Come," he said, pointing. "We will sit over there." Dunn got up and followed DeVito to a leather sofa. They sat and DeVito asked him, "Do you like Dennis?"

"Of course I do," said Dun."

"Tell me, do you have any idea where he is?"

"No, I don't. When he didn't show up that Monday, I called his place figuring he went on a weekend toot and overslept. I called everyday after that."

"Yes you did. I've heard the answering machine tapes."

"Did anyone else call?"

"Some girls complaining about being stood up. That's all." He looked at Dunn with narrowed green eyes, "Would you care for some food or a drink?"

"I would like some tea, if that's possible."

DeVito nodded to Smith. "And I'll have some coffee. Go with the boys to the kitchen and tell the cook. Bring it when it's ready." Smith nodded and gestured for the three men to follow.

"Now, Mr. Dunn, I want you to think and try to figure who might do him harm, at the agency, I mean."

Dunn was surprised. "At the agency? You think someone at the agency would harm him?" Dunn hesitated and then said, "Well, there's no one but Tom Randall and Lydia Cornell working with this new product, and they're the ones involved in the money split. I don't think they'd harm him or even—" DeVito cut him off.

"You wouldn't suspect Randall?"

"No I wouldn't. He and Dennis are different. They've gone out on dates and paled around, but Tom's business ambitious and Dennis is fun ambitious. There's no reason for Tom to do anything; there's no connection."

"What about the Cornell woman?"

"Well, to be honest, she's a different story. First, she's tough as nails and I think she's ruthless enough to do anything. Second, this whole deal with Metro happened because she learned of the chemical analysis."

"The one Dennis lifted from the place in the Village?"

"Right, and when Dennis told me what he did and that it was all Lydia's idea, I got nervous."

"Why?"

"Dennis is the only person who can directly connect her to the theft. Also, there was a death involved and if Dennis ever got picked up, she would be involved. At least he could implicate her."

"Oh, so you're saying she might have reason to make Dennis disappear."

"I guess so, if she wanted to eliminate any possible connection between her and the theft and killing, sure."

"Is she capable of murder?"

"I think we all are if the stakes are high enough."

"Yes, I agree with that." DeVito stared out into the garden as Smith came in pushing a cart holding tea, coffee, and small dessert cakes. He opened two small tray tables and served the food. He left when DeVito told him to tell the cook that Mr. Dunn was staying for dinner. As he said that, he looked at Dunn, who nodded.

Then he gestured to the food. "Come, let us eat and drink and afterward I want to show you my house, that is, of course, if you care to see it and feel well enough. I don't want to burden you."

"I'd love to see the house."

About ten minutes later, DeVito put an arm on Dunn's shoulder as he led him out of the glass walled rooms. "We have had a long and pleasant relationship, Alexander. May I call you Alexander?"

"Of course."

"Good. Please call me Sal. We have had a long relationship, one that has benefited both of us and one you have respected. I admire that and I admire you." They walked a few steps more and then DeVito stopped and looked at Dunn. "And, tonight after dinner, I will arrange a meeting with my doctors. Maybe there is something that can be done that has not been done. We will find out."

CHAPTER 57

Following a hunch, Smith told the large man who was driving to stop at the hydrant so he could watch the doorman through the car's window. This particular doorman was wearing a uniform right out of a Charlie Chaplin movie with more gold braid and brass buttons than a high-school marching band.

The guy looked to be about forty-five and in pretty good shape since he hustled open cab doors and quickstepped all over the building's entrance. Smith was glad to see the guy didn't look or act stupid, because a sloppy, lazy guy would probably have a memory to match. This guy looked alive and Smith hoped his memory was exactly the same.

"Carlo, go ask him when he's done. Tell him we have a friend in the building and need to talk." Carlo got out, went up to the doorman, exchanged a few words and then returned to a seat in the back of the car.

"He's finished at four, about twenty minutes."

"Good, we'll wait." Smith opened his cigarette case, took one out and lit it.

The man in the back sitting next to Carlo asked, "Hey, Smitty, did you ever read the newspaper stuff about what they call second-hand smoke?"

"What?" Smith asked.

"The stuff about second-hand smoke that says you can get sick when you breathe in the smoke from somebody else's butts."

"No, Angelo, I did not read that. But tell me, why do you ask?"

"I was just wonderin' if you knew about it, is all."

"Are you tryin' to tell me I should stop smoking?"

"Well, maybe, maybe just here in the car."

"Jesus Christ, Angelo, what the fuck is it with you?"

"It ain't me Smitty; it's my girlfriend. She's on a health kick, and when I get home she tells me I smell from smoke and makes me shower and change all my clothes."

Carlo laughed. "Anybody who can make you shower and change clothes ought to get a fuckin' medal. Shit, Smitty, you keep puffin' away. You're doin' a public service."

Gruffly, Smith said, "Why don't you two guys shut up and stop tryin' to be my wife, okay?"

The two men in the backseat quickly turned their heads to look out the closest windows. The large man who was behind the wheel chuckled and Smith turned to him. "Gruppo, you got any comments about my lifestyle?"

"No siree, everything's fine up here."

"Good." Smith replied, opening the passenger door and getting out. He ambled to the doorman who had been eyeing the car, but was now watching Smith.

"My man told me you finish at four."

"What's this all about? You guys ain't the cops."

"No. We are not the cops. It's just that you and me, we need to talk, 'cause maybe you remember something about a friend of ours. All I want is some answers to my questions. There's fifty in it."

When the doorman heard the word "fifty," his eyes lit up and so did Smith's because he loved people who loved money. This guy would tell everything he knew, since he knew that Smith knew he'd have to open doors for three days before he'd put away fifty in tips.

"As soon as my relief guy shows, we can go downstairs to the lockers. We can talk there, okay?" Smith nodded and headed back to the car, flipping away his cigarette as he walked.

The four men watched the doorman hustle, open doors, shut doors, get cabs, and take a couple of UPS packages. A few minutes before four, another guy, dressed in the same uniform, appeared from inside the building. He approached the on-duty guy and exchanged a few words. Then the first guy caught Smith's eye and gestured for him to follow.

Smith and the two from the back of the car followed the doorman to a small dressing room in the basement. The two waited as Smith went in with the doorman who, once inside, started to shed the uniform.

"You know who is Mr. DeVito? He's got an apartment on the seventh floor," Smith asked.

"Oh, yeah, I know him. Good tipper. Ain't been around for a while, in Europe or something?"

"No, I don't think he is, and that's what I want to talk to you about. When did you last see him?"

"About two weeks, maybe a bit more. It was Friday or a Saturday. I remember 'cause I was workin' the late shift that weekend. Usually I'm days. Anyway, he comes out, wants a cab. While he's waitin', he tells me he got a heavy scene goin' with a great-lookin' babe. I'll tell you one thing, that guy can get dames. I seen him with babes I ain't never seen nobody else get— beautiful, beautiful ladies. Anyway, I finally get him a cab and away he goes. That's the last I seen of him."

"What kind of cab?"

"What kind of cab? Let's see, it was a Checker. I love them Checkers. I even think I know the hack. Usually works this area."

"Great. Now look, here's the fifty and a card with my phone. As soon as you see the cabby, get his number, or get him to call me. I got to talk to him. You swing that, there's another fifty for you and a fifty for the hack. Got it?"

The doorman grabbed the bill and looked at the card. "Mr. Smith?"

"Yeah, that's my name."

"John Smith, huh, funny, you don't look like a Smith." In response Smith stared at him in a way that got him very deeply involved with shedding the rest of his uniform.

"You call me, right?"

"Don't you worry I'll find that cabby and I'll call."

Three days later Smith returned and was pleased to see a yellow Checker out front. The doorman saw him coming and went inside. Smith followed him to a guy sitting on one of the lobby furniture pieces. The doorman said, "This is the cabby who took Mr. DeVito that night." Smith handed a bill to the doorman, who said, after looking at it, "If there's ever anything else I can do, ask."

Smith nodded and sat down beside the cabby. "The doorman tells me you are the hack my friend used about two weeks ago." The cabby nodded and said, "He told me there's a fifty in it for me."

"Don't worry about money. Help me get some answers, okay?"

The cabby stared at Smith, came to a decision, and said, "Sure, sure. How can I help?"

"First, what day was it, Friday or Saturday?"

"If I got the right guy in mind, it was a Friday night."

Smith nodded and then asked, "Now, go ahead and tell me what my friend looks like." The driver looked up at the ceiling.

"Let's see, good dresser, about thirty-five, forty, tall, smooth hair, suit, white shirt, very pointy collars, no tie, navy blue trench coat, no glasses, no mustache or marks on his face, but one eyebrow sorta curves up at the end, the right one."

"Okay, that's my friend. Now, where did you take him?"

"The Village Plaza Hotel. You know where that is?" Smith nodded and asked, "Did he talk to you on the trip?"

"Are you kiddin'? He was wound. All the way downtown, he's talkin'. Tellin' me about the broad he's got waitin' there. A real score, high class, snooty, but ready to go. I remember so well because I'm thinkin' I'm bustin' my ass with the cab and this guy's gonna be gettin' laid just about the time I'm into a tuna fish at the Bellmore."

"Did he mention the dame's name?"

"No. All he said was that he's happy the scene came off."

"When you got to the hotel, what happened?"

"Nothin'. I drop him off, he walks in the front, and I'm gone."

"Thank you, my friend. You got a good memory. Is there anything else you recall?" The cabby shook his head.

"Okay, here's something for your trouble and my card. If you remember anything to add to what you told me, call, day or night, call. Okay?"

The cabby looked at the fifty, smiled a yard, and then looked at the card. "Count on me, Mr. Smith. You'll hear from me if I can add anything."

Smith smiled and got up, waved to the doorman and walked back to the waiting car. Once inside, he told the driver to go downtown to the Village Plaza Hotel. Gruppo, the driver, cut over to Fifth and took it all the way down. When they got to the hotel Smith went inside. He quickly saw there was no way to get upstairs without being seen by the people at the front desk. The elevators were across an open space and the house phones were alongside the elevators. The entire lobby was open to the crew behind the front desk.

Smith went to the desk and asked to speak to the clerk who was usually on duty Friday nights. He was told that man worked only on weekends and would not be available until Friday. Then Smith asked to see the manager. After a few minutes wait, the manager approached him.

"I am the manager, sir. Is something wrong?"

"Oh, no, quite the contrary. I'm making inquiries on behalf of a friend who visited someone here about two weeks ago. He's from out of town and asked me to come here to see if anyone found his coat."

"Was your friend a registered guest?"

"No. I think he was just visiting someone who was."

"I see, now, what sort of coat is it, sir?"

"It's a man's trench coat, very expensive, navy blue."

"Would you please have a seat? I'll check with the bell captain." The manager entered a small office behind the front desk and about two minutes later, a uniformed employee came to that door, knocked and entered. A short time after that the manager came out with the uniformed man and they both walked to where Smith was waiting.

"This is the bell captain, sir, and he told me no one has turned in any such coat." He paused and then said, "Maybe if you could describe your friend, someone on our staff would recall him. That might help in some way."

Smith described Dennis DeVito as the cabby had and the manger told him he would check with the head of housekeeping about the coat and also ask the hotel staff to see if anyone recalled seeing someone fitting the description. Smith gave the manager his card and left.

CHAPTER 58

Later that night, Cyril called Gert. "My dear, you'll never guess what is happening."

"I'm sure you're right about that, so why don't you tell me."

"Well, earlier today a gentleman arrived at the front desk of the Village Plaza and asked about our friend. He told Frank that a gentleman's coat had been lost and wondered if it had been found. When Frank asked him to describe the man and the coat, well, you can guess whoooo he was asking about."

"No shit. Well, waddayaknow, someone is looking for him." Gert thought a moment and then said, "Damn, Cyril this is a stroke of good fortune. If we can meet, I'll tell you about an idea that's been bouncing around in my head."

"Do you want to meet now?"

"Well, the world won't come to an end, if we don't meet till tomorrow. I'm free at eleven. Is that convenient?"

"Wonderful, but I may have sleep in my eyes."

Gert laughed. "Cyril, you better slow it down. That frenetic, frantic life you lead may kill you in thirty or forty years."

"Ya wohl, Doktor, und vere shall we meet?"

"The Burger and Bun?"

"Oh, Gert really. You should never eat in places like that. God herself has no idea what they put in the meat they serve. They probably would have used our dear departed friend in their mix, if we hadn't done the cooking ourselves."

"Okay, okay, where?"

"How does Breakfast Brunch at the Village Plaza Hotel suit you?"

"God, you're a worse ghoul than I am, but okay. I'll see you at eleven."

"Come hungry. The food is excellent."

Gert hung up and went back to studying the blueprints that had been submitted for the rebuilding of her townhouse. She was stuck on the project's major decision. Should the lab be rebuilt or should she convert everything to living space? When the insurance company guy delivered the checks, he commented on the distinctiveness of a private laboratory. Most labs he knew of were commercial setups or were attached to hospitals or schools. Hers was the first private one he had come across.

Then he asked some major questions. He wanted to know how she was able to handle her teaching load and use the lab. When she told him her lab use was intermittent at best, he asked why she needed one in her house. Then he asked, if she really was doing only once-in-a-while lab work, why not make do with the university laboratory.

She couldn't answer him and had been hung up on the lab-yes or lab-no question for more than a week. Determined to solve the puzzle, she poured a glass of wine, sat down on Sol's sofa and tried to recall the number of times she had used the lab before getting involved with the perfume analysis. When she realized she couldn't remember the last time she did use it, she knew the lab-in-the-house had outlived its usefulness.

Staring at the blueprints, she now wondered what to do with the house. She never needed more than the top floor and that left two floors, for what? After a moment, she decided the second floor would also be hers and that would leave only the ground floor to be a regulation apartment. She thought about Lou and Winthrop getting married and that maybe they would want to move in. She rejected that idea. Maybe she could rent it to a student couple like Paul and Susan. Well, not exactly like them, since they weren't married.

She figured that with a married couple living in the house, she would never again have to deal with a bitch like Lydia. She could pick and choose the graduate couples herself. The more she thought about having a married couple living in the house, the more she liked the idea and she was also pleased that she had finally decided there would be no more in-house laboratory.

And, after meeting Cyril, she would contact the architect and the contractor and tell them she wanted three floors of living space that would take full advantage of the street out front and the yard out back. Thrilled with her decision, she finished the wine and looked around the room as she sprawled on the sofa.

She thought about Sol, of being dead, and her mind filled with questions. What was the big sleep? What was it to be dead? Unavoidable, certainly.

Everyone who had been alive in the past was now dead. Billions and billions of people had been and now were not. Not only people, she realized. Trillions of flowers, millions of wolves, lions, beetles, tons of living things had been alive were now gone. Her zoologist friends told her tigers, baboons, animals like that have no consciousness of being alive. They don't fear life; they don't fear death. They just live.

People are so frantic about death they can't even say "dead. They say "so and so has passed." As if being "passed" is better than being "dead." This endless anxiety people feel about death has left them open to the big con, maybe the biggest con.

That's what she thought about religion, a swindle that used language as its tool. She assumed some animals could communicate with their own kind, but there would never be the likes of after-work bull sessions or philosophical discussions. Only humans used language that way. But if people had no language, they would not be able to adequately share their thoughts and feelings. Each person would be an isolated package much like most animals. But with language, people were able to share their fears.

She imagined the early people shaking in caves, sweating out the long nights, hoping they would not be food for a more skilled killer than themselves. Did the killers worry? Did the giant wolves and saber-toothed tigers sweat out the nights? No, she thought, only the weak got nervous. Only the weak became the victims of the shrewd thinkers who started the con.

It began when a big mouth came along and told those quaking people they shouldn't sweat this life since there's a promise of another life after death. When you are dead, they were told, you will live in a super idea called heaven, or with your ancestors at some magical place.

Why were people so willing and ready to accept the invisible? Why were they so ready to believe the idea of powers that cannot be seen? She poured more wine and smiled at the simplicity of the answer.

You lived through the long, dark night, but in the morning, the holy man said it wasn't chance that got you through. Oh, no, not that. It was the holy man's particular gods that saved you. "Those gods got you through," he said. "They saved you." He told those folks his gods got them through the evil darkness. How could they prove otherwise? Talk about clever.

She finished the wine and realized that glass would be the last if she was going to shower and not fall down in the bathtub. She wondered, so what if I fell in the bathtub and break my head? So I'll be dead, so what? What will change? It's sleeping.

"It's sleeping." she said aloud. You close your eyes and you go to sleep and there's no tomorrow, just a long, long sleep.

There'll be no waking up. There'll be no meeting with Sol and my other dead friends. There'll be nothing, nothing at all. "That's what I believe," she said, dropping clothes as she walked into the bathroom. Standing naked in front of the mirror, she said, "Go ahead and tell me I'm wrong. Is there anyone who can prove my pals will be there when I wake up?"

She tilted her head and listened. After a minute, she turned on the hot water, muttering, "That's what I thought, just a great con, a really great con."

CHAPTER 59

When Gert got to the hotel, she went straight to the dining room, where she saw Cyril at a table in the dead center of the room. As she walked toward him she wondered if he had them move the table or was it there waiting for him?

The other diners stared at him, sitting ramrod straight and tall. He looked like one of those handsome Disneyland animatronics, perfectly groomed, perfectly dressed and poised. Infrequent TV watchers might have thought he was a TV anchor or a super successful male model, all suave and credible. Never lies, sends money home to mom, never overeats, and donates to all the right charities. She laughed. If only they knew.

Halfway to his table, she was intercepted by the maitre d'. "I'm here to meet Cyril," she said.

"Of course, you must be Dr. Lehman, please follow me."

She trailed behind as they crossed the broad open space. Ever the gentleman, Cyril stood as they got to the table and remained standing as the maitre d' helped Gert adjust her chair. When she was settled, Cyril took her hand, made a gesture that looked like he was going to kiss it, but to Gert's relief, did not.

"Hungry?" he asked. When Gert nodded, he turned to the maitre d' and said, "Vincent, what's on for today?"

"I will do the honor of ordering for you. Is that satisfactory?"

Cyril smiled. "Absolutely."

Gert stared at them wondering what brunch would include. But figured she had nothing to lose.

After Bloody Marys arrived, Cyril told Gert the questions asked about Dennis and the man who made the inquiry. "What kind of guy was this?" she asked. "The one with all the questions."

"Judging from his look, his clothes, his mannerisms, the car and the associates waiting in the car, everyone concluded he's regulation crime family and from that, we must conclude our boy Dennis was involved in that enterprise. You probably remember he spoke about his connections and that people would be looking for him."

"Well, I don't understand what the hell a gangster type is doing fooling around at an advertising agency. But I don't think it matters. We have a golden opportunity to create the patsy and have Dennis' buddies do the dirty work."

"I think I have an inkling of where you're going with this. But tell me anyway."

Gert leaned in closer. "I don't know how, but in some way his pals have traced him here to this hotel. If they know that much, they might know he was here to meet a lady. Now, that leads to a potential and dangerous problem."

"What problem?"

"Well, I doubt they know what lady he was here to see, but it is possible they could find out or guess he was here to meet Susan Merrill. If that's the case, the girl's life could be in danger. However, we can lead them away from thoughts of her and supply them with a logical end for their suspicions."

"Yes, when I mull what dear Dennis told us at his questioning, I recall he said it was Lydia's idea to steal the formula and he was no more than the tool to get it. Now, if his pals are smart they will realize the two of them were connected and Lydia would be in danger as long as Dennis could implicate her with the robbery and killing."

"And they would figure she got rid of him to protect herself."

"Yes... that's exactly what I think they'd think. So what you said about a 'logical end' for their suspicions... you meant lead them straight to Lydia."

"Exactly. The hotel staff can describe the mystery lady just enough to make them think she was the one he came to see."

"What do you think they would then do?" he asked.

"Well, they could kill her, and I wouldn't give a good god-damn if they did. Or they might kidnap her, and then try to get her to admit she knocked Dennis off or had it done. She would deny everything, of course, but that's what she would do even if she was guilty." As she spoke a look of satisfaction spread on her face.

Cyril sat up straight. "Doesn't it bother you at all that they may in fact knock off this Lydia person? No qualms?"

"I've thought about it, and I'm uneasy, but then I think about Sol and my unease turns to pure hostility. If these pals of Dennis are really gangsters, they wouldn't hesitate a moment to knock *us* off if they found out what we did to him. So I don't see why I should behave any more ethically or morally than they."

"Yes, I wholly agree and I also must say that sooner or later his pals will come to the realization that dear old Dennis is no more. And if they reach that conclusion while they have Lydia in their custody, I would think they'd finish her and close the books."

"Dammit, that's what I would do."

"Well, if things go as you think, she is dealt with and our revenge is a fait accompli."

"Exactly. That would settle the score and what happens after that, well, I couldn't care less. But, as I said, they might be after Susan and if they are, then we do have a problem."

"How do we protect her?"

"One way, of course, is for us to safe-keep her so they can't get their hands on her."

"That's a very big problem." he said, slouching toward her.

"I know," she said. "That's why I think we must set them on Lydia's trail as quickly as we can. If they get rapid satisfaction, they won't think there's a need for more poking around."

"You're probably right, but I want to think about what you're saying. It sounds so perfect and so easy. Maybe it's just a little too perfect, a little too easy."

"Okay," she said, as the waiter placed plates of crepes on the table. "You think. Me, I'm going to eat."

They attacked the food and didn't talk at length until they had finished. As they waited for their next course, Cyril asked Gert once again if she had qualms about what they had done and what they intended to do.

"No, I don't. I don't believe in religion and I don't believe in an afterlife and I don't follow rules except to treat people as well as I can. If they mess with me, I get even. For me, this entire affair is retribution. It's getting even, no more, no less."

"Were you ever religious?" he asked.

A bit surprised, she said, "I went through the standard stuff when I was a kid, but I never bought it." She paused to take a drink. "You know, I've always heard there are no atheists in a foxhole. Maybe that's true. Maybe there were lots of guys praying their asses off when other guys were tryin' to kill them, but the way the world looks to me, when the shootings over, the praying stops. It's just a handy convenience."

She drank more of the cocktail. "You know, Cyril, maybe if I had been in the army and in combat, maybe then I'd be religious. But, I wasn't in the army and I think religion's a crock. It's a big deal for a lot of people and that's great for them. Me, I think it's a racket. But I do know it helps people, so it's something I don't stick my nose into. It's not my place to bitch about what other people do. They can do what they please for whatever reasons they have, as long as they leave me out of it." She paused. "You know, I don't usually talk about this stuff."

"Oh, really," he said, smiling.

"Well, I never, and I mean it. I never have tried to talk anyone into or out of a religious belief. I think people should be free to make up their minds."

"You wouldn't be a good missionary with that attitude."

Gert laughed and finished the Bloody Mary, as the waiter scooped away the empty plates.

"Would you like to wait or should I bring dessert?" They looked at the waiter and then at each other and realized neither was in any rush. "Let's wait about ten minutes," Cyril said. "And then we'll have dessert, and," he looked at Gert, "Black coffee?" She nodded and the waiter loped away.

"Look," she said, "that's enough talk about religion. Let's get on the case here and figure out how to get the necessary information to the bad guys."

"That's the simple part." He snapped his fingers loud enough for the maitre d' to hear. He came to the table and Cyril told him to tell Frank they would want to meet with him after they've finished eating.

"How do you want to do this?" Cyril asked.

"I think the best way is to describe Lydia in a general way, but be definite enough so the question askers have little doubt."

He drummed his fingers on the table. "You know, we might be able to push it a bit more."

"How?" she asked.

"What if we get Frank to say Dennis was overheard making an in-house phone call? That one of the staff walked by when Dennis was on a house phone and thinks he heard him use a name that sounded like Lara or Laura, or something like that?"

"Oh, that's a great idea."

"Yes, we can have it said that the name began with an *L* and let them supply it."

"That's better." she said enthusiastically. "That's much better. If *they* say 'Lydia' they'll be almost obligated to think they're correct. If they come up with her name, it'll be like they figured it out. Oh, that's great, that's really great." She paused, then asked, "Do you think there'll be a problem getting someone to tell them that?"

As the waiter served the dessert and coffee, Cyril said, "Oh, no, leave that to Frank. He'll take care of it all."

CHAPTER 60

Smith answered the phone, listened very carefully, and said he would stop by the next day around eleven, and then he hung up. Feeling good, he walked from his office to the hallway that led to the TV room where he figured DeVito would be. When he reached that room, he listened to the interior sounds and recognized what he had heard many times before. Mr. DeVito was once again watching the movie *Sahara*. It was his favorite and he watched it at least once a week. Smith had seen the movie many, many times and was fascinated by DeVito's passion for it.

He wondered about the magical element that so enchanted DeVito, since it was just an okay WWII film with Humphrey Bogart, no women, a minimum number of American and British actors of middling fame, an Americanized German actor, and a medium tank. That was it.

Smith often speculated about DeVito's reason for watching it every week and the only guess that made sense to him was that the film, about out-numbered Allied soldiers facing a larger German force, was a fantasy way for DeVito to deal with his endless battle with local and federal law. Smith thought one day he would ask Mr. DeVito to explain why the film so pleased him, but that would have to wait. More important matters were at hand.

Knocking twice Smith entered to see DeVito on the large white sofa that faced a large TV dominating the end of the room. Seeing that set always gave Smith a laugh because it reminded him that he grew up with a ten-inch-screen RCA, which was then considered the absolute apex of technical achievement.

DeVito pressed the remote's pause button and the screen image turned into an eerie, flickering painting of Humphrey Bogart interrogating the captured German aviator. Smith believed what he was seeing on that screen was the exact situation that triggered Warhol's pop paintings. Warhol made permanent what the DVD player's pause button momentarily froze.

DeVito hit another button and the lights brightened. "What is it?"

"I heard from the manager of the Village Plaza Hotel and he told me he had information that might help explain what Dennis was doing there. I told him I would come see him tomorrow at eleven. I'm telling you now so you know what's going on."

"I appreciate that, Smitty. Thank you."

Smith turned to leave but stopped after a few steps. "If I may, Mr. DeVito can I ask what you think happened to Dennis, do you think he's gone?"

"I'm afraid I do. Dennis is not, damn it, *was not* a dummy. He was nasty as hell at times, but smart about doing things. And certainly smart enough about the families not to realize that if he or even you disappeared, the rest of us would think the other families were involved. And, if they were *not* involved, then it had to be quickly understood they were not involved, so nobody would come out shooting for the wrong reasons. Knowing that, he would have let us know if it *was* family business, so it's got to be somethin' else."

"Yeah, that's the feelin' I had also. Something would have turned up if it was a family matter. It's been almost three weeks. That's too long for a war to not start if it was gonna start."

After a long moment, Smith said, "I'm really sorry about all this." DeVito nodded and Smith slowly left the room. Outside in the hallway, he heard the movie resume.

The long, black car sat at the hydrant on the Fifth Avenue side of the Village Plaza Hotel. Smith entered and when at the desk, asked for the manager. The clerk picked up the phone and a few moments later the manager came out of his office.

"Mr. Smith, how nice you are prompt. Why don't you come in so we can speak privately?" Smith walked around the end of the counter and entered the small office as the manager held the door open. He waited until they were both seated.

"What is it you found out?" Smith asked.

"Well, the best I can piece it out is that the desk man saw the man wearing the blue trench coat come into the hotel and go straight to the house phones. The man used the phone and spoke to someone. A bellhop who was passing the telephone area heard a tiny piece of the conversation the man was having. He was speaking to someone and it was probably a woman."

"Why do you say that?" Smith interrupted.

"Well, the bellhop heard him use the word 'baby' a couple of times and I just assumed your friend was not talking to a man using that word."

"Okay, go on."

"That's about it, except the bellhop thinks the man used a name that began with an *L*, a woman's name, like Lara or Lorna."

Smith asked, "Could it have been Lydia?"

"I don't know and from what he told me, I don't think he does either, but I do know he said the name began with an *L*. Would you want me to get him? Do you want to talk to him?"

"Sure, I would. Any problem doing that?"

"No, sir, give me a moment." The manager picked up the telephone and told someone to send William to his office. About a minute later there was a knock at the door. The manager opened it. A small man wearing a uniform stood in the doorway.

"William, this is the gentleman inquiring about the fellow you saw on the phone, the blue trench coat man. Would you please tell him what you told me and also answer any questions he may ask?" The bellhop nodded and entered the room.

Smith looked the bellhop up and down and then said, "The manager told me you heard the man say 'baby' to whomever he was talking to, right?"

"Yeah, the guy said 'baby' and then something like 'you know who is here and ready' then he said a name. Ya gotta understan' I was walkin' by and heard only that piece of what he was sayin' and the piece of the name. The name sounded like 'Lorna' or 'Laura.' I don't know, but I do remember it began with an *L*. That's about it. I hope it helps."

Smith stared at the man for a moment then nodded. "Thank you. Thank you very much. You've helped more than you know." The bellhop smiled at Smith and then looked at the manager. "Can I go?"

The manager nodded and he left the room. "I do hope what he told you is of some help, and I'm sorry we can't do more, but that about covers what we can do."

Smith nodded then said, "Well, there's one more thing you could do."

"What is that?"

"What if I got a photograph down here of the woman I think he spoke to on the phone? Would the desk clerk be able to identify her?"

"Well, sir, I'm sure he would look at it and be glad to tell you if the woman looked familiar, and he might be able to say the woman registered, if he remembered her, but I don't see how he would able to say your friend was talking to that woman."

"Of course, I understand that, but if he could tell me that the woman did register and was a guest that night, that would help a great deal."

"Sir, we will do all we can to help. I know the desk clerk personally and I know he will give you an honest answer."

"That's fair enough. I'll get that photograph and call to arrange another visit. Will that be okay?"

"Certainly, I will expect your call."

Smith hesitated and then said, "Look, I must apologize, for I'm sure you're wondering why I'm making all this fuss over a lost trench coat, but my friend is very attached to it and if the woman has it, he'd like it back. All I did was offer to help and suddenly this thing escalated into a federal case."

"Oh, I know how that happens, Mr. Smith. Little things become big things almost by themselves."

"Yeah, I know, so please forgive me if I'm becoming or have become a pain in the ass." The manager smiled, shook hands with Smith and escorted him out.

Walking back to the car, Smith felt he almost had the answer. When he sat in the passenger seat he asked, "Do one of you guys have one of them new cameras?"

"You mean a digital one, yeah," said Carlo. "I got one of them things. They're pretty nifty. I use it with my girlfriend. You should see some of the—"

Breaking in, Smith said, "Never mind, Mr. Hollywood. Let's go get it. We got to take a picture."

Frank immediately called Cyril to tell him that Mr. Smith had come and gone and was out to get a photograph to show the desk clerk who was on duty that night. Cyril called Gert and filled her in on what had happened. Her first question concerned the possibility that Smith might show a phony picture and if it was identified as Lydia, Smith would know he is being put on.

At that moment, it became apparent to them both the desk clerk would have to know what Lydia looked like. Gert then asked if the desk clerk in question had been seen by Smith. Cyril said he'd get back to her.

A bit later, Cyril called her to say the desk clerk had not been seen by Smith and it was necessary for them to get a picture of Lydia because he had to know what she looked like. When Gert asked why, Cyril told her he was going to be the part-time desk clerk and he had to be able to tell a picture of Lydia from a phony. Gert called Win and got a photograph of Lydia that she turned over to Cyril.

CHAPTER 61

Leaving the driver in the car, Smith and two men walked into the A.T. Dunn agency and saw the receptionist they had spoken to the first time. She saw them coming and was ready to leave her post when Smith raised a hand and loudly said, "Stop!" She froze as he approached her desk.

"Look, girlie, there's no problem. All I want is a picture of Miss Cornell." He held up the camera. "I have a camera and all I want is a picture. So don't run to the bathroom, okay?"

The girl reddened and said, "Will another type of picture be okay?"

"What do you mean?"

"We have pictures of management we submit to newspapers. I can get one of those for you, if that's okay?"

"That would be perfect and I would appreciate it very much."

She excused herself and walked down the hallway into an office and returned with a black and white photo of Lydia Cornell. As she handed it to him, she said, "It even has a brief bio on the back."

Smith looked at the face in the picture. He had to admit Miss Cornell looked great and he could even see the glint in her eye that turned Dennis on.

"Miss, this is perfect. Far better than anything I could do myself. I want to thank you for your trouble."

"You're welcome, sir," she said to his back, for he was already walking away.

Back in the car, Smith used the cell phone to call the hotel and ask the manager when he could see the desk clerk and show him the photograph. An appointment was set for the next evening.

Cyril waited in Frank's office dressed in a far less fashionable outfit than usual. The man he was impersonating occasionally filled in on weekends so it was stressed to him he should appear like he was put out for being asked to come in when he wasn't on duty.

When Smith showed up he was escorted into the manager's office. The three men stared at each other and Smith thought Cyril looked a little stressed.

"Are you okay?" he asked.

"Well, yes, I guess so. It's just that I only work weekends and I like to have my weeknights free."

"Oh, I see, well look, this won't take long. All I'd like you to tell me is if a particular woman was a guest at the hotel the night my friend came here and lost his coat."

Cyril nodded as Smith opened an envelope and took out a picture of Lydia. "Do you recognize her? Was she at the hotel the night in question?"

"Oh, yes, I remember her. It seemed odd to me when she checked in. I figured a woman who looked that good checking in personally would mean the guy would be along later. Usually, the man gets the room and the woman comes later. I remembered her because she reversed the usual, and, she was quite stunning."

"Do you remember my friend coming in?"

"I don't know who your friend is." Cyril said.

"The man who was wearing the blue trench coat."

"Oh him. Yes, he came in like a house on fire. Went right to the house phones, made a call, and then took the elevator up."

"You know my friend is quite a character. Sometimes he wears a blond wig. A pretty good one, matter of fact, and many people think he's really blond. Was he wearing it that night?"

"Blond? I think we're talking about two different people. The guy I thought you meant was tall, thin, smooth longish dark hair, sharp dresser, had that nice blue trench coat. I don't know anything about a blond guy."

"Oh, no matter," said Smith. "That sounds like my pal." He held up the photograph once again. "But you're sure this woman was here at the hotel?"

"No question about it."

"Okay. Look, I want to thank you for your time and I hope this covers your trouble." Smith handed Cyril a folded bill, thanked the manager for his help and left. When then door closed, Cyril plopped into a chair and inhaled deeply.

There was silence until Frank said, "You did that well, I bet he's convinced he's got the truth."

Cyril stood and realized he was still holding the bill in his hand. Like it was cursed, he dropped it on Frank's desk. It was a hundred.

"Why don't you take that and put it in the employee's welfare fund or petty cash or someplace where it'll do some good. Okay?"

Frank nodded. "Don't worry, we'll find a use for it. And, I must say, it went like a dream."

CHAPTER 62

"What do you want me to do?" Smith asked.

"Are you sure she's the one who was at the hotel?"

"The desk clerk recognized her picture and described Dennis well enough to put the two of them together," he said, sipping some coffee.

DeVito shifted his eyes to some small birds at a feeder and his face showed the same concern and commitment as did fathers watching their kids in a park. Birds were the one diversion he allowed himself as he made his climb and to make certain he could always see them, he positioned feeders around the estate where they would be most visible from his glass-walled office.

At each stage of his ascendancy, the constraints on his life grew in proportion to his increased power and prestige. Now that he was a "big man," it was hard for him to go where he pleased and do what he wanted. He was always surrounded by a loyal army ready to do his bidding or if need be, die for him. Almost everyone he knew envied him. But he envied the birds. He was jealous of their freedom and their smoothly joyous flights. Watching them, he felt the regret an adult paraplegic feels watching kids aimlessly run around and away with their youth.

Turning back to Smith, he asked, "Do you have any idea why she would do something like this?"

"I can only guess, but what stays in my mind is the connection to what Dennis did for her."

"Yes." DeVito said, nodding. "He could involve her in dirty business."

"Exactly, that's what I mean. She would probably think that way and his existence would be an endless source of worry. With him gone, the connection to the fire, the robbery, and especially the killing, vanishes."

"Look, look, a cardinal." Smith followed DeVito's finger and saw a brilliant red bird searching the ground under one of the feeders.

Smith nodded. "Very pretty."

Slowly turning back to him, DeVito said, "I can understand her anxiety and her need to resolve it, but what did she do with him? Where the hell is his body?" He hesitated. "Have the cops turned up anything in the rivers?"

"No. There's not a word. He just simply disappeared."

"I wonder how she pulled it off," DeVito muttered, looking back at the cardinal.

"Well, I guess she managed it the same way she managed to get him involved in the first place. You remember I told you that Dennis said she first contacted him to see if he could recommend a thief for the job. If Dennis had done that and not gotten personally involved, he'd still be here."

"Right, right," DeVito said with some sadness. "I guess she talked some other guys into getting rid of him the same way." He turned back to the bird feeder. "She's a tough cookie, huh?"

"Oh, yes. I met her only once, but from that one time, I would say she's capable of anything. Because she's very pretty, she doesn't look tough, but she is."

DeVito shook his head. "It's too bad it has to come to this, but get rid of her. When she's gone, we close the book."

"How should I do it?"

"I leave that up to you, Smitty. You're an ingenious guy, and I know you'll do it right."

"Okay, I'll get right on it." He got up from the chair, turned and started to walk out of the room, but DeVito stopped him.

"Smitty, do me a favor. See if Dunn got back from the hospital, and if he did, see if he would like a visitor."

"Sure. I'll be right back." Smith walked to the main foyer and checked with the men at the front door. They said Dunn had been back for twenty minutes, so Smith headed for the guest room where Dunn was staying. He knocked on the door and waited about a minute for him to open it.

"Mr. Smith, what can I do for you?"

"First off, I hope you're feeling okay."

Dunn nodded.

"Good. I'm glad to hear that. Mr. DeVito wants to know if you feel okay enough for him to come for a visit."

"That would be fine. When does he want to come? But you know," he interrupted himself, "I can visit him. It's not necessary he comes to this room."

"I'll go tell him that and I guess he'll answer you on the house phone." Smith turned away as Dunn said, "Thanks." and closed the door.

It took a few minutes for Smith to get back to the glass room and deliver the message. When DeVito heard that Dunn was back and feeling okay, he called him. As Smith was leaving, he heard DeVito asking Dunn if he would like to have lunch and then watch *Sahara*, the Humphrey Bogart movie. The last thing Smith heard was DeVito saying, "Wonderful, wonderful."

Smith then went to the room he used as an office and thought about Dunn and how well he had responded to DeVito's hospitality. When DeVito's doctors had reported that Dunn was not a medical mistake, but did, in fact, have inoperable cancers, and a very short time to live, DeVito had offered Dunn the option of staying at the estate or going to a medical center. Dunn had jumped at the chance to be around people. He said he had always lived alone but didn't want to die alone in a damned hospital with his finger pressing a call button that no one answered.

Smith thought of Dunn, and of all people for that matter, as a machine with a built-in life span. No one could know when that machine would stop, all that was known was that it would. Dunn's condition was made clear to the house staff, which was told to be kind and comply with his requests. Smith figured DeVito was repaying Dunn for the years of loyalty, and he admired him for that, because lots of guys would write a check for the funeral, walk away, and forget about it.

Sitting at his desk, Smith's mind was filled with the many ways to eliminate the Cornell woman. He laughed inwardly at his thoughts. In one minute he had gone from feeling sorry for one person facing an ugly and untimely death to planning the ugly and untimely death of another. It struck him as grotesquely humorous.

As he pondered the best way to do the job, he picked up the house phone and told the man who answered to find Carlo and send him up. About five minutes later there was a knock on the door, it opened and Carlo stuck his head into the room.

"You wanna see me?"

"Yeah, come in. I want to talk something over with you." Carlo entered and sat in the ornate chair alongside Smith's desk.

"Whaddaya want?"

"Well, we got to get rid of the Cornell dame, and I want you to help me sketch out a plan. I like to think out loud and have someone ask me questions if what I'm saying doesn't make any sense."

"You want me to ask you questions?"

"Right."

"Okay, here's my number one. Why don't I take one of the boys, grab her, cut off her fuckin' head, and dump what's left in the river? That's an easy plan and it gets the job done."

Smith smiled. "You really got the knack, you know. Direct action, do the job, period. But you know, I want we should figure something that would do more than just get rid of her. I'd like a plan that would benefit us with more than just her going bye-bye. And, by the way, I want you should use Gruppo on this."

"Okay, no problem. Now, I've been thinking about this whole mess and I think something has not been talked about. At least, I don't know if it has or not."

"What has not been talked about?"

"Well, from what I've picked up, Mr. DeVito bankrolled the advertising agency when it began and picked Dunn to run the show, right?" Smith nodded. "Okay, so Dunn has been runnin' it since the beginning, right?" Smith nodded again.

"Okay, well with Dunn slowly going out of the picture, who's gonna be in charge?"

"What're you gettin' at?"

"Well, now that I learn we are going to remove the Cornell dame from the operation that leaves only that guy Randall. He's the only other one I ever seen up there. Is he runnin' the joint now?"

"Oh, I see what you're getting at. Hey, you are one smart son of a gun."

Carlo smiled as Smith continued. "What you are saying, I think, is that when the operation began, Dunn was obligated because he knew that without Mr. DeVito's money, there's no action and he's back out on the street. So, as it turned out, Dunn is working for us. But, this guy Randall. He doesn't know about the beginnings, and I'd bet he doesn't know about Mr. DeVito's involvement with the agency or with Dunn. So, if it turns out he's going to be running the operation for us, we have to make a point with him so he understands who is in charge. He should know who's runnin' the show."

Smith had been watching Carlo as he talked and as he continued, Carlo's grin grew until now, as Smith finished, Carlo's smile was wide enough for a toothpaste commercial.

"Exactly right," Carlo burst out. "That's what I mean. We gotta make sure Randall knows who is really in charge even though it looks like he's in charge."

Smith stood and held out his hand. "Carlo, I thank you. I will check this out with Mr. DeVito and be sure to tell him from where the idea came. It may be worth a Christmas bonus."

"That would be great, Smitty." As he walked to the door, he said over his shoulder, "Be sure to call me whenever you want to talk over more ideas. I like doin' this."

Later that night Smith proposed the idea to DeVito, who immediately approved it because he had been planning to turn over the agency's operation to Randall. And now, with Cornell's exit, it was important that Randall more clearly understand his relationship to the business and to the family. When DeVito asked how all of this was going to happen, Smith told him he was working out a plan and would let him know. Before he left, Smith suggested they should have Dunn explain to Randall exactly how the agency began and how the DeVito family is involved.

"When Randall fully understands how the profits are split and the phenomenal extent of business freedom being offered by the arrangement," Smith said, "he will not be afraid to be daring and inventive."

CHAPTER 63

That following week Randall was invited to the estate and had the entire business arrangement explained to him by Dunn and DeVito. In answer to his question about how Lydia Cornell was going to fit into the operation, now that Dunn was retiring, DeVito told him Miss Cornell was leaving the firm in the very near future. Randall was surprised, but offered no objection and when asked if she knew about this decision, DeVito told him she did not know but would know shortly.

The next week Randall was invited back to the estate for a dinner meeting which turned out to be an evening of chit-chat that surprised him, because he didn't think DeVito and Dunn were the type.

Eventually, he returned to the city in a provided car, because it was late and there was no way to get back to Manhattan at that hour. To this day, he clearly remembers telling Lydia he could not get out of the meeting and that she was not to wait up for him.

She didn't. At least she didn't intend to wait up. Since Complete Abandon had become a hot item, her workload had increased, and she returned to Randall's penthouse at day's end feeling like she had put in twelve hours in a New Jersey zinc mine. She was tired and Tom's absence in no way upset her. She hadn't told him yet, but she was planning to move out as soon as she could find an appropriate apartment.

Her share of the earnings was high and she was planning to get her own place because that would be better than living with Tom and certainly better than the time she had spent coping with Gert. She had briefly considered the mid-sixties between Madison and Park and figured that location perfect.

With her own place, there would be no need for anyone to help her. She would take care of herself and be as independent as her money and looks would allow. Tom's penthouse had been just right during the "transition" as she thought of it, and she enjoyed living above the shop-girls and the clerks. She was thrilled that her feelings about others being beneath her would no longer have to be subdued or hidden. Once in her own penthouse, she could give vent to what was an honest accounting and eliminate all the sweetness, the niceness, and the other false fronts she had been forced to maintain. Her day had finally come. All her scheming and planning had finally paid off.

Somewhat glad that Tom would be late she walked onto the terrace and looked into the night sky. It was an unforgiving pool of tar with no immediate pinpoints of light. In the East, a glow she assumed to be Brooklyn, gave the sky a yellow-gray cast. Turning to look to the West above New Jersey, she saw a similar unblemished canvas of dullness. It was a dingy night with clouds obscuring most of the stars. She stretched her arms above her head and figured a quick bath and a good sleep would help her get ready for tomorrow.

As she was about to turn and leave the terrace, a hand closed over her mouth and another grabbed her firmly at the waist. For a moment she thought Tom had returned early and was playing his version of "Rape the Princess," but she knew Tom's smell and the cologne that filled her nostrils wasn't his.

My God, she thought, a robber. Then she thought it could be a rapist. Instantly terrified, she tried to struggle but could hardly move. The hand across her mouth was big and it partially covered her nose making it hard to breathe. What would happen if she passed out? She tried to bite the hand, but there was no slack—she couldn't open her mouth. When she tried to kick behind her, the person who held her pushed her forward and slowly forced her to her knees by putting his enormous weight on her back. She couldn't move. She figured it was a man holding her, and he had to be very big and very strong to hold her as he did. She felt like a small child being held tight and close by an adult.

The man leaned downward on her back and forced her knees and shins into the flagstones of the terrace. Her body was bent double with her chest crushing the tops of her thighs and her chin almost touching her knees. She was forced into a motionless position. For a fleeting moment she envisioned the television sales pitches for defense sprays and various defense courses for women. They wouldn't do her much good now. Trying to free herself, she heaved her body first to the left and then to the right trying to dislodge him, but he didn't budge. How long could this go on? How long was he going to hold her like this? Was this how he got his jollies?

She sensed movement to her right and from the corner of her eye she saw the legs of another man. God, there were two of them. There was just enough light for her to make out his shoes, very shiny black shoes. They looked new. Did they dress for this?

The man on the right asked, "Any trouble?"

The man holding her grunted, "No."

"Okay, just keep her like that. It'll take about ten minutes."

"No problem. I'm okay, and so is she."

Again she tried to struggle, to scream, to move. His weight made it impossible. He had sprawled on her back forcing her to the flagstones and his weight was crushing her so much that she had trouble breathing. It was hard to fill her lungs with his weight on her, and with her mouth inches from her knees she could breathe but could not get in enough air to scream or even talk.

The man to her right put down a bag, a black bag, which he kneeled down to open and from it he took out a hammer, a large, heavy-looking hammer. Still digging into the bag, he took out a long rod. Then he put both tools aside and from the bag took out some large towels and a piece of cloth which she watched him wrap around the hammer's end. Then he stood and walked away. She guessed he was moving toward the edge of the terrace.

There was silence for a moment and she could clearly hear the breathing of the man holding her. Again and again she tried to move, but she was pinned to the ground like a bug in a museum display. Then suddenly there was a sound. It was a thud, a dull heavy sound. The hammer was hitting something. She could feel the vibrations through the flagstones beneath her.

What the hell was going on? The hammering was not constant like someone hitting nails. It was sporadic. There was a thud, then a rest, and then another thud, with maybe ten or twenty seconds between. What was he hammering?

Then there was a sound she couldn't identify. It wasn't the hammer. It had to be that rod. She heard metal on metal, a scratching, screeching sound, then silence, and then after a few seconds, the hammering once again. First the hammering, then the scratching, then the sequence repeated and she lost count. What were they going to do? She started to cry, and in the dim light she could just make out her tears collecting on the flagstones only inches from her face. Then she felt wetness on her ankles and realized her bladder had let go, though she hadn't discerned the sensation of urinating. God, was she losing control? What were they trying to do? This was obviously no rape. If they wanted to rape her, they would have dragged her inside to the bed and taken turns. She knew this wasn't a sexual thing. The man holding her was like an iron statue. He never once shifted his hands from her mouth and waist or his weight from her back.

Over and over she tried to move, to twist her body, but she was frozen. Her toes were tingling, and she knew the blood flow was being cut off. What air she could get into her lungs was cool, and if she could, she would have bargained away everything she had for a deep breath. What were they going to do? Who the hell were they? she asked herself. Why was this happening?

The hammering started again. He was waiting between blows—hiding the noise. Nonetheless, she was hoping someone would hear and call the police or investigate. Then she realized the absolute futility of that hope. This was a city that watched a man kill a woman in the street as if it was a TV show. No, she knew no one was going to come to her rescue. Then she thought Tom might walk in on this. Maybe he would come back in time before they... before they what? she asked herself. What were they going to do? Her mind screamed the question, were they going to kill her?

Finally, she had said it to herself. They might be going to kill her. Why? What had she done to them? Who were they? She realized it was too crazy to be a random attack. Men who were smart enough to get into the building and into the apartment without being seen would probably have devised a better game for themselves than tossing people off terraces. Is that what they were going to do? Throw her off? Then why don't they do it? Why the wait? Why the hammering?

She realized the guy was hammering at the railing. What else could he be hitting? He had to be breaking away the cement supports for the railing. She knew that without being able to see. There was nothing else where he was hammering except the railing. Then she knew. They were going to kill her, and they were going to throw her off the terrace, but the railing would go with her. It was going to look like an accident. Afterward, anyone who looked would see broken cement and figure the railing gave way when she leaned on it. The building was old. The cement work was old. This was a murder. They were going to murder her. Again and again she asked herself why, who? It made no sense.

She heard an airplane and its noise seemed louder than usual. She thought of people killed in plane crashes. If the plane didn't explode in the air, then it fell and the people inside knew they were falling. They knew they would hit the ground and be killed. How long did it take? What happened when you died? Oh my God. Was there a God? Was there a heaven? What happened when you died? They're going to kill me and I don't even know why. I haven't done anything wrong. Why would someone do this?

The hammering stopped and again she heard the scratching of the metal rod and then nothing. There was complete silence until the footsteps. The man was walking back to where she was. She saw him kneel and replace the hammer and rod in the black bag.

"Finished?" asked the man holding her.

"Yeah, she should be no problem… was a good idea."

She listened to them talk. They were as casual and matter of fact as two guys buying watermelons. Then suddenly, she felt a bit of release, an easing off. He was shifting his weight. Then all at once he straightened. He stood up and she came with him. To her amazement, his hands never relaxed their grip. The hand on her mouth and the other at her waist were still as firm and steel-like as when he first grabbed her.

Looking to her right she saw the man who had been hammering. He was standing by the bag. There was something about him. She had seen him before. Where? Then she remembered, in her office. He was one of the men who had come with the fat man asking about Dennis. Why were they doing this? What was it all about? As quickly as she formed the question, she knew the answer. It was about Dennis. This all had to do with Dennis. They must think she had something to do with his disappearance. She tried to struggle. She tossed her weight from side to side and then she felt the man's grip easing just a bit. She struggled harder and tried to bite his hand.

Then she realized she was moving. He was carrying her to the railing. She could see the lights from the apartment across the street. As he carried her closer to the edge, she could see more of the buildings across the street. Maybe someone would see. Maybe there was someone watching them at this moment. They would see what was happening and call out. They would call the police. That would stop them. They wouldn't do anything if someone was watching.

The man stopped about three feet from the railing. She looked down and saw what the other man had been hammering. The cement at the base of one section of railing was gone. There was nothing at the base of the railing's legs except holes, black holes with nothing around them. Where was the cement he had chopped out? Then she saw it to the left. It was piled on the cloth.

The other man walked past them to the edge and looked down. He looked to the left and then to the right. Then turning, he said, "Coast's clear."

The man holding her tightened his grip on her waist and turned a little. He moved her to the right like she was a doll. Moving her as he did brought a field of view into focus she couldn't see before. Now she saw the apartment through the terrace doors. She saw the yellow light above the couch and she saw the bathroom window and thought of the bath she wanted to take. When was that? How long had all this been? Would Tom walk in?

The man holding her moved her more to the right and then threw her at the railing. Like a slingshot, he pulled her back and then swung her forward. She was flying through the air. He had done it like a pitcher at a ball game. He wound up and threw her like she was a baseball.

Everything was a jumble for a moment and then she saw the apartment behind her and she saw the two men. She recognized them both. They were the ones who had come to her office with the fat man. Then she hit the railing and her mind went blank.

For a moment, her forward motion stopped and she knew the railing would hold. She knew it would hold her and she would not go over. She felt a terrible pain in her side. Hitting the railing must have broken something. He had thrown her hard and she hit the metal with great force. It wouldn't matter if she broke something whatever it was could be fixed. With time, the broken bones would heal. What would that matter? If the railing held she wouldn't go over.

But it didn't. Her forward motion didn't stop, it just slowed. She was still moving and she could see the railing moving with her. She screamed and knew she was falling. I'm going to die, she thought. "No, no!" she screamed. Reaching out she grasped the railing. It was beside her and she grabbed onto it. It was hard to see. Her eyes were tearing. How long would it take? How long would it take? She looked down and saw the ground. It was very close.

One end of the railing section hit the ground a fraction of a second before she did. The other end, to which she clung, hit the street side of a parked car. Their combined weight blew out the car's windows in a shower of glass that flew in every direction. The witnesses remembered that most clearly. They said multicolored rainbows of light formed in the air as the force of the concussion blasted the glass into space. One lady said it was a beautiful sight and she was thrilled until she realized what had happened.

Lydia's body looked like it was part of the car and railing. Everything was twisted together. People stared in amazement and then looked up in fear of more things falling, but saw only bleak, impenetrable blackness.

A man approached Lydia's body, thinking it was possible she could have survived the fall. Kneeling down beside the tangle of metal and flesh, he stared into her wide-open eyes and knew he was wrong. There was too much blood and raw flesh. He shuddered when he realized he was looking at pieces of her insides. Slowly he stood and, taking off his jacket, covered her head. As he did that, a police car screeched to a stop about fifty feet away, its siren still screaming, as had Lydia moments before.

CHAPTER 64

Randall appreciated being driven from DeVito's estate back to Manhattan. He liked the idea and the feel of chauffeured limousines. It was a benefit he knew he would enjoy. At about nine o'clock, roughly an hour after he left DeVito's estate, the car pulled into Irving Place, and Randall was surprised to see several police cars in front of his building. He left the car and asked a guy in the street what had happened. The guy who was wearing a bathrobe over pajamas pointed to a smashed car and said someone had fallen from the building.

Not stopping to look at what was lit by a wrecker preparing to haul away the ruined car, he started to enter his building but was stopped by a cop who asked him who he was and where he was going. When he told the cop his name and that he lived in the penthouse, he was told to wait right where he was and not move. A few minutes later, a Detective Saunders came down in the elevator and walked with him into the lobby and told him to sit on one of the available chairs.

Standing in front of him, the detective said, "I'm afraid I have some very bad news, Mr. Randall."

"What is it? What happened?"

"You have a Miss Lydia Cornell living with you in the apartment?"

"Yes I do."

As he said that, Randall realized what had taken place. Chills shot through him as he now understood what DeVito had meant when he said Miss Cornell would shortly be leaving the firm. He was so visibly shaken the detective thought he was going to collapse, so he arranged for the EMT's to stand close by in case Randall needed medical attention.

The detective went on to explain how the railing on the terrace had given way when Miss Cornell had evidently leaned against it. He also said it was

357

all too common for the bricks and mortar of older city buildings to crumble and he went on to tell Randall that the accident had happened several hours ago, just after dark.

He said the precinct police who arrived first had notified the appropriate units and then went into the building to try to identify who it was who had fallen. They took the doorman outside to look, and fortunately, the doorman was able to identify Miss Cornell. Saunders went on to say that when he arrived, he managed to gain entry to the apartment and found Miss Cornell's handbag and other personal items. He told Randall he went out onto the terrace and saw that one section of railing was missing, and that he briefly looked at some other sections that seemed to be okay. He said it was strange that she happened to lean on the one section that let go.

He then reassured him by adding that the police forensic people and the city building people would check again, but they had checked the terrace that evening and found that overall it was safe.

After asking where Randall had been and learning he had been at a business dinner with people who could verify that fact, Detective Saunders told Randall there would probably be no problem for him, and Randall was allowed to return to his apartment with sleeping pills the medics gave him. As soon as he got inside, he swallowed them and waited in the living room for them to take effect.

But before they did, he went out to the terrace to look at the spot that was now cordoned off with yellow plastic tape. He shivered as he looked at the space where there had been iron railing and cement work. Flashing into his mind was a recollection of meeting a guy at a dinner and being impressed with his appearance and manner, but then being startled when the guy smiled and revealed missing front teeth. Randall had been so shocked he never forgot that incident and now, looking at the missing railing, he recalled the missing teeth.

Staring at the open space, he thought it funny he was surprised by what was not there. It was like looking at where a building had once stood, staring, transfixed and gaping at what was no longer there.

He closed his eyes and shivered a bit when he fully realized for whom he now worked. DeVito and his associates, whoever they might be, were now his bosses. For a fleeting moment he thought that maybe he should just disappear. Take off and go somewhere and then he laughed when he thought, all I know and all I have is here entwined with the A.T. Dunn advertising agency. Which is now mine, he thought. I am in charge and I'm not going anywhere.

He realized Dunn had done it for years. He had managed to live with DeVito and not be hindered in the slightest way. Randall nodded and thought, if Dunn could live with the arrangement and be successful, I will also live with it and be equally successful. Why not? I know how to do it and I will. He straightened his shoulders and took a deep breath.

Then, after several minutes of thinking about his situation and staring at nothing, he went inside, undressed, and went to bed. Thoughts of Lydia flooded his mind, and he realized he had liked her and enjoyed working with her because she was smart and tough. But now she was no more and that was that.

Eventually he managed to drift off and slept soundly. In the morning he was happy he had no headache.

CHAPTER 65

Six weeks later Gert watched the contractor's vehicle slowly rumble down the street, turn onto Seventh Avenue and disappear in the sea of traffic. Then, with the same pleasurable uncertainty she reserved for biting into an unknown piece of soft-centered candy, she turned to look at her house, finished in record time, according to the contractor.

The roof line, the eaves, and the top floor looked the same, but she reveled in the changes as her eyes scanned lower. Where a short while before, the second floor windows were closed off to hide the laboratory, now there were great sheets of sparkling glass showing beautiful light-colored curtains. The eliminated street-level entrance was once again available, now with an enameled navy blue and purple door. The windows at that level were also new and shining with curtains visible for all to see. At the top of the front steps, the main double doors matched the street door and like mirrors, reflected the late-afternoon sun. She loved the final touches: the gleaming brass door knobs and kick plates, but best of all, the door knocker in the shape of a microscope that Lou had managed to find.

Gert was thrilled she'd been able to avoid being directly involved, as she had with the previous building makeover. This time she butted out and turned up only to approve specific items or sign checks. Hard as it was for her, she stayed out of it. That was probably the main reason for her joy. By not being caught up with every phase of the reconstruction she was allowed to deal with the finished building as a surprise, rather than as a sweaty job that had finally come to an end. To her, it was no longer just a building. Now it was a house with three floors of living space.

The architect's orders had been to turn the place into a real home, with only two concessions to Gert's whims. One was a full-fledged library-study on the second floor; the other was the retention of the elevator. But now, it was out in the open, not hidden away. She thought the visible acknowledgement of the elevator would be a metaphor for her new approach. She vowed to open herself to what was going on around her.

Everyday and every night she thought about Sol and the clear message his death presented: no one is ever ready for it. Very often even the suicide is surprised by the gripping realization that turning back is now impossible. The idea echoed in her head. With Sol gone and Winthrop finding Lou, her life had totally changed. She had always been alone, but now it was truer than before. What had been was no more. Her world had changed. There would never be those crazy lunches with Sol or walks around the Village or the hurried meetings in one of the lounges. Now she was quite alone and she wasn't happy about it.

Her world had truly changed. The instant she plunged that needle into Dennis' neck, she figured the next dose would be hers. She had done many things, but never had she deliberately and coldly executed another human being. That she could didn't surprise her; that she would—that was the shock.

Her own death had become a daily thought. Should she end it? Would anyone care? Would she care? How many more years would it be before she would hungrily welcome the end? Why wait? The work was done. It was all finished, wasn't it? Wait for what? Wait for a husband, for a boyfriend, a girlfriend, a lover? It was over. Her dreams were empty. Thirty years before she would have had reasons for staying on, but now, all she could ask herself, wait, wait for what?

Then, with equal force she would deny all thoughts about killing herself. She convinced herself Dennis's death and now Lydia's death were merely a redressing of the balance. There was no need to wait for the perverted justice meted out by the politically corrupted system the law had become. For her and many others, justice had become a tangible end people dealt with on their own. If anything, she was proud she had been instrumental in setting things right. She was proud that Cyril and his friends had helped settle everything. She bore no guilt or remorse for it balanced out and she loved it, since equilibrium was the only answer for her. All sides of all equations had to balance out. That was how nature worked.

A flash of understanding had made clear it was foolish to pay attention to death, since no one is ever ready. So the hell with it, she decided. Live in the open, be unafraid, and get whatever there is to get done, accomplished now, because there is no time but now. So, with great force of will she cast out the thoughts of death and got ready for whatever would come next.

Walking up the front steps, she smiled as she grasped the microscope door knocker and gave it two hearty whacks, opened the front door, and entered her new home.

The staircase had been completely replaced as had been the carpeting. Everything was new. Where once the wall of the laboratory had closed off the hallway, there was now an eight-foot arched doorway opening into a bright front room. Then there was the study-library, kitchen and bath, all of it new to the second floor.

The third floor was reserved for her: for her bath, bedroom, for her private sitting room, and it was all very beautiful. The smell of fire was gone, replaced by the odor of fresh paint and new furniture.

She strolled into the front room, admired the soft, overstuffed sofa and plopped into a large chair. From the side table, which held Sol's lung-like ashtray, she picked up the magazine Lou had mailed. It was the latest issue of *MK* with Lou's feature story on A.T. Dunn and Complete Abandon.

Lou had written the story about the perfume at A.T. Dunn but did not mention where it had come from or who developed it. The article also covered the radical approach the perfume had created by being the first of its kind. Metro's development of the Bio/Det concept was also effectively spelled out. Lou had devoted a fair amount of space to the area of biological determinants and had quotes from scientists who testified to the amazing potential that could be available from the process. Many extraordinary projections were made about how this new approach would benefit not only the cosmetics industry, but the pharmaceutical and medical fields as well.

There was no reference to Lydia Cornell or Dennis DeVito, but it did mention Tom Randall, the present CEO at A.T. Dunn. Randall was quoted as saying he was proud to carry on the traditions of the industry as they had been taught to him by his mentor, Alexander Dunn.

Lou had managed to get in several paragraphs about Dunn's funeral at which many executives of other agencies had spoken highly of him and what he had accomplished. They spoke of his willingness to tackle new products with dynamic campaigns and particularly his being brave enough to operate in areas not usually the playing field for advertising agencies.

Parts of Tom Randall's eulogy for Dunn were quoted where he mentioned how proud he was to be able to carry on the tradition that Alexander Dunn had so ably started. What Lou had included was tasteful and did justice to Dunn's contributions.

In addition, there were two related articles in the issue—one dealt with the human sense of smell and how potent it can be when galvanized by a new, strong odor. Another focused on olfactory adaptation and how it would reduce the effect of any new odor after a relatively short time. That combination was given as reasons for the phenomenal instant success of Complete Abandon and the almost guaranteed shrinking of sales yet to come as people adapted to the new odor. As she read, she thought about the public's significant gullibility which would enable the sales of Complete Abandon to continue on a high note even after the perfume was no longer able to fulfill its advertised promises.

Gert closed the magazine, wiggled her bottom in the new soft chair, and looked around the room. It was a far cry from what had been there before. For a few moments, she shifted back and forth from what was now there to what was no longer visible. As she admired the beige and light-blue furniture fabrics, her mind melted them into the dusty metal racks of chemicals and glassware that before had occupied the same space. She looked at the paintings on the walls that previously held blackboards and at the thick carpeting that now covered wooden floors that still bore imprinted scars from the years of bearing the granite-topped lab tables.

Getting up, she walked into the middle of the second floor which held the new bathroom and the library filled with her books and all of Sol's. Plans had been made to donate most of his books to the college library, so graduate students, who would benefit from the scholarship created in his name could also understand a bit about the man whose generosity was enabling their education.

Then she walked to the rear of the second floor where a large kitchen had been installed with its rear wall opening onto a deck that would be glorious in the warmer months. Everything in the kitchen was up to the minute, all stainless steel professional equipment.

She made a cup of coffee and sat at the kitchen table sipping and thinking about the weekend party to come. Cyril had insisted on a housewarming and had invited everyone who was even remotely involved in the Complete Abandon affair. At one time not long ago Gert would have already begun making hors d'oeuvres, the soups and meats, the side dishes and the desserts. No more. Now she called caterers and ordered what she wanted. And it wasn't that Cyril was picking up the tab; it was simply a matter of Gert appreciating the remaining time she had.

An enormous banging sound brought her out of her reverie. She looked left and then right and then tilted her head and listened. The noise surprised her and she had no idea what it was. Then it happened again and she realized someone was using that new door knocker. She walked to the front door and looked through the peephole to see Winthrop and Lou. Gert opened the front door and smiled.

"Well, how the hell do you like this?" She asked throwing her arms open wide. "Isn't it all just beautiful?"

"It looks like a new house. It's hard to believe it was just a remodeling."

"Well, Win, whatever the hell it is, come on in and take a look. I bet you'll be surprised."

They came in with the trepidation you see when people walk into their own first house. They tiptoe in because they can't believe it's theirs. Evidently, it's easier to sneak up on reality than barge in on it.

Pointing, Win said, "Look, the lab is gone. Damn, the wall is also gone. Look Lou."

He walked into the small hallway separating the sitting room from the library and standing between them, he looked left to the sitting room and then right toward the kitchen and its glass doors. "Gert, this is beautiful." Then he asked, "What's upstairs?"

"That's my private world. Another sitting room, my bedroom, and a large bath big enough for anything you can think of."

Win smiled and looked at Lou. When Gert saw his lascivious glance, she said, "Oh, no you don't. That's my personal space. Don't ask to borrow my bathroom for a weekend."

"But Gert," Lou said, "we'd wash the tub. There wouldn't be a ring."

"Speaking of rings, did this character come up with one yet, or is he still trying to get you to accept a Corona cigar band?"

"Take a look at this," she said, thrusting out her left hand. Gert peered at the ring on Lou's finger. It was a thin gold ring that held a deep green emerald in an elegant and unusual setting. Gert was impressed with the setting because of its formality. It wasn't the typical naked rock balanced on a stump of gold. Instead, the emerald was centered in an oval frame of gold with rectangular diamonds down the sides that created a stunning framing effect.

"Where did you get that Win? It doesn't look like Fifth Avenue."

"It isn't. A week after I met Lou, Carlos Gianni, from the Geology Department pops into my office and asks me if I have use for a first-class emerald he came across in Italy."

Gert snickered. "Come on. Came across in Italy? What a load of bull. Win, Carlos is a bandit. He's back and forth between here and Italy three, four times a year. As far as the school is concerned, he's delivering papers or attending conferences, but he doesn't attend anything. He's there picking up an assortment of precious stones. The school regards him as a first-rate geologist, and that he is, but to me, he's nothing more than a sweet, lovable smuggler."

"Come on Gert, that's a harsh word. But be that as it may, I bought it from him and had a local goldsmith create a setting Lou sort of designed, and voila, we're officially engaged."

"Do you really like it?" Lou gushed.

Gert softly enclosed Lou's hand with her own. "It's very beautiful and I am thrilled for you both." She looked at Win. "Did you get a wedding ring too?

"Of course, we're ready for it, are you?"

"You bet I'm ready. Just think of it, on Saturday night there'll be a wedding and a great party." She laughed out loud.

CHAPTER 66

At 9:00 that Saturday morning, Cyril showed up with the caterers. They brought tables, chairs, platters, silverware, glasses, trash cans, coffee pots, and boxes of food.

Gert was parading amidst the sea of boxes, fighting the temptation to open them when she was confronted by a waiter. "Professor Doctor Lehman, Monsieur Cyril warned me to keep you out of things. You are not getting into things, are you?"

Gert's desire to be the prima donna was going to happen. "No." she said, "No, I'm not touching—I'm just watching."

With that, she turned and headed for the front door. As she passed a very large and very new hallway mirror, she stopped to look at herself. Her hair looked okay and she particularly liked the makeup job the local drag queen had done. The only drawback was her shape. The white dress she wore was beautifully made from an exquisite fabric, but there was an awful lot of it. As she stared in the mirror, she muttered under her breath, "Damn, I look like Moby Dick's best girl." Then she turned, opened the door and went out.

She walked down the outside front steps to the street level door and rang the bell. After a moment's delay, Lou opened the door. "Oh, Gert," she said. "Please come in, come in. I was hoping you'd come down. This is all so...so, damn, I'm nervous."

"Honey, there's nothing to be nervous about. Win is a fine man and brilliant in his offbeat way. And, I have to say, you look great. Every man here today will cry when he sees you."

"Oh, you're sweet, but, it isn't Win I'm nervous about. It's me. He's never been married before, I have and I'm worrying I'll screw this up like I messed up my first one."

"How old were you when you married the first time?"

"I was twenty."

"Come on, Lou, at twenty most girls don't know anything about what it means to be married. Now you know. You'll make mistakes, there's no question, but you're a big girl and you know what you want. Mistakes happen, but solutions are all over the place." Gert paused and took Lou's hands in hers. "Look, I may not look it and I sure as hell don't act like it, but as far as you're concerned, I'm as good as your mama. You have trouble, come and see me. Okay?"

Lou encircled Gert in her arms and hugged her. "You're just what I need, Gert. If someone had said that to me the first time and was really there to help, well, I don't think I'd be standing here right now." Still holding hands, they walked to one of the new sofas and sat.

"Your mother wasn't much help, huh?"

Lou shook her head. "No. She wasn't the kind of woman who would help. We never had a decent relationship. I was her daughter and she was my mother and that was about it."

"That's too bad, but it's all in the past. Now everything's different, everything." Gert looked around the room and admired the layout. "Just like all this. You like it?"

"Oh, yes. The remodeling is wonderful."

"Yeah, I'm really happy about it. It's like a brand new place, and it's all mine." Gert got up and started to walk to the kitchen, but stopped and turned. "Hey, I almost forgot to say I really liked the magazine piece you wrote."

Lou smiled. "Thanks. I've gotten a few compliments, but I'd like a raise." Gert laughed. "Hey, you want a drink?" Lou shook her head and looked at her watch. "Gert, what time do you have?"

"Don't get nervous, you have almost an hour." Gert went into the kitchen and returned with an open bottle of wine and two glasses.

"Will you stay with me? I hate being alone right now."

"Of course I will." She poured an inch of wine into each glass and handed one to Lou.

"Here, take a sip and relax."

They both drank and sat silently until Gert burst into tears.

"Gert, what is it? What's the matter?"

Very slowly, Gert put her glass on a table. "It's Sol. I miss him so. He should be here to see all this. We were a pair, Lou. Now that he's gone, I'm alone and... and I miss him."

"But Gert, we're here. Win and I will never disappear and it seems Cyril and his pals are here for you also."

"Oh, I know that and believe me, I appreciate it more than you know. But Sol, Sol was like an anchor for me. He always needed help and I always helped. At times, I felt like his mother." She got up from the sofa, picked up the wine glass and drained it.

Then she put the glass down and said, "Lou, there's an empty space inside of me and I don't know how to fill it. I dream about him. I dream about the two of us walking in the Village, about having dinner, about seeing a movie together. We were together a lot. I don't know how I'm going to deal with him being gone."

"I wouldn't worry right now. You're smart and resourceful. I know you'll figure a way."

Gert nodded. "Maybe I'll adopt Cyril. Can you picture that?"

Smiling, Lou said, "I think it's more likely he'll adopt you."

Laughing, Gert said, "Right, he'll be my mother. That would really be cute."

CHAPTER 67

About an hour later, the second-floor living room was bulging with more than forty people jamming both sides of the room. Standing that way, they created an aisle that led to a small flower-bedecked platform under the front windows. On the platform stood a local judge Gert had collared for the ceremony. The wedding march was playing as Win slowly walked down the "aisle." About thirty seconds later, Lou came out of the study holding Gert's arm and walked to where Win was standing.

The judge stated the usual and necessary legalities, finished, and nodded to Win, who turned to face Lou. He reached out and took her hand. Speaking softly, he said "I've thought a lot about what it means to say 'I love you' and I want to tell you what it means to me when I say it to you." He paused, and then said with great seriousness, "Loving you means the focus of my mind, my heart, and my life is you. I have found you and found myself. Therefore, I dedicate myself to you without reservations." Then he raised her hand to his lips and kissed it.

Delighted by Win's surprise declaration, Lou said, "And I you." Then she threw her arms around his neck and they kissed.

Gert, quite overcome, was blubbering, but pulled herself together enough to shout out, "Judge, is it legal? Did you say all you have to say?"

The judge nodded and Gert yelled, "Okay. Let's stop the wailing and start celebrating. There's food on this floor and there's food downstairs. So, pick your food and dig in."

Laughing, the friends and well-wishers rushed to Lou and Win, offering congratulations and for the next hours, people ate, talked, and listened to the Bossa Nova musicians play their quiet, elegant jazz.

Couple after couple approached Win and Lou to hand them envelopes. Win got a kick out of the envelopes and at one point said to Lou, "You know,

I've been to weddings and I've given the bride and groom an envelope with a check, but it was always a couple of kids and money seemed appropriate for kids starting out."

"So, are you saying that you don't think we're a couple of kids starting out and we don't deserve that kind of gift?"

"No, no, I don't mean that at all. I mean, well, we're not kids."

"Speak for yourself, buster. I feel about seventeen and I'm thrilled. I can't wait to spend some of that money getting new dishes, pots and pans, napkin rings and linens."

"I'd like to go with you because it'll be a new experience for me. I never bought things like that. My usual routine was the Salvation Army and a buck for a box of kitchen items."

"You're a real classy guy." He laughed and took her in his arms.

"Take your time, Win, take your time," Gert called out from across the room where she was standing next to Cyril. Win and Lou walked to them.

"There'll be plenty of time for that," Gert said, almost losing her balance, but Cyril grabbed her arm to steady her. "Are you all right?" he asked.

"Of course I am, but I'm a little drunk too."

Eventually, the band switched to soft sambas and everyone was feeling the rhythm. There seemed to be no fewer people at any given moment, since for every person who left another arrived. The early crowd faded away, replaced by guests decidedly younger and more thoroughly Village. Gert had made it her business to invite everyone who knew Win, her, and Sol. There were waiters, waitresses, bartenders, and a good many students.

One of the students told Gert he had heard that Paul Coleman and Susan Merrill were going to be married. When Gert heard that, she figured she would offer them the downstairs apartment and solve that issue.

A bit later Win and Lou were watching Cyril and Gert leaning on each other. They moved through the dancers to where they were standing. Lou looked at them with envious eyes and said, "You know, I could use another drink, so I'm going to get one." She turned and headed for the kitchen.

As Lou walked away, Gert hooked her arms in Win's and Cyril's and announced, "Come on boys, it isn't right for a newly married lady to drink alone."

CHAPTER 68

The next week Sergeant Murphy strolled into Lieutenant Randolph's office.

"Hey Lieutenant, you remember the case a while back—the one with the burned out townhouse and the dead guy, the professor with the broken neck?"

Randolph nodded. "Yeah I do, so what?"

"Well, that Professor Lehman, the NYU chemist whose house it was, she said we should pay attention to anything about a perfume that does weird stuff. She insisted that an analysis was stolen and that the analysis was for a formula for a special type of perfume. Well, she sent me a copy of *MK* magazine and I just read an article in it about a perfume that does magical stuff.

"Yeah, I remember her and her story. So, what are you saying?"

"Well, I think we should look into this affair a bit more carefully. The perfume mentioned in the article and the way it's described seems a lot like what Professor Lehman talked about. What do you say? Should I dig a little?"

"Sounds good to me, after you finish your coffee and roll, bring me the magazine okay?"

"You got it, Lieutenant."